Ben Pastor, born in Italy, became a US citizen after moving to Texas. She lived for thirty years in the United States, working as a university professor in Illinois, Ohio and Vermont, and currently spends part of the year in her native country. *The Road to Ithaca* is the fifth in the Martin Bora series and follows on from the success of *Tin Sky, Lumen, Liar Moon* and *A Dark Song of Blood*, also published by Bitter Lemon Press. Ben Pastor is the author of other novels including the highly acclaimed *The Water Thief* and *The Fire Waker*, and is considered one of the most talented writers in the field of historical fiction. In 2008 she won the prestigious Premio Zaragoza for best historical fiction.

THE ROAD TO ITHACA

Ben Pastor

BITTER LEMON PRESS
LONDON

BITTER LEMON PRESS

First published in the United Kingdom in 2017 by
Bitter Lemon Press, 47 Wilmington Square, London WC1X OET

www.bitterlemonpress.com

A CIP record for this book is available from the British Library

ISBN 978–1–908524–80-5
eBook ISBN 978–1–908524–81-2

Typeset by Tetragon, London
Printed and bound in Great Britain by
CPI Group (UK) Ltd, Croydon, CRO 4YY

To all those who believe, with Wordsworth,
that the Child is father of the Man

MAIN CHARACTERS

Martin Bora, Captain, German Army *Abwehr*
Frances L. Allen, American archaeologist
Andonis Sidheraki, her Cretan husband
Gottwald "Waldo" Preger, Captain, German Airborne Troops
Vairon Kostaridis, Police chief, Iraklion
Patrick K. Sinclair, First Lieutenant, Leicestershire Regiment, CreForce
Manoschek, Undersecretary, German Embassy in Moscow
Emil Busch, Major, German Army *Abwehr*
Bruno Lattmann, Captain, German Army *Abwehr*
Alois Villiger, Swiss scholar
Rifat Bayar Agrali, "Rifat Bey", Turkish businessman in Crete
Pericles Savelli, Italian scholar
Geoffrey Caxton, English archaeologist
"Bertie", Sergeant Major, CreForce
Margaret Bourke-White, US photographer
Erskine Caldwell, US author

Go back to the target you missed;
walk away from the one you hit squarely.

CRETAN SAYING,
IN KAZANTZAKIS' *REPORT TO GRECO*

A room lit to the most hidden corner is no longer liveable.

WERNER HERZOG,
I AM MY FILMS

Foreword

TO: Colonel Bruno Bräuer, Commander Airborne Regiment 1, 7th Flieger Division, eyes only
FROM: Medical Officer Dr Hellmuth Unger, *Wehrmacht* War Crimes Bureau

Colonel,

In the process of verifying reports of war crimes committed against German military personnel during the recently concluded operation in Crete, the following account came to my notice. As you will see, it is of a completely different – I would say opposite – nature, and, in view of possible pressures forthcoming from Messrs Brunel and Lambert of the International Red Cross, it may require immediate attention.

Yesterday, 31 May, a British prisoner of war of officer rank repeatedly insisted on being heard. Brought into my presence, he handed in a photographic camera, whose contents he urgently asked us to develop. The camera was entrusted to him by a fellow prisoner, an NCO who successfully escaped from the gathering point at Kato Kalesia. The photos (see attached) bear witness to an atrocity supposedly committed by troops belonging to Airborne Regiment 1: hence this preliminary note to you.

According to the officer, whose name, rank and unit I will include in my full report, the NCO told him he fell behind during retreat, and found himself alone, hiding from our victoriously advancing troops in a gully along a road some miles south of the so-called Chanià Gate, leading west from Iraklion's city walls. An amateur photographer, he had a portable camera with him. From his hideout, he claimed he saw eight German paratroopers approach on foot along the road, and enter a property we have since identified as Ampelokastro, the residence of a prominent Swiss national. The men, armed with MAB 38 automatic weapons and Schmeisser submachine guns, reportedly pushed the gate open and disappeared from his view behind the garden wall. Being unarmed and outnumbered, the witness did not dare to draw close. Within minutes, immediately after a single pistol shot, a commotion followed by volleys of rapid gunfire came to his ear. The utter lack of sound after the shoot-out ("not even voices shouting in German", which he fully expected) made him "hope that the paratroopers had fallen into a trap", set by Allied soldiers hiding on the premises or by locals equipped by the British Army.

As reported to the officer, nearly a quarter of an hour went by before the NCO decided to attempt crawling into the garden to see. He met with no signs of life there. A watchdog had been shot dead on the steps leading inside the building, where total silence convinced him the paratroopers had perished or were no longer in the house. Indeed, the garden (as later that day I confirmed in person when I visited the scene) is provided with a back gate, reported to have been unlocked and wide open at the time. As soon as he stepped in, the photographer was met by the ghastly sight of an entire civilian household exterminated by gunfire.

While the eyewitness himself has thus far escaped recapture, the officer who reported the case is presently being held in the Galatas camp.

In the interest of truth, and given the potential repercussions of such a grave incident involving the illustrious citizen of a neutral country, I decided to contact you directly and with every urgency. My full report, marked "Ampelokastro, Eyes Only", will be deposited at your office for you to choose how to proceed.

PART ONE

Setting Off

1

Nul tisserand ne sait ce qu'il tisse.
No weaver knows what he weaves.

FRENCH SAYING

SUNDAY 1 JUNE 1941, MOSCOW, HOTEL NATIONAL,
10.00 P.M. THREE WEEKS TO HITLER'S INVASION OF
THE SOVIET UNION

If Martin Bora had known that in a thousand days he'd lose all
he had (and was), his actions that day wouldn't have appreciably changed. Today things were as they were.

On his bedside table sat a note that read *Dafni, Mandilaria,*
and nothing else. Its heavy, slanted handwriting, however,
lent it a certain importance. From a man whose signature
could mean instant execution, as it had done for some forty
thousand already, even the jotted names of southern wines
sounded ominous.

Bora turned the note face down. He then opened his diary
to a blank page and began, from force of habit, by censoring
his real thoughts.

Maggie Bourke-White keeps fresh lilacs in her room. The scent fills
the hallway on this large top floor; I perceive it whenever I go in or
out. Her husband (see below) doesn't like me at all, and it's mutual;
she's more tolerant, or else has a photo reporter's interest in strange

15

animals, such as we Germans are in Moscow these days. But it's all strange, or else I wouldn't have on my night table a note in Cyrillic that reads *Dafni* and *Mandilaria*. I was quietly in a cold sweat at our embassy last night when I received it from Deputy Chairman of the Council of People's Commissars and NKVD chief Lavrenti Pavlovich Beria. Stalin himself doesn't unsettle me as much as his powerful head of secret police! I, a mere captain occasionally doubling as an interpreter, had additional reasons to be fidgety. Last Friday, returning late from one of the diplomatic circle parties – actually a Russian-style drinking bout of the kind I'm getting rather sick of – something happened that illustrates the strange world we move in. I got it into my head (I was tipsy after all the Starka and Hunter's vodka, but not actually drunk) to take a left on Gorky and head for Triumphal Boulevard and Nikitskaya, where the Deputy Chairman has his city residence. It was two minutes past midnight; I supposed there wouldn't be much going on at that time, even though Soviet officials earn affectionate nicknames such as "stone arse" because of the long hours they reportedly spend sitting at their desks. Well, either those stories are true, or else the NKVD were ticked off for whatever reason: they stopped me around the corner despite all official papers and the *propusk* glued to my windscreen, and gave me (or tried to give me, I should say) the once-over. They made me leave the car and questioned me for several minutes. "Is your name Martin Bora (pronounced Marty'n Bwora)?" "Yes." "Do you reside at the Hotel National?" "Yes." "Then what are you doing here?" "Don't know. Where's here?" "Have you been drinking?" "Yes." And so on. It all simmered down once I pretended to be soused beyond redemption. Had they been patrolmen, I'd have offered cigarettes. As foreign tobacco is at a premium in the Soviet Union, it often opens doors and shuts mouths. But with members of the secret police I wouldn't be so glib. In the end they grumbled an admonition and let me go. Did they believe I'd got lost in the foreigners' district? I doubt it. Will they report me to whomever?

Of course. But we all play these games in Moscow nowadays: diplomats, soldiers, privileged westerners.

Speaking of the latter, just yesterday, as I waited below for the hotel lift, I ran for the fourth or fifth time into best-selling American author Erskine Caldwell. He resides here with his lilac-loving wife Margaret, or Maggie, and enjoys the superlative kid gloves treatment from Molotov's *Narkomindel*. While our embassy personnel have been restricted from travelling outside Moscow, the couple freely (or so they think) ride and fly about for their articles. I am under orders to act engagingly with non-belligerent foreigners, so I always greet Caldwell first.

As usual, the leftist globetrotter who broadcasts starry-eyed reports from Moscow to the US ignored me. But he couldn't very well pretend not to see a fellow who exceeds his football player's height, speaks perfect English and is attired as a military attaché's adjutant besides. Be that as it may, like a cowboy peering into the distant prairie, Caldwell stared elsewhere. I didn't insist. Mrs Bourke-White wasn't with him, but I'd met her in the hotel restaurant before. Perky rather than pretty, she strikes me as intelligent, outspoken, a news photographer by trade who has travelled half of the known world. A Bavarian who deals in optical instruments has been trying to hit on her, banking on his status as a civilian who can boast of the third-floor suite with a grand piano and Napoleonic knick-knacks. It seems the two Caldwells get along fine – although he's rumoured to be short-tempered, and we'll see how long a free-thinking Yankee woman will put up with that. It'd be all plain gossip if I weren't aware of the role these intellectuals play in today's rapid communications. I keep an unobtrusive eye on them through E., a close associate of theirs, whom they trust and at most assume will report to Comrade Stalin exclusively.

Additionally, all of us – Soviets, Germans, others – make expedient use of the motley humanity crowding that repository of émigrés, the dilapidated Hotel Lux, former Zentralnaya, also known as the "golden cage of the Comintern". The intrigue up and down its six floors reminded one of Vicki Baum's *Grand Hotel*. The residents have a desperate need for amenities – what am I saying, the basics as one understands them in the civilized world: soap, toilet paper, light bulbs, etc.

Bribery is not impossible, though the residents know it might cost them their neck. They've been decimated in the last four years, despite every last one of them being communists; I should know, I have to pore over back issues of the now defunct *Deutsche Zentral-Zeitung*, which spewed out their red propaganda for years.

Back to Lavrenti Pavlovich Beria. In his armoured Packard, last night he showed up uninvited at Ambassador Count von der Schulenburg's informal get-together for a few selected guests, which is how I got my homework sketched by him on a notebook page. For whom (or what) is the third most powerful man in Russia requesting sixty bottles of choice Cretan wine?

After a meeting that exuded goodwill but remained tense, we were wracking our brains to understand it (private use, a major bash, a present to US Ambassador Steinhardt?). For all we know, in a roundabout way the wine could be meant as a gift for our own Foreign Minister. Naturally, my superior, Colonel Krebs, agreed at once to send me all the way to Crete to secure the delicacy. Never mind that we've barely concluded a victorious if hard-won campaign to conquer that island.

Officially the airborne operation closed yesterday. As per my orders, tomorrow – the major hailstorm of the past hours having abated – I'm off to Lublin on a Russian plane. From there on German wings I'll continue on to Bucharest, and then south to Athens. At Athens I'll hitch a ride somehow, possibly on one of the seaplanes that fly the route to Crete, or one of the ambulance Junkers likely going to and fro since the battle.

Does being a soldier include such unglamorous chores as providing wine for our Russian allies? Apparently so. Enough for a diary entry. Wake-up time in five hours, 1 a.m. Berlin time, 3 a.m. Moscow time.

MONDAY 2 JUNE

Without daylight saving time, at 3.30 dawn was already breaking in Moscow. Bora pocketed Lavrenti Pavlovich's note without rereading it.

The truth is, what made me curious about his house off Triumphal Boulevard wasn't the accounts of his work habits, but insistent rumours about his penchant for luring underage girls no one hears from afterwards. Improbable? He didn't hesitate to arrest the wife of Stalin's personal secretary, and they say he'll send her to the firing squad! No wonder they stopped me at the street corner.

He felt his jaw for smoothness after shaving, lifted his tunic from the back of the chair and put it on. The task of packing the small bag he'd take for the trip was quickly disposed of. When the waiter knocked discreetly on the door, Bora answered, "*Da, kharasho,*" without opening it, so that he'd leave the tray on the threshold. He'd sent for room service to save time. Because all hotel personnel worked for the secret police one way or another, and a guest assigned to the German Embassy was sure to be carefully scrutinized, Bora waited until the dying footfalls outside told him the man had gone, and then unlocked the door.

Cup in his hand in front of the open window, he breathed in the brisk air, where droplets of moisture coalesced without actually becoming mist. From the street below, it was possible the higher floors of this and other buildings would soon appear swathed in fog. The spires of the nearby Citadel were already. One of the coldest springtimes on record, trees in parks and on street sides still behind in blooming – except for Maggie

Bourke-White's lilacs. *I wonder where she finds them?* Bora neared his lips to the cup without drinking – the porcelain rim was hot enough to scald. Not even by leaning out could he be sure, but his car and driver must be waiting below. Or maybe not; it was still early. Four o'clock was when he'd asked for a shared cab to Leontyevsky Lane, where he was to join embassy undersecretary Manoschek, with whom he'd fly to German-occupied Poland. Unlike him, Manoschek was continuing west to Berlin.

It was good to have at last secured a room with a view after weeks of overlooking the hotel's inner court. Bora searched the bristling horizon of cupolas, spires, towers, flat roofs of immense tenements; an odour of heating fuel and wood stoves lingered, factory smoke and smells, mostly the pungent aroma from the state brandy maker at the other end of the block. About now, from Dzerzhinsky Street's GPU offices, so inconspicuously as to be suspect, a sombre car was no doubt approaching the National. Without smiling, Bora was amused. *Are Max and Moritz in it? I bet they are; I threw those cartoon characters out of bed. There's never a time that I walk from here to the embassy without being shadowed by one or the other, or both: all I can do is go out of my way to leave early and take the longest route possible, down to Spasopeskovskaya Square and Steinhardt's federal-style residence, or all around the Kremlin, crossing and recrossing the bridges before heading again for the Garden Ring. I hardly stop anywhere, take no photos, so they can't very well find fault with me. At most, I slow down in front of bookshops, or the Bolshoi Theatre (under repair), or the costly delicatessen stores on Gorky Boulevard. In the end, the few hundred metres from the National to our embassy swell to two or three miles. I make my shadows earn their daily bread.*

Again he brought the cup to his mouth and took a sip. Immediately the thought "Coffee has a strange taste" bolted through him. Bora, who drank it black and never stirred it, rushed back to the middle of the room, reached for the spoon on the silvered tray and scooped up some liquid from the bottom of the demitasse. He fished out a grainy residue, translucent, amber-coloured. His alarm rose like a spring released. With the tip of his tongue he tasted the particles from the spoon, a small motion that relaxed him at once. Nothing but sugar. Cane sugar, expensive in Moscow – an unrequested, additional touch for the foreign guest at ninety-six rubles a night. *Why, on my monthly pay I couldn't afford to spend more than ten days here: of course they'd sugar my room-service coffee. And they wouldn't be so crass as to poison me with breakfast.*

Bora drained the cup, feeling foolish, but only to a point. *It isn't here that I've learnt to keep constantly on the alert: here I've perfected the lesson. Is it excessive prudence never to let my diary out of my sight, even placing it inside a waterproof bag when I shower? Staying in Moscow makes you paranoid.* Again facing the window, without need of a mirror he deftly looped the silver cord aiguillette over his right shoulder, secured it to the small horn fastener under the shoulder strap, and hooked its end loops to the tunic's second and third button. Below, Gorky Boulevard was in a suspended state between sleep and stirring to life. His late father had known it as Tverskaya, before the house fronts were moved back to double its width, when stores had rich pediments and wooden signs, and long rows of hansom cabs lined it. Today it was a channel for delivery trucks, early buses, "shared cabs", people heading for an early work shift. Bora buckled his belt. Moscow would do without him today, and vice versa.

On the bed, his bag contained no more than was needed for a three-day trip. Glancing at it, it was impossible not to think of his *other* luggage, ready and waiting in East Prussia. But Bora had learnt during this assignment to bridle these and other thoughts, so he immediately shifted the focus of his attention. He no longer surprised himself at his ability to hide his own thoughts from himself, as if people around him could read his mind. So he kept from thinking "East Prussia", telling himself "Russia" instead of "East Prussia", and "diplomatic service" instead of "First Cavalry Division, ready to be deployed".

Lavrenti Pavlovich's note in his pocket felt like something that could spy on him just by being in contact with his body. Bora took it out and contemplated it. Dafni, Mandilaria. *Cretan place names? Does the first suggest a wine with the flavour of bay leaf?* Dafni *means laurel in Greek. They all drink loads, these Russians, from top to bottom. What generals are left over after the Purge swim in alcohol; 35,000 officers push up daisies instead.*

Of all the mundane incumbencies typical of serving in an embassy, a round trip just short of 3,500 miles to fetch wine was nearly mortifying at this time. Manoschek had gone to Germany for a routine visit, but who knew what his true intentions were. He might be carrying documents to be removed in view of the attack against Russia. Between now and then Germans in Moscow would ride to work, buy cheese and champagne on Gorky, attend parties where refusing repeated toasts was out of the question. Bora closed the window. He was aware how, now that Krebs substituted for the ailing General Köstring, the presence of Schulenburg, Krebs and himself justified the Foreign Minister's mocking definition of the embassy as *that nest of Saxons.* Not a criticism, but not a compliment, either. Bora would go out of his way not to show disappointment over this errand.

Minutes before four o'clock he was packed and ready. He set his empty cup and tray outside his door and the overnight bag as well, unlocked. It simplified the business of the Russians looking through it, despite all passes and permits. At airports and railway stations you knew they'd already gone through your things when customs agents magnanimously let you pass without checking. Diplomatic privileges seldom applied to lesser representatives of the Reich, and least of all to their luggage. Even the Ambassador's suitcases had been stopped once. It had taken outraged telephone calls to disentangle matters and caused a paralysis of all trains until a special convoy delivered the sequestered goods. So Bora travelled light, and readily said what he knew customs officials expected him to say.

Surveillance he was used to. When he and his brother were growing up, their rooms had no key, because his general-rank stepfather did not allow the boys to lock themselves in.

Truth be told, Bora secretly contrived to make a skeleton key. He never made use of it: it was enough for him to know he could lock himself in if he wanted to. There were nights when he slept on the floor so that on first inspection his stepfather would think him gone; other nights he simply sat up in bed, thinking. At twelve, thanks to the skeleton key, he'd already laid his hands on most of the forbidden books, kept in a small panelled room next to the library. He didn't necessarily read them: he was satisfied with having bypassed prohibitions. Still, he rarely lied: asked directly, he'd answer with the truth. To his younger brother, he confided all but those things that might force him to lie as well. *I am responsible for my silences and my transgressions*, he told himself, *and cannot involve Peter in them.*

The story of the skeleton key remained a secret to everyone. Bora even took it with him to Spain, only to lose it during the bloody siege of Belchite. That was in '38, and ever since he had felt as though he'd lost part of his private world, as if anybody (who, in the immensity of a land torn by civil war?) could, on finding it, gain access to his most secret self. Stepping out of the hotel room, Bora had to admit how the same desire to protect himself and remain ultimately inaccessible had brought him to volunteer for counter-intelligence. Discipline, self-control, firmness – the qualities his superiors praised in him – matched the unlockable door of his childhood. Bora, however, kept an imaginary key on the side: *I consider myself free to do what I must.* The sole difference was that now he'd do so even at the cost of shamelessly lying.

In the hallway, the flowery scent from the Caldwells' room wafted to him. Bora caught sight of a forsaken, small sprig of lilac on the lift floor, a blooming tip of tender pink. He retrieved it before someone had a chance of stepping on it, careful to tuck it out of sight inside his cuff before reaching the ground floor.

I'll give it back to her when I see her again.

He left the key at the desk and picked up the daily papers. The cream-coloured nude statues buttressing the archway – half demigods, half Saint Sebastian – looked down as he crossed the deserted lobby. Outside, barely short of a cold drizzle, suspended particles enveloped him as he left the multi-storey turn-of-the-century leviathan. The cab, a *marshrutka* limousine usually shared by several passengers but this morning reserved for him exclusively, waited along the roadside. Naturally, so did Max and Moritz, across the pavement in their black ZIS, parked toward Hunters' Row.

In two minutes 600 or so metres were covered. The driver – actually a low-rank NKVD operative who called himself Tribuk – turned left at City Hall and followed the back streets to the German Embassy, so he wouldn't have to turn around to continue to the airport. Being tailed had its rules.

Rain began to fall. Standing under what protection the balcony above the entrance afforded him, the undersecretary waited in a dark trench coat, with two brass-cornered suitcases at his feet. Bora left the car to greet him, and he drawled a lethargic reply to the military salute. "Morning, *Rittmeister.*"

"Good morning, Undersecretary."

"What, no greatcoat?"

"No."

"Sort of cold not to wear one." Manoschek had a gift for stating the obvious. Bora was in fact uncomfortable, but it would be an encumbrance to take along extra clothing for the Mediterranean. He watched the official reach inside his breast pocket. Still bearing the marks of the pillow on his right cheek, he looked as though he could do with some more rest. "Mail flew in for you, Bora."

"Thank you."

Motionless while the driver busied himself loading the suitcases into the car, Manoschek commented, "It appears you're friends with the Chancellor of Freiburg University."

"Professor Heidegger?" Indifferently, Bora reached for the envelopes. "I'm not *friends* with him, I took his pre-Socratics summer course back in '32."

"He's under surveillance, you're aware."

"Has been for the past five years." Bora turned his eyes to the two men inside the idling ZIS and resolved to show no haste to review the mail. "Why do you think I correspond with him?"

It wasn't true. Or it wasn't true in the sense that Bora's messages to the philosopher were part of the close observation – the Gestapo took care of that. Their last exchange had been on the scarcely seditious question of "*appearance* as a privative modification of *phenomenon.*" Seeing that Heidegger's reply had been unsealed, Bora directly put the envelope away, and did the same with the rest of the correspondence from his family, including his brother Peter.

Manoschek wasn't usually aggressive. But he'd drunk too much at the reception the night before, and his sternness served as a foil to embarrassment. He had a boyish face with a button nose; only an incipient double chin lent maturity to his profile as he glanced toward the east end of the lane and the incoming car. "All right," he said then. "My angels are here, we can go." They climbed into the back of the cab from opposite sides, with Manoschek's briefcase between them.

"Care to see the newspapers, Undersecretary?"

The dailies passed from Bora to Manoschek, who at once unfolded them so it would be clear to the driver that nothing was hidden inside the bundle. As soon as the cab moved, Max and Moritz followed, and so did the newcomers who shadowed the undersecretary. The trio of automobiles regained Gorky and made north for Pushkin Square.

Manoschek ran his eyes across the paper spread on his knees. Was he reading, or simply avoiding the idle talk one always resorted to in the presence of Russians? That he waited at the embassy, while he roomed at the Moskva Hotel, could only mean he'd stopped by for documents to take along, certainly not Bora's mail. When a small paper-bound book materialized in his hand – it must have been bothering him in his coat pocket as he sat – Bora succeeded in glimpsing its title before it sank out of sight inside the briefcase.

The Dead Live! Ah, yes, Manoschek relished occult literature. What else did he read he didn't want people to know about? Bora contemplated the string of government buildings sliding past in the rain. *At the second-hand book stalls on Kuznetsky Bridge Street I bought for 30 kopecks (less than 25 pfennig) a book I never expected to find in Moscow: Joyce's* Ulysses *– in the German transla-tion no less, published when it was already banned in its homeland. Has someone from our embassy (it could be Manoschek) disposed of a supposedly obscene, uncomfortable novel with a Jewish protagonist? All I know is that two years ago Wegner, up in Hamburg, beat the Bora Verlag to it (or else Grandfather decided against acquiring it). Whatever, I couldn't pass it up. It's been sitting inside my overnight bag in a plain brown jacket, as I don't care to advertise that I have it* *and haven't got time to begin it. But now, as I head for the Aegean, somehow possessing a book about the ultimate Wanderer of Greek myth makes sense.*

Manoschek put away the newspaper. He asked, "Do you know by heart how to make a Beacon cocktail?"

"I don't. I know it's got egg yolk and chartreuse in it."

"And brandy?"

"Maybe. Question is, in what proportions?" To get back at him for the Heidegger quip, Bora observed, "I try to stay away from cocktails, especially these fly-by-night imitations of American drinks."

"I'd think you an expert, given your familiarity with foreign wines," Manoschek sneered, but he wasn't seeking a fight. Bora ignored him. He met Tribuk's pale eyes in the rear-view mirror, and chose to wrong-foot him by staring back.

They reached and crossed Mayakovsky Square. Trees battered by the recent hailstorm stood over carpets of shredded green leaves and branches. It was here that Bora had turned to drive past the forbidden city house of Lavrenti Pavlovich. The habit of hiding his thoughts had become second nature. He was careful not to glance left, where the Lenin Military Political Academy occupied half a city block, but in this capital of ministries and barracks you'd have to shut your eyes to remain uninvolved. From here on, especially once past the Baltic and Byelorussia Station, offices connected to commercial aviation and aeroplane factories followed one another. It would be Leningrad Boulevard by then, leading out of Moscow.

Shortly before five o'clock they reached Tuschino. The airport, beyond a narrow canal, filled the oblong space in an oxbow of the River Skhodnya. Water fowl, haze rising from the water, seclusion – one could imagine it as the military camp it had been 400 years earlier, in the "Time of Troubles" that bloodied sixteenth-century Russia. Czar Boris Godunov had just died then, the second False Dimitri had allied himself with the Poles and Jesuits. Manoschek was no lover of Russian music; no point in Bora mentioning Mussorgsky's opera on the subject.

With Max, Moritz and the two angels stationed outside, the Germans walked into the terminal. Neither of them anticipated obstacles; all details of their respective destinations had been cleared beforehand. Somehow, however, even leaving Russia with the blessing of the authorities could be difficult. Bags were opened and inspected by a uniformed official (brick-red collar tabs, which meant NKVD), who stopped short of frisking them but made an issue out of an unreadable signature on the permits. It meant a round of phone calls understandably complicated by the early hour. Even on Monday, most offices in Moscow would still be closed. Within minutes, Manoschek, who relied on Bora's knowledge of Russian for his recriminations, was visibly checking his temper to avoid incidents. Only a pink flush in his face revealed his state of mind. As a result, the sleep mark on his cheek stood out like a scar, while on the other side of the counter the Russian stayed stone-faced, with the handset glued to his ear.

Bora refused to become emotionally involved at this early stage of his errand. He was thinking of the scene in *Boris Godunov* (his father, the Maestro, had directed Chaliapin in the lead role), when the enraged Czar is told Dimitri threatens Russia from the west: "Let nothing through, not even a soul from the border: not a hare from Poland, not a crow from Krakow!" How fitting, all considered. A silent consideration escaped his mental censorship: *Forget hares and crows, there will be German eagles invading soon from Poland.*

Comrade "Tichomirov, Yegory Yosifomich" seemed the hardest to get on the line, being out of town – still at his country dacha, most likely. Manoschek fretted. Bora chose to walk to the window overlooking the runway. When a handsome Lisinov twin-engine came into view, leisurely taxiing as it awaited permission to take off, he inwardly lit up. A welcome sight, for a change: if authorization to leave was ever granted, the socialist version of the DC-3 promised to offer the most comfortable leg of the journey.

It was 6.30 before the snag was resolved. On cue, the shared taxi and the two ZIS left together, and the NKVD official strode to unlock the door to the tarmac. "*Dobrogo puty*" was called for, but he kept from wishing the travellers a safe journey, or adding anything to that effect. Whether or not the Germans would agree to separate from their luggage, no one offered to carry it for them. Manoschek stormed out of the building ahead of Bora. "Hell," he said through his teeth as he swung the brass-cornered suitcases, "having to sweat blood for the privilege of travelling 1,000 miles on Russian wings."

Bora caught up with him. "American wings, really, regrettably with a higher range than our best bomber to date." On this side of a smile, he added, "It beats an eighteen-hour train ride to Warsaw any day."

On the rain-wet, silver sheen of the fuselage, elegant cursive letters spelt in red *City of Moscow*. Overkill though it was, the attendant at the foot of the ladder double-checked the passengers' papers before letting them on board.

Once up in the air, through the drizzle the spires of a large reddish church wheeled slowly below; fat green meadows, the houses of Krasnogorsk on the Moskva. A fearless climb followed, bucking and bumping through a layer of low cloud into a blinding sunbeam, only to reach the ragged vapours drifting above. Surely designed as transportation for high officials, the plane's interior was provided with all manner of comforts, and the two Germans had it all to themselves. Drinks were made available to them – tea, mineral water, Gollansky gin in sealed bottles. Manoschek refused to touch anything; Bora, ever since the night of his errand under orders to follow prophylaxis against malaria, took Atebrin with a glass of water.

Before long, the undersecretary was deep in his book on the occult. Too deep, maybe, because he eventually dozed off in the comfortable seat with his forefinger stuck as a bookmark between pages. On the opposite side of the aisle, Bora went through his correspondence and the newspapers (his hunting ground for useful titbits slipped through censorship). Heidegger had attached to his reply a recent essay on Hölderlin's Greek poetry, and how "this essence of sea travellers, lonely and feisty" should not be confused "with every seagoing trip". *Der Nordost wehet*, read the poem, "The nor'easter blows". Relevant somehow, punctual somehow, like Joyce's *Ulysses* in his bag. In the four and a half hours of flight the two men exchanged no more than a few sentences, which was just as well, since – for all they knew – official aircraft were bugged even as their hotel rooms were.

Eventually, the immense Pripet Marshes created a broken patchwork of dark greenery and wide pools below; marking Poland's Soviet-occupied east, water alternately dazzled as it reflected the sun or grew sombre as it became overcast, like a great musky creature whose many eyes blinked open and shut. Bora put away the papers. The view of the marshland quickened his pulse. *I may soon be riding through it with my men,* he thought. *Smiles, diplomacy, slyly tossing alcohol in the flowerpots to avoid overdrinking, careful not to offend our hosts, meanwhile… It's all in preparation for our real plans.*

Lublin was the first landing field over the border of the German occupation zone, on a plain dotted with round lakes. As the Lisinov drew near, two Luftwaffe fighters assigned to the airport took off to meet it. Bora had crossed the area in

'39; he recognized the winding course of the Bistritza, the city slaughterhouse on the side of the road. In those days the airfield had suffered bomb damage; repairs were proceeding at a feverish pace.

Under escort, the *City of Moscow* banked widely to the south, approaching the runway with a tail wind. Manoschek put away the book, yawned into his fist and looked over. On the starboard side, beneath the broken clouds, the roofs of the Majdan Tatarsky labour sheds grew visible, then slid past. "What's that?" he enquired.

Bora bit his tongue. "Clothing works."

What had Heidegger written to him? *It's all in freeing oneself from a concept of truth understood as concordance.* Which meant he could answer "Clothing works" (the undersecretary not being a confidant of his, and the Russians perhaps eavesdropping) when Little Majdan, Majdanek, was well on its way to becoming a concentration camp.

On the ground, a spartan Ju-52 was refuelling. It was Bora's, not Manoschek's. The junior diplomat, with extended stopover time, welcomed the chance to get lunch. An orderly took charge of his suitcases, allowing him to head without encumbrances for the mess hall.

"See you in Moscow, *Rittmeister,*" he said.

Will not, Bora told himself. *You're out of Russia for good, as we prune our embassy staff of non-essentials.* "See you in Moscow," he replied sociably all the same. A few minutes after eleven, Moscow time; ten locally. The half hour needed for the cargo plane to be ready could allow him to get a bite to eat, but Bora didn't care to prolong his association with Manoschek. He set back his watch one hour and waited, pacing around in the chill of day.

*

The southerly that compelled the Russian pilot to modify his landing became a headwind as Bora continued to Bucharest. The expected three and a half hours in the air became four, worryingly close to maximum range. Bora, the only passenger among crates of various supplies, leafed through Joyce's novel so as not to stare at the co-pilot's nervous tapping on the fuel gauge. At 14.48, in the lashing rain, the slippery runway of Baneasa airport felt pleasant under the tyres of the landing gear. It turned out it wasn't the fuel gauge the co-pilot was knocking into reaction, but some other indicator. "Won't be continuing for another hour, *Rittmeister,* maybe two. If you don't suffer from air sickness, you'd better eat; it'll be evening before we get to Athens." Bora did as suggested. A kind of stolidity set in whenever he couldn't appreciably modify his lot. Suspended between north and south, winter and summer, peace and war, he did what was strictly needed, saving energy. An indifferent plate of food and bottled water would bridge him over to Greece, and to an indifferent bed. Tomorrow, Crete. Day after tomorrow, back to Russia. He could nearly see himself from the outside at times like this, moving about or standing still. His thoughts, his censored thoughts became transparent then; there was no hiding them, or from them, or from himself. He padded layers of extraneous ideas over those thoughts, for safety. He ate alone in the mess hall of the Romanian Air Force. With nothing to read but dailies already gone through and the politically dubious Joyce novel, Bora searched his memory for Greek words to use in Iraklion, as if ancient Greek would avail him at all. The sole quotation that came to mind from his schooldays began *Essetai e eos e deile...* something-and-something. The *Odyssey,* maybe. Ulysses had travelled much less conveniently than modern man, for ten full years. *More: he did ten years of war plus ten years of wandering, before making it back to his home, such as it was.* Essetai he heos… *"A dawn will come": who the hell says that?*

It was 450 plus miles to Athens. The Junkers left Bucharest shortly after four, in heavy rainfall. When they reached the Danube, the weather cleared unexpectedly, as if the world were turning a page. Mountains, plateaus, eventually the distant blue of the sea: another dimension opened, where the afternoon grew increasingly bright. Bora reached Athens around eight in the evening, drowsy but not at all tired despite the long journey. *Essetai he heos he deile*: those few Greek verses rolled in his recollection as he dozed off.

TUESDAY 3 JUNE, 6.36 A.M., ATHENS, GREECE

It was impossible or too early to say whether the day would be sunny. Mist rolled in from the sea when Bora reached the harbour and climbed into the rowing boat that would deliver him to the plane. The mode of transportation for the final leg was an ambulance Junkers, an "Auntie Ju" marked by a red cross and equipped with floats. Its crew, making back for Crete after delivering to the city infirmaries German paratroopers injured in the fierce days of fighting, agreed to take Bora only on account of his higher orders.

That the conquest of the island had been a bloodbath, Bora knew from unofficial embassy reports. Sporadic enemy resistance in the hinterland still posed a major danger and would continue to do so. Nonetheless (or because of it), army reporters and photographers were flooding in to present it as a resounding success: after all, the Brits and Colonials had been roundly beaten, losing lives, equipment and vessels in their flight.

Ahead of Bora, the medical personnel had already taken their places on board. He saluted and was at once the focus of their attention; his own, acutely aware of more disturbing odours under the whiff of disinfectant, plunged him for a moment back to Krakow nearly two years earlier, when he'd stared at colleagues torn to shreds in a grenade attack. Nurses, medics, a surgeon, all cramped in the facing rows of stretchers that replaced the seats, were clearly wondering who he was.

There was nothing to be done. Feeling more out of place than ever before in his life, Bora had the choice between taking the last corner available on the backmost stretcher or trying to balance on his feet for the next two hours. Dignity won over comfort, and he sat down cramped, hoping to be ignored. The surgeon, however, scowled at him above his metal-rimmed glasses; the nurses gawked (one was pretty, with the upturned nose of a small dog, the others very plain and sunburnt). When the co-pilot made a last round before locking the door for take-off, the surgeon asked him directly, "Who's the decorative young buck?"

It had been unfeasible to secure tropical wear in Athens. Bora was still wearing his embassy gear, so the comment was justified. The co-pilot leaned over to answer something.

"He's going to Crete to do *what?*" the surgeon remarked loudly enough to be heard by all. Well, he *would* say that. Four thousand German casualties, whose blood and vomit were still staining Crete's rocks and polluting the air inside this plane, and this spit-and-polish intruder was travelling there to procure cases of wine. Bora inwardly blushed at the words. A sudden urge, very much like a yearning to *suffer* in order to be somehow worthy, washed over him; whether his reaction was resentful, childish or both, the surgeon's insult did not sting any less because of it.

No one addressed him during the flight, too bumpy for seeking refuge in reading, much less writing. Before the floats touched the water of Iraklion harbour, Bora unhooked the silver cord aiguillette from the buttons and from under his shoulder strap, slipped it off from around his right arm and put it away.

Essetai he heor he deile he meson hemar… The rest of the verses came back to him as the Junkers bounced and lifted great waves of spray to a rolling halt.

"A dawn will come, an evening, a midday when someone will bereave me of life in battle by the stroke of a spear or a bow's arrow."

Godlike, fair Achilles had spoken them, prophesying his own death as he readied to plunge his weapon into Hector's throat.

2

The splendour of daylight pointed to a place that seemed nothing but a German depot. The harbour was piled with materiel. Bomb-damaged, being cleared now of rubble, the dock lay cluttered with carcasses of fishing boats blown out of the water, sails, masts, oars, crates, containers of all kinds. End to end, three sand-coloured, diminutive Italian cars one could barely fit into reclined on their sides like a disjointed, broken toy train. A British truck and a German tracked *kettenrad* sat parked next to each other under a veil of dust as if they'd been there for years instead of days, or hours. No wind, only powdery stuff still coming down after the air raids and battle. Along the breakwater seagulls picked at floating litter, wary about nearing the shore.

A battered bus with a red cross painted on it idled in the confusion. Surgeon and nurses filed towards it, climbed aboard, were gone. Bora – whose orders were to stay there until his contact arrived – watched, shielding his eyes, as it clattered to town. Sea odours, war odours were strong; the light was strongest of all. June days might be endless in Moscow, but being dropped into this southern light was excessive, like regaining one's eyesight after an extended period of blindness. Two and a half hours south-east of Athens, the muted skies of the north seemed never to have existed. All appeared bright yellow to him. Yet from the air he'd seen green patches besieging the bony spine of the island; he'd seen and recognized the great saddleback of Mount Ida, but also squares of silver-green, olive groves and fields.

From where he stood, the town of Iraklion was difficult to judge. A squat fortress nearby jutted out to sea. Beyond, Bora made out a crowd of mostly two-storey buildings, gaps that marked narrow streets or demolished roofs. He imagined an atmosphere halfway between a Middle Eastern bazaar and an Italian piazza; given Crete's past under Ottoman and Venetian rule, both applied. Around him, only German soldiers were in sight, and heavy equipment that forced him to stay out of the way. Among the makeshift directions to this or that command post, nailed or glued to their Greek counterparts, a sign to his right read, "Look out: live high-tension wires." Bora picked his way carefully along as he reached the low wall bordering the wharf, because being electrocuted while requisitioning wine in Crete was not among his plans for the war.

The name of the contact he'd been given in Athens – a Major Emil Busch, German Twelfth Army *Abwehr* – surprised him given the modesty of his errand, particularly in a place where Air Force Intelligence was expected to serve. Standing where he'd be visible (and all too recognizable in his winter uniform), Bora had no doubt his man was on his way now.

Formerly attached to the DAK (Deutsches Afrika Korps), Busch looked every inch the part: pith helmet, colonial tunic, khaki shirt and tie, canvas top boots tied from knee to ankle. He seemed to have taken along the colours of the desert sand; the whites of his eyes, too, made dingy by the long-term use of anti-malaria drugs. They acknowledged each other routinely.

"How was your trip?"

Bora shook the outstretched hand. "Fine, sir, thank you."

"A bit long, I'll bet."

A raised left eyebrow, as if an invisible monocle kept it up, gave Busch a perplexed or critical glance; his voice, however, expressed nothing but formal solicitude. It did not call for a reply, all the more since Bora didn't feel tired at all. Only overwhelmed by the light. "I'm ready to proceed with the assignment, *Herr Major*. The pilot informed me there's a cargo plane leaving tomorrow at seven. I expect to be on it with the shipment."

On Busch's part, a small delay followed. Less than hesitation, more than an accidental pause. Bora had the distinct impression the interval meant, "That may not be possible", which was odd, since the major had said nothing of the kind. It was just that pause, like a shadow that flits by and leaves nothing behind. From the level of the harbour, Busch led the way towards a tall, modern building on a rise just inland, along a street facing the sea. His gait was slightly off, the left leg pivoted a little outward, drawing a quick half-circle as it took the next step. He spoke up over the harbour noises. "You'll recognize the Megaron. Five floors of hotel frequented by the best society in peacetime." He glanced over his shoulder, "By the way, when were you here last?"

"It's my first time, *Herr Major*."

"I understood it wasn't."

This too sounded strange. What difference did it make? Bora decided not to read more than there was into Busch's nonplussed words. "Perhaps because Grandfather Franz August served as vice-consul in Chanià earlier in his career. My mother spent some years here as a child."

"You don't know Crete, then."

"Not at all. I've only seen old photos of my grandparents' residence at the western tip of the island."

"Hm." At the entrance of the hotel Busch raised his hand in a half-wave, less than a military greeting, in reply to the guards' salute. "That won't help."

Ah-ha. This was more concrete than a pause. Bora followed, glad to get out from under the sun. "Forgive me, but why would I need to be familiar with Crete? I only have to pick up those confounded bottles and wait for the next flight out."

Instantly, and for a moment more, stepping indoors from the blaze of the harbour seemed cool darkness itself. Busch was standing in it, at the centre of a devastated lobby. "…You did, until this morning."

"I only arrived this morning!"

The major summoned him closer. His movements were small, controlled to the extreme, a habit of working in the heat: lifting his forefinger and hooking its tip once or twice did it. "Something came up, *Rittmeister.*" In a lower voice, he added, "You can tell by looking around – I'm sure you saw the state of the harbour from the air – that the last two weeks have not been a picnic. In the middle of all this, counter-intelligence is in the political doghouse. As if our preliminary reports that the locals are fiercely independent meant they'd dislike the Brits and love *us.*"

Underestimating enemy numbers sounded more like it. Bora only said, "It's obvious there was no red carpet waiting."

"Right." Busch inhaled noisily. Although only around forty, he had one of those faces that wrinkle up entirely and age years when grimacing. "I'd rather say no more about it. Follow me, please." *Something came up.* From habit, Bora didn't solicit details when orders were concerned.

Clearly, they'd changed since his departure from Moscow. How, where, by whom, he might or might not be told. They couldn't be worse or less useful than those he presently had, so he kept his mouth shut waiting for more. One step behind

Busch, he crossed the lobby between piles of broken window glass, trying not to think ahead. Compared with Russia, the heat was brutal. He'd reconciled himself to winging it for twenty-four to thirty-six hours in his Moscow uniform, and having it laundered as soon as he returned to the National. Now...

"You'll have to secure tropical gear." Busch seemed to read his mind. "You can't trek around in riding boots."

Trek around? Again, Bora said nothing. They had meanwhile stepped into a large room, a breakfast or dining space freed of tables. Photographs of the Greek royals, taken down from the wall, sat propped up on the floor – a sad-mugged king who'd spent half of his life with the crown in his suitcase, and a childless Bulgarian queen with plenty of lovers. A stack of coffee cups crowded a sideboard. Some clean and bone-white, most of them dirty, they let out a whiff of strong coffee as Bora went past. Sturdy brew, Turkish-style, memories of Morocco and the Spanish Foreign Legion. Either left behind by guests fleeing in haste, or used by troops of one or the other army, that forsaken porcelain heap implied even more than the downed royal portraits.

Busch reached a desk (the hotel manager's?) near the far wall. Crowded with folders, and now topped by the discarded pith helmet, a huge mirror to its right reflected it, opposite a window just as large and paneless, also reflected. Two desks and two Emil Busches, bathed in a pool of splendour by the doubled, unmerciful daylight.

Once he had removed his visored cap, Bora blinked in the glare. *Something came up.* He experienced something just below excitement, a physical unrest on the verge of becoming ela-tion. He thought of Herr Cziffra in Aragon, or Colonel Kitzel in his own hometown, Leipzig: a brand of officers like Busch, who had for the past four years got him in as much trouble as they had kicked him into growing up. Outwardly, he waited without showing any reaction other than to the excess of light. When he estimated that no spontaneous explanations were forthcoming, he only asked, "Where may I secure what I need?"

Busch squinted as he looked up from the desk, as did his mirrored twin. It would have sufficed to pull a curtain across the window or remove the mirror to diminish the glare, but clearly he liked it this way, or used it to unsettle his interlocutors. "Maps I can give you." He took a lengthy sip from one of several bottles of Afri-Cola set on the floor near his chair. "Do you by any chance read Italian?"

"Yes."

"Here you go, then." A handful of folded charts came Bora's way. "Clothing won't be easy just at this moment – you're tall, too."

"And I'm not Luftwaffe."

The half-empty cola bottle – pinched in the middle, with the relief of palm trees on the neck – balanced on the one corner of the desk that was free of papers. "You might have to mix and match. As long as you have the right headgear and insignia… There's a deposit of English tropical uniforms down the street." Busch scribbled on a piece of paper with the hotel letterhead. "See what you can find there."

Bora skimmed and pocketed the note, as he'd done with Deputy Chairman Beria's. "May I know what my orders are?"

"Oh, sure." The major reached for the bottle. He tilted it more and more as he emptied its bubbly contents to the last. "You must have been wondering." Again that snorting intake of air and a tight-lipped stretching of lips that expressed more discomfort than amusement. A manila envelope was retrieved from the pile. Out of it Busch pulled photo enlargements and a folder marked *Ampelokastro, eyes only.*

One at a time, one on top of the other, the photographs were laid so that Bora could glimpse them against the confusion of papers. "And here's the full report, to be read with utmost care. We need answers before the International Red Cross intervenes or *Reichskommissar* Himmler sends someone, and without stepping on the toes of the airborne troops too much. They're foaming at the mouth. How about a cola?"

"No, thank you."

"You should be drinking lots in this weather. I learnt it after getting sunstroke in Egypt. *Nerò* is water, *metallikò nerò* is mineral water, which you should always ask for. As I was saying, our paratroopers have seen their comrades riddled with bullets as they came down or got caught in tree branches; there's talk of torture and mutilations of those who fell into enemy hands, especially the Greeks'. I assure you, the airborne troops aren't keen on anything Greek at present, and you can't blame them."

Without saying it out loud, Bora wondered what chance he had of finding support for an enquiry. *Murdered civilians. Whatever it's really about, things don't look promising; it'll be like pulling teeth. There's little chance truth will be a question of concordance with events or anything else... Professor Heidegger notwithstanding.* He chose not to peek inside the folder, possibly the only way to avoid having second thoughts. "How much time do I have? I'm expected back in Moscow."

"We know where you're *really* expected, Bora. But that's three weeks away. Ambassador Count von der Schulenburg is *au courant,* to use diplomatic French. Colonel Krebs also, and though he isn't at all happy about it, as if wine mattered more than risking an international incident with Switzerland, he lets you off your embassy hook for a week." Busch replaced the empty bottle with a full one, which he opened and disposed of in one long gulp. Stiffness and protocol were not compatible with a belch, and in fact he amicably let go of both. "I'm going to take a leak now. Please review the stuff here and give it back. The photos you can keep, we've got copies. Goes without saying that by now it's well beyond *eyes only*." Halfway to the dining-hall door, he wagged his forefinger one centimetre either way. "And report back here when you're done at the depot: there's more to discuss. We'll find you lodgings somewhere in this building."

In the few minutes he was alone in the room, Bora read the physician's extended report to the head of the 7th Airborne Division. When the major walked back in refreshed, drying his hands on a handkerchief, the folder had already been returned to the desk.

"Questions, *Rittmeister*?"

"I'll have them when I report back, sir."

"Good. Since you'll want to get around independently from the Luftwaffe authorities, I'll work on procuring you a local guide. Without one, you stand to have your head blown off within a mile of the city wall. Come, I'll see you out and point you towards the depot." In the lobby, where the wintry glitter of broken glass resembled and made him long for ice and anything cold, Busch did a sudden about-turn. "In other matters, not altogether unrelated, we lost the von Blücher boys, 'Old Forwards" descendants, all in one day."

Bora halted so as not to collide with the major. "Good God, the eldest was born three or four years after me. I doubt the youngest was out of secondary school."

"Right. Well, they lived up – or died up – to their ancestor's Napoleonic fame. It seems they tried to rescue one another under enemy fire, and fell in succession. That's all the details we have for now. Two were recovered; we're still looking for the body of the seventeen-year-old." Busch resumed walking. On the threshold he finished the commentary, staring at the sea. "That, too, is Crete today."

10.50 a.m. Written while sitting at the edge of a fountain, in a square of Iraklion (or Hiraklion, Heraklion, Chandax, Kandyie, Candia, Megalokastro: the town goes by more names than any place has a right to have).

Half an hour ago, when I reported back from the depot, Major Busch wasn't at the Megaron, so I'm to try again in ten minutes. I can't believe my good fortune. There I was at dawn, mortified at sitting in good health inside an ambulance plane, and on the spur of the moment I get to risk my neck! To date, the worst thing that has happened to me was having my skull cracked by a rock in Poland. (Peter says I haven't been the same since, which of course is pure nonsense. It wasn't rocks that opened my eyes in Poland.)

To summarize things, a British POW accuses German soldiers (First Battalion, 1st Airborne Regiment, 7th Flieger Division) of killing five civilians without an apparent motive in the Cretan interior on 30 May. The matter is deplorable in itself, but not enough to justify the attention (I'm not saying that of the Red Cross, but the *Reichskommissar*'s). Details will no doubt follow regarding the victims' identities. Immediate complications, instead, come to mind: the Englishman who actually took the photos is not accessible; we only have a second-hand report from the officer who heard his story, still detained; the crime scene – if that's the right term – lies at some distance from the city, in a countryside all but pacified. How conceivable is it that alternative culprits pop up, or something else exonerates the paratroopers in a week's time, if at all? Perhaps the whole thing is meant as a show of concern, a flurry of activity to assure the *Reichskommissar* (and/or the IRC) that we've done everything possible under the circumstances.

Meanwhile, among the creature comforts I was given by an assistant of Major Busch's are: the ubiquitous Nivea cream (!), which I don't plan on using, salt tablets, a collapsible drinking cup, a first aid kit and a British archaeological handbook about the island. The latter surprised me at first, but it didn't take me long to appreciate the use of it: I can see it's got detailed information about Crete's geography and the state of the roads (none of them paved in the interior as far as I can tell), and additional maps. It also abounds of course in artistic and architectural data regarding the island's Minoan and Mycenaean past. I was hoping for a more practical guidebook, but I'll work with what I have, and maybe learn something in the process. It's by an Englishman gone native, a John Pendlebury, MA, FSA, who seems to have forsaken the trowel for the submachine gun (an SOE operative? Ten to one) and vanished – or was killed – outside Iraklion's walls a few days ago.

At the former CreForce depot I secured the best provisions, including a Belgian-made 640 pistol (that is, Browning High Power, the sort of weapon I'd kill for, and did get to use in Spain). Also: acceptable clothing, a map case, German mountain Jäger ankle boots (top quality, cleats and forty-four studs under the soles), etc… I'm only missing the fairy tale's thieving penny, which comes back to you when you pay with it, and brings along all the money in the other's pocket. If I manage not to be dragged in front of a German firing squad for wearing parts of an enemy uniform, it'll be strange but enthusing. I'm armed, equipped, have a rucksack. Now I only need my local scout – hopefully someone who understands something else other than a Greek dialect, even broken Italian.

It's hard not to think of Graf von Blücher's sons, three sunny lads if ever there were, from a long line of men fallen in 200 years of wars. I wonder if their poor mother has been told already, or goes about her days thinking them alive and well. Before leaving for the Polish campaign, I asked specifically that any bad news regarding me should go to my stepfather, the general. It'll be up to him to tell Mother and Dikta.

Time's up, must be off to the Megaron again.

"Frances L. Allen: you mean *Francis*, right?"

A dusty telephone had appeared on the crowded desk since Bora's last visit. Busch answered while wiping the cradle and dial with the same handkerchief he'd used as a towel. "No, it's a she. Worked with that Pendlebury fellow, knows every rock and tree in Crete, speaks Greek like a native." He stretched the handset across to Bora. "Will you please untangle the cord? Thank you. She isn't a looker either, so things ought to remain businesslike between you."

"They would regardless, *Herr Major*."

Busch urbanely swallowed a burp. "Maybe. I go by my old Classics: aside from that gadabout Ulysses who screwed everything he met on his way home, even prim and proper Theseus forsook his new Cretan wife after killing the Minotaur, and she'd helped him exit the maze!" He took back the handset and nestled it in the cradle. "Well, what do you say?"

Bora looked up from the scrap of paper with the woman's name written on it. "I wasn't expecting a US national, male or female, to be my guide. I'll take what there is, especially if I have to travel to the interior. What else should I know about the lady?"

"She's from Texas, married to a Greek presently dead or run off – I think the latter, possibly sailed away with the Brits. Politically unsound. A communist, I think. We told her he's severely wounded and in a German hospital on the mainland, depending on our good graces for his life. Otherwise, she might try to leave you in the lurch to go after him. Whatever you do, make sure you don't let on he could be somewhere in the hills; you'd be signing your death warrant."

"I see. Damn it, at least Theseus could trust Ariadne's thread to find his way."

"You can't. Don't quote me, but if she pulls a fast one, don't limit yourself to leaving her behind as he did: we can't afford witnesses, so – American or not – shoot to kill."

"Understood."

"She's being driven now from a gathering point for foreign nationals near Chanià. I'll introduce you this evening." Both Busches – real and mirrored – pulled back in the chair and loosened their collars. "We – well, *invited* her to be our guest in Iraklion on 1 May, after news of the massacre began to circulate. She has been informed she's to assist you in your movements. What? I can't tell from your poker face whether you're pleased, displeased, or equanimous about your new task. Here, a free gadget to sweeten the pill a little." Out of a drawer, a khaki-coloured glasses case was fished out and tossed Bora's way. "Courtesy of an RAF pilot from 30 Squadron, who left them on the runway at Maleme. US-made, unusual green lenses, hope you won't mind. I understand them to be comparable to German quality. At least you won't go blind."

Bora recognized the coveted American brand. Quickly he took the sunglasses out and examined them. "Thank you, *Herr Major.*"

"Enjoy. Now we'll make a few hairy phone calls – or not." A frustrated slamming down of the handset followed. Busch surged from his chair, and so did his mirrored self. "*Sergeant!* Damned telephone won't work! Get back here and fix it on the double! All right, Bora, your questions first."

"The basics: I need to know who actually witnessed the incident, the identity of the victims, the name of my counterpart in the First Battalion, and when and where I may meet the British officer who surrendered the camera to us."

"Fair enough. Come, let's take a walk outside while they fix that thing. I've got a bad back; can't sit too long anyway."

Once outside, they veered away from the harbour and down a crooked street that led downtown. Bora had walked it returning from the depot (a faint, sweetish smell of carcasses still buried under rubble, a stable with a dead donkey in it, wild-looking cats squatting on demolished windowsills). And then, wrought iron balconies, narrow pavements, torn canvas awnings. Busch strolled along with his sickle-step and perplexed eyebrow. "The victims were not a family in the common sense of the word, Bora, or rather they were such in the Latin sense of a *familia* comprised of master and servants. The woman was a housekeeper and the young men hired hands – all locals working for Dr Professor Alois Villiger, fifty-nine, a Swiss national." He pulled out of his inner pocket a grey-blue passport, which he handed to Bora. "You can keep this. See for yourself: a scholar and connoisseur of antiquity."

Bora eyed a few pages of the document and pocketed it. "Like half of the foreign intellectuals wintering in Crete, as far as I know."

"…Point taken. He was also an expert on Germanic ancestry and a consultant to the *Ahnenerbe*, a personal friend to *Reichskommissar* Himmler, who will blow his top if he learns that the Air Force shot him dead."

"Ah." Bora's heart skipped a beat. Even under the shade of his visor, the dazzle of the street was insufferable. Etiquette forbade the wearing of sunglasses while speaking to a superior, so he looked down to protect his eyes and hide his surprise. Despite the difference in the light, smells, temperature and street noises, the moment he blinked other odours and sounds flooded in: the liquor factory behind the hotel, smoke from the distant steelworks, trolleys and buses rattling along Gorky Boulevard. The Kremlin carillon chiming *The Internationale*. Maggie Bourke-White's lilac scenting the hallway. In a bewildering flash he was back in Moscow, and at the same time wondering what he was doing here, being given such news. He had to snap out of it to come up with a reply.

"Forgive me for being cynical, Major Busch. All you'd really need, then, is to dispose of however many copies of the photos you have, and let it go as an unfortunate, unresolved instance of civilian casualties."

"Except that the British officer will seek out the International Red Cross if its personnel don't fly in before he does. His name is Sinclair, Patrick K., a first lieutenant in the Leicestershire Regiment, 14th Infantry Brigade."

"Sinclair. A Scotsman?"

"Don't know. But he's determined, and unless we're ready to silence him too, the cat's out of the bag one way or another. Having destroyed photographic evidence would only make things worse then."

Bora made a dutiful mental note of the odd expression, *silence him too.* "Any news of the actual witness?"

"No. We don't even have a full name for him yet, though we might soon. 'Sergeant Major Powell' is how Lieutenant Sinclair identified him. He managed to slip off and take to the mountains. Both he and Sinclair were in a queue under guard. There was an excess of prisoners in that particular spot, so in the confusion a handful darted away. Of those the guards fired after, three were shot and killed right off. Two may have been wounded: they leapt clear out of sight. What's important is the roll of film, you'll agree."

"I agree to a point. Where's the camera?"

"We lost track of it after the photos were developed for the War Crimes Bureau. We know it was a non-professional affair, a small Kodak such as even we use."

"Does Lieutenant Sinclair know what's in the photos?"

"We didn't show them to him, but yes: Powell told him how the contents of the camera supported his story. Sinclair surrendered the camera to us only against assurance the photos would be developed. He insisted on seeing the appropriate authority as well, which is how he got to make his report to Dr Unger of the War Crimes Bureau on 31 May. Unger had the photographic prints made, and following the directions Sinclair received from the actual witness, visited the crime scene on the same day. As you read, the bodies were removed on Saturday after Cretan police arrived on the scene." A blue awning, deeply sagging but still intact, promised some respite from the sun. Followed by Bora, the major withdrew to it and stood in the shade, by the entrance of an empty shop.

"When will I be able to interrogate Sinclair, *Herr Major*?"

"It might not be feasible to get him here from the internment camp until the morning. He was one of the Brits assigned to Crete well before the invasion, so they'll be grilling him for information. Stayed behind near Iraklion with two men to allow the bulk of his unit to withdraw safely, and paid for it by falling prisoner himself. Remember to do the same, should you find yourself in similar circumstances, *Rittmeister*. Between now and tomorrow I'll schedule other meetings for you. The day is young." Falling prisoner was nothing Bora was remotely contemplating at this time. He prudently faced the street. No local residents were in sight. The town must have been evacuated for the most part; German vehicles and personnel had taken over for now. They'd eventually migrate back from the countryside, the elders and women of Iraklion, but few of the healthy men: they would do what Frances Allen's husband had done: sail away or take to the mountains with shotgun in hand. Then again, some might have stayed in town, hiding in wait for the distracted invader with his back to the street.

Bora said, "I'm curious to hear Sinclair's point of view, or rather our camera-toting Powell's, through him, on why paratroopers should break in to kill unarmed civilians. Strictly between us, I understand a trained commando bursting in with guns blazing if they were under orders of some kind or acted on a tip. Is there a report of valuables in the villa, antiquities and the like?"

"On the contrary."

A warm breath of wind from across the street brought the stench of something dead and irretrievable in the devastation of a building. Bora couldn't help turning his face, but not the major. Busch only perspired heavily, as if all he'd drunk thus far was oozing out of his pores. He gave the impression that one could squeeze him dry like a sponge, and that sunlight might shrink him to nothing. He said, "Villiger kept files, choice artefacts and research funds in a vault of the National Bank of Greece here in town. The *Reichskommissar* himself gave him orders in that regard. Come, *Rittmeister*, let's keep walking that way; there's a street-side canteen where we can get something cool."

They continued as far as, and then went past, the captured depot, a point beyond which Bora hadn't yet ventured. More and more, the street resembled a funnel of liquid sunlight; its narrowness crowded with litter and vehicles dissolved, human shapes melted into it. *Purgatory must be something like this*, Bora thought, *a cramped pass that if we only slide through it leads to the Throne of God. But there'll be no stench of death there.* Grounding himself was still hard; he made an effort to stick to business, such as it had become in the last three hours.

"*Herr Major*, according to the extended report the shells recovered from the crime scene are 9×19 mm Parabellum, consistent with the MAB 38 submachine gun our paratroopers are known to employ. We have photographs. In the remote event I could prove that Germans have nothing to do with killing a Swiss national, it's doubtful I'd have time and opportunity to discover the actual culprits. What then?"

Thankfully, they turned into a shady lane, away from the heat. To all appearances, Busch's interest was drawn to a modest facade whose entrance was marked by an overhang of corrugated iron. Nothing but debris remained of the house next door, pulverized by a direct hit. A forlorn string of braided garlic crowned plaster and broken tiles, making it look like a vampire's final resting place. Busch walked and said nothing. Bora, however, understood from his silence that a surrogate plan was afoot in case of failure. A stab of impatience prompted him to go beyond tact. "Since the major doesn't seem inclined to discuss the likely alternative, I will venture a guess: blaming the locals and carrying out a reprisal on trumped-up charges flies square in the face of the War Crimes Bureau and its interest in this matter. It's counterproductive; it'll further exacerbate sentiments against us on the island at a very bad time. I'll be no part of it."

"Oh?" Busch turned to face him. He seemed genuinely entertained by Bora's words. "Yes, yes, we heard you were one of General Blaskowitz's scrupulous boys in Krakow. We're not in Krakow, and I guarantee that in *three weeks* you'll be eating your self-righteousness. Tell me: you get along with your employer, Count von der Schulenburg – yes?"

Getting along, when referring to a top diplomat and a young company officer in his employ, was an expression wholly out of place. Bora made an effort not to wonder about it. "As you may judge from my present charge, *Herr Major,* I am at the margins of His Excellency's circle."

"Are you?" Busch seemed in no hurry to leave the relative comfort of the shady lane, or else he meant to keep Bora cornered and listening. "His son, Fritz-Dietlof – quite the traditional soldier. Refers to civilians as 'mob', the old-fashioned way. An interesting career, from police vice-chief in Berlin to deputy president of Upper and Lower Silesia, to officer in the 9th Infantry Regiment. Does he frequently phone the embassy in Moscow?"

"I wouldn't know, *Herr Major*."

"No, of course you wouldn't. It isn't part of your job."

Bora's sense of alarm was heightened, but the reason for it was too vague to pinpoint. "Should it be?"

"It should."

The conversation seemed to end there, but Bora wasn't about to content himself with half-words at this point. "Is there anything in particular I ought to know regarding phone conversations at the embassy, or conversations in general?"

Busch looked away from him, and at the ruined house across the street. "Well" – he spoke slowly, conserving energy even in his speech – "it's all right as long as one preaches 'manorial socialism', Prussian-style, in the manner of Luddite estate owners who reject industrialization and city life. That's *picturesque*. The choice of tea-party guests, however – I expect you're not acquainted with Admiral Tirpitz's grandson Harro Schulze-Boysen, or his wife Libertas." (Bora confirmed he was not.) "He works for the Ministry of the Air Force, and we have reason to believe he frequents among others one Alexander Korotkov of the Soviet news service, assigned to Stalin's embassy in Berlin."

The story, wholly unexpected, was so extreme that Bora doubted what he was hearing. "Is this a test?"

"When you're put to the test, you'll know it. Keep your ears open for any father–son phone exchanges between the Schulenburgs, or between the ambassador and senior government advisor Arvid Harnack. We have it from a reliable source in Casablanca that someone in that diplomatic circle is leaking information about our forthcoming Russian plans. I don't know about you, but I make a distinction between intellectual discontent and treason."

And he'd been ordered to act engagingly in public toward leftist foreigners like Erskine Caldwell and his lilac-loving wife! Bora was in a cold sweat.

"I'll keep my ears open, *Herr Major*."

"Good, I thought so. Undersecretary Manoschek thinks highly of you."

"Manoschek!"

"He's not so stupid as you think he is. He kept us informed. When you were shipped off more than 3,000 miles away to fetch wine, we suspected they meant to remove an *Abwehr* officer from the embassy for a few days. When they stuck you with a prickly murder case to solve here, we knew they needed more time before that *Abwehr* officer returned to Moscow. Manoschek is in Berlin to check things out at that end. We keep under strict surveillance all incoming and outgoing embassy phone calls at present." Busch resumed walking. "See there?" He pointed out a shopfront a few doors past the ruined house, reachable by climbing down a few stone steps. "That's one of the establishments where you must go to secure good-quality Mandilaria. Ask for Panagiotis. Now please follow me."

Bora couldn't find one word to say. So this was what the expression "pulling the rug out from under one's feet" meant. *We*, as used by the major, could stand for the intelligence network in North Africa as much as for a pinch of entrepreneurial *Abwehr* officers ranging far beyond their territorial bounds. *He knows about me in Poland, my troubles with the SS: unless he was there, he's unusually well-connected. What else does he know?*

Their destination, a dark little cafe recycled as a canteen, let out a sour, less than inviting odour of spilt beer, piss and whiffs of seafood being fried in olive oil, a fitting image of two cultures forced together by war. Preceding him to the threshold, Busch decided to answer Bora's scruples about solving the case. "Unless light is shed on this murder, *Rittmeister*, a reprisal will follow. There must be culprits; they will be fabricated if necessary." Once indoors, only his voice remained, like the Cheshire Cat's smile. "I bet you're wishing you were still charged with raiding Cretan cellars."

Ten minutes later they were still there. Busch whispered useful details over a large glass of water and mint; Bora listened and sipped an insipid coffee made from instant powder, barely warm. Bitter dark grains, still undissolved, frothed on the surface; he crunched them under his teeth because they were the sole thing in the cup to have a taste. In the dimly lit room, maybe five metres in length, the odour of damp plaster and brick dust combined with the smells he had already perceived before entering. Around a table some mountain Jäger sat guzzling beer directly from the bottle. For all of their apparent relaxation they were armed to the teeth, like dogs placidly chewing on their bone but ready to yank the chain to jump you.

Busch kept his tone to a level that allowed the sharing of news otherwise best imparted in private. "What's the right expression? *In camera caritatis*, between you and me, Dr Unger tells me squads like the one in question, belonging to the same regiment, were involved in post-battle incidents both in the French campaign and here, resulting in the deaths of civilians. It's possible it went as we're told."

"Why should *we* pursue it, then?" Still troubled by the previous conversation, Bora felt something close to resentment. He didn't like drinking places, their odours and their customers.

Glancing to his left, away from the street entrance, through a low back door he could make out a tiled space, the size of a lift shaft, shady like a square well of high brick walls. There, the angle of a little free-standing structure, hardly more than a sentry box, signalled the fetid latrine. A skirting of mildew met the green mush at the foot of the brick wall, fissured from top to bottom as if lightning had struck it and tried to halve it. Out of sight, something made of metal, unhinged or loose, squeaked like a rusty weathervane on the upper half of the wall. "The investigation should rest with the War Crimes Bureau or the Red Cross, Major Busch, aside from the fact that *those in question* may try to sabotage the enquiry in any way they can."

"They'll do that in any case."

"Why not involve the Air Force *Abwehr*, then? It's way out of our competence; lack of collaboration is understandable under the circumstances." Bora tensely squared his shoulders. Ever since he'd entered the canteen something he couldn't quite put his finger on had raised his level of alertness. The habit of keeping physically on the lookout even when his thoughts were elsewhere made him uneasy, but feeling uneasy was not yet perceiving a threat. It had nothing to do with his new task as far as he could tell – any doubts in that regard were wholly rational. Whatever it was that tried to distract him, or gain his attention, had no recognizable source. Here and now, Bora wasn't even sure which of his senses was involved. He said, "As I see it, the *Reichskommissar* wants the truth, regardless of *Reichsmarschall* Göring's Air Force; the War Crimes Bureau is concerned with IRC reactions if there's no attempt to look diligently into things; the LW rejects all accusations and resents any intervention from the outside. Only two out of three want a culprit; two out of three – not the same as above – hope we Germans have nothing to do with the deaths. Are we expected to show we made an effort, or are we serious about this?"

Receiving no answer only increased his restlessness. He understood a change of mood when Busch suddenly switched topic and raised his voice. "The Venetian bastions and gates mark Iraklion's perimeter; it's a spiderweb where if you follow a radius from the centre out, you can't help leaving town and you can't get lost."

"Right." Bora exchanged a curt acknowledgement with two newly arrived lieutenants in baggy paratrooper garb. It would be superfluous to tell the major that if he hadn't lost his way in a metropolis like Moscow, it was unlikely he'd be trapped in Iraklion. The officers reached the counter, ordered beer, and withdrew to a table by the entrance.

"Go and see about the wine after lunch," Busch went on in the same audible tone. "That way you'll have the crates ready to go when you're done."

"I will." Bora put down the cup without finishing his coffee. Seemingly, the extent of his enquiry would remain undetermined for the time being. It might all depend on the "hairy phone calls" to be made once back at the hotel. It was safe to assume they were meant to obtain permission to proceed, clearing the path through Air Force resistance with a general officer's direct order. Not the best way to start an investigation. He'd have to pack in all the necessary groundwork within the next few hours, so that meeting Sinclair in the morning would find him prepared to ask pertinent questions.

The squeaky grating of loose metal out back jarred his nerves. He blamed his state of alert on it, but his physical response was disproportionate to the source. *It's something else,* he tried to reason, *and there's a touch of danger behind it. It wants to be seen, or heard, or smelt. Whichever sense is involved, I must isolate it by a process of elimination. Are the paratroopers behind me spying on us, commenting? Surely Busch's vagueness suggests one or the other. But they aren't the threat, not yet. Whatever it is, it* is *about hearing. I feel I'm straining to catch voices, sounds I don't actually hear. So, what good does instinct do?* "Panagiotis will direct you where there's excellent bottled Dafni to be had" – Busch continued his artificial dialogue. "Once you secure however many bottles you need —"

Bora's alarm peaked. Impulsively, he looked beyond the major's shoulders. *It's not what he's saying, nor the whispered talk around the tables. It isn't* words *at all.* From the cramped little passage to the latrine, the whine of corroded metal kept coming. *Is that it? No, that's not it, either.* The source, however, the locus *was,* there.

Busch didn't have time to finish the sentence. From out back the inaudible crossed the threshold of hearing: the ominous sounds of a hull about to break into pieces, a deep groan of planking and beams under great pressure. In the twilight of the canteen, Busch barely completed a startled about-face before everything in the rear of the building came crashing down. The mouldy brick wall imploded, folded over the latrine and its cramped enclosure. Masonry, baked clay, pieces of blighted plaster painted and unpainted, gutter pipes, roof tiles erupted through the back door into the canteen. Counter and shelves shook, bottles fell. A choking haze blasted in like a volcanic cloud.

Realizing that the cave-in was not actually above them was little consolation to the clients, overwhelmed by scattered fragments and powdered limestone. In an overturn of tables and chairs, Jäger and paratroopers scrambled to the exit, gagging, cursing in the dust storm and shouting obvious and irrelevant comments, such as "Shit almighty, I was just there in the loo!" Bora and the major were the last to emerge from the canteen (after all, you have to show your colleagues how cool-headed the Army is about things). Dust dispersed quickly in the open.

The dazed communication among survivors was reduced to blasphemy and grumble. As they stood in the lane brushing themselves off, cracking and snapping sounds went on for nearly a minute, followed by the metallic clank of falling bricks.

"Is everybody out?" one of the paratrooper officers called, counting heads. "Everybody's out." The impassive Busch had lost his pith helmet in the confusion, and grime stuck to his sweaty head. "So much for that." He might be referring to his headgear or to his interrupted drink. "Bora, let's go back to the hotel."

A preoccupied Bora followed. *The question stands: what good does a sixth sense do if it doesn't shield you from trouble? One might as well turn it off.*

Together they rounded the corner from the lane onto the main street. There, an Air Force patrol did its rounds unaware of the incident. The men stomped as they marched, and sang, "Paratroopers, paratroopers, / right on, 'gainst our foe!" shouting the last three words.

Whether the synchronous tread of boots had anything to do with it, or else cave-ins follow a sympathetic mode in old, crowded towns, just then a row of evacuated houses – thus far apparently unharmed by the air raids – came down one after the other. Their facades slid vertically of their own accord, as if pared away by a knife. Walls in pale, chalky colours appeared in a totter and dangle of cheap furnishings and framed pictures of long-dead relatives or who knows what, an iron bed tilted foot first, half in, half out. From the cascading stonework a bloom of bright dust sparkled and seemed to catch fire in the sun.

The patrol transiting below was nearly crushed by debris. Bora saw the paratroopers scatter, and then react back-to-back in a defensive cluster, as if you could ward off raining bricks. A whirlwind of dust rained over them, engulfed them, drifted here and there. Within seconds the heaviest particles began to settle like foil in a snow globe. In the agitated middle of it, a ghostly figure writhed to disentangle itself from under the rubble. Even from a distance, army trousers and haircut gave him away as non-Greek. Naked to the waist, white with atomized chalk like a fish ready to be fried – Bora wondered if the frying pan in the canteen was still going, a completely ridiculous thought at this time – a British or Anzac soldier crawled out of a basement on all fours but unafraid; his entire self had a look of spiteful defiance when they jerked him up by the arms and pointed guns at him.

"Imagine that. They come up like rats," Busch said through his teeth. "There's got to be hundreds still around, Christ knows how many on the island."

As if on cue, one of the paratroopers obliged the major's curiosity by levelling his weapon and firing at will against something else that moved across the ruins. Feet planted in the rubble, a half-rotation of his torso was all it took. No anger at all in the burst from his machine gun; at most a vicarious comeuppance after being forced to hang fire before an enemy regular. One, two figures trying to scamper off went down, like animals at the slaughterhouse. Greek deserters or conscripts? Civilians? Impossible to say; they only had their underwear on.

Bora heard one of the mountain Jäger in the lane behind him utter, "What the hell...?" and run up to gawk. They all hurried past in a group, as if they could only move or think together. They carried the salvaged bottles of beer with them in hand and underarm, as there was "no trusting the canteen," they said, "with a gas stove for frying that could blow sky-high at any time."

Down the street the paratroopers searched the wreckage. Over rubbish and litter, slowly, braiding a wake of mealy dust, a requisitioned truck with Arabic plates from the British experience in Africa arrived to claim the living and the dead.

"Let's go, the telephone will be working now." No remark escaped Busch on what had passed from the moment he'd seen the Briton captured. He turned around, taking measured, sure steps with his scythe-like gait.

Maybe the two Greeks were not dead, who knows, or not dead enough. Bora heard the pop of handguns administering a *coup de grâce* as he followed the major up the sun-gorged street. *At this very moment they're passing through the narrows of Purgatory, if the Orthodox believe in it.*

At the Megaron, after the phone calls, there was time for a sandwich, and Bora was assigned a room upstairs for the night. Busch yanked open with the bottle opener the second-last Afri-Cola he kept by his desk. "I'm busy until 17.00 hours or so," he said. "Go up and change or whatever, check on the wine and then wait until you're called." The angle of the sun having progressed, there was less of a dazzle around him. His mirrored double looked altogether dim as he joined in the toast. "Oh, wait," he said, calling Bora back. "I forgot to tell you: I've got the name of your liaison in the First Battalion, Captain Gottwald Preger."

"Captain *Waldo* Preger?"

"Why, yes. Excellent soldier. Do you know him?"

"Well, I knew he was in the airborne troops. We used to play together as children."

"Small world. All the better, then."

Bora saluted and left the room. No point in telling Busch he wasn't sure the acquaintance would help matters. Preger was the son of the family gamekeeper at Trakehnen: for all of Nina von Bora's broad-mindedness, the unequal relationship had turned awkward once the boys had grown. They'd last met three years earlier at the Preger home, back from separately volunteering in Spain. National Socialist egalitarianism or not, the old gamekeeper's deference towards young *Freiherr* von Bora had embarrassed them both.

As boys, on account of something or other they'd flown at each other one day and fought like wild dogs. His brother Peter, barely seven, had run home crying, with the result that Bora's stepfather had intervened with the heavy-handedness

61

of a massive, irate Prussian general. He'd literally carried the feisty Martin by the scruff of the neck to the gamekeeper's home, and made him apologize to Waldo's parents. And that was regardless of who started it or where the right lay.

It had smarted at the time, but Bora was used to iron discipline. Climbing to his fifth-floor hotel room, he took comfort in the thought that the reason for the boyhood contrast was lost to memory, at least as far as he was concerned. Either they had been playing rough and things had degenerated, or else there was some sort of juvenile principle involved. At a time when Bora's summers in fascist Rome had weaned him off monarchist ideas, most salaried small administrators still felt strongly about them. It was just as possible they'd thrashed each other over Hindenburg's presidency while playing cops and robbers, or cowboys and Indians. What was certain was that he'd gone to receive Confirmation at St Mary's Church with a black eye.

His room faced inland, and yet the pervasive odour of the sea breathed large through the open window: it rode a briny, warm breeze you could taste like salt on your tongue as you looked out. Above, the brightness of the sky was different from the shore, more tolerable, deeper at the zenith; it paled again at the southern horizon, past the glorious ridges, home to gods and heroes. Beyond the mountains, on the southern coast, lay the Libyan Sea. Between here and there, the forbidding rocky saddle of Mount Psiloritis, once called Ida, intervened with its crags, gorges, caves, plateaus, "impassable and impossible", according to Busch. Anyone who took refuge there, or from there sought the southern mountains, was as good as vanished.

Below, Iraklion sat packed in its fortified walls, a brick belt here and there overgrown with houses like lean-tos around a sheepfold.

This is where I am now, with a task to accomplish. Between now and the day I leave I must put out of my mind all Major Busch told me about Ambassador von der Schulenburg. I must keep from giving it the smallest thought, and come as close to erasing it as possible, without forgetting it. I must be so surgical as to be able to think of Russia, of Moscow, and not think of Busch's words.

Bora turned away from the window, as if only now the room were of any interest to him. A note typewritten in German, tacked on the inner side of the door, explained that toilet paper should not be disposed of in the bowl. Also, that although drinking from the sink was considered safe, it was best to rely on bottled water, or water-purifying tablets. There was a toilet but not a shower; another notice above the sink further informed that water must be conserved by taking a sponge bath (no sponge supplied: Bora made a mental note to secure one). A solitary, good-quality towel hung from the rack.

Enough to make one homesick for the facilities of his Moscow hotel. *See, I can think of Moscow and not of the* other *thing.* On the bed lay a pillow and a light cover, with pillowcase and sheets laundered and folded (but not ironed) at the foot of the mattress. In his orderliness, Bora made the bed tightly, army style, and sat on it to remove his boots.

When he unbuttoned and slipped off his tunic, the limp sprig of lilac fell out of his left cuff. Thousands of miles away from Russia and the branch it belonged to, still blooming in a vase in Maggie's room, it retained the faint echo of a scent. Bora couldn't say why he'd taken it along and kept it, other than that Maggie Bourke-White had answered his greeting the second day they'd seen each other, and young women one way or another stood in for his wife Benedikta, the only one he cared about. So the sprig of lilac represented Dikta as much as it did Maggie the American, a photographer it would be useful to have here now to help him look through the images taken at Ampelokastro. Bora picked the stem up from the floor; it found its place in his wallet, where he carried a snapshot of his wife.

For once he was sexually calm; he'd seen Dikta a month earlier for Peter's wedding, and things between them were strong, fine. Details of the ceremony had kept her busy for weeks; social animal that she was, she'd taken over where Margaretha "Duckie" Hennin's mother couldn't reach, or Bora's own mother Nina for that matter. What Dikta and Martin had shunned in their haste to marry – church, lavish feast, invitations – was organized in the smallest detail this time around. Never mind that Peter, son and half-brother of a landed aristocrat, what was then called a *Schlossbaron*, married into the family of a *Schlotbaron*, an industrialist ennobled by his business. All those who counted in Leipzig and Dresden were in attendance, plus the Hennin relatives and friends from Freiburg and Baden. Dikta, far more beautiful than the bride, made the papers in her Paris gown. Certain like everyone else that war would be over within weeks, she had planned the French honeymoon trip they hadn't had in '39. Bora said yes to everything, but had made no plans.

In front of the sink, he scrubbed up as best he could – to him *washing* meant a shower either cold or very hot: abundant, in any case. Inevitably, soapy water spilt on the floor all around.

After changing uniform, Bora opened the door of the hallway to get a cross-draught that would dry the tiles. His rinsed, well-wrung underwear he placed on the sunny windowsill, held in place by the heavy ashtray he'd found on the bedside table.

The colonial outfit was comfortable, less likely to draw attention. (He'd overheard the jeering comments – "Here comes the cavalry" and "Cavalry to the rescue!" – on his way to the depot.) Without waiting for the floor to dry completely, Bora shut and locked the door to have privacy while he looked through the photos of the crime scene. Busch had given him copies of those surrendered by Sinclair as well as of the batch Dr Unger had ordered to be taken for the *Wehrmacht-Untersuchungsstelle*.

Tolerance for the sight of death, built in Aragon first and amply perfected in Poland, took nothing away from a sense of melancholy bordering on guilt. The mortification Bora had experienced on the ambulance plane returned. Then, he'd felt indebted to his dead and wounded comrades, as if it were his fault that he was yet unhurt. Now he could watch these bodies, unnamed except one, all unknown to him, capable of speaking only through the merciless interruption of their lives, and feel that he should care – that he *owed* them something. The Japanese had a term for such obligation; he'd either read it or heard it from the eastern visitors to Leipzig two years earlier. You owe mentors, elders, all those who teach you: whatever the word was, he felt its weight. *And it must mean something that in German "debt" also means "guilt", and "care" and "worry" are one and the same.*

The black and white photographs showed an execution, nothing less. Blood sprayed on walls and furniture, soaked carpets; violence reflected on daily objects seemed twice as crude and out of place. Alois Villiger lay face up, shot first or in front of the others; the woman, his housekeeper, reclined across the long step that separated the room from a dais-like space lined with bookshelves. The hired hands, little more than boys, had fallen in a tangle of arms and legs as if they'd huddled together like frightened sheep. Through an archway, in the back, another sitting room or study was discernible, but not clearly. More books, a desk, a number of white oval spots – hanging plates? – on the end wall.

Villiger's appearance, as much as the post-mortem images suggested, was wide-chested, on the heavy side but as if deflated somehow in comparison to his passport photo. His meaty head, with sparse greying hair cut very short, seemed small for his size. He'd worn wire-rimmed round glasses – lost in the shooting but lying next to him on the floor. In his shirt and beltless trousers, both soaked in blood, he had a disturbing, aghast look of astonishment and outrage. The woman's foot touched his head, giving the odd impression of an acrobat balancing with arms outspread on top of her partner, poised to fly. Her plump fairness and dainty heeled shoes contrasted somehow with the standard idea of a Greek domestic, and although she appeared to be on the declining end of youth, she must have been her employer's junior by fifteen or twenty years.

Bora set down the prints in three rows across the bed. In whatever succession the individual frames had been captured, he changed their order over and again to reconstruct an actual chronological sequence, as seen by someone approaching from the outside. Paratroopers entering the garden. Outdoors and indoors shots, angle, proximity, the extension of blood pooling under the bodies – he shuffled them until he was satisfied he'd come as close as possible to creating a continuity of frames, like a still movie. On the back of every photo he pencilled a temporary number, and jotted down a few preliminary questions in his notebook. *I'm not sure I can have answers,* he wrote, *unless I confront all those involved, from the paratroopers to Sergeant Major Powell to the War Crimes Bureau physician to Lieutenant Sinclair, who is however only a second-hand witness. There could be others. Worse luck, Sinclair may be the only one I actually get to see.*

Next, he took out the Italian maps Busch had given him. "South of Iraklion, outside the Chanià Gate" were vague terms; Ampelokastro may or may not be actually marked as such, so he had to guess its location for now. The terrain seemed rough between the town and the southern plain of Messarà; names of saints dotted the trails leading south alongside valley bottoms: St Nicholas, St Miron, Mount Jerusalem, Saint John; Bora wondered what glorious antique place names hid under those banal indications of chapels and shrines. Ampelokastro could be along any one of the seven or eight routes leading south from Iraklion.

His eyes migrated west across the narrow, horizontal body of the island as pictured on the map, to the neck of the hammer-shaped peninsula north of Chanià, where his grandparents had lived from 1905 to 1906. It was the dangerous time of the Theriso incident, resulting in the first declaration of Crete's union with Greece. Only eight years earlier, the Turks had killed hundreds of Christian Cretans, foreign soldiers and even the British consul at Iraklion. As far as Bora knew, the family residence had in latter years become home to the Italian Archaeological School. In family albums the gracious house remained safe, locked in time with its airy porches overlooking the garden, carob trees and palmettos, happy dogs and his mother's pony (what was its name?), in view of the sea. These days, there was an internment camp nearby.

Bora glanced at his watch. Five more minutes, and he'd go to see Panagiotis in his shop, and ask about the wine. He'd then wait for Busch's call and the meeting with Frances Allen. There would be occasion to study the maps thoroughly and leaf through Pendlebury's book overnight.

The prosaic task of checking on the underwear laid out in the sun drew him back to the window. There, the hour's incandescence took him like vertigo. He had to pick shapes and distances out of the splendour, through the brackish heat, to steady himself.

No wonder, he thought. *It's like looking inland across the ages, more than I ever did in Moscow or elsewhere. Inland is remote antiquity itself: the place where Zeus was born, the sacred Ida massif. Inland are Ariadne, the labyrinth, the Minotaur, forsaken cities that faced attackers like us more than 3,000 years ago, and their ruins stand while memory of the attackers does not. Losing a battle or a war isn't necessarily the end.*

Sometimes victories – especially early ones – can lead to disaster, acting as deceptive corridors of a maze that has no exit if not through the monster's lair. Victors may write history, but losers are remembered longer, wept over for longer. This small town of Iraklion would fit inside the Kremlin walls. And we're going to war against all *of Russia.*

Pulling back into the room, by contrast with the outdoor light, was like stepping into purple darkness. Bora felt the chair, the bed by groping rather than seeing them. *I wonder why it is that I can let go so easily of a set of orders to accept another: am I such an unthinking, corpse-like, devoted soldier?* Perinde ac cadaver, Kadaverdisziplin *? Or do I grab the opportunity to do more, risk more, for my own motives, putting only the face of zeal on it? Until yesterday I would have carried out Lavrenti Pavlovich's request with anything but a cadaver's pliability. Today I listen to every new obstacle that gets in the way of a hopeless task, and while raising logical objections, inwardly I'm delighted. Clearly, I live for the orders that will be given us in three weeks, but even the fattest fly in the ointment – getting my head blown off outside the city walls, in Major Busch's words – cannot discourage me.*

By and by, the hotel room became visible again, with its notices tacked to door and wall, the maps, the few things that marked his transitory presence in Crete. Bora pocketed the Ray-Ban case before leaving for Panagiotis'.

An undertow of ideas churned inside him as he climbed down the flights of stairs two steps at a time, nearly at a running pace. *Small things always grow larger if you look into them. Much as I don't want to (and I don't want to), I'm beginning to feel an obligation to discover what happened at Ampelokastro. Why? Because, as Professor Heidegger puts it, "Moral conscience shows itself as a call to care." Because I was brought up to care, to carry out my duty, and duty is an obligation, however minor the task appears. Because I owe justice as much as I owe my family, those before me, my teachers and commanders. I owe those I serve with, my young wife. Above all else in the world, I owe Germany. Beyond that, I owe Almighty God.*

3

The only evidence of the wrecked wall behind the canteen was a veil of brick and plaster dust everywhere. In his shop below street level, Panagiotis, dark-eyed and unflappable as if walls came down every day, spoke nothing but Greek, a detail Busch had failed to share. Bora wrote down for him the names of the wines he sought. Trusting his schoolboy knowledge of the Greek alphabet, he specified *oinos* after the names. To his surprise, Panagiotis crossed the word out and wrote *krasì* in its place: *oinos* was what the ancients called wine; now it was *krasì*. He made the German understand by gestures that he kept the bottled Mandilaria elsewhere, and Dafni must be bought from another merchant. A drumming of fingers on his chest meant he volunteered to take care of the acquisition himself.

So far, so good. Seeing a fly-spotted calendar on the white-washed wall, Bora pointed to today's date as the desired time of delivery. Panagiotis shook his head. Shown the day after, again he signalled he couldn't guarantee the deal. Only after Bora indicated Friday, two days from now, and met with another shake of the head, did he recall hearing that Greeks move their heads from side to side to assent, and nod to deny. *Avrio,* tomorrow, they finally agreed in Greek, both kinds of wine to be delivered to the Megaron, already packed in four crates of twelve bottles each, and two six-bottle cartons.

As long as you buy and sell, language is seldom an obstacle. Panagiotis insisted on offering a complimentary taste of his Mandilaria as they parted ways. Bora accepted half a glass, but declined to chase it with a clear liquor he suspected to be ouzo or the Cretan version of it.

Back in his room, he red-pencilled on the map the trails that led inland from Iraklion. Ampelokastro was not marked; he had to circumscribe its approximate location relying on the hints Busch had given him – twelve or so miles south of the Venetian bastions, off the road that left town through the Chanià Gate. The problem was that the road out of the western gate in question forked left several times, and you could head south along any of those trails. Trails – in tall grass, along shallow rivers and through woodland – had been a boyhood passion of his, both at Borna and Trakehnen. Nothing like these winding treks up and down dry, craggy uplands: hunting and animal paths across green stretches of endlessly flat terrain; lonely, treacherous with marshy bogs. During vacations he'd wander for hours, with and without his brother, hardly ever getting lost and caring little that he might. Once or twice he'd returned after dark, finding Nina worried and his stepfather frowning but deep down satisfied that he had shown enterprise and courage. Only once had he taken the wrong turn and lost the way back. Neighbours, farmers living on the estate, those working in the stables had come looking for him in the woods bordering Lithuania. Eventually, he'd spied their torchlights dancing crosswise through the trees, heard the dogs and men calling. To resist the temptation of letting them find him, he'd stepped into the brook he was sitting by, and walking in the wet he made the dogs lose his scent. Only after the dispirited search party turned back at dawn had he followed them from a distance, because the authorities would be alerted next, and he wanted the satisfaction of arriving home before then. To this day, it was one of his favourite nights, sloshing homeward downwind, guided at first by distant flickers and faint barking sounds and then led by his instinct alone. *I'll always get home,* he'd told himself then, *no matter how far I go, no matter what lies between me and my parents' doorstep.* Distance, obstacles, had in one night become superable. *It'll be the same even if no one comes looking for me.*

Bora still thought so. Did anyone search for Odysseus, whom the Latins called Ulysses? No. Not even his grown son, who merely banged on the doors of family friends asking after him. This afternoon, under his red pencil, trails very different from those of his childhood days ran like fissures across Crete's long, narrow body, thin wounds showing flesh and blood through them.

The rap on the door at a quarter to four, too discreet to be from Major Busch himself, sounded like an orderly sent up early for one reason or another. Bora went to open the door with the pencil between his teeth – muttering "Yes?" – and surprise nailed him there for a moment.

The business card held up to him was faded, creased from sitting for ages in a wallet. "*Epitropos* Vairon Kostaridis," the newcomer said, "chief constable of the Iraklion police. They told me you understand Italian. I thought I'd come directly."

He was a round little man, bulgy-eyed, with the sad, pale face General Sickingen at home unfailingly identified with civilians and all others he had no time for, as "they've got stomach trouble written on their mugs". Stomach trouble stood in his military eyes for a spectrum of personality flaws, from apathy to dumb zeal, passing through cowardice and small-mindedness. To this day, Bora had to force himself not to judge men's faces, not to speak of women's, by his stepfather's standards. He took the pencil out of his mouth. In Italian, he only repeated, "Yes?"

because this visit could have as much to do with Cretan wine as with Cretan murder. *Damn it, though: he's the spitting image of Peter Lorre as the child-killer. You'd expect a Levantine to look this way in novels and motion pictures.*

"May I come in?"

"Please."

Kostaridis crossed the threshold. At a glance he took in Bora's discarded uniform and the high-power pistol on a chair, the wet towel, the bed covered with maps and underwear and the ashtray on the windowsill. "*Il maggiore* Busch" (he pronounced it Voos) "was kind enough to tell me I'd find you here, *capitano*, so here I am." He used the *voi* form of address, an etiquette imposed by fascism but harking back in fact to Italy's past. "How is it that you speak Italian?"

Bora folded and put away the maps as he spoke. "Crete was under Venetian dominion centuries ago."

"Indeed." Kostaridis observed the German's motions but kept a pleasant, self-deprecating smile. "I began my career in the Cretan Gendarmerie under Colonel Craveri, who patterned it after the Italian Carabineers at the turn of the century. Twenty-five years ago there were still Italian officers among us. If I may ask, how is it that *you* speak Italian?"

There was nothing to keep Bora from answering that he'd spent many summer weeks in Rome at the home of Donna Maria Ascanio, his stepfather's first wife. Instead – it was his way of drawing lines and defining distances, at least for now – he said, "It isn't relevant, is it? Kindly state the reason for your visit." Without adding that he was in haste (it was not true, and besides, it would give more information than he cared to share), Bora reached for the Browning pistol and ostentatiously started loading it.

No offer had been made for him to sit, and the only chair was occupied by Bora's riding breeches. Kostaridis remained standing. He kept – it must have been a habit – his head slightly tilted on his left shoulder, but not like someone suffering from a stiff neck. "I was first contacted by *maggiore* Voos, shall we say, regarding a shipment of Dafni and Mandilaria." (*Ah, that's how you pronounce those names correctly*, Bora told himself. *No wonder Panagiotis didn't understand at first.*) "This morning, *maggiore* Voos informed Police Chief Signor Polioudakis that for anything regarding the deaths at Ampelokastro" – he pronounced it *Ambelokastro* – "I should confer with you."

Too late, Bora realized that an interruption in his gun-loading could betray surprise, much as he'd caught puzzlement in Busch's delayed response when hearing he'd never been to Crete. So he pretended to double-check the shell he had in his hand before slipping it in with the rest. Silence per se was no sign of eagerness, and would force the policeman to say more. Kostaridis took a step around the bed, where a slight draught from the window relieved the stifling warmth of the room. From his new position he stared with great interest at the field-grey tunic draped on the back of the chair. The Horseman's Badge in gold stood out on it, the only medal Bora wore while on embassy duty. Wholly out of context, he said, "I was a member of the Greek team that won a bronze medal for shooting, thirty metres, military pistol, at the 1920 Olympics with Karainitis, Vaphiadis, Zappas and the Theofillakis brothers. The shooting range was at Beverloo, not far from Antwerp."

Yes, Belgium, the first Olympics after the Great War. They exchanged a look of appraisal across the floor. "Germany was not invited to the Games that year," Bora replied, dryly. The Greek ill-disposed him. He seemed insignificant to him and unforgivably shabby. A badly cleaned stain on his chest pocket betrayed the leakage of a fountain pen; black socks and sandals had more than an occasional familiarity with dusty streets. The young NKVD toughs at the street corner by Beria's house came to mind: sturdy, well-attired, capable of conveying danger; so different from the slipshod, frog-eyed fellow facing him.

The German's lack of empathy left Kostaridis undeterred. He said, "If I understood correctly, *capitano*, my duty is to provide any supplementary information you may need. Frankly, everything leads us to confirm that German soldiers, shall we say, carried out the attack. But I was told no stone must be left unturned in seeking out possible alternative explanations for what happened to Signor Filligi."

"...and Signor Villiger's domestics."

"*And* his domestics."

"They must have names, these people."

"They do. Siphronia was the woman. The hired hands were – let's see." (Kostaridis took out of his pocket a used, folded envelope.) "I've got it written here – Fotis, Panos and Konstandes. I don't think you'll need their surnames."

"They're not house animals. I *will* need their surnames."

Kostaridis read them out loud, and then showed their spelling on the envelope. No change of expression, only that shooter's head-tilt, although Bora's concern about the deaths of four local servants must strike him as unusual.

Bora rode the advantage he'd gained. "Do you have a list of possible culprits for me already, or are you in the process of drafting one?"

"Not a list per se, *capitano*. Rumours —"

"I have no time for rumours, Chief Constable. Either you have some information, or you don't. If you don't, I'll bid you good day." Being rude was not like Bora; being curt when faced with imprecision, very much so. His reply was the equivalent of pushing Kostaridis out of the room. The policeman stopped the door with his metaphorical foot.

"Maybe you should know who Signor Filligi was, and what he did and meant to Cretans."

"How long will it take?"

"If you listen closely, fifteen minutes will do."

It took less than that to summarize two years of the victim's life: Villiger's arrival at the start of 1939, the acquisition of Ampelokastro from an American scholar relocated to the mainland, his interest in antiquities and living remnants of the original Cretan people. Familiarity with the local language did not particularly distinguish him from other intellectual expatriates: the English, for example. He'd been a part of the island to the extent that any foreigner can be accepted by islanders. Nothing extravagant about him except his camera-toting trips. Once a month he hand-delivered the film to Iraklion for development, dined in town, checked on the regular money transfers received from Switzerland through the Iraklion branch of the National Bank of Greece.

Bora didn't miss a word. He actually began taking notes, which was as close as he came to admitting he appreciated the information. "Were you on the crime scene?" he prompted Kostaridis.

"I was. Your army notified us on 31 May, after they'd made a first inspection."

"These photos – were they shown to you?"

"No." And because Bora seemed disinclined to share his own folder, the policeman went back to his subject. "Subsequently, the villa was entered between the first and second day of June, reportedly by German troops seeking shelter for the night. It's to be expected that if they left the door open when they moved on, locals would quickly have flocked in to loot."

It was diplomatic talk on Kostaridis' part. Busch privately admitted claims of pillage on the part of the invaders: it was possible the Cretans had stepped in to finish what the Germans had begun. Different kinds of insects come to pick on the same carcass. "It complicates matters," Bora said, coldly.

"I agree."

"The bodies – where did they end up?"

"The young men were claimed by the families and returned to their villages. The woman, well, she was quickly interred in Iraklion to avoid problems. *Signor* Filligi, as far as I know, a German ambulance took to Chanià for burial with the non-Orthodox and other foreigners."

"'Quickly interred', 'problems'." Bora looked up from his notebook. "What do you mean by that?"

Kostaridis shrugged. "Superstitions, nothing relevant to the enquiry. *Si dice che a volte i morti di morte violenta camminano.* Now, for the alternatives —"

"What do you mean, 'They say that those who died a violent death *walk*'?"

"Nothing but local superstition, *capitano.* For the alternatives it would be wise, shall we say, to keep in mind one name in particular: Rifat Bayar Agrali, whom they address as Rifat Bey. He owns the property bordering Ampelokastro."

"I thought the generic title of respect among the Turks was *Effendi.*"

"A word actually deriving from *authentes,* which is Greek," Kostaridis tactfully pointed out.

"Yes, but the Agrali family gave administrators to Crete, so *Bey* stuck to the clan."

"Should I keep this fellow in mind because he may have something to do with this, or because he's a Turk?"

"I could tell you 'Both', *capitano,* and you'd make a certain judgement call. I could say nothing, and your judgement call would be another. I'll admit that I don't like Turks. This city was ninety per cent Turkish 100 years ago. As our martyrs of 1824 said, 'I was born a Christian, and a Christian I shall die.'"

Bora stopped short of a smile, but liked the answer. "Well, I have no love lost for the Mahdists, myself. They beheaded my great-grandfather in the Sudan." Just then, a sudden gust of wind pulled the windowpanes together, and he had to lunge for the imperilled ashtray before it plunged five floors down onto someone's head. He recovered it, but his undershirt floated out of his grasp into the sun.

"There's a garden below," Kostaridis drawled. "It won't go far."

A quick glance down confirmed the fact. Bora turned back to the room, aware that he'd lost the psychological upper hand and some of his dignity. "So," he said rather more sternly than was called for, "what did Agrali have to do with Villiger, dead or alive?"

"Other than proximity? Sometimes geographic proximity creates problems. And then there are two aggravating circumstances, shall we say. Rifat Bey has a vicious temper. That is number one. Rifat Bey does not like Germans. That is number two."

Bora interrupted. "Villiger wasn't German."

Kostaridis' smile was more condescending than apologetic this time. "Forgive me, but a Greek-speaker is a Greek; a German-speaker is a German. Besides, to us Greeks – Cretan or not – every foreigner is a *frangos*, whether or not he's a Frank by race."

"Good. Fine, then." It annoyed Bora that the policeman was secretly amused. *Of course, I nearly dropped an ashtray and barely saved my shorts from following the undershirt.* "Well, where do I find this German-hating Turk?"

"Maybe you should know more about him, too."

Bora laid the loaded and holstered Browning on the bed. This game of Chinese boxes could be a local habit of telling things piecemeal, or else Kostaridis' affectation, like his recurrent "shall we say". Clearly the policeman was studying him, making judgements, drawing his conclusions. Not one chance he was nearly as sleepy as he looked. *I may have started this conversation on the wrong foot,* he admitted to himself. *I could be making things more difficult for myself as a result.* "I took Italian classes," he volunteered, "but before then, I'd practised it in Rome as a child. I learnt curse words before I knew how to conjugate verbs. Feel free to move my uniform and sit down."

It wasn't much of an olive branch, but Kostaridis showed himself a sportsman. He carefully rested Bora's breeches and tunic at the foot of the bed before taking their place on the chair. "Thank you." He sat hugging his knees with his hands, like an old man, although he must have been between forty and fifty at most. "Sphingokephalo is the name of Rifat Bey's house, on Sphingokephalo Hill."

"I thought all Turks were made to leave Greek soil some eighteen years ago."

"Yes, but after the so-called Balkan Agreement of '34 and the normalization that followed, a few exceptions were negotiated. Additionally, through his mother Rifat Agrali was related to the Turkish signatory. He was born and raised on the island; his family – from Spaniako in the west, originally – owned a chain of emporiums and tobacco stores. They were the local distributors for choice American cigarettes, Anargyros' Murad, for one."

Standing with his arms folded and his back to the wall, Bora nodded. As a young woman his maternal grandmother was nicknamed *Murad girl*, like the rosy-cheeked odalisque on tobacco boxes and posters, and despite her being a Scot, both he and Peter took their dark hair from her. "I'm familiar with Murad," he said.

"Well, *capitano*, when the 'population exchange' between Greece and Turkey was agreed upon in 1923, Rifat Bey lost all he'd inherited from his elders in Crete, and his wife to cholera. Greeks repatriated from Anatolia took over his family business and houses, including Villa Sphingokephalo. What goes around comes around, I say. But there's no keeping a Turk down, is there? While in Istanbul, he took a rich Greek woman as his second wife. In Rhodes, he somehow became a partner of TEMI, the Italian Aegean Tobacco Manufacture. So, eleven years after being expelled, he was just the man who could manage to return to Crete. He couldn't buy back the family business, most of it gone under with the economic crisis. He could and did reclaim his house and property south of Iraklion, buying it from the repatriated Greeks who'd settled there and let it go to the dogs, it must be admitted."

"Not much of a deal, as I see it."

"Wait. He spent a fortune refurbishing the villa, and until last month he could boast of the highest quality Malvasia vines around. Cretan Muslims drink wine, in case you don't know. He has a large garage at Agios Mironas to service his trucks, which regularly ply the routes from Iraklion to his other businesses in the Plain of Messarà, and to Ierapetra. When his second wife died a couple of years ago, he built her a marble monument he hired an English architect to design. *Bellissimo*. You can see it from afar, from all directions. I'm told the villa was untouched by the fighting, although an air raid destroyed his winery, so he's likely to be even less well-disposed toward Germans of any kind."

"I don't see what any of this has to do with Villiger, even if their properties are adjacent."

Kostaridis looked at the ashtray, safely on the bedside table, as if inspiration could be derived from it. "That brings me to aggravating circumstance number three. A small watercourse, shall we say, runs between the two estates." (Bora wondered,

Shall we say *it's a watercourse, or* shall we say *the properties deserve the rank of estates?*) "Saving the Messarà plain and a few other spots, irrigation is a problem on the island. *Signor* Filligi begrudged the water necessary to Rifat Bey's vineyard. You'll object: not everyone involved in a land dispute can be suspected of his neighbour's death. But, *capitano*, a complaint was made against the Turk for opening fire against Filligi himself on a matter of trespassing. And with Rifat Bey there have been, shall we say, *coincidences* before. Three out of four of the repatriated Cretans who'd taken over the Agralis' business died within months of his return. True, he made no attempt to recover the family stores afterwards, but vengeance is a spice you can enjoy without sprinkling it on any food."

Bora sulked. The German word *Gerede* rolled in his mind. Chatter, gossip, hearsay. Too easy, too comfortable. A door opened where he'd not knocked in the first place. To a Cretan official, putting the blame on a Turk was just as expedient as accusing Germans, or vice versa. The truth might lie on either side, or neither. What did Professor Heidegger say? *He who is really on the right scent doesn't talk about it.*

"I don't understand this talk of coincidences, Chief Constable. Either you have reason to suspect the Turk, or you don't. If you believe him an instigator, you must be also implying that he secured assassins equipped with military weapons."

"That would not be a problem in Crete these days. Last time I checked, Rifat Bey had a regular arsenal in his house, including several high precision rifles." When Kostaridis rolled his eyes from the ashtray to Bora, he gave the impression of having just thought of something else. "There's another possible lead as well, linked to the housekeeper at Ampelokastro."

Of course, there we go, cherchez la femme. *I expected you to bring it up, because it's the sort of lead that would take a long time to follow.* Bora fidgeted. "Do you mean a love triangle?"

81

"No-o-o." Again, Kostaridis drawled his vowels. The sound was nasal, accompanied by a raising of eyebrows. "Or maybe yes, who is to say. Maybe even more than a triangle; with women geometry can be funny. In the presence of outsiders Signor Filligi showed none of *that* interest in his housekeeper, but then we know how things are sometimes. He took photographs of her, *questo si?*' On the other hand, he photographed every native Cretan who had blue eyes or fair skin, male or female, no matter how old they were."

Maybe a love triangle, maybe more, maybe none. Annoyed as he was, Bora couldn't object to Kostaridis' other observation. Judging from the crime scene photos, Villiger's housekeeper and hired men were fair, blonde- or red-haired: the right link, according to the *Reichskommissar*'s theory, to the noble "racial ancestors" of the Teutons. "What is your personal opinion, then?"

Kostaridis followed with his eyes Bora's quick move to grasp his linen underpants (sewn by his mother) from the windowsill before another gust took them. He could have looked away. Policeman that he was, instead, he observed things, even the least remarkable ones. So he was all the less credible when he innocently said, "I try not to form an opinion until I have enough elements, *capitano*. Fact is, Siphronia's husband is confined to the colony at Spinalonga. His brothers – I know you'll ask, so I'm telling you beforehand that they're on the run or in hiding – never accepted her being in a *frangos*' employ, and their kin's impotence to avenge his honour. They could have, shall we say, taken advantage of the recent fighting to carry out their brand of justice. It's remote, but a possibility. In the eyes of traditional farm folk, the woman was compromised and no longer fit to be seen in honest company."

And that's an opinion. "Spinalonga." Bora thought of the maps he'd been studying. "It's an island off the eastern coast, isn't it? What colony are you speaking of?"

"The leper hospital facing Elounda."

"What? The lepers, too?" Bora had the distinct impression of being made a fool of. "Why not a three-headed dog while you're at it?"

Kostaridis squared his unhappy face at him, hardly the expression of a trickster who enjoys his joke. "That's a good point about the dog, *capitano*. The dead dog in the garden wasn't Signor Filligi's."

Written at the Megaron, waiting for summons from Major Busch. Megaron is what the Greeks called a house's main hall, the perfect name for a hotel. I don't need a Greek dictionary to remember: I had top marks in Greek. In fact, if to this day I love Classical antiquity, it is in good part thanks to my teachers, especially old Professor Lohse, who died at Missolonghi like Lord Byron, albeit not fighting for Greece's freedom: he had a heart attack, poor man, so thrilled was he to have reached that sacred ground. We boys had these verses by Hölderlin carved on his headstone: "What is it that / chains me so to the ancient / blessed shores, till I love them / more than my Fatherland?"

Speaking of poets, and Byron in particular, I must assume Kostaridis' given name, Vairon, is actually the local spelling of the poet's name. Curious fellow, this Kostaridis. He conceals his cleverness by pretending to be awkward; Ulysses played the harmless fool to get his way, to avoid alarming his wife's suitors before killing them. I bet good old Vairon would be capable of ordering every bone in your body broken to make you talk, if he had to.

I can't figure out whether he believes Preger's men are guilty or not. He'd like to think they are, at any rate. Major Busch tells me there's no doubt the unit was in the area. I'll get details from the paratroopers directly, who to date haven't been heard by the War Crimes Bureau.

The Bureau has its hands full with reports of violence carried out against us by the locals, so that's probably why. The runner-up as most credible culprit is Rifat Bey, the violent neighbour whose anti-German feelings were explained to me as the result of a disagreement the Turk's family supposedly had decades ago with the German owner of the Huck Hotel in Smyrna. How does Kostaridis know? His father worked as a waiter at the hotel, "the best house in town, with excursions to Pergamon and Ephesus". That would imply that – if guilty – Rifat Bey was already hiding in the garden when the paratroopers came through. Possible: he lives next door.

Myself, I'm not discounting the possibility of a raid by Siphronia's brothers-in-law. Ulysses slaughtered the suitors to the last man, although they hadn't technically laid a finger on Penelope, and Grandfather Franz Augustus told us Cretan men learn to handle rifles and shotguns in the cradle. They, too, could have been coincidentally lying in wait in Villiger's garden when Preger's men marched in. Naturally, should Rifat Bey or Siphronia's in-laws be culpable, it'd either mean our camera-toting Sergeant Major Powell told Sinclair a lie, or else he was mistaken. Hard to take German paratroopers for anything else but German paratroopers, though. Only after I speak to Sinclair will I have a slightly less confused vision of all this.

The detail of the dog is marginally interesting, but not to be ignored. I'm not sure, but it looks as though it was shot once through the head. The photo shows it as a fine animal, not pure-bred but a well-kept watchdog; no collar was visible on it, but the fur at the neck showed it had been wearing one, or had been on a lead or chain. In fact, Kostaridis says frightened dogs have been running loose ever since the attack. The pet could be significant in ways that will become clear, or simply have been an innocent animal bystander in the wrong place at the wrong time.

Kostaridis was rather less informed (or more close-mouthed) regarding Villiger's hired hands. None of them was over twenty.

I'm no judge, but I'd call them pretty boys, in a primitive manner. I won't go further in these speculations until I speak to Major Busch again; if there's anything beyond race-related scholarship about Villiger's choice of menservants, he knows or knows how to know.

At any rate, the policeman showed me on the map where Ampelokastro and Sphingokephalo are located, and the "watercourse, shall we say" running between the properties. Their names sound romantic to a German ear: Vineyard Hill, Head of the Sphinx... The contended brook, unnamed on the charts, goes by Potamos (= River), as workaday as you can make it. At a second reading, Villiger's passport is a paragon of banality. The entry and exit stamps show travels fully consistent with one who studies antiquity: Greece, Italy, Turkey. Seems to have toured mostly these countries of late, which makes sense given his work with the Ancestral Research Bureau. He hasn't left Greece in three years. The only curious, but not altogether strange detail is that the passport was issued to him by the Swiss embassy in Athens five years ago, possibly to replace a document lost or stolen on arrival on the mainland.

Punctually at five, an orderly came to call Bora. Busch sat in a wicker chair outside the hotel, in the company of a large glass of ice water. Whether he'd recovered his pith helmet or found another one, his head was safe from the beating sun. "Have you met Kostaridis?"

"Yes."

"And what did you think of him?"

Bora reported his impression of the policeman. "You're wrong," Busch stated. "He isn't clever at all. And his feet stink."

Bora hadn't noticed that detail. It was possible, even probable. Kostaridis' socks and sandals had a forlorn look of overuse. Still, despite his own severe views of shabbiness, the major's comment struck him disagreeably. "There's a detail the chief constable seemed reticent about," he said, changing the subject. "Unless of course he's uninformed, but I doubt it."

Busch faced him with his back to the harbour, where clearing up and unloading went on side by side. Behind him the sea bristled dark blue with blinding white lacy trims in the offing, but lay wine-dark and still in the basin, with the squat Venetian fortress like a giant loaf of bread cooling in the breeze. "What, whether Villiger was queer for his farm boys?"

"Yes."

"You read too much Winckelmann or else you have a dirty mind, *Rittmeister*. Villiger was married to his science."

"*Herr Major*, I had to ask."

"Naturally. I was being facetious. Of course you had to ask. It would be interesting if Villiger's marriage to his science allowed for diversions." They were sweeping up glass shards in front of the hotel, from the many windowpanes shattered by bombs and cannonade. Busch stood up. He gave the impression of being more interested in listening to the tinny clatter of fragments than to the conversation. The sound was cold and icy, just as the pile of glass and crystal splinters in the lobby had seemed wintery, refreshing. In fact, the heat was oppressive. "Who knows," the major added, "maybe all those who relish Grecian antiquities do so because they have a high tolerance for male nudity. But so do soldiers, eh?"

Bora did not appreciate the comment. He spoke quickly to close the parenthesis. "An interesting question arises, at any rate. It seems that no one, not even the photographer, actually saw the shooting. I plan to listen very closely to what Lieutenant Sinclair has to say tomorrow."

"Ah, speaking of which, you'll have to wait until tomorrow to meet the American woman as well. We couldn't find transportation for her past Rhethimno, where she's stuck. It's the way it is. What am I saying, it's a way of life on these islands.

Nothing ever works as planned; what's not done today will be done tomorrow. Maybe. I used to work out of Rhodes before the war; believe me, I know what I'm saying." An about-face pointed Busch toward the street. "I'm supposed to walk for my back, come along. I'll see you across town to the Chanià Gate: it's half a mile from here."

On the way he acted the tourist guide. "Kalokairinou is what they call the avenue leading to the gate, but don't expect a German-style avenue. See, that's the Hotel Knossos. The Brits used to patronize its basement bar. Even Pendlebury, the fellow whose book I gave you. And the Allen woman. They drink like fish, these Anglo-Saxons: we found booze stacked to the ceiling. There was a gang of them, scholars and archaeologists-cum-spies."

"Did Villiger frequent them, you think?"

"He was Swiss, he could do whatever he wanted."

"He worked for us. Don't we have a file on him?"

"We had one. Can't find it at our central office in Berlin, they're looking for it."

A detour around the street where the house fronts had collapsed was taking them down alleys spared by direct sunlight.

"*Looking for it?*" Bora stopped in his tracks. "With a few days to solve this thing, you'd expect the *Reichskommissar* —"

"The *Reichskommissar* will squash you like a bug if it turns out the Luftwaffe killed his scholar. And then he'll try to squash the Luftwaffe."

"Well, *that* makes me feel better, *Herr Major*."

They had come to a small square guarded by a modest old church, reminiscent of a mosque. Busch called it Agios Markos, but Bora had lost any interest he might have had in learning about Cretan sights. Soon enough, along narrow streets, they reached Kalokairinou. The relatively wide pavement and shopfronts seemed citified by comparison.

"The gate's down there," Busch said. He stopped to rest his leg, and used the pith helmet to fan himself. "Through it, you exit the Venetian walls and venture west, eventually to Chanià, hence its name. They also call it Pantocrator Gate. Pantocrator, you know: Christ, ruler of the universe, the One with the terrible frown. Not too far from town you also meet the crossroads leading south to Ampelokastro. It's a hilly countryside, pleasant enough, but over the past two weeks we've fought over it tooth and nail as if it were solid gold."

Bora stuck to business. "Sir, is there a chance I might meet Captain Preger before morning?"

"There is: at the moment he's quartered at or near the city landing field. Tell me, why did you pull a face when you heard his name?"

"I didn't think I pulled a face."

"You pulled a face."

It could have become one of those moments when you have to think on your feet and lie outright, or else act stupid. Bora was halfway into the second option when Major Busch, ever controlled in his gestures, nodded half an inch in the direction of the gate. "Speak of the devil." Kalokairinou lay bathed in the afternoon sun; he must have anticipated or even planned the meeting because from here you couldn't make out the faces of those sitting at a street-side cafe. "There's Preger with some of his airborne colleagues, the self-styled *Elite of the Armed Forces*. I think it's best if I leave you; the gate is just beyond, you can see it from here. Talk to the man. Should miracles happen and should your American guide make it, there'll be time this evening to meet her at the Megaron. Forget what I told you about Kostaridis, too. You might need him to open some doors."

Preger did not stand from his chair. Bora's arrival, expected or not, seemed to stall him between the impulse to get the meeting over with and the desire to delay matters by ignoring his army counterpart, or pretending not to know why he'd come. Beer mugs in hand, cigarette packs on the table, his friends turned to see who it was. Among all of them, Bora included, the prudent mood was of young dogs, different in breed and size, measuring up to one another and calculating the possible outcome of a scuffle.

Preger had blond stubble and surly dark eyes set in a firm, square-jawed face and the same scowl of someone who carries a chip on his shoulder he'd had in Trakehnen, back from Madrid. The scowl had nothing to do with Ampelokastro. Suddenly, Bora was completely sure that Preger's feelings about his old playmate had been dredged up from past memories. There was no getting around it, he had to accept that even if until this morning he'd forgotten their boyhood incident, Preger apparently had not. The taste and flavour of those wet summers in East Prussia, drawing blood by hitting with both fists, rose with a small gathering of saliva in his own mouth. It wasn't the last scuffle he'd been in as a boy (after all, only fighting with a social inferior was anathema in General Sickingen's eyes), but the fact that Waldo had gone off to school at his cousin's in Königsberg afterwards made that particular row somehow final.

He and Bora greeted each other at the same time, by rank. "Will you excuse me," Preger told his colleagues then, and their prompt rising to leave suggested they'd rehearsed the scene. He'd be the one to walk away to join Bora otherwise.

Bora sat across from the paratrooper, and no sooner had he done so than a leathery local waiter stepped out to remove bottles and half-empty mugs. Flies avidly drinking spilt beer were chased off but would return before long.

"I heard you were here on a fool's errand."

Preger's first words were so clearly meant to irritate, Bora reacted by slipping into almost excessive calm. "Now less than yesterday," he answered, "but I'll carry on as I'm bidden."

"Yes, I was informed by Colonel Bräuer."

Preger's burly arms, bare to the elbows with his sleeves rolled back, showed cuts and bruises in the thick hairiness, possibly from dropping with his parachute into shrubs or tree branches. Many paratroopers Bora had seen had similar gashes, broken fingers or wrists. In their sand-coloured uniforms every one of them looked irritable, ill-disposed because of or in spite of exhaustion. Did they really expect the island would welcome them? Without prompting him, Bora waited for Preger to say more. Intelligence reports implied similarly hopeful scenarios for some regions of Soviet Russia, especially the Ukraine. *They're waiting for us; they will greet our men as liberators. But what if they don't? Never mind, it'll take us two, at most three months to reach Moscow. Who'll care then how the Reds see us?*

"Frankly," Preger took up, "I don't get what business of yours it is to waltz in, all spiffy and without a scratch, to run after an Englishman's nonsense." (Being reminded that he was unhurt, as if it were his fault, stung Bora to the quick.) "In case you're not aware, the patrol operating in that sector was ambushed the afternoon of the same day near Stavrakia. On Sunday we evacuated the troopers to the mainland with serious injuries. Not that I'd encourage them to talk to you if they were available. Have you consulted our commander, Major Walther?"

"I did."

"Is he in favour of the enquiry?"

"No."

"And our Group Commander?"

"Colonel Bräuer communicated he isn't favourable either."

"I thought so."

Preger still spoke with the guttural low-German accent from around Stettin; if anything, he stressed it more now than in the past. His older brother had died while a prisoner of the Russians in the Great War: Bora remembered the black crepe on the gamekeeper's door when the news came in 1920. Through his childhood, Waldo wore a black band on his sleeve, and then a black button at his lapel. That marker defined him for all times, shaping his resentment and desire for revenge. Bora had secretly envied that black button as a boy, because his father had died years earlier and not in war, and he couldn't very well wear mourning for his Scots grandfather William George, fallen at Khartoum in 1885.

The angle of the sun at this time of day made every bit of glass and metal glint and shine; on Preger's stocky figure, his wristwatch and the insignia on his side cap caught the light as he waved away the waiter who came to take Bora's order.

Bora called the waiter back and asked for water. "*Neró.*"

"*Metallikó?*"

Right, mineral water what was Busch recommended. "*Metallikó*," Bora confirmed, holding his own under Preger's stare. "My orders originate directly with Major General Student at XI Air Corps level."

It could be the staggering blow that ended the match at the very start. Preger grabbed the cigarette packet and tapped its bottom to take out a smoke. "I know *him* as the commander in chief who authorized 'reprisals and punitive expeditions to be carried out with exemplary terror' in Crete."

"Nonetheless, Major General Student gave me clearance." It had been the third of the "hairy phone calls" from Busch's office. Bora did not add that matters had been mediated by Major Count von Uxkuell, chief of divisional staff, one of those who found fault with Student's punitive orders.

"Don't expect any collaboration from us out in the field."

"I don't."

Mineral water was set in front of Bora. With the change provided by Busch he paid, and after glancing at the filmy rim of the glass, drank directly from the bottle. In their exchange thus far, Preger had bitterly swung back and forth between formal and familiar forms of address, correcting himself whenever he used *du* instead of *Sie*. Bora took the initiative of choosing informality once and for all. "Waldo, it's neither my charge nor intention to blame the killing on our men." (*They're not our men*, Preger specified, *they're mine*.) "In the unfortunate case they broke the rules, and with proofs to support it, I have a duty to bring it up. You'd do the same."

"I wouldn't do any such thing. And you – well, it's *you* who reported that the island was poorly manned and the locals wouldn't fight! Which side are you on, anyway?"

Provocations were best left alone. Bora tried not to take complaints against Intelligence personally, given the short notice of the attack and scarce time available to provide reliable details. Whether or not their information panned out, it was a habit with commanders at all levels to resent IC officers, even if – and *especially* if – they brought sobering news. He swallowed a dose of Atebrin with his next sip. "Short of meeting the rifle squad on patrol at Ampelokastro that day, I'll need an operational report or any other available account. What do you suggest?"

Preger looked away for a long minute, as if the desolate stores across the avenue, with their shutters rolled down, were more interesting than the company he was in. Swallows shuttled back and forth very high at this hour; only their thin cries came down to earth. He moodily chewed on the unlit cigarette, and only because Bora was drinking, and kept his peace, did he at last reluctantly pull out of his pocket a map overlay of the patrol route, and a few lines pencilled by the NCO heading the eight-man rifle squad. "If I wasn't under orders you'd never get this. You won't find anything in it."

Bora read. No incident of note was reported. Ampelokastro appeared among other place names. The locality had been reached at 11.00, and the next goal half an hour later. Or so wrote the NCO. If it actually took significantly less time to cover that distance, one could suspect a delay, even a stopover, a sign that the paratroopers didn't simply *walk through* Ampelokastro. Bora needed his maps to make a judgement call. Granted, there are many reasons at war to lose time en route. He copied report and place names on the overlay word for word, number for number. If needed, he'd time himself walking the same distance. "Thank you." He gave the documents back.

With a twist of his lips, Preger pushed the shapeless cigarette to one side of his mouth to speak. "You never change, do you?"

"It depends, Waldo. I changed in a lot of things. Did I start it, back then?"

"Of course you started it. You were the *master's son.*"

"I don't think I struck first."

"*I* struck first. It was the only way to make you eat your words."

Smiling was better than raising one's voice, and more irritating. Bora smiled. "That, I'm sure I didn't do. What were we arguing about, anyway?"

"As if you didn't remember."

"I *don't* remember. It can't have been that important."

"Of course! And that's how much you've changed." Predictably, Preger returned to military formality between them. "I'm not my father, you know, standing with hat in hand by the door when the *family* motors in for the holidays. I stand *for*, and I stand *by*, what's mine. I'm not going to let my men's actions be censured by outsiders, *Rittmeister.*"

"But it may be best, *Herr Hauptmann*, if we figure out things ourselves before the Red Cross comes knocking for answers." Bora found he could stick to his usual equanimity in the measure his colleague struggled with it. Preger's repeated use of "I", a proud vindication of his present role in the world, discouraged further references to their row as boys. Bora could see, as if it were before him, the Trakehnen square where stood a memorial to the war dead. The name of Preger's brother had been added last, during a public ceremony attended by everyone in the neighbourhood, with then Major General Sickingen in high uniform and all the women (farmers' and landowners' wives and daughters, including Bora's mother) in black.

Christ, he thought, *we're twenty-seven, we're grown men; both his parents have died since. We earned our medals in Spain. As commanding officer of the unit involved, Preger would resent any outsider butting in; he's simply lending a particular colour to his indignation because it's Martin Bora he happens to face. I won't fall for it, I won't. Not that I couldn't belt him again if it came to blows, his street savvy notwithstanding.*

Moving his chair aside to leave, Preger struck a leg of the small cafe table. Bora had to grab the water bottle to keep it from falling. "Just don't expect any collaboration from us."

Chanià Gate was a wide archway in the thickness of the city wall, manned by German troops. Bora's habit in Moscow had been to carry permits ready at all times, but here they paid no attention to him. Once past the gate he turned right and left the road. Up the dirt and grass swatch hugging the western bastions, he walked a few hundred paces to the sea.

Elsewhere, litter from the air raids and fighting created a disorderly maze. Here a small section of the shoaly strand remained curiously clear. Not much of a beach, though. Pebbles reached the water's edge; below the rippled surface, the submerged rocks trembled in a lazy, green transparency. Westward, a spit of land topped by a pyramidal peak jutted out to sea, and the sun would go down behind it eventually; the promontory gave the illusion of a man-made battlement, with a large keep guarding it (it was nothing of the kind, and it had all fallen into German hands). The *real* keep, still snow-capped, was the massif of Psiloritis further back, where the hinterland could still prove dangerous. Bora picked up a pebble and threw it against the necklace of small waves, toward the crisp-edged islet facing Iraklion whose name he'd read on maps and forgotten.

Preger's resentment stayed with him. "Waltzing in without a scratch" was a gratuitous insult, but understandable under the circumstances. Less predictable was the fact that their boyhood incident had made the rift deeper, less manageable. Whether he'd been right or wrong on that occasion, Bora felt guilty about it. *To him, I'm still the master's son. And now I may have to confirm that his men not only shot four Greeks, which is forgivable in the eyes of our commanders, but also a ranking Swiss citizen who under* no *circumstance should have been harmed. It would affect Waldo's career just as he was poised for glory.*

Was it improbable for paratroopers to have overreacted? They were a tough, ideological lot, steeled on the Western Front. What Bora knew about Waldo's adult life came from Peter, who kept track of all those they'd once socialized with, seeing as he was the fellow with the most friends and acquaintances on the face of the earth. Waldo Preger had become a Party member early on. In the summer of '32, he was involved in the Königsberg street fighting; two years later he joined the police force. In this he wasn't alone: several of the airborne troops commanders were former police officers. The story went around – if Peter hadn't been telling a flyer's tall tale – that Preger had punched a man dead during those riots. Rough days, hard to tell where legitimacy stood; amnesty took care of incidents and accidents involving National Socialist hotheads. *My stepfather led a conservative Freikorps after the Great War; there was precious little difference sometimes between their crusade and* skull-bashing in back alleys. And it's Preger's men who are under scrutiny for this murder, not Preger. I will not let hearsay or recollections stand in the way of common sense. He's a former policeman, and has that and other advantages over me here in Crete. He was a bully, and still is. But I'm even more pig-headed now than I was then.

There where the sea was little more than knee-deep, to the right of some jagged rocks breaking the surface, an object Bora took to be tarpaulin rolled back and forth under the veil of water, without washing ashore. For a tense moment he expected to recognize in it a human torso, still clothed, but the folds floated too loosely for that. Not that soldiers on both sides hadn't lost their lives by drowning. It would simply take longer for the sea to give back its dead.

Why had he walked to the shore, anyway? He wasn't much of a sea lover: to him water meant swimming and rowing along lakes and rivers. He couldn't connect the Aegean to any familiar sight; this wasn't his horizon. *Everyone has his – how did Jack London put it? – "call of the wild". To a Greek it would naturally come from the sea, evidence (and lure) of chaos around the stifling world of a reduced homeland. To us, born inland in a cold climate, the closest wildernesses are the moors and forests across our monotonous plains. To our nation, traditionally, wilderness is the East, as anyone born in Leipzig could theoretically walk from his doorstep to the Pacific Ocean – or to the Atlantic for that matter, but there's no wilderness west of Leipzig. Except for Spain, maybe.*

Yes, and Spanish wilderness meant Remedios, whom he still thought about four years later. Bora pitched another pebble, far beyond the rolling tar cloth. Remedios had nothing to do with the sea, she was the opposite of the sea, on her mountain perch at Mas del Aire; but she'd been to him (not to others, regardless of that American communist, Philip Walton, and all who'd climbed into her bed) what island enchantresses had been to Ulysses. What drew him to Spain was pure idealism; to

Crete, he'd originally come to fetch wine, not to lay the dead to rest. Still, he'd arrived from a foreign land, like Ulysses and Theseus before him, both of whom had from time to time met goddesses and monsters. Preger's men, inflamed with battle, caked with dust and blood, could well have misunderstood a word, a motion in Villiger's house, and opened fire. Among his wife's suitors, Ulysses killed even those who were good lads: wandering, like war, made him mean.

Out in the sea the tarpaulin kept lazily ebbing and flowing: Bora reached for a flat pebble to toss at it, then changed his mind. He'd never seen himself as a wanderer, yet he never stayed put.

There's no moss gathering on this stone; it keeps on the move, though not always rolling. It's cast at times, thrown a distance, or sunk. It tumbles, it falls, it is washed ashore... that's movement, too.

He discovered that he was road-weary after all. The trip had been long, uncomfortable for the most part; there was nothing much he could do to advance his task before the morning. He'd go back to the hotel to sleep if he thought he could sleep while there was still light in the sky. Weariness made him agitated, besides; he'd lie there worrying, and that would be all.

Dark, stringy algae and small chalk-white shells dotted the strand under his feet. If he closed his eyes, the rhythm of the swell came like liquid breathing. Deep, unfamiliar. None of this was his own; the closest seashore in his childhood had been hours away, the North Sea when in Leipzig, the Baltic when in East Prussia. He could turn his back to the water and feel none of the regret seafaring men must experience when walking away from it.

A casual glance landward revealed that Kostaridis was watching him from afar. In his irritation, Bora appreciated the fact that he didn't try to disguise his presence. Under the arching light of the afternoon, the policeman kept to the verge of the strand, so that his sandals wouldn't pick up seaweed and gravel.

Hands in his pockets, he greeted the German with the southern tilt back of the head, a raising of his chin. And when Bora came within earshot, he said, "*Capitano.*"

"*Epitropos.* May I help you?"

"No. *I* may help you. You wish to go to Ampelokastro, no? I have arranged it. In the morning we can go there."

Were he in a generous mood, Bora would have told himself that such are the epiphanies of the gods, or of the gods' messengers, appearing when needed in the least probable disguises. "I have meetings scheduled for the morning."

"But *maggiore* Voos said they will not be until well after midday."

"Did he?" Bora wondered when Busch and Kostaridis had discussed things, and why a lower-ranking official should be told what was his privilege to hear first.

"*Sì.* If we leave early, we can get back to Iraklion by noon. And I can show you where Rifat Bey lives, too."

"I suppose you've arranged for transportation as well."

"No, no." Kostaridis hedged self-consciously. "Your army will provide a vehicle and escort."

"It'll be quicker if you just tell me at what time you'll be picking me up tomorrow morning."

"Will five o'clock do?"

"It'll do." The studded soles of Bora's mountain boots captured what sand there was, in from the pebbly shore. He stomped to shake it off. "Well, aren't you coming back to the hotel? I expect you'll be holding my hand all the way there, or will happen to be going my way."

"No. I will see you tomorrow."

Bora must have seemed slightly surprised. Kostaridis shrugged. "I stay here, I watch the sun go down. It has been rising and sinking thousands of years on this island, on this sea. It comforts me to participate, shall we say, in eternity in a small way. Whenever I can, I stand in this spot and watch the sunset like an old man."

The sound of the evening swell had been changing ever since Bora walked to the waterline. The rush of small breakers as they started to fringe rocks and shoals came to his ears, but it wasn't enough for him to want to look back. "Aren't you afraid someone will pick you off, standing alone and working with Germans as you do now?"

"No better way for a man – not just a Cretan, or a Greek – to die than watching the sea. Surely you've thought out what you'd like to be be watching when you die."

Bora frowned. No. He'd decided, four years earlier, what he'd be thinking of at the moment of death, whom he'd be thinking of. It was Remedios. The place was irrelevant. Even the time mattered little, even though he had so many hopes and expectations these days, in this season of his life, dying in Crete would be most unwelcome. He turned in the direction of the town. "I'll see you in the morning, then. Five hundred hours sharp, in front of the hotel."

"The tar cloth out there – it would float if it were empty."

What else does he notice, what else does he understand? Bora started for the battlements, toward the gate. "Yes. I thought there was a human torso inside it. I think it might be a severed arm instead."

Busch wasn't at the Megaron. Bora ate quickly in the improvised mess hall below, then climbed to his quarters. The room was still warm from the heat of day; little chance it would cool off overnight. The bed, too short for a tall man, meant he'd have to lie askew or crumpled on the mattress. Until dark he reviewed the maps, memorizing routes, place names. From the slim dictionary of modern Greek supplied by the major, he spelt and repeated to himself the handful of sentences that might be useful during his stay. Even after dark, with a riot of stars outside, the swelter and a short mattress kept him awake, so he opened the *Archaeology of Crete*. There was a photo of John Pendlebury MA, FSA, "Formerly curator at Knossos", on the flyleaf: the sort of fair, athletic fellow Professor Villiger would gladly list among his racial specimens; or had listed, who knows? They could have drunk gin and tonic, ouzo or cognac in the basement of the Knossos Hotel together no more than a month ago. Bora began reading, intrigued by the appendix to the chapter on Crete's geography, where the author had personally entered walking times between locations. He circled and marked statements and notes there and further into the essay; at Early Minoan III he fell asleep with the book on his chest, and dreamt of losing his way.

He was crossing a field of tall grass – oats? rye? – along a dirt road shaded by oaks, straight like an arrow. The field (a real one, known since childhood) edged the Krumm property and ended at the horse chestnut planted by the Modereggers, whose pretty daughter Peter had fallen in love with – a relationship the general put a quick end to. Everything in the dream was as he remembered near Trakehnen, the soft boggy soil and the phosphorescence of new stalks against a stormy summer sky. Crane nests topped distant chimneys and forsaken smoke-stacks, a flat horizon rimmed the world on all sides. But where the peat fields should be, the blue line of a mislaid southern sea took their place. Someone waited for him on the shore, so he headed for the sea. But however far he went, up to his waist in undulating green blades, the turquoise-blue swatch of water stayed far away and unreachable. The road, the oak trees went on and on alongside him, even when in reality he should have long ago come to the next village or farm. One thing he was sure of: Waldo Preger was the man waiting for him on the shore of the unlikely sea.

Bora woke up at 4.30 a.m. with a start, wondering why the Russian waiter hadn't knocked with his morning coffee. For a few confused seconds he didn't know where he was, or why. He got out of bed, washed and shaved like a sleepwalker.

If I only knew why Waldo and I fought. It would help me understand, it would help me understand – what?

4

As a rule, Bora put no stock in Mediterranean punctuality. He was all the more surprised when, at ten to five, he saw Kostaridis – wearing exactly the same clothes, socks and sandals of the previous day – waiting in front of the hotel. It would have been civil to ask the inspector whether he'd had coffee already. If Bora chose not to do it, it was because he had a northerner's prejudice that showing familiarity to a southerner results in unwanted liberties.

Kostaridis caught him off-guard. "Have you had your coffee? A man can't start a day's work without a good cup of coffee."

Bora didn't answer. He breathed the unfamiliar sea air and made no effort to look less grumpy than he was. The first blow of the day had come when Busch, already up and about to motor west, told him, "Off to Chanià, see you this afternoon at 17.00. I'm awaiting further data on Prof. Villiger from the head of the *Ahnenerbe*, SS Oberführer Prof. Dr. Walther Wüst. For your information, yesterday paratroopers from the Third Battalion of the 1st Airborne Regiment carried out a reprisal at a small place called Kandanos, 180 executed. The day before, a similar action was taken by the same unit at Kondomari – and their army reporter immortalized this on film. I'd be careful about rubbing the airborne up the wrong way if I were you."

Pointless advice for an investigator, whose presence is an irritant per se. Bora watched the sea, pearl-coloured at this hour. He had to admit that the great water surface, so untroubled, so placid, had a calming effect: no wonder Kostaridis would choose it as his last living glimpse. As for Bora, always in haste, time was the existential question: how much time would he have to do what he hoped to in life? There were moments (this was one such) when he felt he had 100 years yet ahead of him; in other moments, only a handful of hours. Neither prospect troubled him particularly, although the idea of decades to spend without knowing how made him thoughtful: war as a career had been ingrained in him since childhood, but wars don't last a century as in the old days. Rubbing Preger's men up either way sounded irrelevant, an infinitesimal part of a much larger game.

Within minutes, a motorized platoon of Jäger heading for Messarà arrived to pick them up. Fully armed and in battle gear, they'd provide a safe ride to Ampelokastro. "There's our patrol from Agios Andreas," the platoon leader informed Bora, showing him the place on the map. "They're due to come down that way around 14.00. They'll bring you back to Iraklion after you're done."

Under normal circumstances and on good, paved roads, the twelve or so miles separating the city from Ampelokastro could be travelled in half an hour at most. Factoring in dirt lanes and danger, this time might double, or worse. The track inland didn't seem promising once they left the walls and turned south from the westbound route. The Jäger kept silent and on the lookout – four personnel carriers in all, with Bora and Kostaridis riding in the third vehicle.

On the westbound route, close to Chanià Gate, was where the scholar Pendlebury had reportedly fought and been badly injured. If he'd died of his wounds, Major Busch said, his grave was somewhere at one of the many crossroads. The longing to be hurt stayed with Bora in the shape of guilt. He rolled it in his mind and looked at it from all sides, like an object that must be opened in order to understand how it works. It could be harmless, a dud, or else potentially dangerous and not to be tampered with. How many times had he picked up shrapnel as a child, dug for spent shells, scraped around for relics of the war around Trakehnen… Country boys and unwary farmers lost limbs and eyesight to unexploded devices, a reminder that some objects are best left alone, with their potential for satisfying curiosity still inside.

Crete provoked recollection. Like a memory machine, its antiquity and starkness dredged up images and feelings from the past, pieces that belonged to him and had been dismissed, or so he thought. Every step Bora took was fraught with an anxious sense that it had an analogy with something experienced years earlier. Heat, dust, the meagre vegetation of summer reminded him of the Sierra near Teruel. Of Spain, where he'd fought a year without a scratch – exactly the expression Preger used to rile him. There, up in those mountains, Remedios initiated him into undreamt of sexual practices, telling him that he was *worthy of it*. "Why?" he'd asked.

"Because you'll suffer much."

"Because you'll suffer much," she told me. I haven't seen it thus far, however you want to define suffering. I don't know how worthy I really was, either. To be sure, learning to outlast an orgasm and keep going was a big thing for a lad of twenty-three brought up not to curse, answer back or masturbate – although through the years, two out of three I did learn to practise. For some months afterwards, he'd thought himself special because he was destined to suffer – as if it weren't his human lot after all. *Yet there are those who don't get hurt, and you wonder whether they're at ease or uncomfortable with their state.*

Soon they took a southbound road. All around, the parched air, brittle like old paper, dried his throat and lungs when inhaled. Bora told himself he'd taken Remedios' words for a prophecy, but was it really? Villiger and those with him at Ampelokastro had once and for all resolved the issue of suffering: and now a man who hadn't – who longed to be hurt – had come from the other end of Europe to solve their murder.

Close to an hour was what it took to travel ten miles. The sun, already high on the horizon, baked the crusty sides of the road; clods larger than a man's fist, hard like rocks, forced the light armoured carriers into a painfully slow, jarring ride. Automatic weapons at the ready, the motorized Jäger sat looking right and left at the barren stretches of land, marked by lonely, dilapidated huts and stone fences built without mortar. Whenever the ruts made the surface impassable, one after the other the vehicles braved the slopes on either side of the road, at risk of overturning. Narrow spots came up where the passage was reduced to a convulsed bed of shingle, over which the carriers listed like clumsy boats. Dust alive with sand-coloured crickets hovered all around, the harsh pitch of cicadas dressed meagre shrubs and rare trees: elements that for thousands of years had belonged to the place and the season. The variables were a smell of fuel and overheated engines, the clank, roll and thud of pebbles as they cannoned under heavily treaded tyres. Its own aggressiveness gave the platoon away.

Where the path widened ahead, unexpectedly a swarm of tropical blouses pointed to a German roadblock, or another such impediment. The head vehicle braked, halted in idle. Bora checked the place against the map: they weren't at a crossing exactly, more like a fork in the road, manned by paratroopers. Waldo Preger led them, khaki blouse and narrow-rimmed helmet on his head.

Bora left his seat, but not the side of the vehicle he'd been riding in. Whatever was going on, if it was the sort of operation that culminates in a reprisal, being there as a witness, in the company of a Greek official, would only complicate his role in Crete. He knew himself well enough to see – as if from the outside – the frowning stillness disguising his own unrest. Any sign of imminent violence, however, was lacking among the paratroopers. They hung around in their field outfits, the loose smocks – bone-sacks, they called them – buttoned around their thighs so as to resemble shorts worn over trousers. Preger himself – feet apart, hands on his hips – was stationed on a boulder higher than the road, like a sea captain surveying his crew from the bridge.

Goddamn him, I bet there's nothing going on. Preger's done this on purpose. If he can't keep me from looking into things, he'll slow me down all he can. Waiting for the platoon leader to clear matters with the paratroopers, Bora kicked the closest tyre in frustration. By the map, they were still two or three miles from Ampelokastro, in the middle of nowhere. *Now we'll have to waste an hour or more while Preger pretends – what? To be making the road ahead safe?*

He exceeded in optimism. Soon the dusty Jäger non-com joined him. "Sorry, *Rittmeister.*" He apologetically shook his head. "We'll have to leave you here, there's danger of anti-personnel mines ahead. Road's off-limits for the next few hours. You'll have to continue on foot." Which may have been what Preger had told him and he actually believed, or a story he had agreed with him he'd report, given that in Crete paratroopers and mountain troops seemed to work hand in glove.

Bora wouldn't give his old playmate, was looking over his shoulder in Bora's direction, the satisfaction of seeing he was furious. "Very well." He grabbed his rucksack from inside the vehicle, followed without haste by Kostaridis. The exchange had been in German, but evidently Kostaridis understood the situation, and probably the motives behind the hold-up as well. He indicated a rather forbidding incline to the left of the road, barely mitigated by a goat trail that zigzagged upwards like a scar.

"This way, *capitano*. It's a bit long, though."

Bora stepped in front of him to start the climb. "Are you armed, at least?" he said through his teeth.

"What for?" Kostaridis shrugged. "If my fellow Cretans or the English want to pick us off, they'll do it from a distance, with rifles that a handgun isn't about to stop."

They were already clambering through a herd of spiny, yellow-flowering bushes when the Jägers' vehicles below them ground into reverse to reach a wider place, where they could change direction and return north.

Bypassing the road meant taking to the wild hills, trusting Kostaridis' sense of direction (trusting him *at all*!), wasting precious time. If they came to grief, it would be Bora's fault for going along. He was nervous in the measure that he wanted to make it quickly to the crime scene. More energetic than his companion, he overworked himself in the first ten minutes, after which he had to stop in the brutal heat for Kostaridis to catch up with him.

Spain had been wild in '37, but this terrain was harsher, even lonelier than the Aragon hills, like a carcass picked clean by scavengers. Bora paused because he did not know the way, and because elementary prudence required that he observe Kostaridis, in case he showed any alarm.

"Just because I keep going, don't think there's no one around." Kostaridis disabused him of the idea. "But we must continue as if we didn't care." He'd taken off his jacket and slung it over his shoulder, like a farmer going to the fields. "If you see a mirror flashing on the ridges or hear voices far off, don't worry. They're only signals. When they're about to shoot you, they give no warning." On cue, a cry muffled by distance, as of someone plunging into an abyss, wavered across the thirsty air. "Hear that? It isn't for us, it's meant for somebody down Bisala's way."

Bora wasn't so sure, but there was nothing he could do about it. In the next few minutes, other isolated calls rose far away – boys' or women's shrill cries, as from disembodied creatures. *Easy in a place like this to believe in spirits that inhabit nature*, Bora thought.

They kept to the sloping sides of the hills to avoid becoming easy targets on the ridges. It was a precarious balancing act, especially for Kostaridis' sandals. There were turns where, far below, they could see the road they'd be following had they not been prevented from doing so. Distances trembled with heat where the mountains began, mountains faded into the bright sky behind them; only the protection provided by his sunglasses made it possible for Bora to stare at the rugged rocky horizon, or at the sky.

"Did Professor Villiger own a car?" he asked Kostaridis, turning to him. "How did he travel to Iraklion?"

"He seldom did. Unlike most villa owners who spend part of the week in town, renting an occasional room or as guests of friends, he stayed put. Came by bus to Iraklion once a month to do chores, his banking and dine at the Megaron or Knossos Hotel." (Bora noticed Kostaridis pronounced the name Knossos with the accent on the last syllable, not on the first as in classical Greek.) "For longer trips around the island one usually travels by public car or rides a mule, depending on the itinerary. To catch the bus near Keramoutsi, I expect he walked. Did I tell you that two weeks prior to his death he enquired about passenger ships leaving Crete?"

Bora turned, and risked stumbling. "You *did not*. Leaving for where?"

"Nowhere specific. Leaving Crete. Africa being out of the question because of the war, I'd say that either he was looking into a trip to Turkey, or to another non-European country."

"He dealt with the National Bank, right? Has anyone looked into his account or deposit box?"

"Oh, yes." Kostaridis took advantage of the questions to catch his breath. Hoofing along the scrub of the incline, where slippery rocks made it necessary to grip with both hands, he'd had to put his jacket back on. He dripped with sweat. "It was done on the first of June."

"The first of June was a Sunday!"

"It wasn't done, shall we say, during regular banking hours. I believe it's called a victor's privilege. When I checked on it, the paperwork relative to his deposits wasn't there. To the best of his memory, the clerk told me the last amount was in excess of 10,000 German marks, none of which the professor reportedly turned into ready money. But every first Monday of the month, considerable sums of cash in German marks arrived for him from an undisclosed account in Rhodes, by special courier. That's possibly why his safe-deposit box was emptied, and at present there's no deposit left at the National Bank under Signor Filligi's name."

Possibly? Ten thousand marks are a German general's yearly pay. Bora balanced in a crouch to remove burs from his socks. "When we first met you only spoke of 'regular money transfers' from Switzerland!"

"You seemed somewhat impatient to wrap up the conversation, *capitano*. Besides, I didn't want to give you all the bad news at once."

Fuck. Bora cursed to himself without saying the word, staring at the policeman. *Another hell of a detail to look into.* If Villiger's official employer was *Reichskommissar* Himmler, deposits – routed through Switzerland by way of Rhodes in order to avoid incidents – could be hefty. But to this extent…? And if for whatever reason large amounts of cash were stashed in his deposit box at Iraklion, no surprise that it had been opened. He stood up quickly, losing and regaining his balance in succession. "Cash and valuables could attract many, not excluding bank employees. When you say 'emptied', do you mean 'opened with a key' or 'broken into'?"

"I mean to say that Signor Filligi's deposit box was simply opened by German paratroopers, who were in possession of the key, on the morning of 1 June. The bank director had to unlock the doors for them." Kostaridis mopped his neck with a crumpled handkerchief. "Fifteen more minutes." He sucked in his breath. "Then you'll be able to see the villa way down there."

So it was. Still distant, eventually Ampelokastro came into view, on a shelf less elevated than the travellers' lookout but higher than the road leading to its gate. From where Bora and Kostaridis stood, a spiderweb of other trails and mountain roads showed, criss-crossing the dramatic landscape in all directions. No vineyards grew around Ampelokastro despite the meaning of its name, only solemn olive trees twisted by time into fantastic shapes. Through Bora's green lenses, even in the bone-dry light of day, their pale heads of small leaves resembled schools of silvery fish. Tall, long-maned palm trees gave the enclosed garden the look of an oasis, but an oasis you see in films, built to suit. The two-storey stucco house, of a fading oxblood red, sat half-seen behind the luxuriant greenery. To someone drawing close from the same level, nothing but the roof would be visible above the garden wall. It remained to be seen where Sergeant Major Powell had supposedly been sitting with his camera when he watched Preger's men march down and walk through the gate.

At the bottom of the gully separating Villiger's house from the opposite hill, a small river or seasonal brook – the contended Potamos – had carved a deep bed, lined with dwarf willows and water-seeking grasses. Rifat Bey's Sphingokephalo must be the pale ochre, sprawling house built on that ridge, steeper and nearly bald, behind a long terrace parapet over-looking the valley. Rows of vines covered the rolling ground beyond the dour profile of the hill, as far as the eye could see. South, west and eventually up the mountains, more ledges, yellow bushes, sparse huts or chapels perched on spurs of rock, white and opaque like wave-tossed shells.

Out of the depths of that solitary vista, a savage male voice called out. Impossible to locate as echoes rebounded and mul-tiplied it, it tore the heat-trembling air, answered by another further off, and by more echoes. The voices of hunters, of fishermen crying out to others that the prey was approaching the net. "That might be for us," Kostaridis commented with a fatalistic twitch of his lips. "We'd better go down. It's safer."

It took another quarter of an hour, during which Ampelokas-tro disappeared from view as Kostaridis hiked the back road through a defile so steep and confined both men had to balance by propping themselves on the rock walls with their hands, and squeeze sideways as it tapered off to a crevice at the lower end. Bora removed and hand-carried his rucksack in order to fit; at his request, and not only because he knew the way, Kostaridis preceded him.

Watching the policeman press on like a cork caught in a bottleneck, Bora felt no sympathy: his own knees and chest rubbed against the scraggy stone wall. Because he couldn't reach for the holster on his left hip if he needed to, he'd driven the pistol into the right pocket of his shorts, where it bulged and chafed his thigh. *By God, if this is some form of trap the Greek's drawing me into, I can't even shoot straight.*

A trap, at least for now, it was not. From the high ground they reached a knoll where Kostaridis said, "See? If you go down that way, by and by you find yourself on the road, but south of Ampelokastro. You have to backtrack and enter the garden through the rear gate."

"No. I want to enter as Sergeant Major Powell did, from the front."

"This way, then."

They rejoined the road from Iraklion – by Bora's map still nearly a mile away from Ampelokastro. The dusty verge of the road was alive with insects; a solitary cicada opened the chirring season far afield. A few steps beyond, as they passed an unremarkable spot, Kostaridis said, "See that shrub? Your War Crimes colleagues notified us that when they first drove to Ampelokastro, they passed by two dead Englishmen about there. Shot point-blank. No papers, no other identification on them, except their uniforms."

"*Two* dead Englishmen: is that all?" Bora looked indifferently toward the place indicated. "I've seen photos of German paratroopers robbed even of their boots."

Kostaridis ignored the provocation. "Yes, well. Dead soldiers were popping up everywhere during those first days."

"God will know them even without a name on their graves, *Epitropos*. Any of us might end up that way."

Bora's watch read 8.35 when they reached the garden gate, both the worse for wear. Kostaridis had a hole in his sad-looking left sock. He pulled the tip of it and tucked it under his big toe as Bora pretended to look elsewhere. What small, cottony clouds had topped the mountains had long since evaporated; the bright sky crowded everything. The moment Bora took off his sunglasses, even the faded colours of summer exploded into radiance all around, whites turned incandescent: as upon his first arrival, he struggled not to feel blinded by the excess light.

The road from Iraklion lapped the gate in a shallow curve; there, it widened into a sandy space before skirting the property along the brook and heading south. The segment along the garden wall was dilapidated; it made sense now why the paratroopers had entered the garden, to bypass the crumbling spot. Bora followed with his eyes a second trail that came down from the foot of Sphingokephalo Hill, passing over a reedy culvert and across the brook. If the report Preger had showed him was correct, that trail came from the west, and the paratroopers had arrived from that direction. A man concealed in the muddy brook bed could crawl into the culvert to avoid detection and then emerge far enough away to fix the soldiers' movements on film: the angle from which the photos were taken confirmed that possibility.

An overheated Kostaridis fanned himself by the wide-open garden gate. Once they had walked past it, he pointed out the gravel, combed and mounded by the tyres of ambulances or other vehicles that had manoeuvred in and out. A bucket by the front steps must have served to wash the dog's blood away. "It wasn't there when we first came," he told Bora. "But who knows how many have since passed through here. See, they also piled up the gore-soaked carpets out there and tried to burn them. Good thing they stopped halfway. Look at the trees' lower leaves, they came close to torching them."

Bora had replaced the pistol in its holster, but kept it unlatched. "The loose dirt in the flowerbed? Were the two dead Brits buried there?"

"No, we took them to town. I bet it's where they buried the dog."

"Was the dog killed by one or more shots? I couldn't tell from the photos."

Kostaridis' thumb pointed to his own forehead. "Single pistol shot."

The front door was ajar. From the outside, there was no evidence of a broken lock, but looking closer there were signs it had been kicked in. Bora used the toe of his boot to push it, and stepped in first. No vestibule, no hallway; he found himself directly in the large room where Villiger and the others were killed. An indefinite odour, best left unexplored, hung in the air. Blood had dried on the flooring and walls. That soldiers had camped here overnight was proven by the scatter of empty food cans and bottles, but there had been looting as well, before, during or after the Germans' bivouac. The place Bora knew from the photographs was hardly recognizable: it looked as though it had been abandoned for years. The furniture was gone, except for the pieces built in or too large to drag out through the door; books – taken off the shelves to search for valuables behind them? – lay in heaps. Wading through the broken odds and ends dropped by pilferers, Bora paced all around the killing area, where blood had seeped through the carpets to the floor. The image of a carcass picked clean came back to his mind.

He refrained from comments only because German soldiers had participated in the raid one way or another. A quick look revealed that the kitchen and pantry had been ransacked as well.

Foodstuffs, pots, plates and tableware gone, curtains stolen from the windows: only the layout of the ground floor resembled the photographs. "Upstairs?" he asked.

Kostaridis wiped his eyebrows with the back of his hand. "Bedrooms and library." He kept his voice low, to avoid the slapping echoes of an empty room. "*Capitano*, it's the habit of our peasants to take what the dead no longer need. Times are meagre. If there was anything useful, it's gone."

"It depends on your definition of useful. Most of the books seem to be here. Fine editions, too."

"I mean money-wise and in terms of clues."

"Clues? Does it mean you no longer believe it was German soldiers who did the killing?"

"I don't recall ever saying I did. But soldiers might kill for reasons extraneous to war. Don't you agree?"

I never would. Bora did not speak the words, but they were contemptuously stamped on his face.

"You would, you would." The sweaty Kostaridis widened his eyes, Lorre-like, and was for a brief moment repulsive to the eye. And then, placidly, as if he was referring to Bora's opinion on the matter: "...agree that soldiers might kill for personal reasons, I mean."

Next, softly for two men, they moved around and busied themselves with the evidence still there, especially the lead fragments embedded in the walls. Somewhat reluctantly, and only because he had no acceptable reason to avoid it, Bora shared with Kostaridis the photos taken by the Englishman and the War Crimes Bureau. "See? Villiger must have been standing in front of the woman when he fell. Not that it necessarily means anything."

"Or maybe it does, *capitano.* The field hands huddled instead of trying to get away, and that's why they're so tangled together. That, too, may mean something, or not."

Bora retraced his steps to the front door. "I'd say the first round was fired from about here; it wasn't exactly done close up. Provided the victims were all in this room, it would take seconds."

"Right. And whether or not you're aware you'll be shot, there is no getting away from submachine guns." Kostaridis pinched his old trousers at the knees before crouching to study the wall. "Same sort of weapon, used from different standpoints." He fingered the bullet holes. "My initial thought was that only one of the attackers opened fire. After seeing the wall close up, I conclude at least two of them did. And although number two might have hesitated, opening fire after the victims were already falling, both exhausted their ammunition."

Bora had reached a similar conclusion the night before. "I wonder if the dog was killed first. A stray that wandered into the garden might not bark at the coming of strangers, but once the shot that killed it was heard outside the door, you'd think the boys at least would seek refuge upstairs."

"Maybe." Backing away from the wall, Kostaridis kept looking at the bullet holes. He stumbled in his open-toe sandals across a hefty paperweight shaped like the Colosseum, no doubt a souvenir from Rome. He gasped the next words in pain. "Maybe they killed the dog last."

"No. Powell heard a single shot before the wild firing. A watchdog would race at strangers and be killed much closer to the gate, or even outside of it. A stray might cower, but wouldn't wait around in the racket of gunfire until they shot it, too."

"Anyway, *capitano*. From past experience as a marksman, I know that with a firm hand you can centre a moving target on the front steps even before crossing the gate. I think they mistook it for a watchdog and killed it as they approached the garden."

"Could be." Through an archway Bora crossed into the study, which in the photographs appeared as an indistinct background. Plundered like the rest, it was kept shady by the trees outside. More empty bottles (beer, wine, soft drinks, a single Rodinal container) lay discarded on the floor. What in the prints he'd mistaken for oblong plates hanging on the wall turned out to be in fact chalk moulds of human faces: a miscellany of Villiger's Aryan Cretans, no doubt.

Bora lifted a mask from its nail. The holes in the nostrils suggested it had been modelled on a living person, breathing through straws inserted in the nose. A hand-written label glued inside bore a number, location and a generic description:

"Twenty-year-old farm girl, area of Agia Paraskeve. Eye colour, No. 5. Hair, straw blonde". Another mask read, "Fifteen-year-old street urchin, Iraklion. Eye colour, No. 3. Hair, dark blonde", and so on. A third face, a young woman's, so closely reminded him of Remedios that Bora hastened to look for written indications. But the label was incomplete, and only read in pencil "Shepherd girl, outside Gonies?" A question mark, and no details given. To the right of the masks, a framed photograph showing rows of glass eyes illustrated the grading system: 5, Medium Blue; 3, Light Blue... On the list, developed by a long-dead Swiss researcher who'd read his dissertation at Leipzig University, Bora's green eyes registered a six. Or was it a ten?

Christ, as if it mattered where I fit. This taxonomy makes as much sense as judging a racehorse by the colour of its mane. But he looked to see where his wife's eyes and his mother's eyes ranked in the diagram. And wasn't it true that his stepfather, a superb rider like all the family, used horse terminology as he pointed out the boys to guests visiting the estate? "There they are: the seal brown is Martin, my wife's son, and the sorrel is my Peter." *For him, colour did not mean quality necessarily, but belonging: I'm not his son, after all.*

The noiseless Vairon Kostaridis, so far down the chart as not to count, joined Bora in the twilit study. As he walked past, his shabby figure was intercepted by a sun blade from the curtainless window, a single luminous shaft that burrowed through the thick of garden trees. When he stepped beyond, it beamed freely. To Bora, the white scalpel of light seemed capable of burning a hole through the wall like a blowtorch. *That's how the Eye of God,* he thought with a shudder, *will sear and wither our man-made categories. How can we be so foolish as to ignore it?*

"If you look outside, *capitano*, that's the Sphingokephalo memorial up there."

Bora drew close to the window, but not so close as to enter

the sunbeam. High above the palm trees, the sugar-white monument appeared as if suspended in mid-air, a small round temple watched by its mythical animal guardians. Grieving and honouring the past, too, is a human artifice. Directly below, in the garden, Bora's attention rested on the gaping rear gate. It was through it that Preger's men claimed they'd passed without stopping at the villa. On his map he'd marked in red pencil the locality they headed for – Skala. He planned to walk the distance himself before returning to Iraklion.

It was the first time since their arrival at Ampelokastro that Bora and Kostaridis paused in their search. For no reason other than they had nothing to tell each other, they stood side by side at the window in complete silence.

But both men remained vigilant. When out of the stillness a thud, so muted it would otherwise escape notice, reached them from upstairs, it startled them entirely.

A step, a book fallen flat on the floor... Bora looked up at the ceiling. He could have kicked himself for not inspecting the second floor right off, but it was too late now. A rush of considerations shot through him – *If they wanted to attack us, they could have, and didn't. They're hiding from us, or didn't hear us, or they heard us and stupidly betrayed themselves* – in the time it took him to nod at Kostaridis. Kostaridis, staring motionless at the same ceiling, really did look like Peter Lorre as the child murderer, hopelessly trapped by his adversaries at the end of the movie. "The library," he mouthed.

A resolute about-face, front room, stairs. Bora released the safety catch of his pistol as he climbed two steps at a time, with the policeman at his heels. The instant he reached the upper floor Kostaridis directed him to the sole one of three doors that wasn't wide open, and Bora kicked it in.

Standing by a towering bookcase with overfull shelves, a man in shirtsleeves and linen trousers froze at the sight of

118

the gun. It was all that kept him from dropping a boxed set of volumes, a pile of which sat on the library table within his reach. At his feet, a cloth-bound dictionary lay where it had given him away by falling.

"I was tidying up," he stammered to Kostaridis in Italian. "Recovering texts I lent the professor... I didn't hear you come in."

Possible. The door was soundproofed by padding; a true library door. Had it been locked from the inside, there'd have been no kicking it open. Bora holstered the gun before stepping up to the stranger. He flipped open the volume at the top of the stack, revealing Villiger's ex libris glued on its frontispiece.

In his rolled-up sleeves and canvas shoes, the man facing him had a holidaymaker's toasted look. Bulgy-necked, with neatly combed-back hair, he seemed surprised at the sight of the frontispiece. "I can't believe he glued *his* ex libris over mine." It sounded like a lame excuse. Assuming the German didn't understand his words, he stared at Bora but addressed Kostaridis. "I am Professor Pericles Savelli, formerly of the Archaeological Museum in Rhodes. Whom am I addressing?"

Kostaridis did not answer. To a questioning glance from Bora, he confirmed the man's identity with a blink of the eyes.

"*Ma insomma*, who's he? What does he want here?" Savelli insisted.

Bora blandly replaced the volume on the shelf. "*Capitano Bora, esercito tedesco.*"

"He speaks Italian!" Savelli said, as if a large animal had just shown itself capable of articulating a sentence.

"He does," Kostaridis drawled. Searching around the room with his crafty, somnolent eyes, he added, in the same vein, "And you, Professor, know *me*."

"*Va bene, e allora?* What next?" Savelli took a resentful step sideways, to put more space between himself and Bora's looming presence. "I'm within my rights, gentlemen. The front door was unlocked, the place was deserted, so... It's natural, isn't it? I heard the news of the *disgrazia*, after all."

Calling the massacre an "accident" might be Italian understatement. "Who told you?" Bora cut in.

"The expatriate academic community in Crete is a small one."

Villiger, Pendlebury, Allen, Savelli... Bora latched his pistol holder. "It seems to be growing by the hour as I learn about it, and that doesn't answer my question. Who actually *told* you what happened here?"

The gap opened by the removal of several editions caused a slender quarto to fall flat on its shelf; other books came to lean sideways against it. Spines bearing Greek, German, English authors' names, mostly followed by the dotted initials of academic titles, shifted behind Savelli's head. *A man's death*, Bora told himself, *may also be signified by the disarray of his punctiliously sorted books.* In the rummaged library, only the massive, built-in desk kept an appearance of normalcy.

A frown of alarmed spite came and went from Savelli's face. If he wondered what role a German officer played in all this, he knew better than to ask outright. "I live just over the hill in Kamari. My landlord informed me after witnessing the commotion when the police and ambulance came. A friend retired from the Italian Archaeological School confirmed the news. It's *brutto, brutto*. As foreign nationals you understand we're all concerned. First the rumours about the disappearance of the English scholar, Dr Pendee-bury..." (Bora noticed he mangled foreign surnames like Kostaridis, the Greek way) "and now this *disgrazia*."

The emphasis on the words "ugly", "accident", like the tone used to pronounce them, sounded affected, artificial. *But is there a natural response to violent death?* Cocking his head, Bora read the leaning title of Winckelmann's fundamental essay on ancient art, in the recent Phaidon edition. "How well did you know Professor Villiger?"

"Ah, not well, not so well – *buongiorno* and *buonasera.*"

"You barely exchanged a good day, and he lent you books?"

"No, no, no! I said *I* lent him books, as a professional courtesy between colleagues."

Kostaridis nudged Bora's elbow. A moderate prod, which Bora resented but understood to mean he needed to step away to hear some whispered communication. "I'll give you details later, *capitano*, but the Iraklion police was notified about this gentleman by the Italian Carabineers in Rhodes. Money questions."

Bora turned back to the scholar, whose book-picking had started again. "Your late colleague – where and when did you last meet him?"

"When?" Savelli took a deep breath of air to gain time. The baring of teeth gave a moment of glory to what must be an expensive set of dentures, somehow appropriate to a literate's mouth. "About six weeks ago, during Orthodox Easter week, in Iraklion. He couldn't wiggle away, there were others present. See, I asked him about – my books." *Vice versa is more likely*, Bora judged. "Imagine, he denied having them. I said I'd be passing by Ampelokastro anyway, and would pick them up. He told me he was very busy, and planning a trip besides."

So, Villiger meant to leave Crete at least as far back as April. This was new information. Kostaridis did not react to it (he stood by the built-in desk, opening and closing drawers as if their smooth functioning fascinated him and their contents meant nothing), but Bora wanted to know more. "A trip where?"

"He didn't say. Naturally I took it as a brush-off, but he was jittery."

"Jittery as in impatient," Kostaridis spoke up, "or jittery as in scared?"

"*Dio santo*, what do I know about that? Within a week, all hell broke loose and every one of us had to lie low because of the fighting. My landlord can confirm this is the first day I have put my head out of the house." Encouraged by the safely holstered gun or by Kostaridis' negligent attitude, Savelli stood his ground. "Look here, gentlemen, I'm the damaged party in all of this. I'm only taking back what's mine." The bound set of volumes joined the stack on the table. "Civilization as we know it is coming to an end, if we innocent scholars can be killed or abused in our homes, and stolen from to boot."

Oh, do me a favour, Bora thought. Generational annoyance with older men and their idea of rules made him sneer to himself. *Civilization as you know it* is *coming to an end, and good riddance*. From the titles pulled out so far, he could not make out Savelli's specific focus of research. "May I enquire what your speciality is?"

"My speciality? Young man, I worked with the great Halbherr, with Maiuri, with Jacopi: the entire Aegean is my speciality. I dug at Tavernais no later than this spring. And I'm not leaving here without my books."

"No." Bora laid his hand on the stack. "I'm afraid there have been enough independent withdrawals from this house. Make a list of the titles that belong to you, I'll make sure they're returned."

"What? I don't remember all the titles!"

"List those you recall, then."

Savelli made a choking noise. "This is unheard of! This is an outrage! I'll bring it up with His Excellency the Italian Governor, General Ettore Bastico, I'll ask for support from the Italian commander in Crete!"

"I'm shaking with fear. Be my guest."

During the exchange, Kostaridis kept his equanimity. Leaning against the desk, with his thumb and forefinger he scrupulously reshaped a lonely cigarette fished out of his pocket. He stuck it, still slightly bent, in his mouth, lit it and looked around for an ashtray to place the spent match in.

It was an odd, infinitesimal gesture of regard in the middle of chaos. Bora caught it out of the corner of his eye, and was intrigued. Kostaridis could have tossed the match on the desk or dropped it anywhere on the floor. Unknowingly, he had been waiting for a sign that he could trust the policeman, and that refusal to litter a ravaged room came close to doing it somehow. When Kostaridis' cigarette went out after the first drag, Bora decided to be gracious, and stretched his lighter out to him.

"And *please* do not smoke," Savelli complained. "I moved this far south on doctor's orders; I'd rather not breathe tar and nicotine while I'm being insulted."

Kostaridis shuffled to the window, opened it, and continued to smoke.

One by one Bora gathered up the ex libris and re-stacked the volumes under Savelli's angry stare. "When you prepare the list, please include author and publishing house."

"I protest! Do you take me for a librarian? This is – really, this is untenable!"

"You're free to turn me in. Remember, Bora is the name." Bora punctiliously righted the bookmark sticking out of a nineteenth-century volume, whose ex libris indicated a proprietor – Marcel Amédée Duvoin – who sounded like a Frenchman. "Chief Constable," he said without glancing at Savelli or Kostaridis, "will you escort the professor out of the house?"

Shouted recriminations about *stolen books* and *stolen ideas* came to Bora's ear while the scholar was dragged below. Stolen ideas? Did Savelli mean plagiarism? Likely another empty claim. And yet, resentment between scholars could run deep. Decades before, the Bora Verlag had entered a controversy by publishing Dörpfeld's field notes on Troy after the death of his great mentor, Heinrich Schliemann. The debate surrounding the site of the ancient city was still raging at that time; it mattered that an important Leipzig publisher had chosen to support the Schliemann–Dörpfeld thesis versus the French and American school. Careers and recognition were furiously made, risked and lost in the process. There was no telling to what excesses academic infighting might lead.

On the stairs, Savelli's complaints rose in pitch as he felt bolder with a Greek national. He was shouting by the time he reached the ground floor.

All the more surprising was the silence that followed. Either the professor had run out of steam, or else Kostaridis had seen to it that he shut up. Bora stepped to the windowsill, to look into the garden below.

The two were on the gravel path. Kostaridis, a cigarette stub still in his mouth, was unceremoniously searching the Italian's pockets. His frisking was quick, professional; you could judge its purse-snatcher lightness from up here. When something small rapidly passed from Savelli's pocket to his, after which they parted ways, Bora pulled back promptly.

He was systematically searching the books on Kostaridis' return. One at a time he held them upside down, fanning them so that bookmarks or sheets inside would fall out. Villiger, he thought, must have used just about any piece of paper to mark his pages, an unusual trait in a pedantic researcher. From the flapping leaves rained down receipts, postcards, snapshots, business cards, even the occasional bookmark. Bora swept them up as they touched the floor, and drove them into the large pockets of his British Army shorts.

"Has the Italian gone?"

"Yes." Kostaridis didn't bring up the object he'd taken from the professor, and neither did Bora for now.

"Savelli is an Italian surname, but Pericles – spelt with an S – sounds Greek."

"No, no. He's one of those Italians with cultivated Grecian names."

In no particular order, Bora replaced the books on the shelves as he finished looking through them. "You said you'd been notified by the Italian police in Rhodes. Why didn't you tell me about him earlier?"

The Greek shrugged his shoulders. "You're right, I should have. But it didn't seem directly related to the murder. Five years ago Savelli came here from Rhodes, where he'd worked for a time as vice-director of the Archaeological Museum. He'd got into hot water, shall we say, and was sacked on account of some missing gold coins. Although it was never proven he had anything to do with it, the Italian colonial authorities claimed the coins turned up in a British private collection, whose proprietor Savelli knew. Oh, and he also ran into trouble with officers of the local Italian garrison (I believe it was the 9th Infantry Regiment of the Regina Division at that time), over a cabaret artist who performed at the Circolo della Caccia in Borgo Sant'Anastasia. And —"

"Please tell me everything at once without my having to prompt you."

"As you wish." Kostaridis said it as if getting to the point were a waste of good storytelling. "The artist, one Signora Cordoval, was a favourite with the officers and frequently their guest at Villa Fiorita, incidentally not run by a Greek national but by a shady character, an Egyptian who went by the name of Jalloud. Have you ever been to Rhodes? They don't call it the Island of Roses without a reason. Foreigners have been living it up in its hotels, pensions and clubs for some thirty years. Italians mostly, but Egyptians and Turks as well. If you like *dolce far niente*, that's the place."

"I don't like *dolce far niente.*"

"Right. That's what I thought. Well, the star of the Italian-occupied archipelago formally accused the professor of man-handling her in a fit of jealousy. It must be said she betrayed him famously. The head of the local Carabineers bragged to me that he could personally vouch for it. But on the other hand Savelli had the gall of violating the superstitious rule of – do you know what *seradura* is?"

"I haven't the faintest idea. It sounds like *lock* or *locking* in Italian."

"It's what Sephardic Jews call the superstition of closing up a house during someone's 'unexplained' illness. For a given time you're supposed to cloister the sick alone except for a healer who performs all kinds of rituals, from anointing him with sugar and spices to administering crushed resin and ground coffee." Kostaridis opened his arms as if to concede a point. "You smile, but Signora Cordoval didn't find it amusing when Savelli hammered on the door of the house where her old father lay infirm, and broke a window to get in when they wouldn't open to him."

So the singer was Jewish. Bora made a mental note. On another shelf, books on racial theory gave him a taste of Villiger's other field of interest. "You keep saying *Signora* Cordoval, but what was her given name?"

"Signora *was* her given name. It's common among those people."

"Ah. Did the father, the old man, die as a result of the infraction?"

"No, but Savelli had to run from the Jewish quarter for dear life, chased down Calle de los Ricos by those who lived there. This is to tell you, *capitano*, that he's no respecter of rules. He demanded that Signora give back the money he'd spent on gifts, and especially a family brooch. She turned him down, and shortly thereafter – given the story of the missing artefacts – he repaired to Crete in disgrace, as an independent scholar. At the police we heard no more of him until four years ago, when the artist came to Iraklion on tour. We were called to the scene because he broke into her dressing room to recover the famous brooch, claiming it belonged to his late mother."

"Ah, yes. *Mamma. That*'s Italian."

"In the end she agreed to give the jewel back and he had to pay good money for damages to the theatre, and her wardrobe. And besides —"

Bora interrupted what he recognized as another pointless round of drivel on Kostaridis' part. "All right, all right. So, Savelli is a tightwad, a brute and – because it takes one to know one – he claims to have been stolen from when he's suspected of selling ancient coinage. The police of two nations are on to him. Scholarly diatribe or not, I doubt he could manage to get five people killed for a handful of books and papers."

"Well, this is not a paperweight."

Out of Kostaridis' pocket, the cylindrical case of a photographic roll appeared, which he held between thumb and forefinger. "The professor swears it's his, of course. See for yourself: there are similar empty containers in the top drawer of the desk. This one is full, and might contain another set of pictures of Cretan peasants, or something else entirely." He turned to watch Bora furiously rifle the desk. "*Signor* Filligi must have kept the roll well hidden, because when we searched the room empty containers were all there was."

Cardboard boxes and aluminium cases of Agfa Isopan camera film filled the drawer. Bora looked up from them in frustration. "Damn, no one mentioned this desk in the reports. I wonder what else is gone. Didn't you tell me Villiger took his film to Iraklion for developing?"

"I did. Ever since Greece entered the war, the owner of the camera shop has been reporting on foreign customers to the police. That's how we learnt of the many photos Signor Filligi took of the locals."

"But some he probably printed himself. In the study downstairs I saw an empty bottle of Rodinal, which is a concentrated developing agent. He must have owned a camera as well, or more than one."

"*Poios xerei* – that's 'Who knows' in Greek. You'll see it's a useful expression in Crete. We got here late, *capitano*." If frogs could smile, they would smile from ear to ear like Kostaridis, without showing their gums and without amusement. "I can tell you that Rhodes' reputation for *dolce far niente* does not exclude its use by all kinds of people as a place of intrigue. The more time you have on your hands – you know, idleness being the devil's workshop, and all that. The Italians recruited their spies among intellectuals, who'd naturally be acquainted with the expatriate society *and* the military."

Just like Villiger, who worked for Himmler… Bora had to admit there was nothing of interest left in the desk. *Aside from the culprits and Powell, between the War Crimes Bureau and the Greek police, the camping soldiers, the thieving peasants and the Italian professor, there's no telling how many people trampled through Ampelokastro before this morning.* "Why didn't you detain Professor Savelli for questioning?"

"For three reasons: first, he's not a suspect; second, he's not the type who'll take to the mountains in any case. Third, his landlord is a police informant and would have tipped us off if Savelli had acted suspiciously at the time of the murder. Besides, espionage" – he used a word Bora had never pronounced – "isn't anything our district is equipped to handle. Anyhow, from the professor's rental at the outskirts of Kamari, on foot it takes fifteen, twenty minutes to get here. You've seen how distances don't really matter in Crete: it's how long it takes you to get from one place to the next."

If only the same could be said of investigations, where time matters, and how! Bora did miss his carefree task of fetching wine for the Russians. *I'd be heading back to Moscow right now and my biggest worry would be not overdrinking at embassy parties. Here I am, into the only week at my disposal, when a month wouldn't be enough to understand what happened to Villiger, let alone to pursue all the possible leads.*

"By the way, is it espionage?" Kostaridis asked, suavely.

Bora had no answer, and wouldn't have given it if he had one. *This is hopeless,* he glumly kept thinking as he went tramping through the bedrooms, a needless survey after they'd been emptied by scavengers. Not a piece of furniture, no bedding or clothes left.

"They'd already been raided when I saw them," Kostaridis commented. "The housekeeper slept in the house, but there's no telling if the field hands ever did: there's a hut in the olive grove with pallets in it. I'm willing to bet they only came in for their wages at the end of the month, which is probably why the door was unlocked, and they were all caught together. And if you have been wondering whether there was anything more between master and male servants, my reply is that we do not know."

They returned downstairs, Bora visibly preoccupied, Kostaridis uncaring that his big toe showed pitilessly through the black sock.

With a crime scene gravely tampered with, and intimate details of Villiger's household unknown, it would be much easier to confirm the official story and blame the paratroopers. *There's still that one needle in the haystack, but Major Busch is deluded if he believes I'll be able to track down a runaway such as Powell has become, with or without the American woman's help. He's the only one who could give me details on the actual timing of the*

shooting, on the murder scene minutes after it happened, and gener-
ally corroborate what Lieutenant Sinclair understood from him. It's
a temptation to say, "Preger's men did it: overreactions and mistakes
happen in war. This is as far as I could get in a week; I'll see you
after we conquer Russia."

More scraps of paper and cards emerged from the books
piled between the bloodstains and the bullet-scarred walls. Bora
gathered them automatically. Then he joined Kostaridis as he
crossed the littered floor and went to stand in the patched
shade of the garden. The odour of wilting grass and sun-dried
earth flowed in from the olive grove all around, a sleepy scent
that made one feel lethargic.

Not Bora, whose zeal was only whetted by disappointment.
Carelessly taking out of his chest pocket the Ray-Ban case, he
said, "The Jewish cabaret artist, where is she now?"

"Don't know."

The promptness of Kostaridis' reply surprised him. "Are you
telling me you don't know because I'm German, or because
you really don't know?"

"Is the information relevant to the enquiry?"

"I don't think so."

"Then I don't know where she is, and that's all."

"I can find out, you're aware."

"'Find out' where she is, or whether I'm lying?"

"Both."

"In that case, it makes no difference what I say now."

"Have it your way." Bora started for the front gate. "I'm just
fishing around for ideas." He put on the sunglasses, aware that
Kostaridis might take it as a move to conceal his eyes. Which,
after all, was exactly what it was.

The matter of trust surfaced openly when the policeman
stepped aside to let him out of the gate first and Bora declined
with a smile.

"Is that why you pointed your gun at me back there in the defile, *capitano*?"

"I don't care for traps. Why, do *you* trust me?"

"It's irrelevant: I'm a fatalist."

"I'm not. Spain and Poland taught me I must keep an eye on my fate."

Years later, when asked about the episode, Kostaridis would observe that his first impression of Bora had been of someone still *intact*. As if nothing had yet touched him, and his life had unfolded within a circle of physical and psychological safety. It surprised him to hear that the German already had two military campaigns behind him. *Good for him,* he recalled thinking without envy. *There are some who go through life unscathed.* But the disenchanted earthiness of his culture suggested that – in a war that would last until the adversaries wore one another out – sooner or later the bill would be presented to Martin Bora.

Once they left the shade of the garden, the parched daylight flew at them, reverberating from the gravel of the road. Tall, blooming henbane, with black-hearted yellow flowers and toothed leaves, grew on its verge. Insects teemed over the dusty willows and grass along the brook. No bird sounds. Perfect silence, lack of wind. Moments in which time became its own seal and no longer seemed capable of past or future.

The question of trust given or not, received or withdrawn, was a tightrope Bora had been trained to test before walking: with Kostaridis he felt he was back to the preliminary stage. He stepped away from the policeman to size up the bare rock wall beyond the brook, with the ochre-yellow parapet crowning the top. Close to home, the Sandstone Mountains had provided just one of the hiking opportunities for him, even before Spain had him crawling up and down the Aragon heights. And in the Grampian Hills he'd learnt fell running from his Edinburgh cousins. He could at a glance judge the relative ease of the climb. *Do I really keep an eye on my fate, or want to?*

From somewhere else Sphingokephalo Hill might well resemble the profile of a lion with the head of a woman; from here, it hardly deserved the name. Regardless, anyone looking down from it was in the ideal position to observe and hear the goings-on at Ampelokastro. The villa's terrace hugged the rock like a battlement, anchored to the building and on the ledge probably eight or ten feet higher than the ground it stood on.

Bora preceded Kostaridis across the hump of packed earth and decrepit masonry that bridged the cement culvert. "Time to go and check on the Turk," he said, and passed the straps of his rucksack over his shoulders. "I'm climbing directly from this side."

"Why? By the regular road we can be there in fifteen minutes."

"I can be there in six or seven."

Kostaridis shielded his eyes to look up the incline. His attitude was that of one who concedes there's no teaching the futility of needless exertion if exertion itself is seen as a merit. "You had better watch out: he doesn't like surprises."

"See you at the top."

The Sphinx's head – or its neck, at any rate – posed no difficulty to an ascent. Midway through the clamber, Bora found a hold secure enough to pause and look at the vineyards that formed a partial green belt around the hill. The destroyed winery Kostaridis spoke of must be in town, because all seemed to have been spared here. As for Ampelokastro below, it came more and more into full view: the palm trees, however, shielded the garden. You might see men walking through the front gate, and that was all. The culvert, and anyone hiding in the muddy bed of the brook, might or might not be visible from the top of the hill.

Bora climbed without effort, and kept asking himself questions he'd have to turn over to others, Major Busch first among them. *What exactly did Villiger do for the* Reichskommissar *? Did it entail more than just measuring skulls and eye colour? If his field hands were receiving their wages when they were killed, does it follow that the attackers knew this, or did they accidentally catch the whole household together? No cash was found on the scene as far as I know, or was stolen before the photos were taken. If Preger's men really had nothing to do with this, I have one chance in a million of finding a solution.*

Only the last stretch, chipped smooth with a pickaxe to discourage intrusion, gave Bora the thrill of risk, but by then the terrace was at hand. He vigorously hoisted himself up and gained the wide parapet. Simultaneously, from a glass door that banged wide open, three large fawn-coloured dogs, with black faces and curly tails, lunged furiously at him. Bora, who'd barely risen from a straddle to an upright position, nearly lost his footing; driven back to the edge, it was a miracle that he didn't fall backwards. In a frenzy of barking and growling, the charging dogs resembled the three-headed hound of hell. *Christ, they're foaming at the mouth. If one of them jumps up, they all will, and I'm screwed.* Bora groped for his holster until he found the comforting bulk of the pistol grip.

"Ouzo, Mumia, Almansour!"

From the terrace door a deep-voiced hulk of a man came out, himself brandishing a pistol. "Ouzo! Mumia, Almansour!"

Rifat Agrali had the physique you'd expect of an Ottoman in a Mozart opera, down to his portliness and moustache, except that he was blonde. As he stepped out into the sun, his whiskers glittered like sheaves of pale straw. "Ouzo, Mumia, Almansour!"

Instantly the animals turned away from the parapet and trotted to sit at their master's feet. "*E tu, inglese, che vuoi?*"

They faced each other, right arm extended and gun in hand. Bora did no more than let go of the trigger. Whatever the circumstances, being asked in Italian what he wanted was less of an irritant than having a weapon squared at him. He said, in Italian, "I'd have shot them, you know."

"And I'd have shot you right after."

"I doubt it."

"You wouldn't if you knew me."

Neither was willing to put away his weapon first. Bora recognized the blowback pistol. *M1922 Subay army model*, he told himself. A good piece, related to the Browning used at Sarajevo to assassinate Franz Ferdinand and start the Great War.

While he stood still in a firing stance, from a few feet away Rifat Bey's eyes were as sourly green as Bora's, a six or a ten on Villiger's chart. "German, are you? I thought you were an Englishman at first." And "You're no paratrooper, at any rate. Why didn't you come to the front door like most human beings?"

"It was quicker to climb the cliff." Bora slipped down from the parapet onto the terrace, careful not to set off the dogs once more. From where they'd been ordered to sit, they could go from the floor to his throat in seconds flat. "I was at your late neighbour's just now."

"So." The Subay kept Bora under aim, although the hairy arm holding it relaxed. Rifat Bey walked around him and glanced below. "Who else is with you?"

"*Epitropos* Kostaridis, from Iraklion."

"You keep such bad company?"

"And worse."

At last, Rifat Bey stuck the handgun in his belt. "That slug. What does a *frangos* like you have to do with Cretan police?"

"I'm looking into what happened at Ampelokastro."

"I wasn't here when it happened."

Bora slid his pistol down the holster without latching it. "You and your neighbour didn't get along, I hear." In his peripheral vision, behind the Turk he caught sight of food and water bowls in a corner of the terrace; and unless he was mistaken, inside the glass door there was an army rifle – a Great War era G98 – leaning on the floor against the wall.

Rifat Bey seemed aware of what had caught Bora's attention. "I ought to set the dogs on you and the two-bit copper, the *sbirro*. Didn't he tell you I wasn't here when the Swiss died? I wasn't here when the battle began. I was at Zimbouli."

"And where's that?"

"The 'Place of Hyacinths', my town house near Iraklion." Seeing Bora take a step sideways, he whipped out the Subay once more. "No. Don't you move. You stay right where you are; you're not coming any closer to my house."

Bora did not argue the point. Judging by the way the dogs pricked up their ears and curled back their upper lips, Kostaridis must be approaching Sphingokephalo. As he'd reckoned from below, the terrace stood on a base maybe eight feet above the level ground of the hilltop. From where he stood, an incline of agave-studded land was visible, with a path leading up to the front of the villa. The inspector laboured under the sun with the weary deliberate pace of a postman, or a door-to-door salesman. He'd covered his head with a kerchief knotted at the corners and carried the jacket draped on his left shoulder.

When he reached close enough to stand below the parapet, he called out, "Agrali, hold the dogs, I'm coming up. And thanks for leaving a few kegs to step on."

Rifat Bey leaned out to look at him. "What d'ya want, *sbirro*?"

"Cool your heels, Agrali." Kostaridis' jacket appeared on the parapet, followed by an arm and a leg. Eventually, the entire policeman emerged. "I'm here on business, with the captain. Be neighbourly, and I'll pretend I didn't see what you stuck in your belt."

"This?" The Turk grinned as he tapped the Subay. "This is my worry beads."

"Your *worry beads*." Kostaridis had removed his socks. Barefoot in his dusty sandals, to counterbalance the impression of inadequacy he put his jacket on, over his sweat-drenched shirt. "You wouldn't know what happened to Signor Filligi and his household, those three handsome boys included?"

Rifat Bey pointed with his chin at Bora. "He already asked. What do *I* know? Why should I know who did it, and why?"

"We heard he'd been jittery of late," Bora mentioned, "and was planning a trip."

"Good! Good that he was jittery, and good that he was planning a trip. I should be so lucky, that the *frangos* son of a bitch would take a long trip."

Kostaridis stepped around to shake dust from his sandals. "In a way he has – indefinitely."

"I wipe myself of it, *sbirro*. German soldiers ruined my winery; this one comes up from below like a burglar. Why shouldn't Germans have killed that water thief? I give you both one minute to turn tail and get out of my property before I let the dogs loose."

Bora wasn't taken in this time. It was all about intimidation. The Turk was openly aggressive, so much so that it might be a way to exaggerate and defuse his hostility at the same time, concealing other, more devious levels of dangerousness. As for Kostaridis, he kept even now an air both clandestine and submissive, the air of one who has crumpled his animosity into a lump so tight that it may be carried unseen in a pocket, so to speak, and be pulled out at the right time wholly by surprise. Preger – well, Preger's resentment toward the world, at least the world of civilians, to which their childhood belonged – was exhibited like a proud badge. Bora wondered what impression *he* might give others.

"Speaking of dogs," he said, "I noticed four bowls but only three dogs. Are you missing one of them?"

"Yes, I'm missing one of them. I also lost my winery, thanks to you."

Bora chose the conciliatory route. "I'm sorry about your winery. It so happens I'm in the wine business myself, at present."

"It can only mean you're here to steal it."

"Not even close. I'm buying it bona fide from Panagiotis in Iraklion."

"*Dishwater.*"

Bora was about to reply, but then he thought it might be true, that Major Busch may not be such an expert after all.

"Panagiotis' Mandilaria is dishwater, I'm telling you."

"Why, are you a producer of Mandilaria?"

"No, but his is swill."

"I'm also looking for Dafni."

"Panagiotis doesn't make it. And don't trust him if he tells you he'll buy it for you from a friend, either." A brief toss of his head and a whistle under his breath sent the dogs filing indoors. Rifat Bey pulled the glass door closed behind them. "How much do you know about wine?"

"Enough not to make blunders when I order some at the table, but no more than that."

"You don't know anything about wine, I can tell. Ask the *sbirro* if it isn't true what I say, that the best Dafni *and* Mandilaria in Iraklion are sold by the Spinthakis widow near Agia Ekaterini *djamé.*"

"It's true," Kostaridis agreed, although he turned up his nose at the way Rifat Bey still gave the old name of *djamé*, mosque, to St Catherine's. "I'll show you where it is when we go back."

And here they were, talking about wine while the question was murder. Preliminaries, Bora understood, meant to reduce mutual hostility and clear the path for a serious conversation at some other time. "There was a dead dog at your neighbour's," he told Agrali.

"I know. I buried it. Not mine."

"And did you enter the house, while you were there?"

Rifat Bey turned to Kostaridis, who had spoken the words. "The minute's up. I'm calling the dogs."

"And your thugs too, I saw them looking out of the windows as I climbed the path."

"Fuck you, and my thugs too."

Bora watched them spar, aware they wouldn't get more from the Turk at this time. *I'm not like them at all,* he reasoned. *My aggressiveness is not so close to the bone. Mine is a reaction. Against the wrongs done to our Fatherland after the Great War, against those nations that smother our vital space, and against demands that we keep justifying ourselves to the world as Germans. My private self gives way to the needs of my role as a soldier. What do I want, for myself? I have no time to think about it; my psychological space is all taken up. I have the young, handsome wife I desired, and that's plenty.*

"Let's go, *capitano,*" Kostaridis grumbled. "Agrali, I'll have a bone to pick with you when you come to town."

Rifat Bey sneered. "And go down the regular way, where I can see you."

The crack of a rifle, surely the German-made weapon Bora had seen through the glass door, came from behind as they walked away from the residence along the exposed path. Bora's first response was to turn around, a move Kostaridis prevented by grabbing his wrist before he could do so. His hold clamped hard on him like a manacle.

"Don't look back, keep going."

"He fired on us, are you deaf?"

"Sure, he did. In Crete you don't show that you're afraid."

"I'm not *afraid*, I'm furious."

"Let's go."

The sharp whine of a second shot pierced the air even closer. Bora hunched this time, just short of a stumble. "Christ, he nicked my head!"

"Are you hurt?"

"...No. I don't think so."

"Keep walking, then. He'll respect you for it more than he would if you fired back." In the same even-minded tone, Kostaridis added something in Greek that sounded like quiet blasphemy. "Well, the bullet did tear the skin a bit. Quite a scar you got there."

Bora irritably rubbed the side of his head. It was the surgically stitched wound from his Polish days, when a hail of rocks had welcomed a group of German officers riding down a street in Krakow. It had bled and hurt, but was nothing compared with the retaliation that followed. He didn't like being reminded of it. He wiped the smear of bright blood on his shirt – hardly the kind of heroic injury he darkly longed for. *"A dawn will come, an evening, a midday / when someone will bereave me of life in battle..."*

Regardless of what Kostaridis had advised, he glanced over his shoulder toward Sphingokephalo. From the terrace, Rifat Bey kept them under aim through the scope of the high-precision Gewehr 98.

Bora was tempted to respond with a well-directed shot, but even a Browning high power didn't stack up to a marksman's rifle, so he reluctantly gave up the idea.

It's all been done for thousands of years, he thought, *provocation and response, or lack thereof: Kostaridis is right in that. During the hour of Greek literature, while my schoolmates took en masse the part of the Trojan defenders, I was solidly on the side of the aggressors.*

Achaeans over the people of Asia, Achilles versus Hector. Those warriors far from home, led by revenge for the rape of Helen, had all my sympathy. And notwithstanding Professor Lohse's deeply moving declamation of Hector's farewell to wife and child, I'll take Achilles' angry solitude any day.

5

Being thrown out of doors was not an experience he was familiar with, surely not twice in the same day. Seeing his Moscow uniform, boots, briefcase and the rest of his belongings lying in a heap on the pavement in front of the hotel, Bora vaulted out of the personnel carrier even before it came to a full stop. Everything was piled there where glass from the broken windows had been swept yesterday, looking just as forlorn. A newly stencilled sign by the entrance – *Headquarters, First Battalion, 1st Airborne Regiment, 7th Flieger Division* – said all there was to know about his new status in Cretan society. Bora was in a rage, but there wasn't much he could do about it. He swept up the pieces of his uniform, his briefcase, maps, what few basic toiletry items he'd brought along, and walked in to rest them on the floor just inside the hotel entrance.

As if on cue, an Air Force major – Bora was only later to know it was First Battalion Commander Walther himself – stalked out of Busch's office wagging a "no" with his forefinger to keep him from leaving his things there. Bora saw red. He came within an inch of creating an incident but held on to his temper somehow (*I've got a case to solve, and I've got Russia to invade*). "And *stay* out!" The commander's shouted words followed him as he recrossed the threshold.

When a never before seen Greek concierge rushed out after him to apologize, because the captain "must believe it, the hotel management had nothing to do with this", Bora stared at the laundry bag in which the man offered to collect his odds and ends. "I'm afraid your cases of wine are gone, too. I *told* them it was reserved, but…" Without finishing the sentence the concierge handed him a sheet of paper folded in two and stapled together.

Here in the street, whatever they thought of the scene, the Jäger who'd driven Bora to town put their vehicles in reverse and left the way they came. A handful of paratroopers looking out from the hotel seemed to be enjoying it instead. Bora had to put on the best possible face in the presence of other Germans, and of Kostaridis besides. He removed the staples and read.

It was a telegraphic note from Busch. *Unexpected urgent transfer to the mainland. Meet Lt Sinclair at 17.00 hours, Iraklion Airfield. Frances Allen under custody at the Hotel Knossos.* Whatever he jotted down next, he'd comprehensively cancelled with the fountain pen, until the paper had nearly torn through. The hour of writing (8 a.m.) was marked at the close of the note, along with a meaningful, *You're on your own now. Good luck. Radio Athens if you're in a pickle.*

PS Your "Scotsman" could be as black as the jack of spades for all we know: the K in his name stands for Krishnamurti.

So, Busch had been sacked. It was conceivable that the *Abwehr*'s poor showing before the campaign had put in motion devious methods of retribution that cost men in the field their posts. Unless, of course, the intermediate Air Force commands chose to behead the team investigating the massacre, or other reasons (Casablanca- or Moscow-related?) were behind it. Whatever. No word on where the paperwork the major had shown him might be. With Busch gone from the island, Bora's support system was down to nil. Anger (or else the sun beaming straight down) made the nicked side of his head throb as he looked up from the note.

Only now did he notice the luxurious, customized Italian sedan parked by the kerb, with a German airman behind the wheel and worry beads hanging from the rear-view mirror. Two feet away from the car, Kostaridis observed, "Alfa Romeo 6C, six cylinders, 2500." He said it as if he'd stayed behind to admire the expensive piece of machinery, when he'd clearly been watching what was going on in front of the hotel.

Bora avoided his glance. He was not about to beg for help. With urgent appointments to keep, however, and an alternative base of operations to secure, his choices were limited: leaving aside the airborne troops, it was either the Jäger or the Cretan police.

"Should we see about lodgings?" Posing it as a question, Kostaridis saved him from having to ask a favour. "I can send for a car at the police station."

Bora fretted. "I have thirty minutes before I meet the British officer who turned in the photos, and then I must reach the Hotel Knossos."

"To stay?"

"I don't know if I can stay there. I'm to see an American detainee, a woman called Allen." It was more than Bora would otherwise have shared, but he was hard-pressed. He inwardly cheered when Kostaridis seized a youngster who'd been gawking at the Alfa Romeo and sent him running for support.

"They'll be here in ten minutes," he assured Bora. "...Allen, you said? An American married to a Greek?"

"Yes. Do you know about her?"

"I can tell you about Sidheraki, her husband. He's been in and out of jail the past ten years, for political reasons. Belongs to the KKE of Nikos Zachariadis."

Bora gathered his belongings and turned his back on the Megaron, the place of his public humiliation. "The communist party leader? My information is that we transferred Zachariadis to Germany when we first landed in mainland Greece, months ago."

"Allow me to say the Metaxas government made it easy for you by having him already in custody." Kostaridis studiously undid the knotted corners of his handkerchief so he could mop his face with it. "Make no mistake, *capitano*, I'm an anti-communist. Thanks to Metaxas we closed down hashish dens and got rid of rabble and bouzouki music. I realize Germany is marching along with the Soviets at this time, but a man's ideas are a man's ideas." (*If he only knew where I'll be riding three weeks from now,* Bora thought.) "So I kept an eye on Andonis Sidheraki, even though he's settled down since he married the American. It seems her British colleagues cherished him, because he's got an eye for antiquities; they say he can spot an ancient site better than anyone. Besides, Sidheraki follows the Siantos rather than the Zachariadis party line. 'Old Man' Siantos is more anti-fascist than anti-capitalist and anti-British, as Zachariadis always was. I can tell you plenty about Sidheraki, but he isn't the man you're looking for."

"No, and as far as his wife is concerned, he's in our hands."

"You're aware of course that he ran off the moment your troops reached the island?"

"I am." Dignity being all he could hang on to at the time, Bora went out of his way to conceal the discomfort that sweat and sunburn were causing him on the blistering pavement. In the harbour below, the clearing of wrecks continued on and off the docking area, as if nothing but German men and machinery populated Iraklion. The sea beyond the flurry of activity lay perfectly blue, trimmed with lazy afternoon waves. He'd jump in it with his clothes on if he could. "I'm also aware," he added, "that some less anti-communist colleagues of yours left the jail door open, and many other comrades took to the hills. Never mind; our leverage with Miss Allen is that Sidheraki is wounded and in a prison camp on the continent. What else should I know about him, just in case?"

"He's self-taught. Could easily revert to his pre-marriage fanaticism. Daring, reputed handsome. Younger than his wife." Amused at his own comment, Kostaridis blew the dust of the trip from his nose into the crumpled handkerchief. "To us, she swore her husband knew nothing about the arms found at their place near Knossos."

"*What* arms?"

"Ah, you weren't told. Well, six brand-new MAB 38 submachine guns."

"Brand new as in 'never used', or —"

"No, not so new. Obtained somehow."

Bora's surprise made it difficult – even silly – to stand there ramrod straight, as if being drenched in perspiration were a natural condition for him. "I doubt she was the one collecting weapons we Germans bought from the Italians!"

"Well, shall we say that as a US citizen, she could have got off scot-free had she not protected him." The frog-like smirk returned to Kostaridis' face. "That's wifely affection for you. What can we do? Greek men make good lovers – or so women and goddesses always think."

"This changes things considerably. MAB 38 guns were used at Ampelokastro."

"But Sidheraki had already left home when Signor Filligi was killed."

"Or he simply kept out of sight. When did you search his place?"

"Let's see. Must have been the 31st."

"A day *after* the killing."

"Yes, but I really don't think —"

"Sidheraki must have fled in a hurry, if he didn't bother to take the guns with him. Where do you suppose he went?"

"*Capitano*, you could drop 10,000 men and make them disappear on this island. There's no way of knowing. He could have joined the bands in the interior or embarked with the British. He could be hiding in any village, or even in Iraklion. If your leverage on the American woman is to make her believe you've got him, you had better be able to maintain the ruse."

Bora pressed him impatiently. "Do you have a photo of this Sidheraki fellow? If I ask her, she'll suspect he's not in our hands at all."

"The photo in his police file is dated, won't do much good. He came and went so much that we didn't take a new one of him every time." Kostaridis folded and refolded the wet hand-kerchief before driving it into his pocket. "Wait, we picked up a boxful of papers from his home. We'll look through them when we reach the police station."

"*Epitropos*, I don't have time. And where's your damned transportation?"

"*Calma, calma.* There it is." Kostaridis pointed at a modest, unmarked car coming up the street. "Not a customized Alfa Romeo like Rifat Bey's, but it'll get us there." He good-naturedly shook his head. "No wonder he was sore at you Germans; it's the only one registered on Crete."

The way to the airfield was littered with enemy vehicles unfit for reuse. They sat or lay there waiting to be scrapped, minus their tyres and whatever else could be unhinged, unscrewed or pulled off. The image of scavenging returned, with humans as insects whose business it is to demolish. Dusty hollyhocks, bombed-out buildings, metal roofs glaring like mirrors on both sides of the road: the geography of summer war set Bora on an anxious, imaginary bridge between his memories of Spain and the anticipation of what Russia would be soon. He rode the brief distance not knowing what to expect from Sinclair, or from himself in regards to Sinclair.

Dust billowed around the car as it sped on. One of Kostaridis' men drove, a small fellow whose eyes in the rear-view mirror were bloodshot and slightly mad. At one point – they were past the turn-off for Knossos – the sight of wooden crates disgorged from an overturned vehicle made Bora cringe. The lost wine meant for Deputy Chairman Beria came to mind. It was no small matter: there'd be repercussions if he failed to procure sixty more bottles of the desired vintages. A bad report from Colonel Krebs, not to speak of Ambassador von der Schulen-burg, could hurt his fine record thus far and haunt him into his assignment with the First Cavalry Division.

Indifferent to Bora's and anyone else's troubles, the sea stayed to the left of the road throughout, deep blue, true to itself.

"There." In sight of the airfield, Kostaridis pointed out a long, single-storeyed wooden shed, windowless on the side closest to them, whose sheet-iron roof must make it into an oven at this hour. "I think that's where you're going."

Bora hoped it wouldn't be so, but of course it was.

Kostaridis let him off at the gate. "On my card you'll find my office phone number. Call when you're done; I'll come and pick you up. To save time, I'll fetch the box of Sidheraki papers and show them to you as we drive to the Hotel Knossos afterwards."

"*Grazie, eucharistò.*"

It wasn't lost on the policeman that Bora thanked him in Italian and Greek, even though he might be doing it because it annoyed him to show gratitude in his own language. "*Parakalo.* Where should I leave your things?"

"Please take them along. I have what I need in my rucksack." Which was a sign of trust, if not outright esteem.

147

When first meeting someone (the practice embarrassed him a little, since he'd developed it long before starting counter-intelligence work) Bora routinely let his interlocutor believe that he knew less than he actually did. He had no specific reason to hide his fluency in English from Sinclair. It was, rather, that penchant – less than a bad habit – typical of one trained to operate undercover.

The moment after identifying himself and his role there, he asked for an interpreter from English. The airfield being one of the places where prisoners transited, a specialist was on hand, and so Bora was flanked by a young *Feldwebel* with a bureaucrat's face, who walked with him toward the guarded shed. "There were close to seventy prisoners until yesterday," he volunteered. "We keep nabbing them in the hills and gathering them here before they go off to Galatas." (Galatas, a postcard from his grandparents' days. Tatties, that's what it was. Tatties was the name of his mother's pony.)

Tall, in his late thirties but youthful, stiff-shouldered, Lieu-tenant Sinclair was standing in the empty room, and turned slightly towards the door as the Germans stepped in. There was something gangling about him, like in a quality colt, but contrary to Busch's predictions he looked every inch the Brit-ish officer (or sportsman) you'd expect to see in propaganda photos, ruddiness of cheeks included – of the sort that easily becomes a flush. Only the moist, dark sheen of his eyes and his neatly trimmed hair gave him away as an Anglo-Indian. At once Bora noticed his left arm was contused; between army shorts and khaki long socks, his knees were bruised. The watch had been snatched from him, judging from the cuts and ring of pale skin around his wrist. His elbow had bled, and recently too.

They exchanged a terse military salute – palm of the hand downward in the German, outward with thumb slightly bent in the prisoner. Bora, who'd summarily dusted off the day's grime before entering, rested his rucksack on the floor. The heat in the room reached the limit of endurance. Even with two gridded windows open, around midday it must pass this limit, and the windows were closed now. One could only admire Sinclair's effort to keep up appearances in spite of it all: the suede of his non-regulation *chukka* shoes was spotless; he'd shaved immaculately and conveyed the impression of discipline and good breeding.

Bora began with the expected enquiries about the prisoner's conditions, asking whether there was anything he could get him. *As if I could get anything for anybody; I don't even have a bed to sleep in on this island, and I'm wearing looted British Army shorts besides.* The plan required that he neutrally observe his counterpart while addressing him in German and pay close attention to the interpreter, nodding only when hearing in translation what he'd caught perfectly in the original.

Sinclair answered that he did not need anything. "Not even your arm attended to, or a wristwatch?"

"No." Despite the interpreter's presence, Sinclair looked directly at Bora when he spoke. "Just what happened to your arm, and to your wristwatch?"

Sinclair did not reply. He was at the same time urbane and stand-offish, as you'd expect of one who is in enemy hands and on principle refuses to show cordiality, much less intimidation, in the presence of his captor. Bora sympathized, convinced as he was it could never happen to him (it would soon enough, in very different circumstances, on that Russian front he anticipated to conquer in a matter of weeks). He suspected the prisoner had been roughed up and stolen from, possibly after he resisted questioning or some treatment an officer would regard as unacceptable.

"As you may have been informed," he said, "I'm not here to interrogate you – my Air Force colleagues will attend to that if they haven't already. I am interested in the circumstances that occasioned your report to Dr Unger of the War Crimes Bureau, namely the entrusting of a photographic camera to you, and what your fellow Briton shared regarding its contents."

Sinclair tightened his lips before speaking. "I shan't be able to add to what was already reported. Dr Unger took my deposition to the last detail."

"The photographer's full name is missing."

"That's because the man never told me. It was all rather frantic – you know POWs are discouraged from talking to one another. I assumed he'd found himself in some rough spot, because he was bareheaded and only wearing his undershirt (Sinclair called it *vest*, the British way). To me, he identified himself as Sergeant Major Powell."

"Any other details?"

"Five nine or five ten in height, I'd say. Slight build, sandy-haired. Gloucestershire man, judging from his accent – that's all I noticed."

Speaking of regional accents to a German who supposedly does not understand English seemed superfluous, but then Sinclair's own speech was faultless. Bora listened carefully. *RP English*, he told himself. His Anglo-Indian status notwithstanding, Sinclair must have attended good schools in the mother country, as Received Pronunciation rinses off whatever provincial inflection one might have. *We were taught RP English at home, although with Grandmother Ashworth-Douglas Peter and I occasionally roll our Rs like Scotsmen.* At a closer look, it was possible Sinclair had been injured during the fighting. The bleeding on his elbow could be due to recent manhandling of a scab that had just begun to heal. "That is fine," Bora insisted, "but it will be useful for me to hear whatever else you recall that might further the enquiry."

Sinclair must have learnt to check his temper very early; Bora recognized from experience the self-control that became second nature. "Sir," he coolly pointed out, "you read in the report how Powell and I met. It was a matter of minutes. Men of all ranks, from different units, were herded together at gunpoint directly from the battlefield. The conditions of our exchange were such that they barely allowed him to sum- marize what he'd witnessed, in broken sentences at that. He seemed – well, he seemed fearful that we might all meet the same fate. No sooner had he handed me his camera than he sprinted off. There was considerable commotion and gunfire as the guards noticed the getaway. I saw Powell being struck in the arm, I don't know how seriously, but he succeeded somehow. I was jostled, fell on my arm, and fully expected the photographic equipment would be destroyed or taken from me." Tactfully, Sinclair did not mention his missing watch, although Bora understood it might have disappeared at that point. "Therefore, I chose to surrender the camera at once, and asked to be heard by a commanding officer."

"So I was told. Did Powell specify where he was when he took the photos?"

"He spoke of a garden villa by a ditch or river, off the Chanià route about ten miles south of Iraklion."

Right. That's how the War Crimes Bureau identified the place as Ampelokastro. Bora nodded. "And how did Powell know which unit the paratroopers belonged to?"

Sinclair squared his shoulders even more, a further stiff- ening of his posture. "He did not. He simply said they were German paratroopers. Your command might have identified the unit from the area in which they operated. I hope you understand, Captain, that it is my intention to provide infor- mation only in the measure it'll secure swift action against those who flout the rules of civilized war."

It was a legitimate reaction against any attempt to force out of him sensitive data about the British Army. Bora waited until he heard the translation of Sinclair's words before speaking in a conciliatory way. "I was hoping you'd provide information in the spirit of serving the truth."

"That goes without saying. But truth is a debated notion."

Yes. Yes. How did Professor Heidegger put it? It's all about freeing oneself from a concept of truth understood as concordance.

"So. A philosopher?"

Sinclair's dusky eyebrows joined above his nose in a frown. Between forehead and lips his features turned foreign, then just short of exotic. For the rest, he still looked like a Lowlander whose hair had been painted black. "Truth is not the exclusive province of philosophers."

"Well, if we come to an agreed-on definition of the word for this particular instance, I'm willing to pursue the truth whatever it may turn out to be. The chips *have* to fall where they may, in our German backyard if they belong there." Because the interpreter hesitated to translate the last part of the sentence, Bora irritably insisted, careful, however, not to betray his knowledge of English. "And tell the prisoner that my working definition of truth is *correct representation of what happened.*"

The frown stayed on Sinclair's face. "I related what I was told by the man on the scene, whom I implicitly trust as a fellow soldier and an Englishman. Powell was shaken, I repeat. In my view, the gratuitous violence against those civilians made him most uncomfortable about captivity. Avoiding it was his aim, and naturally I would not have discouraged him. I'd have attempted an escape myself – my right and my duty as an officer at His Majesty's service – had I not felt this criminal matter needed to be followed through."

It took a respectable amount of fortitude to choose imprisonment over freedom – albeit a risky one – without even having seen the photos, on a runaway's word. Bora observed the prisoner, and then looked away from him. There was pride there. Whatever difficulties Waldo Preger might have encountered or perceived as the son of a salaried man, they were nothing to what Sinclair probably still met as a half-blood. A draftee in his mid-thirties, he must have distinguished himself and have the right connections too, to serve as company officer in a British unit. Still, he couldn't have been to military school, or else his rank would be higher. Collegial empathy was not advisable with a prisoner. Bora briefly lost himself staring at a spot in the floor planks, where, through a hole in the metal roof, a sunbeam projected a coin of fiery light (the dim study at Ampelokastro came to mind, the faces on the wall, the empty categories invented by men, the chalk mask resembling Remedios, *Shepherd girl,* followed by a question mark)… In lieu of sympathy, he chose a more superficial view of the man facing him. It must sting, being behind barbed wire less than two weeks after comfortably sitting with a glass of gin or ouzo in some friendly Cretan cafe, as Busch had said of the archaeologists in the basement of Hotel Knossos. Who knows, the proud-mannered lieutenant might have met Miss Allen or Pendlebury there. Sidheraki, who wasn't British and didn't rank as high as the rest, would have likely waited outside. Colonial ease, and *dolce far niente.*

Dispassion allowed Bora to regain his *Abwehr* mode of courteous impartiality; a full step below indifference, it danced on the verge of becoming either benevolent or inquisitorial. The heat in the shed, that until moments ago had made him physically unwell, became simply the environment in which his calm mind reasoned unperturbed. Although he already knew the answer from Busch, he did ask, "Lieutenant, were you shown the photographic prints?"

"No."

Bora didn't enquire whether Sinclair wanted to view them. He'd taken along the folder in his rucksack, and – given the lack of horizontal surfaces in the room – held it open so that the prisoner could see.

"Good God. A woman, young lads – it's a slaughterhouse."

"Yes." It would be justifiable to point out that mutilated corpses of German paratroopers had been discovered in Crete, but Bora chose not to.

"Who were these people?"

"Civilians." No more details were needed. Using a translator defused reactions, gave Bora extra time to calibrate his words. He shook his head as he studied the photos. "Cleaning the blood from the grout might be impossible."

The irrelevance of the comment brought a vivid blush to Sinclair's finely drawn cheekbones. "I don't understand what you mean."

"Just what I said. The spaces between floor tiles have absorbed too much blood by now."

"Does it even *matter*?"

Bora faced the interpreter. "Tell the lieutenant there are moments when I'm literal. It is a fine floor, and in my observation badly ruined by staining."

"*A fine floor*?" Sinclair's resentment brimmed over. "I hope yours is a provocation, Captain. Whether you were called up to serve or are a professional soldier, you cannot treat a war crime so glibly!"

"*If* it's a war crime." Bora shuffled the pictures. "Believe me, I can quote by heart the articles of the Geneva Convention. You'll find no one on this island as *super partes* as I am, Lieutenant Sinclair. And in case Dr Unger hasn't informed you, the German Army itself has demanded this enquiry. I need additional details, because the fact remains that neither you nor Sergeant Major Powell did actually *witness* the killing.

His, graphic though it is, is *ex post facto* evidence. The photos suggest that he first captured on film the troopers entering the garden. After the shooting, he passed by the dead dog on the front steps and walked in. He hoped, as he told you, to find the troopers ambushed to death by Greeks or Britons hiding in the villa." Bora displayed each image and paused to allow for translation. "At the unexpected sight of civilian victims, he took a number of snapshots before leaving the way he entered. When he noticed the rear garden gate unlocked and wide open, he photographed that as well, and finally the dead dog. He must have been rather upset by then. The last image is blurred, possibly because his hands were unsteady." He closed the folder. "That's all we have for now, Lieutenant. Not proof, not even *close* to proof."

Sinclair visibly struggled to keep his composure. "Are you proposing alternative interpretations of this massacre? The chips *should* fall in your backyard. I will not stand for a cover-up by Germans of a German war crime!"

"I'm sure." That's where Bora wanted the prisoner. In a state of heightened concern that nothing would be done. He replaced the folder in his rucksack. "*Feldwebel*, open the windows, it's too hot in here. And remind the prisoner that I'm literal when I have nothing else to go by. Tell him I'm aware British officers and men, especially those who were already stationed in Crete, discussed beforehand the likely routes of withdrawal, and escape in case of capture. The best way the lieutenant can help me go beyond a literal interpretation is to tell me how I may find Sergeant Major Powell."

Bora was bluffing on the matter of escape routes, but it made sense. If he was right, there had to be people acting as go-betweens with the Cretan resistance.

Again that frown and dark rise of blood to the cheeks, as if Sinclair's exotic half surfaced when he was indignant. "So you may send your death squads after His Majesty's soldiers? Supposing him still alive, I don't know where Powell went. I wouldn't tell you if I knew, and you can't expect me to tell you."

Bora buckled the flap of his rucksack before slinging it across his left shoulder. "Well, that's that, then. Things stop here. I will recommend that the War Crimes Bureau return the photos to your High Command to do with them as it pleases; we have nothing to do with the killing as far as I'm concerned, and I doubt that either your superiors or the International Red Cross will be able to prove otherwise." He turned on his heel and started toward the door. "We're mopping up the island as it is, Lieutenant. It doesn't help your cause or mine to have Powell caught, shipped off or worse, without being able to detail his story." Through the grid of the window, he called to the sentinel outside to have the door opened.

Five seconds, key turning in the lock. Door yawning onto the heat of day, ten seconds. Sinclair's voice reached him as Bora began to leave.

"I must have your word of honour as a German officer and a gentleman *super partes*, that you will share the one lead I'll give you with none of your comrades. Not even with your interpreter."

Bora awaited the translation. He did not turn away from the door but took one step away from it, addressing the *Feldwebel* with his back to Sinclair. "Tell him I give my word of honour."

"*Latine loqueris?*"

Surprise made Bora slowly wheel around this time. "*Loquor.*"

The meaningful Latin words dropped out of Sinclair. "*Domenikos, qui et Minos. Sutor ad Chanioportam.*" And because Bora gave a sign he understood, he added, "*Quidam abiectus, turpis, indiciorum cuicumque pretio venditor.*"

Kostaridis was already waiting at the gate when Bora left the shed. Enthusiasm is difficult to conceal, so the German lost time fumbling with the straps of his rucksack to regain an acceptable appearance of self-control. Minos... He actively searched his school recollections. Wasn't Minos the fabled Cretan king who had the labyrinth built? Stepfather of the man-eating Minotaur, an errant husband cursed by the gods to emit lethal snakes and scorpions with his ejaculation. Minos, one of the judges in Hades... The idea of a low-life informant, abject and money-hungry though he might be, and bearing such a nickname, excited him far beyond prudence. Kostaridis must know all the ruffians in town, so it was best to keep mum in his presence, and find a way to slip off in search of a man who probably had been smuggling goods and people for years.

Buying information without cash, however, would be impossible in Crete as everywhere else, if not more. *Echo paradhes*, "I have money," was the first sentence Bora had mastered after the Greek words for mineral water. But he had less than fifty marks to last him for the rest of the journey, and no contacts who might subsidize him at short notice.

Kostaridis lifted his chin in a concise southern greeting when Bora approached the car. He stood unmoving by the open door, indicating he expected the German to enter first, a policeman's precaution.

The first thing Bora said, hunching his shoulders in the cramped back seat, was, "Where's the National Bank of Greece? I need to go there."

Kostaridis gave him a frog stare. "Bank's closed."

"Well, I need to get in, *Epitropos*. See that you get me in."

"*Now?*"

"The moment we reach town, yes. Did you bring the material from the Sidheraki home?"

"Yes."

While they rode back to Iraklion, the policeman lifted a few snapshots from a box of papers, line drawings, field notes from various archaeological sites. He flipped through them quickly, setting two aside. "Here," he said, "a group shot: the English archaeologists, plus their Greek helpers. Not the best quality, sun's on their faces. This" – he placed his forefinger on the most tanned of all, a shirtless man with a moustache and a broad smile – "is Andonis Sidheraki. You can see him in this other picture too, holding the pickaxe. He's about your age, I'd say. Over ten years younger than his wife."

Next to Sidheraki, a couple of horsey blonde women in straw hats drew Bora's attention. "Is Miss Allen one of these?"

"No. They're Englishwomen. She isn't there. She must have been behind the camera."

"May I keep them?" Bora asked even as he slipped the snapshots inside his chest pocket, so that Kostaridis had to agree. "Tell me, is it possible that Sidheraki joined a rebel band back there?"

"If he hasn't left Crete, I'd expect nothing else."

"A communist band, maybe?"

Kostaridis thought for a moment. "Not if it's Satanas'."

"Satanas as in – the devil?"

"*Kapetanios* Satanas Grikorakis. Worse, as far as Germans are concerned. No, I don't think Sidheraki would join him. His family and the *kapetanios*' folks have been feuding ever since the Turks left Crete. They may all be anti-German, but they'd as soon cut each other's throat over matters that have nothing to do with Germans. Why do you ask?"

Bora didn't say. He looked out of the window towards the brilliant blue line of the sea, a belt around the land and a restriction he wasn't yet used to. Hope and worry were tightly braided within him as he told himself it was a tall order and a dangerous one to try to find a lone man on Crete.

As for Kostaridis, he knew a reticent witness when he saw one, so he changed the subject. "If you give me the roll of film we took from Professor Savelli, by the morning I'll have it printed."

Bora handed it in. "Might as well."

The National Bank of Greece was housed in one of those bureaucratic constructions from the turn of the century, solid and moderately ornate. It could have faced any central street in any European city. Padlocked and awaiting German administrators, it should be off-limits to all, but Kostaridis had a crowbar, and his ways. He posted his uniformed driver at the corner to signify the official nature of the operation, and proceeded to unnail a boarded window on the side of the building, exposing a blasted grill and broken glass pane, witness to the street fighting two weeks before.

Bora used the crowbar to knock off the jagged remnants of the glass pane and hoisted himself onto the street-level windowsill. Grasping the bars of the grill above the blasted area, he squeezed in and landed feet first onto a sea of broken glass. Kostaridis heard him curse in German from within, but it didn't sound like he had been injured.

"Coming in?" Bora extended his right hand out to help the policeman climb through. "I wouldn't want you to think I'm here to steal."

In fact, he had no clear idea of what he wanted out of the break-in. Any ready cash in the bank must have long since disappeared. A glance at Villiger's safety deposit box, raided by German soldiers, would not serve the investigation: if Preger's men had merely crossed the villa's garden, they had nothing to do with it. It stood to reason that other soldiers – those bivouacking overnight, for example – had lifted whatever of value there was, among them Villiger's camera (or cameras),

159

and the key to the safety deposit. Bora was following a hunch that was actually no more than his need for Greek money.

In the vault, the built-in rows of deposit boxes had the looks of a beehive ransacked by bears. Most doors were open; the few still locked might simply be unused. Bora threw a glance at the stack of ledgers lying around. "*Epitropos*, would you help me look for the book of safety deposit rentals?"

Kostaridis said nothing. He stuck a German cigarette in his mouth and before long provided the required ledger.

The list of renters, partly typewritten, partly in longhand Greek, consisted of an alphabetical series of entries, many crossed out in red pencil or blue ink. "These," Kostaridis explained, "indicate clients who withdrew their valuables a year ago, as soon as the war started."

Alois Villiger's name appeared under the second letter, *beta*, pronounced by Greeks as a V. His last visit to the deposit box was recorded on 16 May, perhaps the same day when he had checked on the ships leaving Crete. A look at the box confirmed thieves had emptied it without forcing it; the key was still in the lock.

Bora kept searching through the list. It was not so extensive that he couldn't hope to find other recognizable names, and in fact under *alpha* he found the name of Rifat Bey Agrali, whose two boxes had been voided by the proprietor on 21 May. Under *delta*, only a handful of surnames were listed, one of which was French-sounding: Duvoin, Marcel Amédée. Duvoin. At first Bora passed it by. Then he recalled reading it on one of the ex libris at Ampelokastro. Another expatriate book lender of Villiger's? Maybe more. To his great surprise, Villiger's own name appeared as additional renter of the box. The line had not been crossed out.

"*Epitropos*, have you ever run into a man called Duvoin before?"

Kostaridis said he did not remember, but didn't think so. "*Capitano*, whatever you have in mind, it's my duty to inform you that the seals were placed on this building by your own army. Trespassing is one thing, but —"

"Breaking and entering is more like it, *Epitropos*. You taught me that."

With the key to the Duvoin deposit box in hand, Bora walked back to the vault. The lock had not been tampered with, the key turned smoothly, and the door opened flush with the built-in shelf. Bora pulled out the long, flat metal case housed inside. A bench next to the wall provided the surface on which to rest it, so he could lift the hasp and pull back the case lid.

Inside lay a mid-size manila envelope which, when hefted, suggested contents of folded papers or documents. Bora undid the string around the fastener to open it, and the first things that slipped out were large-denomination Reichsmark and drachma banknotes. The German marks alone amounted to a thousand, nearly six months' peacetime pay for a captain. Bora set the currency aside, and reached in for the rest. Blank forms. One, two Swiss passports. Between their grey-blue covers, they were registered in German–French–Italian, under two different names. One of these was Duvoin, Marcel Amédée, born 1891 in Küssnacht, residence given in Lucerne, 13 Löwenstrasse. Profession: antiquarian bookseller. Entry and exit stamps indicated trips to France, England, Germany, Italy. Clipped to the back cover were a typewritten sheet, business cards from Libreria Bemporad, Antiquarian Section, in Florence; from Banca Popolare di Milano, Agenzia Macello e Scalo Bestiame; Joseph Baer & Co., Publishers and Booksellers (est. 1785), Frankfurt am Main. The other passport had been issued to one Steiger, Federico, born 1886 in Zurich and resident there on Pelikanstrasse at the Hotel Pelikan. A commercial traveller in silk textiles, he appeared to frequent trade fairs in

Germany (Leipzig Fair ticket) and Italy, and it had also been stamped in Belgium, China (Shanghai city map with two streets underlined) and the Soviet Union (last exit stamp, 1930). Both passports, and the identity sheets – *Legitimationskarte* – stored inside them, bore Alois Villiger's photographs.

Bora's mouth went dry. He put everything back in the manila envelope and down the large right pocket of his British Army shorts. He was in a hurry to be on his own and think of a way to inform his *Abwehr* counterpart in Athens (hopefully Major Busch) of the unexpected development.

"Anything I should know?" Kostaridis – who might have seen him handle the papers – looked in from the door.

"No."

Iraklion, late afternoon of 4 June. This important diary entry will be long. It's being written in the room Kostaridis found me downtown off Avenue 25 August. A good thing too; I desperately needed to wash and I'm burned to a crisp besides. So much for my refusing to use Nivea cream. The furnishings are basic, the view nil, but at least I can't be thrown out on my ear.

My head is reeling. Whatever Villiger did for the *Reichskommissar*, it went far beyond the study of racial characteristics. Is that why his file has disappeared from our Berlin office? Why then isn't the SS Central Security Service in charge of investigating his death?

Three aliases – or two at least! A scholar's identity is more difficult to improvise than the others (businessmen who travel widely can more easily disappear into the woodwork), so I assume that, of the three, he really was Alois Villiger. The biographical note at the foot of one of his essays (I tore out the page and took it along from his library) gives detailed information anyone could check, especially university colleagues and administrators. First studies at Basel Seminary, then Friedrich Wilhelm University, Berlin; fieldwork with Italian and German archaeologists, apprenticeship with classical luminaries Antoine Meillet and Charles Bally, the latter incidentally "private tutor to the royal princes of Greece".

Textiles, antiquarian books and racial studies are curious occupations for one who might have once intended to become a Catholic priest. It's *imperative* that I try to contact our office in Athens, and get the ball rolling in the direction of knowing who (or what) Villiger was. The list of deposit box renters produced nothing else of worth, but – cut off from my support system as I am – it goes without saying that the money is a godsend. Especially the drachmas, which I plan to use soon.

Summarized below are the events of the day preceding my three-way talk with Sinclair.

1. Agrali's potshots aside, it was an uneventful return from the countryside. Predictably, the motorized patrol from Agios Andreas denied reports about the road being mined, and we travelled it back to town without complications.

2. The surname Duvoin, which occasioned my opening of the deposit box, surfaced as I leafed through Villiger's books at Ampelokastro, while Kostaridis frisked the Italian in the garden. Savelli's claims of being "stolen from" may not be unfounded: I found his name penned on the frontispiece of a handful of volumes, and other surnames as well: the above-mentioned Duvoin, Fermor, Guarducci, the ubiquitous Pendlebury. Even Frances Allen, whose middle initial, L., as I learnt, stands for Liberty. The English having done most of the excavations on the island, it isn't surprising that their names predominate. As I keep sifting through them, a few intriguing details emerge from Villiger's makeshift bookmarks: in addition to postcards, calling cards, plus phone numbers and addresses pencilled on pages of desk calendars (leads impossible to follow at this time), the significant items are bank deposit slips and receipts. These were issued among others by the Greek branches of Banca d'Italia and Banco di Roma, plus the Heimsauer & Bröck Handelsbank in Lucerne, where one of his aliases supposedly

resides! This is a significant Swiss concern founded by Theodor "Tuck" Heimsauer, married to Great-aunt Victoria Mary Ashworth-Douglas. The bank functioned as intermediary when my grandparents divested part of their art collection during the Crisis of '29. Keeping all three branches of the publishing house open and fully manned cost them, and that's how some fine Renaissance paintings now hang in Berne and Geneva. Poor Great-uncle Theodor – at fifteen I toured the capitals of eastern Europe with him, and my parents were afraid I'd get in trouble, so he worried from when we flew out until the day we landed again (he could relax: girls, especially ones my age, definitely took second place to sightseeing). It would all change a few months later in Rome, but learning the ropes with a stunning thirty-year-old was hardly *getting in trouble*.

Anyhow, some of Villiger's payments (which date from 1938) up to the year 1939 were routed to Crete through Turkish banks in Rhodes such as Notrica & Menasché or Isaac Alhadeff. A clever use of Jewish-owned lending institutions: was it to circumvent possible problems and disguise Villiger's *real* work for us? Of the many scholars subsidized by their governments to scrape through Hellenic ruins – important though our Aryan roots may be – our man was far better paid than most.

A note about Rifat Bey: when I insisted, he wouldn't describe his missing dog to me; he said he doesn't know what happened, and doesn't want to talk about it. I think he's lying, but that's no help. Given that three or four men, presumably the Turk's hired hands, spied on Kostaridis as he approached the house, it would have been imprudent trying to force our way in. Whether or not Rifat Bey had any role in the shooting deaths, I bet money he did more than bury the dead dog. He probably helped himself to some of Villiger's property: one more reason not to let us indoors. At about noon, after we slogged back down from Sphingokephalo, I noticed Kostaridis had brought nothing to eat. "Feeding the hungry" being one of the acts of corporal mercy I was taught as a child, I offered some of my canned meat and zwieback. He'd have none, because on Wednesday some observant Greek Orthodox refrain from eating. Apparently it's in remembrance of the day Our Lord was tried. I'm neither Orthodox nor excessively pious, so I dug into my ration while he smoked. German cigarettes apparently don't fall under the commandment of fasting.

3. Finally, as planned, I walked from Ampelokastro to Skala, the location Preger's men supposedly reached after leaving the garden (and before being ambushed at Stavrakia). It took me twenty-two minutes one way, but I did not have all the gear they carried, and the danger of ambush must have been more serious on 30 May. Half an hour sounds about right, so it seems the paratroopers' platoon leader told the truth about this at least.

Now for the lead I cajoled out of the straight-shouldered Lieutenant Sinclair: this cobbler (*sutor*) who lives by Chanià Gate, Domenikos a.k.a. Minos, *qui et Minos* to use the basic Latin Sinclair and I adopted to keep the interpreter from understanding, draws me like a magnet. For him, I gave up meeting the Allen woman tonight. If the cobbler is what I think, a ruffian who sells people and information for money, I'll get him to point me in the right direction. I remember this kind of human dregs from Poland, where the likes of him were called *szmalcownicy*, or something very like it. I'm pleased to say I kicked one of them down three flights of stairs in Krakow.

Not that our camera-toting Powell would have necessarily met Minos in person, but by the end of May the English, routed everywhere on the island, no doubt secured local channels who could direct them to safe havens in the interior if need be. Major Busch admitted there are a number of runaways out in the mountains, wearing Greek garb but still very much British at heart. I am determined to seek Minos tonight, which brings me to describe my logistics. I find myself in a summer rental for tourists that went understandably unlet this year. In fact the whole house is unoccupied. In case I wanted company, though, given that balconies and small terraces connect properties here, I could easily climb into the house next door. The rub is that two loafers have magically appeared at both ends of the street. In a strange way it makes me homesick for Moscow, as I recognize plain-clothes men at first sight. It remains to be seen whether Kostaridis wants to watch over me, or wants to watch me at all. I can't leave the house in daylight without being noticed by his goons, so I'll wait until dusk sets in, and then off I'll go. With the curfew, I won't be able to ask the locals for a *tsagkares* (read: *tsangaris*, shoemaker) near Chanià Gate. Still, luck is supposed to help those who dare. This is turning into the best thing that has come my way since Poland!

PS The alley (*sokaki*, in Greek) is named after Ulysses' homeland, Ithaca, or Itaka. Kostaridis says Italians used to live here at the start of the century. Funny, all the more since Itaka is the nickname we Germans use for our Italian comrades, *Ita*lienische *Ka*maraden.

PPS Losing the wine is a potential disaster. It seems the airborne (not necessarily Preger's men, although…) had a festive lunch with it, taking along what they didn't consume at the table. I can't possibly return to Russia without it. Hell, I'll worry about it after I'm done with Minos and the entire Villiger affair.

Forcing the lock of the apartment next door was hardly a challenge. Well after sundown Bora entered it and found to his delight that it featured a balcony on the next alley over. He climbed down from its railing to the balcony below, and from it jumped onto the street. He'd studied on the map the web of old streets that crept toward the Venetian walls on both sides of Chanià Gate. He could reach the gate, closely guarded at this hour, without difficulty, but not having a precise address posed a major obstacle. Curfew had emptied the streets of civilians. Life went on in wine shops and cafes behind closed or half-open doors. Curtains or shutters protected windows on all floors; armed sentries watched over buildings where Germans noisily gathered, toasted and drank. Avenue 25 August, bisecting Iraklion, had best be avoided, and also the wider thoroughfares. Bora walked, ready to tell any fellow German with a military police gorget around his neck whatever story necessary to be let through. One street corner after another, his path became darker and more solitary; Greek voices replaced German sounds, the pavement grew uneven and odours unpleasant. Recesses in the stuccoed walls let out an acrid, fishy smell of male urine.

In normal times, in a normal city, a cobbler would have a name in a phone book and a sign outside his door, but that would hardly be the case in 1941 Iraklion with a man like Domenikos/Minos. It was possible he worked out of his house and was intentionally lying low, especially if he indulged in clandestine activities. *That's the best way to hide.* Buried in thought, Bora stepped in and out of a puddle best unseen and unexplored. *So, what's the second-best way? To be in a place frequented by many. In Crete, as everywhere, that would include wine shops, cafes, eating places. And brothels. Didn't Sinclair describe the man as "turpis, abiectus"? The adjectives suggest such an association. If that's the case, with all the new customers in town a whorehouse will be in full swing at this hour.* Or so Bora lightheartedly resolved. Keeping away from larger thoroughfares and to the narrow winding streets, which he knew (or assumed) to lie north of Kalokairinou, made him lose his way and go in circles. *That's what a maze is – this town is a postage stamp, and I get lost in it.*

Starlight and a waxing moon evoked rooftops, crossroads, but left alleys and back lanes steeped in darkness. Bora resorted to his lighter to discern street signs whenever a briny gust from the sea did not funnel inland to snuff the flame. Sometimes only by a given odour did he realize he'd walked past a doorway. Once or twice he had more than an impression of being watched. Nothing easier; walls had more than ears in this country: every door, every window apparently shut was a peeping eye. It was that Greek way of looking through the fissure of an eyelid, from under the lashes. *Thank God I hid Villiger's passports and the rest, and have nothing on me but money that they can go for.*

Until he reached what he recognized as the Armenian church Bora wasn't sure he was heading in the right direction. The Chanià Gate – *Chanioporta* – lay somewhere ahead, slightly to his left in the city walls. Walking to the shore the previous afternoon, he'd glimpsed the dark repair shops, tinkers' and joiners' cubbyholes carved into the Venetian bastions, crannies where who knows how many people could work, live or hide. What if Powell, wounded as he was, had hobbled back to Iraklion, and was only steps away from him? He could wander aimlessly without ever finding him. He reached Kalokairinou Street and crossed it not far from the cafe. It seemed years before, and only a day had passed.

When the soldier on guard by a small post (or commander's quarters) searchingly flashed his torchlight on him, Bora decided to make the most out of the incident.

His direct question, plainly spoken, drew no open reaction from the soldier. "Officers only, sir?" he staidly enquired.

"No. Isn't there one by the gate?"

"There is. You have to keep south and go down Ainikolioti, by the keg-maker's. But that's for locals mostly. You don't want to go there, Captain. There's a much better house two streets down that way; Italians run it."

Bora thanked the soldier and walked where he was directed, save changing course once he was out of sight. *This is totally irrational, there's no ground to believe I'm right, but a brothel is a place where you can ask about a seedy cobbler and not raise eyebrows.* Bora wasn't worrying yet about what language he'd ask in.

Those girls understand all languages if you have money, and I have both drachmas and German marks. Echo paradhes: *I have money.*

He missed Ainikolioti Street the first time, ending up in an alley that blindly met the ancient rampart. Retracing his steps, he skirted the city walls for several minutes before he distinctly heard laughter and women's shrill voices from somewhere in the neighbourhood. It became a matter of trusting the sounds, the ribbons of dim light through shutters and under doorways.

At last Bora reached a place where half-finished kegs and barrels sat like paunchy monks at the side of the street. A wide, wooden awning such as he'd seen elsewhere in town, extending far out from the house, created the impression of a free-standing roof over nothing. Just ahead, voices (Greek and German, with Italian expletives thrown in) came from the upper floor of a two-storey building. The words *ficken* and *puttana* floating down left no doubt as to the nature of the establishment, and suggested two things: either the soldier on guard was wrong in saying it was mostly patronized by locals, or else their percentages had changed. No direct entrance to the brothel was visible from the street. Bora had to shake his lighter before the flame came alive, as the gas in it was running low. In front of him flickered a scurfy, whitewashed partition, no more than eight feet in height, screening the space between the house in question and an adjacent building. Twin posts topped by chalk or cement spheres framed a flimsy wooden door that gave way the instant Bora pushed it. Again, he had to use the lighter to make sense of what lay behind, and what he was getting himself into.

The space between the two houses extended maybe twenty paces in length, unpaved and wholly dark. To Bora's right stood a door painted crimson or oxblood, whose glass fanlight was shaded by wrapping paper. From a shuttered window above came the muffled grunts of a male – nationality unknown but

169

imaginable – exerting himself as drunks do when they can't reach an orgasm. The sounds were laborious, uncouth. The moment they'd grow closer, and more explosive, a German Army condom or the neck of a Greek uterus would be receiving doomed Aryan sperm. Bora didn't fully articulate the thought but it crossed his mind with some embarrassment, as he turned away to check what was on his left. A wooden step and an narrow unpainted door faced him, with a hand-painted cardboard sign that read *Tsagkares*.

So, he'd guessed right. Only now did he wonder how the English got to communicate with Minos: either he spoke a few foreign words or else they depended on one of their Greek speakers, like vice-consul Pendlebury or other patriotic and meddlesome young scholars. But no, these people could direct the runaways themselves; they knew the island like the palm of their hands. And besides, they'd been the first to seek the mountains with rebels armed and organized by them – unless they'd been wounded (or killed) outside Chanià Gate like John Pendlebury, MA, FSA.

Bora knocked. Nobody answered, but he heard steps rustle to the door from within, and then hastily withdraw. Giving himself no time to think, he tried the lock, opened the door and walked right in.

Inside, the final spurt of light from his lighter drew the impression of a low-ceilinged labyrinth of small rooms reeking of glue, leather and dirty clothes. Bora stumbled against something, a stool or worktable, and knocked it over. He couldn't see a thing; there was a draught from the far end of the house that did not relieve the stench but would blow out even a perfectly functioning lighter. Whoever had come to the door kept still, away in the dark.

A fine kettle of fish, his stepfather would contemptuously say when the boys did something stupid. But Bora had put himself in the kettle, and there was no turning back. Calling out "Domenikos" (*Remember, in Greek you pronounce it Dome'nikosh*) might or might not be a good idea. Another misstep made him lose balance and he tripped down to a lower level, a space where the ghost of an outside glimmer leaked through the half-opened window. *It comes from the fanlight over the brothel's door*, he thought. *Not enough to see.* "Domenikos?" he said into the darkness. Next door, across the interspace, the drunk kept grinding, over a woman's titter and whispered Greek prattle, "Oogod, oogod, oogod…" Choked moans definitely gave him away as a German drunk. *I can't see how God enters into any of this.* Bora's skin crept as the rhythm accelerated and the craved achievement seemed at hand. *Do we sound so foolish when we make love?*

The muzzle of a pistol against the nape of his neck came just as an unanticipated male solidarity made him slightly excited, and the touch of metal did nothing to curb the reaction. Most Cretans being short, it was probably his having stumbled down that allowed the man behind him to be level with his neck. A crude voice muttered a question in his ear, likely asking who he was. Bora didn't understand, but ventured to say "*Englesos*" because – unseen – he could easily pass for an Englishman. Even as he said it, the idea raced through him that it might be a mistake. *Cuicumque pretio…* A man selling to anyone for money. For all he knew Minos might now be vending Englishmen to Germans, alive or dead.

Things were moving too fast, or the absolute wrong way. "*Echo paradhes*," he said, and held his breath waiting for a reply. Fitful gramophone music and muffled stomping came from the ground floor of the other house, while the frantic drunk was a groaning breath away from ejaculation.

"*Echo paradhes*," Bora spelt out, because the gun stayed stuck to his head. And whatever shameful reaction the brothel sounds were causing in him, it precipitously abated when he felt a second man grope into the pockets of his army shorts. But the money sat in his chest pocket, so the gun slide was pulled back, chambering a round and readying to fire.

Dark, dark, smell, sounds. Suspended, instantaneous loneliness. The trappings and locus of his death manifested themselves to Bora, who'd imagined them very differently when speaking to Kostaridis, though he had said it didn't matter where he'd die. This was where it would happen. He wasn't even thinking of Remedios with his last thought: just that he was turning around and striking with his left fist. He missed. He missed the armed man and the groper jumped at him. Bora flung the attacker off, managed to take out his Browning, but hung fire. *If I kill him, there goes my possible lead. If I don't...* A point-blank shot exploded anyway, although Bora didn't feel pain and was sure he hadn't been the one pulling the trigger. Flash, blast, a ringing in the ears. The trappings and locus of his death... The bedroom next door went suddenly mute; laughter below it faded and died out. Only the insipid dance music grated away on the gramophone. *I screwed up someone's orgasm,* Bora thought, as if that mattered in the situation he was in. Within seconds, the glare of a torchlight knifed through the room and Kostaridis' voice bellowed, "*Stassou!*" to keep someone from fleeing. "*Chorophilakì, stassou!*"

The cone of light pooled downward to reveal a man crumpled at the foot of the steps and feebly moving; it then swung to the wall, where a light switch came into view and was flicked. Despite the shouted halt, somebody was noisily slamming a window open in another room and escaping into the night.

"*Ma vi pare il caso di morire ammazzato a Creta dopo che l'avete presa?*" Kostaridis' words, rattled off at him in Italian, had the merit of plunging Bora from stress to extreme anger.

Furious, he missed his pistol holder twice before being able to put away his gun. The impulse to lunge at the inspector as he prodded the wounded man was hard to resist.

"Is he the cobbler?"

"What do you want a cobbler for?"

"*Epitropos*, is *he* the cobbler?"

"He isn't. The son of a whore got away. Now we won't have him as an informant any more, thanks to you. Who gave you his name, anyway?"

Bora seethed. "I'm telling you nothing. *I'm telling you nothing.* You butted in on purpose to keep me from doing my job."

"I don't think you even know what your job is."

"Were you following me?"

"What do *you* think? I was."

The wounded man was not so badly off that he couldn't crawl to his feet. Kostaridis turned him around and kicked him towards the door. "He can go. He's Minos' idiot brother." When they stepped out, the space between the houses was windy, dark and fresh. The brothel's windows were all open when Kostaridis flashed his light on the facade. Clients kept out of sight, but the women were curious. An agitated hag with skittle-shaped teats leaned out, with two wild-haired girls behind her, whose breasts were plump and round instead. White, firm like those on Agrali's marble Sphinxes but with large brown buttons topping them. All called to the idiot and made obscene signs to the policeman. Bora felt drunk, although a sip of Panagiotis' wine was the only alcohol he'd touched since leaving Moscow.

Kostaridis yelled the whores back into the house, before reinforcing his lesson to Bora. "Are you crazy, walking in like this? You don't go into such places at night! You could have died! If you wanted to negotiate with the cobbler you should have gone through his mother, who runs the whorehouse. The old cunt is the go-between for business with him."

At least he didn't think I was looking for a woman here, Bora thought.

"What did you want to see Minos for?"

"I'm not telling you."

But they started back toward Ithaca Street together. Admitting foolishness was not something Bora was ready to do. He'd given his word to Sinclair that he'd keep the matter of the cobbler from other Germans; not from Greeks, who seemed to know about him anyway. At one point, he resentfully mumbled, "I need to know where the Englishman who took the photos might have escaped to."

The only sign of irritation on Kostaridis' part was that he walked quickly, just short of a marching step, with arms bent and elbows out. "I could have told you that, without your raising this hell." (In Italian he said *casotto*, which meant confusion but also brothel.) "Runaways seek the foot of Psiloritis and the highlands around it. Forget about flushing them out ever. The Venetians couldn't, the Turks couldn't, you won't. That's where Krousonas is."

"Krousonas. I saw the name on the map."

"Well, that's no place you want to go to. I wouldn't go myself. It's Satanas' backyard."

After the judge of Hades, Satan himself. Bora was about to say something when the policeman prevented him. "Look, *capitano*, Krousonas is off limits: if you go there, I wash my hands of you." And because he heard the German snigger to himself, he blurted out, "There's nothing to laugh about. What happened tonight was stupid. It could have ended badly."

"I'm laughing because I'm provoked." In fact, Bora began to find irresistible the story of the Greek brothel, and of a gunshot ruining a compatriot's long-suffered climax. *Well, Dikta and I are champion fuckers,* he grittily congratulated himself. *We don't sound so foolish when we make love, and compared to us, any brothel is small fry*. But Bora still needed to spread his irritation around, so he pulled out of his pocket one of the calling cards found in the Duvoin–Villiger deposit box, and placed it in front of Kostaridis, where the glare of his torchlight made it readable. "See? I told you I'd find out. Turn it around."

Kostaridis peered at the small print on the back of the card. In Italian, it read: *Daughter of Mazaltov Cordoval and Esterula De Raffeul, Rhodes. Her father runs a lucrative perfume business on Piazza del Fuoco near the postcard shop of the Modiano family and the moneychangers Harran e Mizrahi.*

"I don't understand. What's this, *capitano*?"

"You know very well what it is. It's the Jewish cabaret artist's."

"Yes, but what will you do with it?"

"I'm not telling you."

Truly, Bora hadn't given any thought to it. He'd been careful not to write in his diary that most of the calling cards found at Ampelokastro were of a similar type, and Signora's whereabouts were far removed from his interest at the moment. *Which is lucky for her*, he thought, and snatched the card from Kostaridis' hand.

Once in his room, he filled the tub with cold water, and fell asleep in it. At some point during the night he must have got up and flung himself on the bed, because he woke up there in a daze when dawn was first breaking. He'd dreamt fragments of events of the endless day before, Rifat Bey and the chalk faces, the Jewess in Rhodes, the Sphinxes with breasts like the young girls at the brothel. Sinclair wasn't in the dream, nor Minos. A distant day with Waldo Preger was.

As every summer, there are seasonal workers from Poland who come for the harvest. Big men and women, tall and blonde. Waldo dares me to "go see the Polacks" in the shacks they occupy at the edge of the Modereggers' farm. He's been there before, and knows there's the risk of being chased off with a stick or a wooden flail. So we go, keeping low behind the hedge so they won't see us from the fields. We reach one of the sheds and peer into one of the windows. There, a young woman is breastfeeding her child, bare to her waist in a pool of morning light. Waldo nudges me in my ribs but I drop back, because it's not done. So I sit in the grass with my back to the wall of the shack, while my playmate stands on tiptoes and keeps looking. My heart is in my mouth, because in fact I'm also still looking, with my mind's eye. I've never seen a woman's breast before, and my head's on fire. I hardly hear the hubbub that follows shortly thereafter. Waldo has already taken to his heels when I realize the woman's husband is upon us with a riding whip, shouting in his incomprehensible tongue, and dart off barely in time to avoid being lashed with it. We run through the fields, Waldo and I, zigzagging among the men and women reaping wheat, but only when we dive beyond the fence that borders his father's yard are we safe. And it's a good thing Herr Preger isn't home, or there'd be hell to pay. For both of us it's the first of many forays "in the Polack burg". I don't follow Waldo when he crawls inside to spy, but I can't let his challenge go unheeded, so I stand between the shacks where clothes hang to dry on long, tense ropes. Unnoticed by me, a woman steps out from behind a wet shirt and gives me a slap across the face that makes me stagger. On the spot I don't know how to react, but immediately her man comes out and rages at her, not at me, because I am the master's son. He strikes her, and I shout at him that he's got to stop it, that it's really my fault. In his rage he forgets that I'm the master's son: he lifts me off my feet and tosses me across the threshing floor onto a heap of hulled wheat, where I sit until my head stops spinning.

PART TWO
Wandering

6

*I am twelve, and I don't like girls yet. I am twelve, and every other
Sunday I serve Mass at St Mary's. I am twelve, and I have growing
pains. I am twelve and my stepfather takes me downtown to the "Cheka
Trial" against communist assassins who plotted to kill General von
Seekt. At the Spring Fair Grandfather Franz Augustus buys me and
Peter the first Leica cameras ever produced. In the same year Field
Marshal Hindenburg, a distant relative, is elected president of the
Reich, and my stepfather becomes Lieutenant General. I am twelve
and visit with Peter the new Leipzig Planetarium at the Zoo. Next
year I shall begin classical studies at a private school, and if I apply
myself, I will be allowed to play on Father's Blüthner piano. I am
twelve, and seasonal workers from Poland...*

No. No, it wasn't on account of the seasonal workers. While
he shaved, Bora was still racking his brains to remember the
reason for the fist fight. *It makes no sense to think that it would
help me understand what happened at Ampelokastro. Why do I have
the impression it will? Here it's murder, one way or another. It was just
boys' feistiness then. What's more significant is that I chose to forget.*

Disparate, irrelevant details of those summer weeks at
Trakehnen floated back to his mind. But *those* weeks, *that* day
fifteen years earlier continued to escape him. Even the place

where it had happened, although it could be one of three or four: the shady meadows along the Rodupp Canal, the edge of the property by the Moderegger land, the old chapel, or the abandoned factory beyond the marsh where Pastor Wüsteritz hanged himself over a rumour about young girls, they said; but most probably because his grandson had drowned the year before.

Bora perfectly remembered instead the Pregers' living room, with the hunting trophies of six generations of Pregers (and Boras, and Sickingens). There was a mantelpiece clock, and embroidered doilies everywhere. There was Herr Preger, with astonished and guilty eyes even though the young culprit was apologizing in front of him. And there was Frau Preger, who twisted her hands over the kitchen apron, because they'd come unannounced. Waldo wasn't there; only the black-edged photograph of his brother, who had died in the Great War.

His stepfather had instructed him along the way and now, after a grumbled greeting to those present, he did not say one word. It was up to him, Martin, to explain and apologize.

I should at least remember the apology, if not the explanation; but I only recall the surroundings to the smallest detail, the scent of oiled furniture and the waxed floor, the milky froth of embroidered curtains against the windowpanes, the low beamed ceiling, the adults' hands. And the looming presence of his stepfather behind him.

The latter had seemed to him then – but no, only after the fact, now that he reviewed the scene in his mind and judged it as an adult – a metaphor of his life from now on: the weight of his family name, of his birth, of army honour and tradition behind him; in front of him, those for whom those burdens belonged elsewhere, while they were what he *was*: those to whom he was apologizing even though – he was sure of this, and Waldo confirmed it – he hadn't been the first to lift his hand. But perhaps he'd started it verbally, for all that he was in the right.

I was in the right, whatever "right" was when I was twelve. But I shouldn't have gone from words to blows to defend my ideas with Waldo Preger. With an equal in rank it would have been a glorious fist fight, an acceptable settling of scores. With Waldo, instead... What was the transgression for my stepfather? "Dirtying my hands"? "Lowering myself" to someone else's level? Haven't I been arguing with him for the past ten years about all of this? He can no longer take me by the scruff of the neck and call me back to order, but I can trespass as before, and more than before, in an army that is not egalitarian, and yet light years away from his views of the officer corps. In his time an officer could never marry a girl as uninhibited as Dikta (he and his colleagues laid her easy great-aunts, but marriage was out of the question); in his time, it would be obligatory to use a nobleman's title on his documents and in conversation. I have a good memory; I can't understand why I don't recall the argument. Did I put it out of my mind for some reason? Clearly so. Later that summer Peter broke a leg falling from his horse, and we were all very worried for him: that's the only incident that sticks in my mind. I could ask Waldo directly, if I wanted. But I don't.

Bora prepared to leave his lodgings, thinking of the reflection of water in the canal, the summer insects, the festive bliss of scuffling with his cousins or swimming or climbing, doing everything with ferocity and excess of energy. Which was after all what he did in bed with Dikta, an unbridled parenthesis in the otherwise severe routine of his life. Yes, back then – imperfectly – he'd felt that outmoded things and behaviours stood behind him, not yet questioned but to be questioned soon, today no longer a matter for doubt but heated confrontation. *If he could, General Sickingen would wrest me from her the same way, by the scruff of my neck. But I need some disorder in my order; I need to escape with my imagination at least from the iron-clad rules with which I grew up. My natural father – the Maestro – did it with music, travels, with the scandalous relations he had with strong and sensual women, and not only in Russia. I do it with Dikta and in the solitude (much more shadowy than the banks of the Rodupp) of my mind.*

The army depot, where he'd secure what he needed for the next three days, hadn't yet opened. Bora was still chiselling away at his mental block when he reached the square overlooked by the Hotel Knossos. By the fountain, a gloomy Kostaridis was making it obvious he was waiting for him. "I wash my hands of you," he said, concisely repeating his opposition to a trip inland. "Here are the prints from Savelli's roll of film. Should you revise your plans, you know where to find me." *Does he ever change his shirt?* Bora impatiently took the envelope from the policeman. "Anything of interest?"

"Look for yourself."

The photographs were disappointing. Routine shots of what seemed to be Cretan ruins, of clay figurines, long-beaked ewers and other artefacts, they could have been taken by the Italian scholar just as well as by Villiger. To be sure, Savelli had got into trouble in Rhodes on account of antiquities. One image stood out among the rest, the stolen snapshot of a showy blonde woman among flowerbeds, on a terrace or promenade overlooking the sea. Bora turned it towards Kostaridis. "Is this a local Aryan, or the housekeeper Siphronia?"

"Neither. That is Signora Cordoval."

"The Jewess from Rhodes?"

"Savelli's girlfriend, right. It must be true what he told me, that the roll of film is his, and he'd been carrying it around in its sealed container for a long time."

Possible. Or not. We don't know when Signora's calling card came into Villiger's hands. Bora studied the photograph. *Just like the books at Ampelokastro, which were Savelli's after all. I took him for a liar because I was prejudiced, but he may be far worse than a liar.* "This terrace she's standing on – is it Crete or Rhodes?"

Kostaridis shrugged. "Could be either. Remember she was here four years ago, when they argued about the heirloom brooch."

"I don't see why Savelli would take a picture of her at that time."

"If you look closely, there's the jewel pinned on her blouse. Maybe the professor captured her on film without her knowing, so he could have – shall we say – a proof of her fraudulence. Or else the picture was taken in Rhodes, when they still got along."

Bora pocketed the photographs. "I'll keep these for now. Just to make sure, can you call Savelli in and have him confirm the story?"

"No."

"No?"

"No."

This morning Kostaridis was more than a little testy. Bora saw him in a different light, and it was annoying that he had no means of reducing the policeman's resistance at the moment. "Why not?" he insisted.

"Because I have more important things to do."

He's right, and I deserve it. Christ, I must really come across as arrogant. I haven't even thanked him for saving my skin last night. Bora hid his embarrassment by glancing across the square, toward the graceful Italian loggia where shadows were blue at this early hour. "Thanks for intervening last night, by the way."

He fully expected Kostaridis to repeat his advice and say *Don't go to Krousonas,* or something of the sort. The policeman did not. He tilted his chin as he walked away, as curt and dis-interested a leave-taking as a southerner can manifest.

In the modest lobby of the Knossos – cleared to allow for the transportation of office furniture – there was an odour of dust being swept from one place to the next. Along the wall crates of empty liquor bottles waited for removal, some of them betrayed by their labels as leftovers from British occupation. Bora showed his papers, and didn't have to wait long for Frances Allen to be escorted from her room.

When he eyed her across the floor, the first thing he noticed was an unruly brown curl on her forehead.

Like in the English nursery rhyme, he thought. *I wonder if it means that when "she's good, she's very good, and when she's bad, she's horrid".*

Tanned, petite, wearing dungarees, from where Bora stood her face seemed plain, even unfeminine: someone's ordinary cousin, with a man's watch on her wrist. Bora felt none of the shivers of self-control needed to interact with handsome women. He'd seen army nurses wear the same look of disenchanted, controlled lack of emotion. As a citizen of a non-belligerent country, she could not be held as a prisoner. It was her marriage to a Greek suspected of being a guerrilla, and the weapons found at her house, that justified the prohibition on her leaving the premises.

According to Major Busch she'd been told she was to meet with a German officer and put herself at his disposal. As she returned Bora's look, the absence of coquetry was fully in order, yet there was something off-putting about her too. Not antipathy exactly but resentment (*She believes we wounded her husband and have him in hand*). Lack of fear, to be sure (*She's a scholar in the field, travels and is used to roughing it. She looks like a woman who has a temper*). Bora had the impression she'd be interesting to confront in a rage. Good. Friendliness from or towards one he might be forced to kill was not advisable. And in general he much preferred not to be found attractive by women. As introverted as he was judged desirable, he maintained a wall of impenetrable courtesy around him, wholly polite without giving any impression of being partial to the one facing him. He could afford it. He'd never had to pursue girls, except (maybe) Dikta, because Dikta had immediately taken him to bed and then disappeared for weeks.

Bora gestured for the guard to leave the American. Close up, Frances Allen wasn't ugly, she simply wasn't attractive. Whatever Major Busch meant by "looker", with her wiry bobbed hair, narrow mouth and tan she did not fit the bill. And she showed all of her forty years.

Exposure to the sun had aged her skin, freckling and spotting her cheekbones. She wore no bra, a fact that – even without paying particular attention – Bora couldn't help noticing.

Dikta's bras (all her underwear, in fact, lace, silk and satin) set off her nakedness like bezels do to gems. The lack of such an undergarment struck him as slovenly, not at all attractive. But, he found himself thinking, *she wears nothing under her blouse*, because, after all, a woman without a bra does set a man thinking.

Rightly supposing she wouldn't shake hands, he gave her a military salute and wasted no time in introducing himself. "My name is Bora. How do you —"

She interrupted. "Ah, like the late US senator who didn't want us to enter the Kaiser's war."

"Minus the final H, and no relation."

"Is there a first name to go with it?"

Bora was taken aback. "Yes, Martin. And how do *you* wish to be addressed? Ma'am, Dr Allen, Miss Allen…?"

"My name is Mrs Andonis Sidheraki."

"That's a bit unwieldy. Would you settle for Mrs Sidheraki?"

"If I must. What do I call you?"

"You may call me Captain Bora, or *Rittmeister* Bora."

Small, no bra, no make-up. Broken nails. That sun-crisp layer of skin and the rebel curl. She had to raise her face to speak to him, but did it only halfway so she wouldn't have to look him in the eye. "Where's my husband?"

Bora repeated what Busch had instructed him to say. "On the continent, under our care."

"Where exactly?"

"On the continent, under our care."

Between her eyebrows, a deep furrow endured, one of those expression lines unlikely to leave a face after a number of years. She must be used to frowning, either in concentration or because her nature was bent on disapproval. "I believe I will do nothing unless and until I have proof that my husband is alive."

Bora had imagined she'd say something of the sort. "Well, Mrs Sidheraki, I don't have time to give you such proof, but I have time to inform my colleagues on the continent that you refuse to collaborate." The tranquillity that came from feeling no attraction made things easier, Busch was right about that. "My schedule is tight, so please let me explain what I plan on doing with your assistance over the next three days. If you satisfy, it will be to your husband's advantage. Have you had breakfast?"

"Why?"

"I thought we might discuss things over coffee and canned gingerbread, which is the best I can offer."

"I don't think I want to have breakfast with you."

"But you will."

In the hotel basement hall, the German brew was bad, the gingerbread a step below passable. Bora hadn't eaten a full meal in over twenty-four hours and found both excellent. Frances Allen took only black coffee. If she was wondering about Bora's mastery of the English language, she gave no sign of it. Between indifferent sips, she kept her hands in her lap and looked elsewhere in the room. When Bora addressed her, she replied briefly in her south-western lilt, without seeking eye contact.

Like most foreigners in Crete, she'd heard of Villiger's death. No comments came from her in that regard, but there would be time to sound her out for an opinion. Bora brought the cup to his lips. *I need her: she criss-crossed the island many times, speaks the dialect like a native, and surely knows farmers and shepherds along the way. Her husband is from the Iraklion region, so she is familiar to those she'll ask.*

Not one to waste time or sugar the pill, he told Frances Allen what he expected: for her to play a role in the solution of a possible war crime. The challenge, if anything, was to enrol her as a guide without revealing how little he knew about the island. It was evident that Busch had only partly briefed her: news of a trek inland (Bora didn't pronounce the word Krousonas) to seek contact with a British runaway caused the line between her eyebrows to deepen.

"When do you plan on leaving?" she said.

Bora glanced at his watch. "It's eight o'clock now. In an hour's time at most."

"Fine."

Physically, she reminded him of Maggie Bourke-White. *She's like Maggie minus the lilacs, and her writer husband. But less feminine. She's angry because she misses her husband and worries about him, that's understandable.*

"I'll be sending a man to collect you."

"Fine."

Bora finished his coffee. Her lack of curiosity about details was not a sign of acquiescence, much less passivity. Her detachment, welcome as it was, bordered on abstraction; it had the effect of making him feel wrong-footed. So far, only Dikta had succeeded in doing so. Four years earlier, when he'd finally been able to reach her by phone weeks after their first, glorious intercourse, "I'm sorry, who are you?" she'd said, pretending surprise even though he had clearly introduced himself. "Ah, yes, the lieutenant from the dance party in April. How are you?" She'd easily agreed to a date the following day, during which they'd outdone themselves in his parents' country house. Then she vanished again with that Willy from Hamburg, whom she couldn't seem to bring herself to leave. *If I should ever find myself without Dikta, God forbid... We depend on each other sexually, I'm too spoilt to make do, and so is she. If she left me (it could happen: in Krakow I was afraid for a moment – for more than a moment), I don't know what I'd do with myself.*

"We'll be walking a good part of the way, Mrs Sidheraki. Is there any equipment you'll need?"

"I have all I need."

Bora nodded to the soldier waiting a few steps away to escort her back upstairs. He stood from his chair when she did, and watched her leave. *Major Busch was right: she's likely to drop the ball of yarn midway through the labyrinth to make sure I don't make it back. If she pulls a fast one, he said, shoot to kill. Would I do it? I would.* The thought floated through him along with a separate, bittersweet ache for Dikta, whom their third time in bed had conquered. "Martin, you're ruining my fun with Willy," she told him. "I could be foolish enough to fall in love." And she had written him a postcard after two weeks of total absence: *Without you, it isn't fun any more.* From then on they'd "stock up", as they laughingly said the nights they spent together, for the times when they'd be apart. Married for nearly two years now, Bora expected to meet her for a few hours in East Prussia before moving out, and "stock up" for the duration of the Russian campaign: one, two months at most. Then, after beating the Reds, one more supply, for wherever war would take him next.

Bora climbed to the lobby two steps at a time. *Hell, I should be thankful I have a whole war ahead of me. Prisoners like Lieutenant Sinclair are stuck for the duration. I wonder what he's thinking this morning. Does he regret giving me a clue to find Powell, which means: does he regret trusting me to such an extent, on my word? We're both officers, readers of the Classics. The tie goes beyond our respective roles at this time of the war. And he doesn't know it, but on Mother's side great-grandfathers Ashworth-Douglas and Carrick served Her Majesty in India during the First and Second Opium Wars. That connects us, unless there were native ancestors of Sinclair's among the Sepoys who mutinied some eighty years ago.*

The twang of a Berlin accent reached Bora as he left the hotel with his eyes on the list of supplies needed. Looking up from the sheet, he recognized the red-headed officer dismissing a non-com just outside.

"Bruno! What are you doing here?"

Bruno Lattmann, a colleague supposedly assigned to the *Abwehr* post in Tunis, wheeled around at the question. "No. What are *you* doing here?" He had an African tan, a duffel bag at his feet and seemed to be either arriving or ready to leave. As soon as the non-com was out of earshot, he added critically, "I thought you were in Moscow and Busch's replacement not due in until tomorrow."

"I'm on an errand. Thank God, I thought I'd have to go crazy trying to contact Athens for it. I need urgent support. Can you help?"

Lattmann, although visibly glad to see him, frowned a little. "Depends. We're setting up a sub-post on this island, but won't be immediately operational. I'm just passing through on my way to Athens, working on a shoestring as it is." They'd last seen each other a month earlier at Peter's wedding, where they'd respectively been witnesses for the bride and groom. He knew Bora well enough to wonder at his agitation. "Tell me quickly what you're doing and what I have to check on." Having heard a concise summary of the case, he took a couple of quick notes. "Fuck it all, don't you know there's an International Red Cross team flying in today? You had better leave Iraklion before it gets here; they'll tan your hide if they find you. For the rest, I'll see what I can do. No promises, though. If there's no file —"

"Oh, there's a file somewhere. I'd like to know when and why it disappeared from our central office."

"Well, you and the Lord Jesus. I'll see what I can do, Martin." Lattmann craned his neck to look across the square, beyond the Venetian fountain and its weather-worn lions. "A car is coming to pick me up any time now and take me to the airfield."

Bora handed him the passports he'd found in the safety deposit box. "What about these?"

"Open them, Bruno."

Lattmann changed expression, and even ceased cursing. Before putting them away, he anxiously reread the aliases jotted down in a diminutive notebook "M.A. Duvoin, eh?"

"Yes. Marcel Amédée, M.A. Duvoin."

"Hm. Hm. One thing I can tell you already. Maybe. It's just a guess at this point, and I don't know what you can do with it even if it's right. The initials M.A., pronounced Em-ah... Sounds like Emma."

"Who's Emma?"

"Let me flip the question around: weren't you part of the retinue during the Führer's state visit to Rome?"

"I don't much like the word retinue, but I was."

"Go back to your notes, then. Emma is a Comintern code-name that popped up a year and a half ago in connection with Rome."

So Villiger wasn't ours, or not ours alone. Rome, the Colosseum paperweight... but Villiger the antiquarian might have bought it all the same. Bora had to take a deep breath to keep calm. Comintern, Communist International – the coordinating centre of all Stalinists: huge as the agency was, in the sense used by Lattmann it could only mean the umbrella for Soviet espionage.

"Or I could be completely wrong, Martin, and it was Heini Himmler who gave your dead Switzer two extra *noms de guerre* to play with. Well, there's my princely coach." A rickety car skirted the fountain and drew close to the officers. Lattmann shouldered his duffel bag and shook hands with Bora. "In either case, it won't do you much good. Here and now there are as many good reasons to kill somebody because he works for us or against us, as there are because he's simply in the way of a pissed-off paratrooper."

Bora's mind uneasily went back to the morning he'd left Russia, when – in a somewhat complacent way – he'd written a diary entry about intrigue in Moscow. He took Lattmann aside, away from the car. "Off the record, what do you know about Major Busch?"

"Only that he was here and was sacked. He's in Lublin now. Why?"

"Run me a little private check on him. See if he had contacts in Casablanca, and what, if anything, he's got to do with Moscow."

Lattmann shook his head. "I'm not touching Moscow these days, sorry. Ask for something else."

"All right, forget about 'Moscow these days'. Just for the hell of it, then, see if we have Federico Steiger in our archive among our *old* Moscow informants, or as a Hotel Lux resident there. He figures as having travelled to the Soviet Union, and to China, too."

"China where?"

"Don't know. Port of entry, Shanghai."

"I thought *you* wrote a paper on Shanghai."

"That was about the Japanese siege much later; it has nothing to do with it. See if Nanking Road and Wongshaw Gardens mean anything to us. Steiger underlined the addresses on the 1927 city map. You'll find it in the passport. Both are in the so-called Shanghai International Settlement, home to most of the 40,000 foreigners in town back then. It was also one of the largest collection points for White Russians after the October Revolution."

"What a pain in the arse you are. I'll do what I can. Anything else?"

Bora showed him, without letting go of them, the forms and typewritten sheet found with the passports.

"What's this?" Lattmann spoke under his breath. "Blank visas?"

"Blank 'Aryanized' visas. Plus names and addresses of wealthy Greek Jews, who must have been paying to get out or save their lives ever since we took Greece and its islands. He had loads of their calling cards in his library."

"Martin, you know you have to turn these in."

"No, I don't."

"I haven't seen any of it, then."

Lattmann stepped to the car and threw his duffel bag onto the back seat. "Well," he turned around to add, flippantly as he always did when he was nervous, "I guess it's pointless to tell you, but don't go off at a tangent."

"I think that's my speciality. Have a safe trip, Bruno."

"No. *You* have a safe stay."

Anxious as he was to pick up his supplies (and to avoid Red Cross officials), Bora stepped back into the hotel for the time needed to slip his diary out of the rucksack and reread his sparse peacetime entries, often as brief as a one-liner. He'd been among the 500 who'd travelled with Hitler in '38, sitting in the second of three trains that sped to and across Italy between 3 May and 9 May. Officially he was there as an additional interpreter. In fact, he'd done some busy legwork in and around the Vatican, especially the Collegium Russicum, seeking discreet information on the presence of foreign agents at the Jesuit school created to convert the Soviet Union. Lattmann's suggestion that he check his notes, as if he carried around such details, would have made him smile at another moment. With investigative time being so short, he was ready to rummage through the entries. After all, it had been his habit – and still was – to drop cryptic hints into his daily accounts, purely for personal use and future reference. *4 May 1938, afternoon. The Führer and Duce at Centocelle for Fascist ceremony. I lunched with Father Leiber, S.J., of Gregorian University and Father MacGregor, of the Scots College in Rome, at Hotel Miramare in Ostia. Afterwards, back to Rome; at the Congregation, a <u>fascinating</u> look at the contribution of Baltic students, especially those from Estonia. Weather warm but pleasant. Early dinner with Italian colleagues: excellent choice of wines, although I wasn't as impressed by the Swiss chocolate pudding as they were.*

Aside from Father MacGregor, friendly to the German cause, and the Jesuit Leiber, who had the pontiff's ear, the real hints in the entry were others. The underlined reference to the Congregation meant Bora's call at the Russicum, the Congregation for Eastern Churches, where an Estonian seminarian was suspected to have contacts with Moscow. Bora remembered only the man's surname, Kurtna, and that he was about to go on leave in his homeland. His own recommendation on returning to Germany had been that he be at once enrolled or else put out of commission. The last he'd heard about Kurtna was that he worked for Cardinal Tisserant, head of the Congregation, and newly for Dr Bock of the Institute for German History in Rome, a cover for the *Abwehr*, which did not mean he wasn't still passing information on to Moscow. As for the chocolate dessert, it stood for a conversation with his Italian counterparts regarding Swiss espionage in Rome, and its British and Russian ties. A Swiss citizen, codename Paolo, real name unknown, resided at Ostia in the hotel he'd lunched in with MacGregor. By all accounts, he was the most important of them all, likely to replace Leonid Bondarenko, embassy cultural attaché (and likely Comintern head operative), once the war with Russia began. Bora passed the information on to Berlin, but had been unable to see the agent in person. At the time, the codename Emma was unknown, but operatives could function under several different ones.

What did Villiger of the *Ahnenerbe* have to do with any of this?

It was a gun-toting member of the German *Feldpolizei*, not a Cretan policeman, who stopped him at the corner of Ithaca Street. "Sorry, sir. You'll have to go around."

"Why, what's going on? My lodgings are on this street, I need to pass."

"There's been an incident. Two locals dead."

"*When?*"

"Around seven. We were notified by local police. Seems they were plain-clothes men assigned to picket an officer's – well, I suppose it must have been *your* billet, Captain."

"Yes, yes, it was. What then?"

"Fearing you'd been targeted, the local police went up to search your quarters. Now we're combing the neighbourhood, but it looks like a drive-by shooting, not much of a chance we'll catch them. When did you leave the premises, by the way?"

Bora had to shove the worrisome conversation with Bruno Lattmann to the back of his mind. "They were alive when I walked out at quarter to seven." He cut matters short. Kostaridis' bluntness made sense now: in one blow he'd lost two of his men. *Whom I never asked for.* Bora tried to draw a line between himself and any sense of guilt. *He forced them on me, and they weren't even clever enough to keep me from sneaking away last night.* It might be because he was preoccupied, but the nagging germ of a doubt, which he smothered before it took shape, suggested another remote possibility. What if Kostaridis… No. Too egregious, too gratuitous. It was true that the shooting gave Cretan and military police an excuse to search the houses on the alley, including his apartment. Luckily, according to his Moscow habit, he never left behind what he meant to keep from others. Notes, Villiger's passports, anything sensitive, he'd taken along this morning. "Look," he told the military policeman, "I need to pick up some things in a hurry. Either you take me there or let me go on my own."

The man let him pass. Pools of blood on the pavement at this end of the alley, and midway alongside it, suggested that one of Bora's guards might have been taken by surprise where he stood, but the other must have reacted by running over and presumably firing back, before being felled in turn. The thought of two human beings, killed while standing watch on the empty quarters of an enemy officer, made him angry. *If they have families, Kostaridis will have to explain to them that they died for no reason at all.*

One flight of stairs up, the door to his billet had been kicked in. An overly zealous intervention, given that assassins would hardly lock up after a hit. *Kostaridis must have a copy of the key, since he got this place for me. So he wasn't with those who came on the scene, and that's why they had to break in. Or was it our military police who applied their usual thoroughness?*

All appeared as he'd left it, but experienced searchers leave no trace. Bora refilled his lighter and used it to burn the typewritten sheet of names, flushing the ashes down the sink in spite of Greek regulations. He picked up his container of Atebrin, a Russian wrist compass (embassy party Christmas gift), and left. Below, he gave orders to gather his belongings and transfer them to the headquarters of Cretan police, under the personal responsibility of *Epitropos* Vairon Kostaridis.

*

The soldier at the depot read out loud from Bora's list. "1,500 gr canned meat (750 gr meat with vegetables); 4,000 gr preserved bread; 1,500 gr zwieback; 900 gr Dextro Energen; 1000 gr dried fruit; 400 gr sugar; 12 packages lemonade powder; 18 packages soluble coffee; salt tablets; water purification tablets; 50 cigarettes. Esbit cooker No. 9 and fuel tablets. Anything else, *Herr Hauptmann?*"

Bora double-checked the supplies as they were placed in his rucksack. "No. These," he said, setting aside the dried fruit, lemonade powder, sugar and zwieback, "pack separately in this canvas bag. They should come to just over three kilos." *She'll have to do her bit,* he told himself. *I'm carrying the rest, in addition to everything else we'll need for the trip.*

The coast was clear when he stepped outside. On his way from Ithaca Street to the former British depot, upgraded to distribution centre for German supplies, he'd been intercepted by Waldo Preger in a captured Humber staff car, newly marked with the paratroopers' divisional crest, a yellow comet on a sky-blue background. Preger followed him to his destination at walking pace, only to continue down the street and park in front of the closest *kafeneio.* Now he'd apparently moved on.

The day promised to be hot. Already the shade had lost its azure tinge, and girls walking out into the sun seemed to catch fire in their bright summer dresses. They were the first women Bora saw strolling in town, and paradoxically the everyday nature of the sight made him feel more, not less out of place. Occupied countries, he remembered from Poland, mark the solitude of the invader the moment they regain apparent ordinariness. *First the hospitals, then the brothels, then the cafes and shops: we fill them in progression, as armies always have. For all I know, lonely Mycenaean and Roman soldiers stopped to drink and bargain over souvenirs in Crete thousands of years ago, and perhaps were sent here by their superiors to buy wine, too.*

A few minutes before nine, other than collecting his travel companion at the hotel, Bora was ready to leave town.

Well, almost. The matter of obtaining a ride was formally ensured by the handful of typewritten passes (in Greek and German) that Busch had provided him with. The major's foresight extended to papers securing free access to depots, prisoners of war, a return flight on any aircraft leaving Crete at any time, and permission to take along as needed one Frances Allen, US national. Money, Bora had procured independently. The only fly in the ointment was the lack of an available vehicle and driver.

Unless the worst came to the worst, at this point of his mission Bora would rather avoid asking the Air Force or Jäger for help. The same went for Kostaridis. On the other hand, with the scarcity of private trucks and cars in circulation, short of commandeering a vehicle, driving it himself and leaving it behind where the mountain trails began, there wasn't much of a choice but to *walk* out of Iraklion. After all, in his estimate (based on maps and Pendlebury's notes), on foot and without stopping, even dangerous Krousonas lay less than five hours away. Bora still leaned toward this option as he came into view of the hotel, unaware that two incidents in succession were about to solve his dilemma. Granted that Preger had as much right as any other German to find himself in the Venetian-built square, his being parked in front of the Hotel Knossos spelt trouble now that Bora could least afford it. By nature he was inclined to face obstacles even when they implied physical confrontation. *But*, he told himself, *it's not a good time. Waldo thinks I'm rooming there and is waiting for me to go past so he can provoke me. He can't do more than that, under orders as he is not to work against me, which doesn't mean he won't try to delay me.* This was the first incident.

Bora calmly turned back from the square. On the assumption that most hotels have a service entrance in the rear, he

197

retraced his steps to the depot. From there, past the church of Agia Ekaterini ("The best Dafni *and* Mandilaria in Iraklion," he recalled hearing from Rifat Bey, "are sold by the Spinthakis widow near Agia Ekaterini"), he covered the short distance to the back of the Knossos, and to a double door leading directly into the basement of the hotel. A few steps from it idled a delivery truck, from which cases of wine were being unloaded under the scrutiny of a German guard.

This was the second incident.

Forty seconds before nine, Frances Allen was escorted to the truck. Bora climbed in after her and was motioning at gun-point for the captive driver to start the engine, when Rifat Bey trundled out of the hotel basement shouting in Greek. Bora stuck his hand out of the window and flashed the appropriate authorization in front of the Turk. "*Diritto di guerra,*" he told him in Italian, and "*Vai, vai,*" to the driver.

The wine grower was still raging as they rounded the corner toward Kalokairinou.

"He understands Italian," Bora observed. "I don't know why he addressed me in Greek. Just for the record, what did he say?"

Frances Allen flicked the rebel curl away from her forehead. "You should drop dead if half of it comes true. The nicest thing he called you is 'bastard son of an infidel German whore'."

The truck was a Greek-assembled, good-quality American Diamond T with the Petropoulos bell-and-circle brand. So far, Rifat Bey must have kept it hidden to keep it from requisition. Amber worry beads dangled from its rear-view mirror, and it was further personalized by good luck trinkets and bright-coloured woollen tassels across the dashboard.

Once out of the Chanià Gate they drove past the turn-off to Ampelokastro and followed the coast for a time. Bora looked out, toward the blue swatch of water, here and there crisply trimmed in white. *We'll soon leave it behind,* he thought, *but on an island you never forget the sea, which means you never forget your limits; and yet, within them, every man's a king, as England goes to prove.* In his old school books it was a different story: here live the French, they said; here the Poles; the Danes there, the Austrians, the Swiss. Limits and borders everywhere, and the recurrent, unspoken German desire to break through them.

Whether she wanted to avoid the sight of British vehicles torn apart and the improvised graves by the road, or else refused to engage with those sitting at her sides, the American kept her face low, and her lips tight. When Bora addressed her, she frowned and did not glance over.

"Mrs Sidheraki, which is the closest ancient site of some importance along this road?"

"Týlissos. Why, is that where we're going?"

Bora spoke looking at his map. "For now, yes."

"You mean that's all the driver needs to know."

"I mean that's where we're going for now, Ma'am."

"Very well." She pointed to the place on the map. "It's ten miles or so ahead, on the left of the road." And she instructed the sweaty, worried-eyed man at the wheel, who chewed on his moustache and hadn't said a word since he'd been commandeered.

Before long, the road gradually started climbing; it curved over dry slopes of reddish earth, studded with olive trees as Bora had seen in Spain, and in Morocco before Spain. Through the open windows the endless call of cicadas was like the buzz in one's ears after a sharp blow, as if the world itself had been stunned and now rang with pain. Frances Allen obstinately kept from looking at either man. If she'd looked out of the corner of her eye, on her right she would catch the swarthy figure of the driver anxiously grasping the wheel; on her left, the side of the German's head, shaven army-style, and a firm, less than friendly profile.

Bora appeared to ignore her as well. In fact, far from dulling his reflexes, service at the embassy in Moscow over the last months had made him nearly overreactive: he kept on the alert for any unexpected motion or secret word whispered to the driver. Whether or not Powell and other runaways had sought Psiloritis, or the foot of Mount Pirgos or the barren sides of Stromboulas, it was here – where town life, such as Crete knew it, ended, and the arid lonely stretches began – that questioning should start. You get into labyrinths in all kinds of different ways, and find they do not necessarily have visible walls. Bora turned the map around, unfolded it on his knees. The spot where the British prisoners, Sinclair included, were gathered when the camera changed hands, was marked in red. It was a gully south-east of Kato Kalesia, on a southbound route that ran more or less parallel, twice removed, to the one they presently followed. In between lay the road that wormed south toward Ampelokastro.

Less than two hours from Villiger's house, on foot and without rushing, across fields and ridges, Powell must have stumbled into his captors while he sought the shore. With the red pencil Bora had carefully highlighted the road they rode along now. Chosen because it seemed the most promising, it led away from the cultivated plains and orchards, where German patrols hunted for anything and anybody of use to them.

Ten or so miles into the trip, as they rounded a wide curve, Frances Allen opened her mouth. "The modern village of Týlissos is ahead. Ancient Týlissos, instead, is down that way." Before them, dipped in sunlight, a handful of whitewashed low houses were like a sprinkle of sea salt on a gentle rise. To the left of the road, a steep trail where a breath of sea wind, funnelled into dust devils, sought the lower land; shrubs studded with yellow flowers, dry grass and a fury of cicadas pointed the way.

Bora gestured for the driver to stop, although the man understood enough Italian to get the meaning of "*Ferma qui*". Dust hovered around the truck when Bora ordered both his travel companions to get down. The driver feared the worst and looked terrified; Frances Allen squinted in the sun and waited, without shouldering her canvas bag. A quick circle of the German's hand in the air meant the truck should go back where it came from, and the driver did not wait for the gesture to be translated into Greek. He hopped back on, manoeuvred in reverse just enough to turn around, and sped off. The truck came briefly back into full view as it trundled toward Iraklion, already several curves away and soon to become a speck trailing dust.

"He won't believe for a minute we came to sightsee. Did you make him get down too because you were afraid he might start back with me?"

Her voice was terse, a flicker away from spite. Without looking at her, Bora opened his rucksack and took out the lightweight items for her to carry. "I reserve fear for better things, Mrs Sidheraki. Please take these and lead the way. I'm curious about the ruins."

A small quince tree shadowed the site, where it seemed that every cicada in the island had sought refuge. Stonework surfacing from a clean cut in the arid ledge bore embedded shells. Bora followed two steps behind as Frances Allen walked toward the paved area. *Metis*, he thought, the acute ability of invention, far beyond mere lying, was Ulysses' talent. He'd always favoured Achilles – bare-faced against the enemy, aware of his own inescapable end – but had to admit that Troy fell to the sinister gift-horse, not to loyalty and brawn.

Piece by piece, behind her back, he quietly began to take off all visible identification. He unbuttoned and removed the right and then the left shoulder board, folded his side cap and drove it inside one of his pockets, along with the identification disc. Soon the unmarked khaki uniform (in part British Army issue or pattern, like his sidearm) was all that tagged him as a military man. And his bearing, his size, his looks. There was no disguising those. But his perfect English, as native as his German, would provide the next level of deception.

Frances Allen displayed no overt surprise when she turned and saw the change, only that nervous gesture of raking back the curl from her forehead.

"If they ask about me, say that I need to reach someone inland. Nothing else."

"Not that you'd know the difference, if I did or not."

Bora faced her, straddling the ancient floor with unaffected self-assurance. "It's best that I get there and back in one piece. Now, since we're here, please tell me something about this place, what it was, whose it was."

She drove her hands into the pockets of her dungarees. Half-turned from him, with her white-socked, sandal-shod right foot she pointed to a course of finely joined blocks, and the structures beyond. "Wall," she said. "More wall."

"Is that it?"

"Steps, cistern and wall."

"I see." Bora strapped his rucksack on. "I understood bronze cauldrons up to fifty kilos in weight were discovered among these ruins." He took a few steps around, until he reached the place where a recess in the masonry formed a shelter from the wind. "What's this?" He nodded towards unexpected candle stubs and traces of tapers and candle wax on the stone floor. "Do people gather here at night?"

"No."

"Well, it can't be ghosts, Mrs Sidheraki." She didn't turn around to look, and he did not insist. "Very good, then. Shoulder your bag. We won't find what I'm looking for by following the north–south routes, such as they are: the slopes seem more favourable, so we'll stick to them unless we obtain strong alternative leads. Now you'll start asking questions for me in the village ahead."

5 June, south-west of Týlissos village, in a spot marked as Chorafi on my map. Noon. We halt for a bite and to get away from the brutal heat.

Thus far, three old people in and around Týlissos have given me a foretaste of what I'm likely to be up against: two of them locked themselves in their huts and there was no luring them out again; the third, who must have been already grey-haired when the Turks lost Crete to Greece, said he's heard and seen nothing, and would have me believe he doesn't know the island has fallen to us. There's no calling them *koumpares*, either, a sort of endearment they got from the Italians, which means "godfather", short as I understand it of addressing them as *mou derphé*, "brother", which however Miss Allen couldn't use with them – and they'd laugh if I tried it. I hope to do better the further we get away from the coast, to isolated farms and villages where travellers still receive *some* hospitality. Maybe. Goatherds on ridges, the moment they catch sight of us, run off, followed by their devil-headed animals with bells around their necks.

I don't think these peasants have changed much ever since Grandfather was here. One of them at least must have been a young man then. They hate the Turks and they dress like Turks, wear Turkish moustaches and guard their women like Turks. Frances Allen married into folks such as these, letting go of whatever she'd been before. I bet she'd have been a nurse in the Great War, were she five years older. You wonder how Sidheraki proposed to her.

While digging for antiquities, leaning on a spade in the hot sun, or sitting by the fire in the evening. I bet *she* proposed to him. Yes, she'd laid her eyes on him; decided she'd have him. She did all the thinking, all the wooing, and he just said yes. His sisters, if he has any, don't like her. His mother hates her, calls God's curse upon her. Gloats and at the same time weeps over the fact that they have no children. Well, Father doesn't like Dikta either. Nina is too tactful to say. Only Grandmother Ashworth-Douglas is firmly on Dikta's side, although she puts it in a quizzical way: "She's exactly what you need at this time." Grandfather on the other hand declares her the most beautiful girl in Leipzig.

Frances Allen doesn't smile at those she meets; married women don't play coy with men. To me, she's still giving the cold shoulder. She replies telegraphically to a direct question, keeping mum the rest of the time. She might think it annoys me (it doesn't; I'm indifferent to her moods), and since I am myself rather taciturn, we walk and hike hardly exchanging a word. My stepfather is loud, like most men of his class and profession (Peter takes after him); I'm like Nina, who seldom raises her voice – or needs to.

Frequently in the past two hours, zigzagging across the undulating countryside, we came upon shards, scatterings of material and surface remnants of structures that must be familiar to her. If I asked, "What is this?" she dropped a Minoan or Greek place name and the name of the scholar responsible for the dig. Thus, I heard of Hatzidakis, Manolatos, Pendlebury, and of course the father of them all, Arthur Evans. But never an articulated explanation of the city or palace unearthed, as if I couldn't possibly – being a German and a soldier – understand it. Never mind. She won't ruffle me, she won't. I instructed her to inform those we meet from now on that: a. She is an American, married to a man from the Iraklion *nomos*; b. She travels with somebody who is seeking a Briton called Powell, and can pay for the information (I gave her Greek currency for the purpose); c. only if and when the contact seems to be promising, she's to mention that we're also looking into the deaths of civilians at Ampelokastro.

When I specified that she's to make sure they pass the word on to others, I prompted the longest conversation we had to date.

She told me peasants will spread the rumour regardless, and it's only a matter of time before every sheepfold in the region is alerted. "But they'll wonder why I am travelling with a man who isn't my husband."

I observed that through the years they must have seen her walk and work with other men, Pendlebury, or his British colleagues. Her reply:

"But you're not one of my colleagues. You're a stranger. If they knew who you really are, they'd turn tail all the more and wouldn't tell me a thing, even those who're aware I'm married to a Cretan."

Threats aren't my style, but I reminded her that her husband's life depends on it, so she had better find a way to make those we meet stay and talk. "All I want is a clue to where there might be Britons," I stated. "I'll take it from there." And because she insisted that country folks are afraid of me, I added, "I'm alone, am I not?"

"You're a stranger, and a soldier: alone or not, that's one too many."

Bruno told me not to go off at a tangent. A tangent? Passing myself off as – no, letting those we meet *believe* I'm a Briton or, worse, a German deserter, is the height of recklessness. I stand to be shot by either side unless I tell a credible story. Documents and papers will avail me nothing with illiterates. Out there, hundreds of enemy officers and soldiers are biding their time, waiting for revenge. And that's leaving aside the mountain men Pendlebury and his pals have been fomenting against us and training for months; *they* would gladly cut my throat.

Only Major Busch and Patrick Sinclair could vouch for my intentions, and they aren't here to be asked. Kostaridis, too, unless he intentionally directed me to where I might get killed. I may look neutral from the outside, but everything in my rucksack is German, and my diary – half of it written in English – is a double-edged weapon. Should we fall into the wrong hands, they'll search me before they search my travel companion, if at all. So – God forbid – like it or not, depending on circumstances, I might have no choice but to lock my diary and give it to her.

Bora thought he'd *learnt heat* in Spain, and before Spain, in his weeks of Moroccan training for the civil war. Learning and mastering, however, are very different things. Summer was nearly three weeks away and already grass and flowers lay prostrate, dry. Cicadas called to one another from one stunted growth of trees to the other, favouring the occasional dark cypresses and leafy carob trees to the sparse bushes and sun-baked hedges, which granted neither shelter nor safety to insects or birds. It was an archipelago of isolated leafy spots, on dry ridges that mirrored back and forth those clumps of fresh greenness in the faded heat, and the endless buzz of cicadas. Incredible how Spain differed from this, even though the upland echoed Aragon. Here everything was solitary but bore the mark of ancient hands, the imprint of ancient feet. In Aragon the signs were rarer, and solitude more (or less?) profound.

The going became steeper. At one point, a German cargo plane banked overhead as it prepared to land in Iraklion, bringing supplies or coming to pick up casualties. Frances Allen glanced at it as she cupped her hands to drink at a roadside fountain. Bora prudently stuck to mineral water in his canteen. Through a broken terrain, seamed with dry torrent beds, they reached an olive grove and a single-floored, lonely house in the middle of it. The grove, according to Frances, belonged to a widower distantly related to her husband, one of those who sold shards and metal objects found who knows where. "We've met before, he'll recognize me."

As it happened, the old man was sitting by the door. A large basket stood between his knees, which he seemed to be weaving or patching up with willow branches or other such flexible twigs.

"*Ya sou*," she greeted him from afar, waiting for a response before she entered the speckled grey-blue shade of the trees. Clouds of small insects hovered all around; a sweet scent of wild mint awoke at every step.

The old man interrupted his work and shielded his eyes to identify the newcomers. Bare-headed, he wore a dazzling white shirt and baggy blue *vragha* that tightened at the knees. He silently tilted his chin toward Frances in acknowledgement. Bora, he surveyed critically and did not greet.

"What's 'cousin' in Greek?" Bora enquired before they drew close.

"*Xadherphos.*"

"*Xadherphos*, fine. Tell him in advance that's what I am to you."

While Frances Allen rattled off in the local dialect, the old man heard her out, his eyes still turned to Bora. Reserve and mistrust lodged in the deep folds of his forehead, at the whiskered sides of his mouth. His hair was silvery, thick like an animal pelt, neatly cut. He rested a willow twig on his knee and let an interval filled with golden fruit flies go by before answering at all.

Frances translated. "He hasn't seen anybody unfamiliar pass through here. He saw aeroplanes two weeks ago. He says that if you're my cousin from Londhra – which means England – how is it that he's never seen you with me before?" (Actually, the old man said "good-looking cousin", but she failed to add that).

Bora stared back at the farmer. "Say that I never had to come inland before."

"He wants to know why you're armed."

"Because men travel armed; as a Cretan he should know that."

"Says it's an English gun that you carry."

"It is."

"Wants you to show it to him."

"What? I will not."

"It's courtesy among men to allow your weapon to be admired."

Pauses seemed to matter here. Bora did not answer at once, nor did he look away from the old man. In the sun, where he stood, the soil was deeply fissured, and a warm, lulling breath seemed to rise from the cracks. Unhurriedly, deliberately he unlatched the holster. "First the information I want, then he gets to touch this."

A negotiation of sorts followed, which apparently led nowhere. The old man kept his eyes on the Browning. Then, as if it were a whip, he lashed the air with the long, pliable twig in his hand. Bora did not openly react. In fact, unprepared for the gesture, he had to master the odd sense of confusion the soft sound, the serpent-like motion, caused him. He was suddenly caught up, cast somewhere else, at another time; it was an instantaneous, fleeting split of the mind. *The last one who did this in front of me was Remedios, way up on Mas del Aire. She whipped the air with a willow twig and drew a magic circle in the dust that made me her prisoner.*

"Captain, did you hear me?" Frances Allen repeated something he hadn't heard at all. "He says my husband wouldn't like my going around with a cousin, even though he carries an English gun."

Bora tumbled back to reality as quickly as he'd slipped away from it. "Does he believe I'm an Englishman?"

"He does."

"Then convince him it's very important that I get to talk to the *Enghlesoi*. Will money help?" More dialogue, and all the time the old man watched Bora. *He has the advantage. Sinclair must have felt as I feel now, being talked to through someone else. It keeps you dangling.*

"Captain, he'll take money to tell you where you should go to find one who might direct you. But he won't accept money to keep his mouth shut about a cousin who walks day and night with a married woman. First chance he has, he'll tell Andonis."

Well, Christ, that's all I need. Sidheraki may be dead and his wife thinks we have him, but what if he's alive, hasn't left the island, and is hiding somewhere around here? If it should reach his ear that she's with an unidentified "cousin", I might have that other predicament to face. Bora showed the wedding ring on his right hand. "Explain that I have a beautiful wife of my own, and pay him."

Frances pulled out a couple of banknotes from her pocket. Bora noticed she'd divided the amount so that no one would be able to see she had plenty, and now squeezed the paper between her fingers with the careful, avaricious gesture of one who regrets parting with money. She handed the man one bill and waited until he pointed towards the upland, presumably giving directions, before placing the second bill on his open palm.

All Bora understood was the word *mandra*, which he'd read in Pendlebury to mean a shepherd's hut. And by the way in which the man's fingers paddled the air repeatedly in the direction of the upland, he imagined it meant it was at a good distance from here.

"There's a fellow who keeps his goats past Agios Minas, on the south slope of Mount Pirgos. They've been buying meat from him lately, so he probably meets foreigners. His name's Kyriakos, and he's got vicious dogs."

I faced those before, Bora thought. He unholstered the Browning and held it out grip first to the old man. He was ready to react in case the weapon were turned against him, but all the old man did was stroke and handle it easily, before giving it back; then he reached for his crotch, smiling a meaningful toothless smile.

Bora was provoked. "What did he do that for, what does he mean?"

"Only that you've shown you have what it takes, letting an old fighter, an expert shooter as he is, handle your gun." Frances' next words to the old man seemed to flatter him, judging by the way he laughed and shook his head.

"Now what did you tell *him*?"

"That he must have gotten himself a young lover, because his clothes are too well taken care of for a man who lives alone."

The Pirgos Massif rose to less than a thousand metres, but from little more than sea level and as abruptly as it did, its name, meaning *tower*, was well deserved. A saddle joined it to the pyramid of Stromboulas, closer to the coast. Together, they formed the dark rampart Bora had seen the first evening, when he'd walked to the shore by himself.

The climb started in earnest a few minutes away from the west margin of the olive grove. Before long the canteens were nearly empty, and though she assured him there were wells and troughs ahead, Bora wasn't optimistic. He watched the American energetically keep up with him and even hike ahead, now that her small size and lighter weight became an advantage. Her vitality irritated him. *Damn, does she ever need to empty her bladder? I have to hold it until she holds it, and do everything quickly while she goes behind a bush, keeping an eye peeled if she tries to sneak away with that excuse.*

In case someone were spying on them through field glasses, Bora had to keep safety in mind and avoid wearing his side cap, although spending hours bareheaded in the Cretan sun was less than advisable. Even Frances Allen had resorted to a faded visor cap, of the sort favoured by aeroplane mechanics; the head covering Maggie Bourke-White wore on war fronts, as he'd seen in magazine photographs. *This story,* Bora thought, *began with photographic images, and those who take them. Somewhere Sergeant Powell licks his wounds, thinks himself safe, and wonders (or not) whether the prim Anglo-Indian officer he gave his camera to followed through by denouncing the deaths at Ampelokastro.* Villiger, Powell, Sinclair, Savelli, Kostaridis, Busch and the War Crimes Bureau, and soon the International Red Cross: the thing connecting them was photography, for different reasons. Had cameras been available to him, wouldn't Achilles have shown his fellow Achaeans the gory shots of Hector, dragged by his horses around Troy? He would have, and bragged about it too. Only Ulysses, made now haggard, now splendid by the gods, could get away with not resembling his passport photos. Alois Villiger instead – failed priest, racial photographer, antiquarian, scholar, salesman – had boldly or imprudently used the same photograph on different documents.

"How do you say 'bad dog?'" Bora broke the silence, just to let Frances know he wasn't panting, either.

She kept her face to the steep climb. "*Paliòskilo,* but it'll do you no good if it's set on you."

Animal noises ceased as they left the sparsely treed land below. Cicadas and the rare songbird grew inaudible, hawks – lanners or peregrines, Bora couldn't tell – silently rode the warm air currents overhead. The click of small rocks tumbling under his feet, or the woman's, only underlined the quiet. Any other sound, human voice or otherwise man-made, would carry a long distance in such a complete stillness.

Twice during the ascent, prolonged calls were heard in the countryside: men crying out to one another or to their flocks, two syllables meaningless from a distance or without meaning altogether, sounds recognizable to those they were meant for. Bora pricked up his ears when he heard them. Frances, who presumably understood, pretended nonchalance. *They might*

211

be following us, following us from the start, waiting to see where we go or just watching us, or else planning an attack. As long as they tell the Enghlesoi, *it's fine with me. I'll worry about how to handle the situation once I reach them or they take me to them.*

Before the climb turned them away from the coast, Bora looked back to catch a last glimpse of Iraklion and the blue horizon. That was how he caught the plume of dust racing along a dirt lane down in the valley; more likely than not a military vehicle, speeding inland for whatever reason. Soon the distant, scattered rattle of machine-gun fire, crisp like the drumming on a typewriter, came from the same direction. Infinitesimal, ant-like human figures sprang up half-seen against the pale earth, hunted, as it seemed, by the dust-raising vehicle, smaller than the smallest toy. Frances Allen, too, anchored between rocks, turned at the sound and was looking.

Peter, who flew a bomber, pragmatically said that distance blunts drama: Bora thought of his brother's words, and how admittedly there was no taking sides from up here. You just didn't know. Chased by the bouncing vehicle, the dots ran and fell. A burst followed by a louder sound, like a firecracker going off inside a box, gave away a building hit by grenades, or where explosives had been activated from inside. Flames were invisible in the brightness of the early afternoon. Only smoke billowed white from the demolished building, but it, too, was a diminutive cloud in the landscape.

Frances Allen angrily resumed her climb. Bora did not follow at once. He ran his eyes across the terrain until he identified Sphingokephalo, and the monument to Agrali's dead wife, like a forsaken bit of sugar. Ampelokastro lay behind the hill, invisible from here. *It has to mean something that from afar you can't judge who's who in a dispute – or in a crime. But if taking sides becomes impossible, your conscience secretly knows.*

7

5 JUNE, 3.45 P.M., MT PIRGOS, SOUTHERN SLOPE.

Agios Minas was no more than a square masonry box set on a perch, overlooking a vista of treeless sun-baked ravines, the colour of rust. Like San Martin de la Sierra in Spain, where Bora went to sit and think many times, the chapel stood like a solitary Christian wart on the pagan body of the land.

Seeking the higher ground, Bora and Frances Allen hiked past the chapel together but apart, without saying a word. *Animals travel in the company of others, eat or drink together in the same apparently uncommunicative manner.* Bora was annoyed. It troubled him that she wore no underclothes, on principle. In Aragon, Remedios was always naked under her cotton dress; the first time, when she'd squatted behind her door in a fiery blade of sunlight, it had been enough to lift the hem above her parted knees to see. Bora had never forgotten it. It had been more than staring between a woman's legs, no news to him anyway at twenty-three. It had been glory disclosed, a blooming epiphany beyond specks of golden dust circling. He'd understood what goddesses are about, how they mercifully, on occasion, for no apparent reason, manifest themselves to mortals who then lie with them. At a price. You never think of the price beforehand, busy undoing your breeches or whatever stands between you and entering them. In the middle of it you don't think at all, your mind glows until it is incinerated, you're furious muscles and bone and blessed wetness at last. Afterwards, when you're too blissfully tired to think of the price, it is exacted. When they stopped to refill their canteens, there where a thread of mountain water fell stingily into a stone basin, the travellers neither looked at each other nor exchanged comments, and their hands carefully avoided contact.

For Bora, it was a natural way of doing things, because he resented being touched. By upbringing and from habit, physical contact was for him an extreme resort, necessarily aggressive or sexual. Frances Allen fitted into neither category (that is, of objects and people to strike or covet), so he rigorously avoided her. To tell the truth, as a boy he'd ardently desired his stepfather's embrace, an unthinkable expectation from a Prussian general. He still cherished the day and hour of the two occasions – the first when he'd manifested his decision to follow a military career – when the old man had briefly held Bora's hand between his. There was a single exception to Bora's rules of contact: at home, his mother Nina occasionally hugged his shoulders while he sat, and leaned her cheek on his head. Neither aggressive nor sexual, they were for him moments of inexpressible joy.

It was slow going, buffeted by a nor'easter Frances Allen called *meltemi*. Was it the same Greek wind of the poem, quoted by Heidegger? Bora did feel like the lonely, feisty traveller. *Travel enough, and you become a Wanderer.* The afternoon reached the midpoint before they came into view of the *mandra* indicated by the old man at the olive grove. From now on, the heat would take a different character, losing intensity according to the sun's changing angle.

Kyriakos' dog was huge, stiff-haired, blind in one eye. The sightless pupil had the tinge of milky tea, and whether or not the injury derived from a merciless blow, it made Bora feel uncomfortable to the edge of sadness. Around its neck the dog wore a yellow rag and a studded collar with small mirrors hanging from it; clearly it'd been left behind to watch its master's hut. It raged, pulling the rope that secured it to a ring by the entrance, and effectively kept strangers from entering. The narrow ledge of rocky dirt in front of the hut and the few implements lying around pointed to continuous human frequentation, so it must be that the man was away with the herd. Bora leaned over at his risk to reach for an empty, dark red tin marked Fray Bentos, on the ground just beyond the range of the straining dog. He smelt it and tossed it back.

"Kyria'kosh!" Frances Allen's repeated calls and the loud barking had no effect; no one answered or came to see what it was.

"Damned mutt would wake up the dead. Now what?" Bora was filling a chipped bowl with water for the dog. He pushed the bowl with a stick to within its reach and stepped away from the *mandra,* signalling to his companion to do the same. The animal relented a little. While it drank, Bora pored over his map, of little help in an area marked as unpopulated. "Are you familiar with this side of the mountain?"

"I climbed to a site near Gonies, further up. There are no towns, if that's what you mean."

"The odd house, maybe? Any place where we may ask about the goatherd?"

She pointed to a sharply profiled rock higher up. "There, where it narrows into a bottleneck. No name to the place; locally they refer to it as *mesa pharangi,* 'inside the gorge'."

A perfect place for runaways to forage, Bora considered. *It wouldn't be worth our army's while to scale the mountain to find them, but until yesterday at the latest the Fray Bentos tin contained 'prepared beef', Commonwealth issue. Kyriakos sees foreigners, and how!* His eyes returned to the map. Krousonas lay forty-five minutes away by serpentine trails, maybe two miles as the crow flies. *Mesa pharangi* was already Satanas' turf, but there was no backing down at this point.

Maybe thirty crumbling houses sat in rows facing each other along the rock-strewn passage, where the *meltemi* did not reach. Due to the crags looming opposite each other, at this hour half of the hamlet sat in the blinding sun, half in the shade. Bony mongrels, forewarned by Kyriakos' watchdog, trotted around announcing visitors. A handful of women dressed in black seated by the doorsteps disappeared inside; doors drew shut after them, or faded cloths were pulled across to hide the interior. It was even worse than in the Spanish mountains, because here women didn't spy on you from behind the louvrework.

No sign of men; not even boys, not even elders. Soon the mongrels made themselves scarce. Emptied first by emigration, now by war, such dying places were unlikely to shelter runaways from outside the island, or outside the region, even. Rebels, freedom fighters, bandits, *sphakiotes* might come and go from here, but to Bora's judgement the English kept to the rugged cliffs above. Of course, the injured Powell could have avoided the high road to escape, and made off in the valley, seeking the impervious defiles of the south or the Libyan Sea. *No. No, he's out there*, Bora tried to convince himself. *And without knowing, he's waiting for me.* Frances Allen finally gave a sign of weariness, the first since they'd started out. She sat on a low wall, removed her sandals and turned her socks inside out to dispose of burs, pebbles and dust collected during the climb. Meanwhile, Bora walked down the uneven strip of land bisecting the village.

Right and left, doors and all other openings remained shut. Bora acknowledged the denial as he went past. Small, flat-roofed, no doubt heirs to the ancient dwellings of Crete, the whitewashed house fronts had blue, deep blue, light blue doors – the same hues as the eye chart in Villiger's house. It was less hot than it had been, but he was overheated. After hours under the pitiless sun, blood roared in his ears – the stunned, not unpleasant sensation of one who is about to pass out. Now and then colours floated and swam before his eyes, and quick movements caused him to lose balance.

Bora walked, counting the doors that watched him and said no. Closed doors and windows, he knew, could be unnerving. In Trakehnen there was a vacant farmhouse with dormers set in the slope of its front gable; the dormers, not uncommonly for the region, had eaves that curved like beetling brows over them. As a child, he was afraid of it, "the house with eyes". All the more he'd forced himself to walk past it, with a trembling heart. Once, with the late sun striking the small windows like eyes that flashed wide open, he'd run off and never stopped running until he reached the family gate. Seldom closed, the gate was closed that evening, and he'd frantically scaled it to gain the safety within. When the farmhouse mysteriously burned to the ground two or three years later, he'd breathed easily, but not without a feeling of guilt. He'd secretly imagined that his own fear, and his own will, had caused the blaze.

The doors of *mesa pharangi* said no to him. To his right, on the upper floor of a house in no way distinguishable from the rest, only a solitary, narrow window remained open. A bone-white girl looked out from it.

The narrow chin, the cloud of red hair, the low-cut cotton dress: there were no two in the world like her. Across the fiery air, suddenly Bora *knew* her. No two in the world like her, no two in the world like Remedios… *"Shepherd girl, outside Gonies"… Gonies is somewhere, not far from here. What did Kostaridis say? "Surely you've thought out what you'd rather be watching when you die."*

Love and terror sat on her shoulders like doves.

The moment his eyes met the girl's, Frances Allen came up to him from behind. The pale girl sank back into the room, drawing a blue curtain across the window to shut him out.

She's gone. She's gone. Bora had to fight a demented need to strike the American for approaching. The rage was short-lived, and left him something very much like the bleeding pain of a heartbreak. If he'd been by himself, he'd have taken time to knock on that door, climb those stairs, despite his orders and his hopeless task, to make sure it wasn't – or it was – Remedios. *Because when she comes to me again it's because I'm to die: her face is to me the magnificent face of Death.*

Startled by his reaction, Frances stepped back, out of his reach. "I'll ask around for Kyriakos. Are you coming along?"

Bora poured what water remained in his canteen over his head.

Wherever they knocked, either no answer came from within, or it was uttered as a brusque denial. Invariably, the female voices sounded old, as if the sole young woman among them were the redhead Bora had seen, or thought he'd seen. *She'd never answer the door as long as Frances Allen was with me. More than that; if I was with anyone, I'd walk into her house and find it empty.*

At long last, one of the doors opened. An ancient woman – it turned out she was Kyriakos' great-aunt, as this was the goatherd's village – peered from a dark interior. Frances explained that Kyriakos wasn't at the *mandra*.

"No? Well, he must have gone with his goats onto the mountain. Who wants him? What do you want him for? If he's got the herd with him, he comes back before dark. If he's alone, after dark."

Apopse, this evening. Bora knew the word. Frances reported with her usual concision. Even when he went to sell, Kyriakos returned for the night. "She says that he usually stops by her house before going down to the *mandra*, but we're not to meet him at *mesa pharangi*. She'll leave word with her neighbour for Kyriakos to come to the hut she has not far from the *mandra*. At dusk we can go with her and wait for him there."

"Should we trust her?"

"Don't ask *me*."

Bora did a quick reckoning. It made no sense to go elsewhere if Kyriakos was the one with the information. It was now close to seven; the risks were not appreciably lower if they kept wandering until dark. "Tell her we'll do it. There's only an hour or so to kill until then."

The low wall where Frances had sat earlier seemed to have no other function but to serve as a bench. About twenty feet in length, it ran parallel to the street, dividing it. It was closer to the row of houses facing where the old woman lived; three vigorous fig trees spread over it, and it was as good a place as any to while away the time. Bora reached the wall, freed himself of the rucksack, pulled out his diary and began updating the day's entry. *Finally,* he thought with male insolence, *the American's enamel is cracking. I may be tired, but she looks fagged out and under the weather.* Almost instantly, though, he regretted his own callousness. *Hell, I'm losing my manners. After the heat and the long hike, we could both use a pick-me-up.*

From his supplies, he took out a spare canteen where he'd already dissolved a water purification tablet. He sprinkled instant coffee into its lukewarm contents, sweetened it, and shook it well. He then filled the metal cap and gave it to her, while he sipped directly from the canteen. Frances sniffed the drink, touched her lips with it, and immediately tossed it away with a disgusted face.

Addendum to daily entry. I'm an officer and a gentleman and don't use the term lightly, but she's a bitch, and no mistake. Milder or more erudite terms don't do justice to my companion's peculiarly American brand of rudeness. I wonder how Sidheraki tamed her – if he did. Kostaridis may be just gossiping (Greeks probably frown on fellow nationals who marry out of the fold); on the other hand, I can see her setting her compass on the suntanned demigod wielding a pickaxe at the dig. As for Andonis – well, marrying an American is the dream of many a European male. I wonder if she planned to take him back to her parents or disappointed him by deciding to set up house in Crete. Kostaridis described their place to me as little more than a two-room affair with a stable and six Italian MAB submachine guns, in the outskirts of the most famous archaeological site on the island, the Palace of Knossos. A "routine check" according to Kostaridis, but if German soldiers carried it out in the company of Cretan police, it was because the latter had tipped us off about Sidheraki's political activities. For a Greek national, the find would mean the firing squad. She's an American, neutral and untouchable (for now), all the more since she was away in Iraklion at the time of our landing. Both Cretan and German authorities took the lenient view that she was unaware of the weapons' presence. Why? Kostaridis' uncle Nikolaos sailed to New York from the Cretan village of Rapania some thirty years ago. Having told me so in passing, he denies it influenced his decision to buy into Frances' innocence. As for us, we needn't irritate the United States at this time. I simply keep in mind that MAB guns were used to fire the rounds that killed the Ampelokastro household.

It was the sound of food cans hitting the ground that made Bora look up from the page. He turned around, only to see Frances Allen busy groping through his rucksack.

"Hey! What are you *doing*?"

She continued to dig. "Have you got a spare undershirt in here?"

Bora wrested the rucksack from her hands. "Leave my things alone! What in the world has got into you?"

"Not *into* me: I just got my period, you dolt. I need something for it. I'm looking for an undershirt, or anything else cottony. Give it to me. Come on, give it to me."

Bora did not move. "Why?"

"Oh, cripes! You wear a wedding ring, you know what a period is, don't you? Have you got a goddamned spare or not?"

"I have." Rolled into a neat cylinder, the undershirt came her way.

"Is there any string, too?"

"Only extra bootlaces."

"They'll do. Give me."

Bora did as he was asked. "Here. Don't bother to say thank you."

"Later." She straddled the wall and clambered out of sight between two houses, over a dry hump of rocks. "I'm in a hurry."

Bora carefully rearranged the contents of his rucksack. Such small privacy was granted in the army; he was protective of the few belongings he carried along from time to time. Objects didn't feel the same to the touch after someone else intruded. He replaced the canvas-bound diary out of reach at the very bottom, with letters and his family snapshots inside it.

Of course he knew what a period was. But privacy surrounded his wife's and his mother's lives at certain times of the month; a look or a word was enough to exclude men automatically from those *indispositions*. It took him nearly two minutes to realize that it might all have been an excuse; that his guide could be running like a mountain goat out of his reach. He scrambled to reach the back of the house, ready to chase her. When he saw her squatting a few paces off, fumbling with the makeshift sanitary towel, he sank back. He waited around the corner without spying but at hand, in case she took to her heels.

She found him sitting on the low wall when she returned. "I'm afraid the undershirt won't be much use to you when you get it back," she plainly informed him.

As if I'd want it back after you'd used it, you hag. Bora couldn't find a reply unkind enough, so he said nothing.

"And I'll take some coffee now."

"Not if you have to waste it."

"I won't." She drank this time, not one but three capfuls. "Well, what do you want me to say? That I owe you?"

Bora had to bite his tongue. He screwed the cap back on and put away his canteen. "If it's any consolation, Ma'am, I don't like you either."

The words had their effect. Confirming their mutual aversion was useful, as truces can only be declared after you agree that you're in conflict. Frances Allen surveyed the rucksack, safely between Bora's knees. "I noticed you've got cigarettes in there." She chewed a cuticle off her thumb's fingernail. "What'll it cost me to have a pack?"

Bora fished out a ten-pack, which he laid on the surface of the wall between them. "They're army issue, and I'm not venal."

"Matches, too."

He handed her his lighter, "But I'll need it back."

She lit herself a cigarette and for a while took slow drags, looking at the line-up of houses and closed doors across the street. Partly turned from her, Bora resumed writing his entry, locked his diary, capped his pen and put everything away in the rucksack.

"You're the orderly type, aren't you?"

"*Very* orderly."

"And very organized, I'll bet." When she sneered, a web of small wrinkles crowded the outer corners of her eyes. "That's why you presume you'll find your man in three days, out of the hundreds who're dead set on eluding your army."

Bora buckled the flap of his sack "I may *not* find him. As they say, I'm giving it my best shot. God had better be on my side in this one."

Behind them, where the western ledge rose high, the arc of the sun dipped slowly. It already grazed the stony rim, so that only the houses at the foot of the opposite ridge were still bathed in orange light. Over the wall where they sat, and across the width of the street, there pooled a warm blueness; the interlacing branches of the fig trees no longer cast a shadow. Like a shrinking cloth, sunlight withdrew to the threshold of the house right in front – where Kyriakos' great-aunt lived – and began to creep up its front. Bora sat easily, stretching his legs, but his shoulders were unrelaxed and his pistol holster was unlatched.

"Are you sure?" She spoke with the cigarette in her mouth (she did have a smoker's mannerisms, and a smoker's dusky voice).

"About what?"

"That God would even consider being on your side. I mean, everyone knows yours killed the folks at Ampelokastro."

Bora stared ahead, at the margin of sunlight inching up the facade, hemming whitewash and blue door as the *pharangi* gradually sank into shadow. *Her house further down, the house of the red-headed girl has long been on the evening side. It is evening itself. She's just a redhead, a Greek girl, but had another woman not been with me, had I journeyed alone, she would have been Remedios, and I'd have been lost. Being saved by the presence of this rude fellow traveller is nothing to brag about.*

"'Everyone knows' is hearsay," he pointed out. "With five people dead, I'm seeking proof."

Again that sarcasm, that web of fine lines around her eyes. "Oh, a *humanitarian.*"

"Anything but, Mrs Sidheraki. I attended with profit four military schools."

Inside the houses, fires were being kindled for the evening meal; the scent of burning twigs and leaves escaped somehow, perhaps from back windows or chinks – no chimneys were visible. To Bora's nostrils, it overlay the acrid whiff of cigarette smoke next to him. By and by, the limpid air grew fumy. When a rifle shot lost in the countryside rang across it, like a rock thrown into a pond, the sound created ripples; it travelled in rings and circles of echoes.

Bora paid attention, and waited. The message of an isolated shot can be construed in many ways: but whether it kills, misses or simply warns off, it seldom partakes in an integrated relay of information. Musically, it equals a single, sharp note from which no melody can be learnt. Two, on the other hand, or three... A second report, like a pebble of sound sinking in a pond further away, was followed by a fainter third one, which overlapped its echo. *They're not hunters, they're signalling to one another across longer distances, which voice alone cannot bridge. Who, what about? Those who eyed us from the ridges and shied off, the old man with the immaculate shirt in the olive grove, those who frowned and said they know nothing... It could be any or none of them. Recurrent calls, rifle shots – it is Allen and I who are notes: they provide the stave.*

Frances ignored the gunshots, like a native accustomed to weapons being discharged for any mundane reason. She'd removed her visor cap and leisurely savoured each breath she took from the army tobacco, looking up at the opaque intricacy of fig leaves above. "Most foreigners have a skewed idea of Crete and what Cretans are like." She thought out loud. "They see the dilapidated mountain villages, the bare feet, the sheep coats, the occasional drunk sleeping in the sun, and they forget that their ancestors ruled the Mediterranean." Like her attitude, her speech was also unhurried, full of round vowels, no doubt a feature of southern upbringing despite her college education. "When Ulysses wanted to impress his audience he pretended to be a Cretan prince. Words so identified with Greece by lovers of the Classics, like 'cypress' or *thalassa*, the sea, are in fact Cretan in origin." She glanced over and flicked ash from the tip of the cigarette, a gesture Bora found mannish in her. "But you wouldn't understand."

The sunlight was now reduced to a ribbon edging the roof, as if a blue tide were about to submerge the house across the street, and those on either side. Elsewhere on the mountain, the advanced day must still be radiant, vistas enormously clear into the distance. Here evening had the advantage. Bora sat up and straightened his back. "Well, we Germans haven't forgotten Crete's greatness, apparently, if we seek to count it among our ancestral homelands."

"Ha!" She pinched the cigarette butt between thumb and forefinger to smoke it to the last. "That's why you sent Wimpy Villiger here, with his unfailing camera and hare-brained hypotheses. He wasn't welcome, you know."

"In your British-led midst? I expect not."

She let some time pass before answering. As if squashing an insect, she put out the bit of consumed paper and tobacco on the surface of the wall. Mechanically, she pushed the bottom of the straw-coloured pack to extract another cigarette. "Oh, it wasn't even politics." She seemed to be weighing whether or not she'd give in to a second smoke. "John – Pendlebury, that is – argued with him over chronology, because Villiger held on to the old dating system created by Aberg, no longer acceptable. Villiger was an amateur."

"Of the bungling type or of the Schliemann type?"

The question suggested some familiarity with her field, which she chose to disregard. "He didn't discover Troy, if that's what you mean. He knew his Early Minoan ware, his Middle Minoan frescoes. But he had a ready-made thesis rather than a hypothesis, which got in the way of his scholarship. That's how John saw it." The first-name basis with Pendlebury was interesting. Bora took one of his mental notes. "They had a couple of rows, after which your champion understood he was *persona non grata*, so he stayed away from us. The times he came to the Knossos he drank at a table on his own, reading or taking notes to look less conspicuous. But he stood out anyway, as all of us – locals and foreigners – were all jolly and pretty loud. John definitely spooked him. When British officers first came from Souda last winter and offered a round of drinks over something or other, he crawled out of the room. That's the last we saw of him at the Knossos. Never mind that some of them physically matched his northern ideal!"

"Why *Wimpy* Villiger?"

"Oh, well, *I* called him Wimpy, because he reminded me of the comic strip character – you know, Popeye's oafish friend, big body, small head. The name stuck among us."

Bora nodded. *For whatever reason, she's talking to me.* He could feel heat leave his body as the temperature around began to slacken, a sensation between pleasure and discomfort. That's how embers inside a cooling furnace must radiate what remains of their fire. *I doubt it's gratitude for the undershirt or the cigarettes I gave her.* In shadow, the lime-based wash on the house fronts turned azure. No. The right term was glaucous, the colour prevalent underwater. *Mesa pharangi* was a sunken village, much as the palaces along the coast were swallowed millennia before by seaquakes. *Maybe it's because women become difficult before their period comes, and then they mellow out? Useless information so far, except for the report that Pendlebury "spooked" the victim.*

He said, "But you lent Villiger at least one book. I saw your name on a text in his library."

"Did I? I don't recall." She placed a second cigarette in her mouth and solicited the lighter from him with a half-curl of her fingers. "Thanks. It must have been before John put him in his place."

Pressing her for details might make her silent again, so Bora let her go through half of her smoke before skirting the subject. "I gather that yours must have been exclusive drinking parties at the Knossos. But it can't be a state secret, chatting about archaeology over brandy. Of course, your Greek husband participated with the rest."

"Andonis is not the drinking type."

"And you are?"

She defiantly blew smoke through her nostrils. "I could outdrink *you*, Captain."

"I'll take your word for it, Ma'am." Bora didn't show that he was amused, much less what he was thinking. *I wouldn't advise you to try it: after the stint in Moscow, I can drink men twice your size under the table.*

"What's the use of talking, anyhow? Both John and Villiger are dead."

"We have no confirmation about Pendlebury, but Villiger is definitely dead. At least one of the two is beyond reproach."

"You'll know whether you killed John Pendlebury; he had a glass eye."

"Really? I wasn't aware *we* killed him. No business of ours, shooting scholars who stick to scholarly business." Bora checked the time on his watch. Kyriakos was late; he must be returning without his herd, which meant he wouldn't arrive until dark. If he was anywhere on this slope, however, no matter how far away, he'd have heard the rifle shots. And he might decide to stay away. *It's difficult, getting down to business with her. She strings me along with the hope that we won't harm her husband; she doesn't believe me, much less trust me.* "I'm no expert," he decided to add, "but I have the impression that archaeologists – whether or not lit with a sacred fire – are competitive prima donnas."

She shrugged. Whether or not she was used to working while smoking, it was clearly her habit to speak without removing the cigarette from her mouth. She said, "If they discover an important site or artefact, naturally they will share none of it with anybody until it's published under their name."

"I noticed that in Pendlebury's *Archaeology of Crete*, the accurate line drawings are mostly the work of female colleagues, whom he generally refers to as 'Miss' or 'Mrs'. And that, I suppose, regardless of their academic titles."

"Is that important?"

"I'm asking. Rank matters in my profession. What I'm also wondering is whether those two, the Swiss and the Englishman, ever transcended an intellectual disagreement."

She looked at him as if curious to know where he was going with this. "Villiger worked for your Race Office, it was a known fact. I told you we didn't care for his company. Is that *transcending*?"

"Hardly. Just for the record, do you mind telling me how you learnt about his death, and when?"

"We heard that his country house was attacked, and everyone in it killed."

"*We* as in – you and your husband?"

Her distrust became a hard, dry look. "You're not going to lead me into a trap. Andonis left home the day you invaded. News of the killing reached town last Sunday."

"But by then you were already in German custody, were you not?"

"I was *arrested* by that fascist kowtower, Kostaridis, and turned in to your command. Regrettably, German is a language that must be mastered by anyone who delves into archaeology. I overheard two of your men" ("They're not my men," Bora commented) "say that paratroopers killed a Swiss citizen at Ampelokastro, and there might be repercussions."

"Is that what you heard?"

"As if you didn't know."

It was news to Bora, in fact. To sound her out, he switched to German. "Actually, Villiger and his household were killed by Italian weapons, such as were found at your place."

She fired back in the same language. "Well, maybe the Italians killed him, then."

Sure, at that time the Italians were moaning and groaning about being assigned to Ierapetra, clear across the island. And Sidheraki might have left home, but not his activism: Kostaridis says the weapons were new, but not unused, when their house was searched twenty-four hours after *the murder.*

"That's unlikely, Ma'am. Speaking of Italians, there's another fellow you might have met – a scholar called Pericles Savelli, who used to work at the museum in Rhodes."

"*Savelli?* No. The only Italian I knew of, in spite of his surname, was the late Professor Halbherr. Cretans say that he can still be seen riding his coal-black mare at midday."

"They would, wouldn't they?"

"I'm sure you have your own superstitions." She didn't put out the cigarette this time. She sent the stub flying through the air with a flip of two fingers. "Before you think we ostracized Wimpy Villiger, keep in mind that he *never* invited us colleagues over, which is uncommon among expatriates. In March, when John and I decided to drop by unannounced, his field hands shouted us away without letting us set foot inside the gate."

"Did they set a watchdog on you?"

"No, there was no dog around. Just those blonde-haired young ruffians. The Turk on the hill next door was much more neighbourly."

"Ah, Rifat Bey."

"Something like it. Now, *he* has dogs, which he keeps tied up. We drank wine and raki, and he showed us interesting surface finds from his vineyard."

Bora nodded, but was thinking, *Which is more – or less – than he showed Kostaridis and me.*

"He told us Wimpy had been crossing the property line to dig for artefacts in his absence, and when he caught him red-handed he opened fire on him to make him quit."

"I believe it."

"He hated his guts, I think."

"But he welcomed two strangers like you into his house."

"Well, not *into* his house. We sat under the trellis outside. In town we heard we shouldn't take it personally, as he stopped having company when his wife died."

"So you see there are reasons why a man might not invite people over."

They'd been silent, and Frances was about to consider a third smoke, when Kyriakos' great-aunt appeared on the threshold of her little house, like the witch in a fairy tale. In the gathering dusk, she summoned the American with a wave of her hand, and Bora came too. They were told how to reach her place outside *mesa pharangi*. She would join them there, as soon as she had finished her chores and talked to her neighbour.

"Are you two married?" she asked Frances Allen, who did not translate for Bora. But he understood the word "cousin" in her reply, and the implied expectation that they come across as related, if not exactly familiar.

The old woman's hut (she called it *kaliva*) could be reached by leaving the gorge from the side opposite to that by which they'd entered. Passing in front of the house where he'd seen the red-headed girl, Bora couldn't help glancing that way. *Yes, I have my own superstitions.* A candle, or oil lamp, or small fire burned upstairs; the blue curtain let the glimmer through, like a vigilant eye. It wasn't quite dark yet; an indoor light should not be so visible, but it was.

Outside *mesa pharangi*, evening was still to come. A diffuse luminosity filled the air with the transparency of glass. Where the sunrays still reached, yellows took on a sulphur tinge, greens turned golden. A cut-out of sea visible from here trembled like molten lead. The higher massif facing Pirgos to the south – Mount Voskerò – allowed Bora to orient himself even better than his compass. The name, Allen said, had to do with pastureland. If place names didn't lie, and if Kyriakos hadn't gone to sell meat, he could have brought his herd to feed on Voskerò. But then he'd already have come back.

Beyond a chain of rolling hills below, directly to the east, sat Kamari, the village where Savelli said he roomed. North of it, Sphingokephalo emerged, an island from a sea of vineyards, whose greenness the shadow cast by the mountain dulled into grey. The ochre house crowned its top, and just below, on a separate knoll, the white curd of the Sphinx memorial still glimmered.

"What are you looking at?" Frances Allen enquired, and when Bora told her, she came back with a snub. "That tacky imitation temple!"

Maybe. Despite the Turk's hostility and contrary advice from Kostaridis, the day before Bora had refused to leave Sphingokephalo before visiting the monument. At midday, the sunlit whiteness of the marble had made it into a beacon of snowy light, a clump of ice or frozen cloud nesting on its conical height. Lizards zigzagged up the dusty climb, from one meagre stringy-leafed bush to another. Bora recalled how at first sight the four lion-bodied women, crouching towards the cardinal points, had seemed identical to him; their faces, however, showed a progression from serenity to desolation. They guarded a tall, plain sarcophagus under a circular canopy, and he'd sat there a few minutes, staring down at Villiger's house. The cut just received from Rifat Bey's grazing shot stung on his temple. So he'd gathered on his fingertip a bead of blood from the broken flesh and left it as a signature on the marble step. Tonight, while dusk swallowed the landscape, the familiar, incomplete film culminating in Villiger's death still rolled in his mind. In a freeze-frame, the runaway Powell crouched in the ditch and craned his neck to spy on the German patrol; in another, the paratroopers came slogging through, armed to the teeth; in another yet, the garden wall screened from view what happened once they crossed the front gate. Bora recalled how, from his lookout near the Sphinxes, he couldn't see the window where Kostaridis had first pointed out the monument to him. The garden palms seemed to conceal Ampelokastro altogether, yet from below a gap in the leafage allowed a view of the facing hill. *A tacky fake temple? Maybe. When you walk around it, at any point at least one of the Sphinxes looks your way, and everyone knows the Sphinx asks impossible questions; if you fail, you die.*

It came to him now that trees and shrubs not only screened the villa from above; they could also, on the ground, conceal others from the patrol passing through. Men lying low in the garden could then go in for the kill. *Maybe there aren't wrong answers: only wrong questions.*

A slippery spot forced Bora to regain his balance by treading on a growth of wild marjoram or thyme, he wasn't sure. He smelt the spiciness of mashed leaves. Evening made scents – and feelings, and reason – more acute. The slope at this end of the gorge was tricky; soon he and Frances had to watch their steps to avoid falling headlong.

The old woman's hut sat on a ledge at the end of a tumbledown trail no wider than two feet. It mostly resembled an oversized kennel built with pale fieldstone. A gnarled almond tree, long past blooming, grew next to it, and the usual scrub of spiny bushes, thistles and burs. Kyriakos' *mandra* was unseen but had to be further down; not far, as Bora recognized the incline negotiated on arrival.

"Wait here," he told his companion, and slipped the gun out of its holster. He reached the door, which was ajar, pushed it with his knee, and looked in. Only after he was satisfied there was no one hiding inside did he hunch to keep from striking his head on the lintel and walk in. Stepping back out, he found Frances Allen sitting on a flat rock by the entrance, with a cigarette between her lips. She'd dropped her sack on the ground and now motioned for the lighter.

Bora stretched it her way. "Here, but it's the last smoke of the night. I don't want anyone to smell us without even seeing us."

"Any other orders?"

"Yes. If you have to do any grooming, please do it while there's still light."

Whatever snide comment Frances might have had on the tip of her tongue, she kept from making it. She returned the lighter and put away the cigarette. She was about to shoulder her sack when Bora intervened. "Leave it here, if you don't mind. Take whatever you need, but not the sack." She irritably fished out toilet paper and a handful of white cloth, which was how Bora knew his ill-fated undershirt had been cut into strips. It also meant she owned scissors, or a utility knife. He'd worry about that later. He was tempted to suggest that blood – menstrual blood, too – was sure to attract dogs, and she had better dispose of what she'd finished using. But he felt that would be too much. He handed her instead a full canteen and a bar of soap in its neat Bakelite box. On her return, they ate a quick meal. Afterwards, under her scrutiny, Bora rinsed the food tins and put them back in his rucksack along with the forks they'd used. He'd flatten the containers with a rock and bury them in the morning. Frances did not offer to help. She sat circling her knees, and as he'd given

233

her permission to smoke the last cigarette of the day she seemed better disposed towards him, or else the waning light mitigated the scowl on her face.

Bora took advantage of the possibility for a new conversation. "Just for the record, do you suppose Dr Villiger could have been trafficking in archaeological finds?"

"You ought to know if he was. He worked for you. Or do you really believe photographing peasants is what he was really doing?"

"I wouldn't be asking if I knew."

"I told you how the Turk opened fire on him. And John was furious after hearing reports that Wimpy paid peasants to bring him things from remote burial sites."

Both circumstances would make Villiger jittery, not to speak of his three passports and whatever else he was up to in Crete. In retrospect, his cover as travelling scholar smacks of those we call kaltgestellt, *dormant agents waiting to be activated. Is it a coincidence that he was "planning a trip", as he told Savelli, and looking into sea travel two weeks before our invasion? If he was ours, he had good reason to stay away from the Brits. If he also worked for the Reds, he had good reason to stay away from us and from the Reds.* Bora contemplated a handful of dim lights trembling into existence across the fields below. Iraklion was a distant scatter of dots, half-seen twinkling by the invisible sea. The photos of ancient artefacts in the roll seized from Savelli – it might be worth showing them to Frances Allen tomorrow. He crouched on his heels, feeling in his muscles the weariness of the day.

"I imagine there can be valuables, easily moved, found in such remote sites."

She leaned her back against the stone jamb of the door. "If you mean those that can easily be pocketed, the most desirable are gold-leaf jewels and such. Many were discovered in Mokhlos, quite a distance from here, to the east. Early Minoan, mostly,

2500–2200 BC. The votive, toy-shaped double-axes in gold, too. Faience plaques. And then seals for signet rings, in agate or haematite, representing animals fighting or flowers – coveted by museums and private collectors. But you have to know your seals; it's their antiquity and not their semi-precious material that makes them valuable. Farmers and shepherds – call them unscrupulous or ignorant or simply in need of money – will grub in the their backyard or pasture, messing into holes or through masonry to get them. They'll do it on commission, too. There's no teaching them that an object removed from its original site loses its documentary value, not to speak of the wanton demolition of ancient structures." She made her smoke last, judging by the frugal draws that revived the tip of her cigarette. "Is that why you pretended to be interested in antiquity – because you wanted to know about Villiger?"

"That, too. But assuming that being German means being dense is – what did you call it? – a skewed idea. My grandfather encouraged Arthur Evans when he first started his archaeological work at Knossos."

"Your grandfather *encouraged* Evans? Right! You're just pretending."

"I'm not. Grandfather lived in Chanià at the time, knew him and eventually published the four volumes of his *Palace of Minos* in German. He still tells of how upset Evans was that his old man gave him a sister at seventy years of age. In fact, she's only a year older than my mother."

"You could have read all that in books."

"Save the family details, I *could* have."

"But it doesn't change a thing. For all your standing up when I stand up and all your good manners, culture doesn't make you better."

"Forgive me for saying it, Mrs Sidheraki, I believe it does."

*

Mount Pirgos, after 8 p.m. I write this final addendum as long as I can see the page. The place where we wait, and might spend the night for all I know, has been appropriated by Kyriakos' great-aunt, but – I have this from Miss Allen, who just heard it from her first-hand – it used to belong to the town whore. *Porne* is the polite Greek word, though I'm sure there are less friendly local terms for the profession. She's reportedly gone up in the mountains with the *Enghlesoi*, or to town with the *Yermanoi*. Understandable: there are no males left at *mesa pharangi*! The advantage, as I see it, is that inside there are pallets (mattresses would be a big word) for the women to sleep on. I don't want to catch fleas or worse, and besides I mean to keep an eye on the door, so I sit outside. If Kyriakos is told by the old woman's neighbour that he's to stop here before he returns to the *mandra*, I'll be the first to hear him approach. I'm willing to bet he's long known the way here, and that there have been a few scuffles among customers in front of the *porne's* door. Didn't Philip Walton and I fight like dogs over Remedios in that Spanish cemetery? We did. That brawl, its reasons and its outcome, I remember full well. But with Preger, it was before girls.

After darkness overtook slope, mountains and valley alike, a welcome cool breeze rolled from the interior. Still parched from the day, Bora wished he could take his clothes off to enjoy it fully. But he crouched there, dressed and watchful instead. As planned, he let the two women sleep inside, in a windowless inner room, and he stood guard on the threshold. The door was ajar: at any time he could step in to check on things. He did silently remove Allen's sandals from her side, to discourage her from trying to sneak away.

Waking was no chore. A few minutes at a time, with his eyes closed, were all he needed to recover from the day. Shepherds, warriors, wanderers had kept watch for thousands of years in places like this, maybe in this very place. The waxing moon, four days away from fullness, was already high; it weeded out the crowd of stars and mitigated the dark. According to Frances Allen, the transparent air and the moon's paleness indicated a change in the weather, of rain coming. If so, there was no other sign of it. Beyond the dimly perceivable landscape of ridges and dales, an irregular mountain range, higher at its southern end, rose in the distance to separate the Iraklion district from the eastern third of the island, which the Italians were meant to administrate. *It seems peaceful, but the moment the village dogs bark, we'll be in for whatever comes down the mountain. It could be Kyriakos, or someone else entirely.* Bora couldn't have slept even if he had wanted to. As usual around this time, he passed the blade of a safety razor over his cheeks and chin to keep a perfect shave. Habitual gestures, which could be interrupted any time. The night before their death, Villiger and the others at Ampelokastro were as steeped in routine as he was now – unless the battle for Crete, drawing to a close, kept them alert and fearful. Who knows, by then, the two British soldiers Kostaridis spoke of could already be lying dead and robbed of all identification not far from the villa, a reminder that war reaches everywhere. Who killed them, and had the household heard those shots? Unless the field hands, with orders to keep strangers away... Stray, exhausted soldiers can be surprised and overwhelmed. Yes, Villiger's field hands, or Rifat Bey's thugs, could have ambushed the two Britons. Or else they were additional victims of Siphronia's in-laws, ready to take advantage of the convulsed situation to settle the score with her. They were shot point-blank and robbed, Cretan style.

Losing one's honour is a sensitive subject, not just for women, and not in Crete alone. Hadn't he gone with Waldo Preger to see where Pastor Wüsteritz hanged himself, beyond the marsh and past the "house with eyes"? The suicide was no longer hanging from the noose but the overturned stool he'd used still lay there, as did his shoes. In the gaping void of the abandoned factory, the boys were startled by a flight of doves that sought the paneless windows to escape. "It's the devil," Waldo had superstitiously said, and Martin had answered, "God won't let the devil use doves." *We were both wrong that time.* Crouching by the *porne*'s hut, Bora didn't fall asleep, he simply went from an image to the next as the mind does, wandering so far that it might as well leave the body. If he closed his eyes he no longer imagined himself in Moscow; Moscow and Russia were at the opposite edge of the universe: it seemed impossible that God willing he'd soon ride across its borders with an invading army. This was Crete, where time stood still. *This island is like a wheel, where time circles round. Crete is a time machine where recollections keep churning, and wherein I've fallen at my own risk.*

It was nearly three o'clock by Bora's watch when he heard the mongrels restlessly barking up at *mesa pharangi*. He slipped inside the hut to rouse the women. Despite the complete darkness of the back room, he could tell them apart by the different odour of their sweaty clothes. "He's coming," he leaned over and whispered to the American. "Be ready at the door." Frances Allen stirred out of a deep sleep and – crawling towards the exit – stumbled over the old woman, to whom she was saying something in Greek when Bora went out again. If he strained his ear, he could make out from above the small sounds of one who tries not to make noise but cannot go wholly unnoticed; pebbles clicked and rolled under his feet. Silently, Bora hiked a short distance up the trail to a spot he had kept in mind, where the shrubbery would allow him to wait undetected for another to go by. It would not trick aggressive sheepdogs; still it would give him some space to manoeuvre.

There were no dogs, but Kyriakos was not alone. Two men picked their steps in the dim starlight – the moon had since set, and even across the valley nothing but a sprinkle of campfires flickered far off – and only when they were close did Bora perceive that one of them carried a shotgun. Whether the goatherd had become suspicious because of the change in routine, or the old woman's neighbour had forewarned him, he'd brought someone along. But he could also simply be travelling with a friend or relative of his.

Bora waited until the men reached the hut, and from the few words exchanged it became evident there was mutual respect between Kyriakos and his great-aunt. An oil lantern was lit, and gave out sprays of uneven glare on those around. On the doorstep, Frances Allen looked like a gorgon, her wiry hair tangled with sleep. She must be wondering where her travelling companion might have gone, but for Bora it would pay not to be found with the others.

Yet, not to appear openly hostile, he called out in English "I'm here" while stepping down to join the group, so the men wouldn't feel he had tried to catch them unawares from behind.

Kyriakos was the one with the shotgun. He held it so that, if needed, he could let off the contents of both barrels on Bora. "*Ya sou,*" Bora said in a conciliatory tone. The swap of stares in the broken glare lasted a matter of seconds. Then Frances spoke up. "Kyriakos says we should all go inside," and, "Where are my sandals?"

Inside the two-room hut, at first all five sat around on the dirt floor in the kitchen-like front space, but after the preliminaries the sleepy old woman went back to lie in the inner alcove. Kyriakos, like his watchdog, was blind in one eye. Big, scarred and shaven-headed like a convict, he kept dully staring at the American and asking the same questions (who were they, what they wanted here, etc.), to the extent that Bora began to think he was mentally unsound. The other fellow, perhaps twenty years of age, could easily be Kyriakos' own son. Same size, same shorn skull. He meekly squatted there without opening his mouth, looking down like someone ashamed or unused to people.

The lantern had been fashioned out of a can, punched with holes. The speckled light that resulted made all faces into an impressionist play of dots. Across Kyriakos' knees lay the shotgun, at an angle that still guaranteed he could fire in split seconds and not miss. Bora looked away from it. *I'd have to be Buffalo Bill to draw ahead of him. I won't show I'm afraid by keeping the Browning at the ready, either, so I must accept sitting under aim, though it would blow quite a hole through me.*

As long as the questioning came from the goatherd, there was no advantage to the travellers. Frances Allen succeeded at last in probing a sentence or two out of him, but not before a Greek banknote came out of her pocket.

"He says he doesn't know where the English are. He doesn't sell meat to the English. He doesn't sell meat, period. He sells cheese."

"Well, to whom does he sell cheese, then?"

More cajoling followed. "To anyone who'll buy it, he says." Frances Allen spoke, fumbling with her blouse. She seemed to realize only now that buttons had come undone and her cleavage was showing. Bora had been too absorbed to notice, but it was probably why Kyriakos was staring and drooling and the boy was looking down. The proof of it was that once the blouse was buttoned up to her neck, the goatherd snapped out of his spell.

Now that presumably he was no longer aroused, though, he was alarmed. Obviously, he didn't trust either visitor – especially two *frangoi*, especially Bora. He took the money, but didn't want to give any information. Bora suspected he planned to keep them there until daybreak, until reinforcements came or a trap was set. Finding a way out of the impasse would not be easy. *He denies dealing with the English, although the British-issue food can I saw at his place suggests he's lying. But I can't very well make him drunk and blind his remaining eye with a burning branch as Ulysses did with the Cyclops. Making up my own story is really all I can do.* He turned to the American. "Tell him we know he's been selling to the English, and that the Germans know he's been doing it. *Don't ask,* Ma'am, just tell him."

An agitated, brief exchange brought a result Bora did not expect. "He says he's been selling not to the English, but to the Italians."

Italians this far north? It's odd, but you never can tell with Italians. They could be scouts as much as deserters. Very odd, but ten to one I'll be able to buy information from them.

"Wait," Frances Allen added to her translation. "Kyriakos wants to know how come you know what the Germans know."

"Say I ran away from them. If he takes us to the Italians, or tells us how to get there, he can have another banknote and two packs of cigarettes."

"*Two* packs? One's plenty."

"Whatever."

The negotiation was quick and inconclusive. "Says he'll think about it and let you know later, when it gets light."

Risky or not, there was nothing else to do for close to two hours. Between now and then, Bora and Kyriakos sat keeping an eye – the right word as far as the goatherd was concerned – on each other. The boy eventually lay on his side and fell asleep. Frances Allen, too, began to nod after a while, so Bora told her she could retire. She mumbled, "Okay, wake me up if you need me, or something," and curled up where she was, like Kyriakos' son.

Bora, on the other hand, had no difficulty staying awake, considering how he could be shot at any time, by Kyriakos or someone else barging in. There was no guarantee they were facing a simple herdsman: he and Allen could have already fallen into the orbit of Satanas' band; Satanas might have been informed and be already on his way, with or without his British comrades-in-arms. Awake but less than clear-minded, Bora couldn't rouse himself past regret for having got himself into a trap. *What was I thinking? A whore used to live here. Every male around knows the way to this hut. I turned so many corners in the labyrinth, I couldn't retrace my steps if I wanted to. There's no magic ball of yarn to follow to the exit.* If the mongrels resumed their barking at *mesa pharangi*, or the watchdog tied to the *mandra*'s door started howling, it would be an advance sign that strangers were approaching. As it would if the crickets and other insects chirping outside went suddenly quiet. *If they capture me, whether they kill me or not, I'll have failed in my task. And I won't see Moscow again, won't ride into Russia. I'll have thrown away my war in this godforsaken place. No. No. I wish it were godforsaken – there are gods and spirits here, or else I wouldn't have seen Remedios looking down from the window.*

An hour dragged by, and nothing happened. *I am twelve,* Bora thought, *when General von Fritsch becomes head of our Military District IV, Dresden. I am twelve and only two years ago one American dollar was worth 4.2 trillion German marks. I am twelve, and secretly weep for joy when for the first time my stepfather calls me "son" in public.*

The musky odour of unwashed bodies, sleepers' breath, women's odour stagnated in the hut; a reek less identifiable – but one could well imagine its source – rose out of the *porne*'s bedding bundled against the wall. Kyriakos' seeing eye, unmoved, unblinking, made the weary Bora guess at one point that he was able to sleep open-eyed like a fish. Sitting cross-legged put a strain on his back, but he couldn't relax for fear of dozing off. As it was, surreal, bizarre images crossed his mind, of maze-like trails, bottomless wells, of the goatherd and his watchdog mangling and blinding each other in a fury. *I am twelve, and hear at home that Herr Hitler will ruin the Fatherland.*

No external threat materialized. The only distraction overnight was provided when the old woman stirred in the back, stepped through the room like a ghost and went outside, hitching up her black skirts. In the murmur of crickets, there followed the trickle of urine just past the threshold, and her deep sigh.

FRIDAY 6 JUNE

As God willed, the low door looking east took on the colour of mother-of-pearl. No *Kapetanios* Satanas, no wild cries, no shooting far or near. Leaving behind the three sleepers and the nearly exhausted lantern, Kyriakos stood, leaned the shotgun against the wall, and preceded Bora out of the hut. There he boldly pissed in the morning breeze while Bora – aching with the long immobility – lit himself a cigarette. Strong and foul-tasting, it was what it took to wake a man up. When Kyriakos drew near and grabbed the pack, Bora pretended to resist, before slowly relinquishing the hold on the plain container for mixed "oriental and non-oriental tobaccos".

Unable to communicate, they smoked side by side under the almond tree, Kyriakos holding the straw-coloured pack to his good eye, Bora looking at the far triangle of the sea glittering like foil. The eastern mountain range delayed the sunrise, but the sky around it was on fire. How did the poets ever come up with "rosy-fingered Dawn"? If dawn had hands, they were ablaze. In the warm light, Kyriakos' scarred face was both brutal and miserable. Wasn't it a goatherd who betrayed Ulysses on his return, siding with the suitors? And wasn't there a muscular beggar at the palace, who wrestled with the disguised hero over food scraps? In hand-to-hand combat, this large and apparently sluggish man would be a dangerous adversary, even for Bora.

Minutes later, hearing Frances Allen's and the old woman's voices inside, Bora took out the compact Esbit cooker, little more than a metal reverse trestle that half-opened on its hinges, and used fuel tablets to build a brisk fire in it. He was stirring instant coffee in hot water when his tousled travel companion emerged from the hut.

"Morning."

"Morning."

"How do you feel?"

"Rotten. Look, I've got to *go*. Can I have my sandals?"

Bora handed her a full cup. "Sorry, no. Later, when you're done."

She snatched the cup, gulped down its contents and tip-toed barefooted around the hut, muttering something that distinctly sounded to Bora like "goddamned Kraut".

As for Kyriakos, he was thoroughly fascinated by the fuel tablets, but wouldn't touch the German brew, so different from Greek-style coffee. His barely-awake son, scratching and stretching, was sent lurching down the goat trail to the *mandra*, presumably to fetch coffee grains and feed the watchdog.

The shotgun was once more at the herdsman's side when Frances Allen returned from her reduced grooming. She found her sandals by the fire, and before resuming her interpreter's duty, she grumpily buckled them on.

Bora was impatient. "He promised to let me know when it got light, and it's light now."

"It doesn't work that way around here, Captain."

In fact, the conversation went nowhere until the younger man brought the essentials to prepare Greek coffee, and the thick liquid filled very small cups. Except for Bora, they all drank, and Frances Allen began to translate.

"Kyriakos says he doesn't know if you're English or not. He believes you're running away from your own, 'whoever they are', or you wouldn't be looking for the Italians. He doesn't care about that. He doesn't care what any of us do, English, Italians, Germans. We're all *frangoi* and due to leave sooner or later. He says the wild goats will live in Crete long after all the *frangoi* are gone. Only the mountains will last longer than wild goats in Crete."

Bora seethed. "That may be his philosophy, but if he doesn't believe I heard from the Germans that he trades with the English, tell him I saw a can of English food near his *mandra* yesterday. Tell him I want to reach those who gave it to him."

"He says a German soldier gave him canned food in exchange for his cheese."

It was possible: enemy depots had been raided right after the landing. "Well, damn it. We're back to square one. What about the Italians he deals with – how do I find them?"

Kyriakos listened to Frances' question. On his haunches by the small fire, he'd maintained an image of passivity, bordering on inertia, throughout the exchange so far. But when his son, who'd been idly standing behind him, leaned over and reached for the cigarette pack, in an unforeseeable reaction he surged to punch the boy in the face, so hard that knuckles met cheekbone with a cracking sound. The boy spun around and – big as he was – fell flat on the ground.

Bora had been refilling his cup. Scalding his fingers with hot water and reaching for his pistol all happened in one fluid move. Right arm outstretched, he sprang up in a firing stance. He saw a bloody froth bubbling from the boy's mouth where he lay, between the fire and the almond tree, but that he was alive and coming to.

"Christ, if he does it again I'll open fire on him."

The line between Allen's brows deepened like a cut. "You'll do no such thing. You don't step between father and son in this country."

"If he does it again, I'll open fire on him."

Notwithstanding the slow return of the Browning to its holster, Kyriakos acted as if Bora's anger escaped him, or could be safely ignored. He resumed his slack seated position. Like a deflating bag, packed until now with hot air, he relapsed into stillness as though nothing had happened. But his inaction was no longer believable, and neither was Bora's self-control.

Nothing was said about the incident. Mortified more than hurt, the big-boned boy crawled under the tree, where the old woman wiped his face with the hem of her skirt. "That's the last time he takes me by surprise," Bora warned. He was unready for his own wrath, as if frustration about his task (and Waldo Preger) were spilling over to other areas of his life. "Will this beast tell me where the Italians are, or do I have to shoot the three of them?" Frances Allen stared at him.

"Did you hear me? *Get him to tell me!*"

She showed no more surprise than she had when Kyriakos had struck his son, except that she grew pale under her tan.

Bora read what passed through her mind, and her hesitation, her fear infuriated him. "*Get him to tell me where the Italians are.*"

She picked her words as slowly as she'd just tiptoed barefoot on the mountainside.

"They keep moving along the slope of the mountain that looks to the south-west, but camp in a place called Meltemi."

8

"Cripes. Cripes. I think you're just waiting to get what you want from me, before you *do* it."

It took Bora a good hour after they left Kyriakos to convince Frances Allen that he had no intention of killing her. He was far from sincere, but pleasant and trained enough to appear persuaded of his own words. "That's nonsense, Ma'am. Back there, you understand that I couldn't afford not to react strongly. He struck the boy without motive, was armed, and had to know we wouldn't be so meek as to be next."

"*We?*"

"Well, you and I are together in this. And you're from a neutral country; Germany has no quarrel with you."

"Which is why you locked me up."

"I assure you, that was because of your husband."

She shook her head and avoided looking his way, but inwardly leaned towards believing him, Bora knew. It was possible that she was used to quick-tempered men. Didn't her husband keep an arsenal at home? As for him, his embassy work had taught him to layer a certain polite stolidity over his orders, to let nothing escape he didn't want to. Friendliness and impenetrability were his daily bread in Moscow, and today, in front of the American, stood an attaché's assistant as much as the boy with the secret skeleton key.

When they stopped to fill their canteens where a spring-fed cement tank brimmed with water, she'd already regained her insolence. "Don't you go thinking I was really scared back there. I criss-crossed this island for fifteen years by myself." She spoke with a cigarette in her mouth, while using his soap to lather her neck. "And you won't be the one who gets my goat."

"I'm not familiar with the expression."

"It means 'irritates'."

Frances Allen was studying him, and Bora let her. He had everything to hide, which was like saying he had nothing to hide. He stared at the broken reflections in the water, where suds created milky eddies. He looked away because the wetness let the hard knobs of her nipples show through the cloth. The place indicated by Kyriakos was distant, unmarked on the map. They'd climbed for the past hour, and were supposed to reach higher: very slow trekking, and circuitous as well. This tank, trough or more likely what remained of a wash house serving forsaken hamlets and huts, was the largest body of fresh water he'd seen in inland Crete. Bora felt his whole body thirsting and uncommonly sensitive, an after-effect of his lack of sleep, or tension. He fought the troubling, fragmentary recollection that had surfaced in his mind when he and Kyriakos had confronted each other in the *porne*'s hut. *I am twelve, and hear at home that Herr Hitler will ruin the Fatherland.*

His travel companion's attitude had changed ever since the morning incident, losing none of its hostility but becoming more duplicitous, astute. There she was, someone's plain cousin. Marrying a Greek peasant, it went without saying against her family's wishes, seemed to have given her a dual nature, making her into a hybrid creature like a centaur or a faun. All considered there was a slight danger under it all, in that wildness. From now on, she might dare him, or show him how far she'd strayed from bourgeois rules. A box whose tight locks have snapped lures more than a lidless box. Bora felt safe in his wife's love, reciprocated. But what if Frances Allen tried seduction? Her middle name *was* Liberty.

"I thought you were looking for a Briton," she said, carefully holding the cigarette with her wet fingers and blowing out smoke. "What good are Italians to you?"

Bora kept his eyes on the water. "They're much more like Greeks than we are. 'Same face, same race', says *Epitropos* Kostaridis. They 'get along'. You've taught me that by now; those we left word with along the way – even those who wouldn't give us information – have started a grapevine. I rather think the British will find us if I don't find them, and the Italians might know about it." He handed her the lighter, stored his sunglasses in his rucksack and calmly unbuckled his holster belt. "Are you done tidying up?"

"Yes."

"Good. Step back."

Bunching belt and holster in his raised left hand, Bora jumped clear into the tank, and sat soaking in water up to his neck. He needed to lower his body temperature, and if she took it as a worrisome hint that he was aroused (he wasn't), it would serve her right.

Frances Allen finished her cigarette with her back turned to him. When he left the improvised bath in his drenched clothes, she was sitting on a rock, gloomy under her visored cap. "Here." Without looking, she tossed the lighter his way, and Bora promptly caught it. "We had better start again."

Cotton dried quickly in the morning heat. Bora only had to change his wringing wet socks to keep them from sloshing inside his ankle boots. He noticed Frances Allen kept a closer eye on him but could not judge whether she was alarmed or intrigued. Two hours after stopping at the water tank, they came to a particularly bare and windy crest, without trails or tracks. If their next goal was called Meltemi, like the sea wind, it stood to reason that it would be buffeted by strong currents, and have a northern or north-eastern exposure. The breeze was therefore welcome as a pointer in the right direction.

Rounding the mountainside according to Kyriakos' directions, however, the wind fell the moment they reached a more sheltered, level area. Strewn with pottery shards and sun-dried tiles, it bore traces of razed constructions, and was edged towards the valley by the stump of a stone wall, no higher than three courses. Frances Allen, in a tersely communicative mood, called it the Upper Palace. "One of the most elevated Minoan sites to date, John's work. I didn't realize you could reach it from this side."

Everything looked bright yellow when Bora removed his sunglasses. "I have seen this place before."

"When?"

"I'm not sure. As an illustration in Pendlebury's book, maybe."

She made a schoolteacher's sour face. "That's impossible. The site hadn't been excavated two years ago, when *The Archaeology of Crete* went to press."

"That may be, but I remember seeing that wall, just as it appears from where I'm standing. Unless..." Bora took out of his rucksack the photos developed by Kostaridis and glanced through them. "Ah, here. That's where I saw it." He showed a couple of prints to Allen, who seemed even less pleased.

"Where did you find these? We only started work here this spring."

"Really. Did you allow visitors to the site?"

"Well, we're in Crete, you don't see any fences around. Farmers and shepherds constantly rove the countryside, we can't keep them out."

"I meant other scholars."

"Not without invitation and hopefully not while we're not here. It wouldn't be collegial. Who gave you the pictures?"

Bora only said he'd got them in Iraklion, which was technically true. If Allen was telling the truth, both Savelli and Villiger could have flouted collegiality by coming by to snap photos of the site. He held the negatives against the light. The images of the Upper Palace were the first in the roll, a fact that potentially made a difference. It meant that, contrary to what Savelli had told Kostaridis, the film hadn't sat in its sealed container for more than two or three months at most. Did that qualify as "a long time"? Bora handed the remaining prints to the American. "What can you tell me about the rest?"

She looked. "This was taken at Agios Silas. This one – Arkhanais, for sure. Tavernais, where the Italians were digging. The shard deposit near Kanli Kastelli. Hey, here's *my* work: the Butterfly Double-Axe Tomb, my best find last April. I didn't even let John photograph it! The photos of the artefacts – I can't judge the exact provenance of figurines, ewers and seals: Cretan material, but they could come from the antiquarian market or illegal excavations."

Tavernais. Wasn't Tavernais where Savelli bragged he'd been digging? *Did he suspect Villiger had photographed the site and planned to use it in his publications? It would explain why the Italian had been trying to secure this roll of film, though Villiger was well past plagiarism.* Bora dutifully pencilled the locations behind the images. "So you'd say all the photos were taken on this island?"

"Those of the sites at least. Who's the gal?"

"I was hoping you might tell me. Women always notice women."

"Because men don't, eh? No, I don't know who she is. Flashy for a Cretan."

"It seems she's a much-admired cabaret artist, Cordoval by name."

"Never heard of her. But I don't patronize nightclubs and such." A closer, tight-lipped look followed on Allen's part. "Is she a natural blonde?"

"Good question. I'm wondering if you recognize the terrace she's standing on."

"Somewhere at Palèkastro near Iraklion. That's Kastelli Hill in the background. Why?" So, Kostaridis – who should be familiar with the place – had been reticent about it, or lied outright. Bora looked up the town on his map and pencilled "Gulf of Iraklion" behind the photograph. If Signora Cordoval had recently visited Crete, there were interesting implications. Even a year ago, before the start of the war in Greece, it would have been dangerous for a Jewess to go about, all the more since she was popular across the archipelago. Standing in plain view, too... He studied the image, an unlikely portrait among shots of antiquities.

Somehow, the calling card with details about her family reached Villiger, and ended up in his deposit box. What does it mean, and does it have anything to do with... ? Anyhow, either Signora was briefly in Iraklion and is now gone – and Kostaridis doesn't know about it, or knows and didn't tell me – or she's still in Crete, under an assumed name and powerful protection.

It was a long shot, but what if her patron were the well-connected Villiger himself? She was a blonde specimen, after all – she could *pass.* The obvious runner-up was Professor Savelli, if they had made up and he'd incidentally let her keep the contended family brooch. *The picture isn't posed, however: she doesn't seem aware she's being photographed.* Bora put away the photos except for the woman's snapshot. *What if Villiger took the photo, but his interest in her was anything but scholarly? Witness the family details penned on her calling card, plus the blank Aryanized visas, money routed through Jewish-owned banks in Rhodes... Damn. Damn.*

"Mrs Sidheraki, would you say that these flowers in the picture are hyacinths?"

Frances Allen impatiently glanced at the image again. "They are common hyacinths. If you have any more idle questions, please ask at once."

"Where do we go from here?"

"Up."

Place of Hyacinths. Wasn't it what the Turk called his residence near Iraklion? Common or not, they fill the terrace where Signora is standing... Forget Villiger and Savelli. If that's the case, Rifat Bey's missing watchdog might not be missing at all, but protecting another house, where a dangerous lover is kept!

They left the site walking side by side, with the American indulging in the archaeologist's habit of searching the ground with her eyes. But it was Bora who picked up a fragment that he showed on the palm of his hand.

All the plaster-faced bit of masonry had painted on was an eye. A fierce animal eye, limned by two wavy lines in dark blue.

"It's the eye of a bull or a Minotaur," she said, giving it back. "Frescoed images of the sacred bulls flanked entryways once. Their images stayed long after the palaces fell into disuse and were forsaken. Those who came later were superstitious, didn't understand, feared them: the painted guardians made taboos out of the ruined mazes of corridors and rooms. Newcomers didn't dare enter for ages."

"What should I do with this?"

"Leave it there or keep it; we'll never find the rest." She stepped ahead of him to resume the climb. "Mediterraneans believe eye amulets are good luck."

Bora half-smiled. "Ah, I need good luck."

"Pocket it, then."

*

The ascent grew demanding, along a steep ridge in full sun, where lack of vegetation forced the climbers to grope for a hold among rocks not always anchored and steady. Bora let his companion precede him, ready to catch her in case she lost her grasp. Despite her sandals, however, Frances Allen hardly missed a move. Years of practice across the island gave her a goat-like instinct for the smallest ledge and foothold. Her small, sturdy figure kept moving, now sideways, bent double, now on all fours as the crest required. Clearly, out of spite or pride, she fought her own weariness.

Bora kept up. He didn't mean to stare, but when a coin-sized dark stain formed and began to widen on the seat of her dungarees, embarrassment nailed his eyes to it. She had to be fully aware she was bleeding heavily, but there was no pausing where they were. Bora forced his attention on the rock wall in front of his face, to avoid being seen to be gawking in case she looked over her shoulder. The only relief was that the strong wind had subsided, either because of the hour or because a stony vertical brow to their right protected this side of the range.

The painted masonry piece in Bora's pocket pressed against his thigh; it caused a sharp throb that had the power of distracting him a little from his fatigue, and kept his senses acute. When the faint sound of an aeroplane engine bounced back from the mountain, he caught it at once, although it was difficult to understand where it originated. Turning as much as he could, he faced an overly bright sky that tricked the eye. It stretched seemingly empty, and by the time the aircraft appeared, it would be too close to avoid being spotted by the pilot. To Bora, it sounded like a small reconnaissance plane, which could only be German or Italian – more likely the first. Still, on this errand he had no desire to be noticed from the air, not even by his own comrades.

The slope he and Allen were labouring on offered no protection. Only a squat, wind-tossed pine tree to their right, perilously clinging to a rocky shelf and misshapen by the strong mountain winds. Bora called out and gestured to the American to move diagonally and precede him under its leafy head. Haste is no friend of precision. She stumbled, nearly lost her footing, reached the broken shade barely in time to avoid Bora's landing on her.

A Fieseler Storch emerged from the blue like a pin pricking through fabric. It was German, and judging from its slow banking across the face of the mountain, searching for something or someone. Odds were, it had taken off from Iraklion's airfield, acting on someone's report. Bora must admit he and his companion could have been spotted by a German patrol down in the valley, too far away to intervene directly but fully equipped to pass the information on to pilots due for their daily rounds. The impervious nature of the Cretan hinterland demanded aerial reconnaissance, often in concert with scouts on the ground.

I don't need to run into other Germans at this time, Bora thought. *I don't want to give explanations, and having them around would scare off those I'm going through all this trouble to meet.* "Please stay down, Mrs Sidheraki," he warned her. "The closer to the trunk, the better."

If Frances Allen wondered why he was dodging his compatriots, she didn't ask. Busy digging through her canvas bag, she nodded, distractedly. As soon as the aeroplane, which was right above them, veered away to start another circle, she said, "Turn your back. I need to change."

"All right, but keep in mind it's got dorsal armament. It could pick you off from up there."

"I won't leave this spot if you turn your back."

"Keep talking, then. I want to make sure you're near."

Bora crouched facing away from her. He was tempted to think that at this point he could probably continue on his own even if she got away. Overhead, the scrawny aeroplane, more insect-like than similar to its stork namesake, braved the updraught with careful bucks of its square-tipped wings. Dancing on its sturdy landing gear, it all but hovered in place, drowning out the American's voice off and on as she recited, "Four score and seven years ago, our fathers brought forth…"

Bora listened. *The damned Texan is intrepid, a bigger headache for me than if she were the fainting type. If she had something physically attractive about her, I could offset my dislike with the indulgence we men dumbly end up feeling for good-looking pests. Not so, and her manners don't help either.*

Light and wieldy enough to sweep low, the Storch plied the width of the slope. At one point, it seemed to change its mind and give up the search. It sheered behind the vertical brow of the mountain and its rasping hum changed pitch, grew fainter.

"We are met on a great battlefield of that war…"

Behind Bora's back, Frances Allen must have moved about or changed position, because some rocks were dislodged and went rolling down. From the corner of his eye, Bora saw a dust trail form as they cascaded, displacing more and more pebbles. At that moment, the aeroplane re-emerged from behind the stony brow. Lower still, it wove a figure of eight that allowed the pilot to draw near and observe the crumble of rocks.

"The brave men, living and dead, who struggled here… Shit." Allen's earthy comment reached Bora before the sound of the swerving engine blotted it out. "Shit, has he seen us?"

"He may have. Why couldn't you stay put?"

"Go to hell, I'm doing my best."

"Are you decent? I'm turning now." Bora actually only half-turned. Evidently, the pilot's attention was up. He was suspicious, and might now be debating whether to have his gunner open fire on the lonely tree. An experienced rear gunner could well strike a target on the ground. Bora put down one knee to steady himself, pulled out the Browning and looked right and left for ideas. A tottering outcrop, an unfettered boulder could serve his purpose. Worse luck, the barren incline seemed solid except for the place Frances Allen had kicked loose. Visions of what a burst of cannon fire could do to their flimsy shelter sobered him considerably. In Poland, he'd driven on a carpet of body parts after roads had been strafed; fleeing civilians lay torn to shreds, horses with bellies gutted by shrapnel kicked desperately in blood and dust. In that otherwise sweet September, whenever he could, he stopped to finish off the animals at least. He'd had to do it with human beings later, elsewhere. The sight stayed with him as a reminder of what war ought not to be, and is.

"...we here highly resolve that these dead shall not have died in vain."

While the Storch headed away to complete another round, Bora did spy a seam out in the open, the faintly distinguishable rim of a vertical cleft, where rain was likely to channel during thunderstorms. He waited for the aeroplane's pitch to rise enough to cover the report, and fired a single shot into the pebbly rim. Rocks detached, cannoned against one another like billiard balls, and started a slide that from the air would hopefully mimic a collapse caused by sound vibrations.

Twice the aeroplane shaved the area where the rocks kept tumbling. Bora sat back and felt he'd forever recall the glint of the cockpit, memorize the flash of black and white crosses and letters under the wings and on the fuselage. The dorsal gun did not rotate to seek a ground target as the Storch righted itself, made a wider circle, returned. Twice it repeated the same manoeuvre, but already the crew's interest had decreased, shifted toward searching further on, towards Mount Voskerò.

The buzzing figure-of-eight dance transferred over and beyond the top of that mountain before Bora resolved that he could breathe out and relax.

Frances Allen squatted with her back to the tree trunk, and was rinsing her hands with water from her canteen. She'd changed into a pair of loose khaki shorts not unlike those Bora wore, unbelted and reaching to the knee. She'd tightly bundled her stained dungarees and now stuffed them inside her bag.

Bora meant to act obliquely upon his embarrassment. He was on the verge of saying he regretted putting her through all this, but something told him he had better not show sympathy at this time.

"Give me the goddamn lighter." She spat at him. "I'm going to have a smoke right now and right here, whether you want it or not."

Bora handed her the lighter. "Those were Abraham Lincoln's words at Gettysburg, weren't they?"

"*Oh, screw you.*"

At midday, they were high enough to have a wide stretch of blue sea in view. The silent treatment was operative again; they stopped for the time needed to drink and munch on canned food, avoiding each other's face. Bora updated his diary. Their progress having brought them halfway around the mountain, once more a strong wind blustered against them. It accompanied them as they found and followed a narrow track specked with goat pellets, bending slightly downward and leading into a gully.

The passage was partly shaded even at midday. Fig trees and yellow-blooming spiny bushes lined it; young oaks filled its bottom. The impression was of unexpected wildness and seclusion. At one point of the track, just as unpredictably, the weather changed as the wind took a southerly direction. In minutes, clouds were racing above the travellers, a swift suspended vapour that trailed a wake close to the ground, like shredded fog or odourless smoke. Bora and Allen found themselves descending into circling whiteness, on unseen ground.

Meltemi is the breeze from Anatolia and it gives the place its name, but this is not a nor'easter. How strange – like Homer's kingdom of the winds, Bora thought. He sniffed the moisture that rose from below and felt sticky, like a spider's web on his face.

"It's somewhere around here," Allen grumbled at his side. "I don't know what to tell you; that's all Kyriakos reported."

Holding the folded map away from the wind, Bora scrutinized their general location, an area unnamed, unmarked but for the symbol of grottoes or caves.

What now? Calling out in Italian – or any language, for that matter – was imprudent. From a place like this echoes would carry far, to God knows whom. On the other hand, Kyriakos said the Italians moved about, so they might not be within earshot at the moment. And what sort of Italians would they be, anyway? Erring on the side of judiciousness was advisable. Bora balanced on the reduced trail to fish out of his pockets his shoulder boards, cap and identification disc, and retrieved the diary he'd already set at the top of his rucksack. "Please," he told Allen, "put these away for me for a while." Last, he moved his wedding ring from his right hand (where Germans wore it) to his left.

They were descending into an opaque funnel where nothing but an occasional leafy twig or fleeting rock formation surfaced from the fog. Villiger's world of bookshelves, racial categories and bloody death was remote from all this, although as the crow flies none of Bora's places on Crete – Ampelokastro, Sphingokephalo, Sinclair's cell, Kostaridis' office – were more than fifteen minutes away.

A sharp modulated whistle vibrated through the vapour like a needle, a warning signal if ever there was one. Its origin Bora located more or less at a forty-five degree angle above the trail, to his right, where nothing but a rock wall should be. A similar high-pitched sound answered it from below, as if the needle were threading back from an incline lower than the trail, at the bottom of the wooded gully where the fog thinned. Not for a moment would Bora have mistaken them for animal sounds. The next step took the travellers below the reach of the clouds, into a space where they became a suspended ceiling above them. Tapering rock walls pitted by holes and clefts, and moist-leafed shrubs encircled them. The simultaneous click of weapons from ledges all around revealed men who kept them under aim.

Long hair, unkempt beards: these weren't just soldiers who'd been on the lam for a week or two. The growth and filth of months were on them. Now, what would Italian soldiers – even deserters – be doing here in the mountains in this state, when they'd reached Crete *after* the Germans? Stared at, Bora stared. Homer's man-eating giants – what were they called, Laestrygonians? – came to mind, or the mythical guardians of Helios' cattle, fierce islanders such as Ulysses met once and again at his own risk, lying and bluffing his way through.

Something like a storm of cogged wheels clicked inside Bora, because he had to think fast, fast, figure out things in seconds flat. *If not Italians, who the hell are they, and why did the goatherd mistake them for Italians? They're not colonial troops fighting with the British, either; and they aren't Cretans.*

"*Atureu!*"

The voice, meant to halt him where he was, did more than that. 1937, different and merciless mountains. Bora felt a second heartbeat start to pulsate in his throat. "Jesus Christ," he said under his breath – in English or German, he wasn't paying attention, as he wasn't paying attention whether Allen heard him or not. Atureu? *"Atureu" is not Italian for "Stop there." And it's not Spanish, either. "No te muevas" would be Spanish. Remedios, is that what you were telling me without words, from your window at* mesa pharangi?

There had been, and there would be, many more occasions for him to risk as much as he did now, throwing himself headfirst into whatever it was that he didn't fully understand but had to be dealt with. *It can't hurt, and I'd do it even if it did.*

"*Salud!*" he called out.

Practised among leftists in war-torn Spain, the form of greeting was political, hence risky; tempered by the show of both unarmed hands, it would sound less provocative to a right-winger if misunderstood. There was a brief pause before the man who addressed him, still aiming the SM Lee-Enfield rifle but slightly pacified, asked in Spanish who he was.

Bora promptly said, "*Soy inglès, y ella es norteamericana.*" ("I'm English, and she's American"; he didn't know whether, as a Texan, Allen spoke Spanish or not. She did appear confused for the first time.) Thus far, he'd rightly guessed the men's political leaning: it remained to be seen whether communists or anarchists. It made a difference, since during the civil war they'd cut each other's throats in Barcelona. And their regional identity mattered too, as it often was an insult for a Basque or a Catalan to be considered a Spaniard, and vice versa. "*Ustedes son españoles? Vascos? Catalanes?*" Bora scrambled through what he recalled from having had soldiers from Catalonia among his men. "*Sou catalans? Jo no entenc català. Parleu castellà?*"

No answer. The men muttered to one another, remaining where they were, here and there on the rocky shelves like figures from a nativity scene. "*Entonces,*" a stocky fellow with the bluish beard of a Moor said in Spanish, "why aren't you with your fellow *ingleses,* and how have you come here?"

261

"I'm trying to reach my fellow Englishmen," Bora told them. "What do you want with us, then? And who is she?"

"*Quiero señas.*" Specifying he was only seeking directions, Bora was all too aware of the appreciative glances going Frances Allen's way. "*Està es mi mujer,*" he made up on the spur of the moment. "*Ya vivia en Creta. La llevo con migo porque està embarazada.*" He added he'd been taken prisoner by the Germans days earlier, and escaped by killing a guard, whose equipment he'd stolen. With a slow gesture, he unholstered the Browning by the grip and laid it on the ground at his feet.

The bluebeard hopped down to recover the pistol; he looked into Bora's rucksack and took out the first cigarette pack that met his fingers. The others kept their rifles levelled at the newcomers and ready to fire.

"*Per què es parla castellà? Por què hablas espanol?*"

Of course, they would ask how it was that he spoke Spanish. Determined to get his gun back one way or another, Bora found such a level of cool fabrication, he no longer felt the anxiety of a moment ago.

"I was in Aragon in '37," he began, telling the truth. All he had to do was to turn around his experiences and those of the enemy he'd fought over those many months and knew very well. "Above Teruel at Palo de la Virgen, on the Sierra de San Martin, among those of the man they called Felipe."

"*De veras?* Felipe who?"

"He was an American, Walton by name. Tall fellow, quick temper. We fought the fascists of Riscal Amargo. *Habia un alemàn con ellos.*" (Bora *was* that German, of course.) "Felipe held the line in the calle de Villanueva during the battle for Teruel."

Again, the men did not respond. They exchanged sentences in a language Bora identified as Catalan: which, as far as he could judge, meant they were most likely anarchists. Better that way; they were less inflexible than the Reds. They kept muttering, glancing at one another, and especially at Frances Allen. *Now she is experiencing how uncomfortable it is not speaking the language, not understanding whether what's being said has anything to do with you. And it's best if she doesn't know.* Bora shook his head, adding a philosophical consideration to his memories of Spain. "The Republic would have won, had there not been infighting."

Indefinite though it was, the statement called for comments, revealing of his counterparts' creed. Infighting and the settling of scores *had* weakened the leftist front, but a Third International communist would insist that a lesson had to be taught to deviationists, while an anarchist by contrast would curse the Stalinist repression.

Clever and suspicious, the Catalans anticipated his question. "Which side were *you* on?"

Bora thought briefly. *As an English volunteer it's unlikely I'd be a Stalinist; were they of that persuasion, they'd already have shot me if they had taken me for an anarchist. On the other hand, if they size me up as a member of the International Brigades, they could assume I was after all Stalin's fellow traveller.*

"I didn't wear a *boina negra*," he said.

The black beret was a badge of obeisance to Moscow. Bora was hoping his steady-eyed, nearly smiling countenance would convince them he was one of those idealistic strangers who'd simply dived into civil war to protect a progressive Spanish government against fascism. The Anglo-Saxons in the lot were seldom traditional communists: libertarian when not anarchical, they'd helplessly watched Spanish republicans demolish one another in ideological feuds. Typical enough, this disagreement on everything: didn't Kostaridis say that Frances' husband would never join Satanas' men? "I began at the Lenin Barracks in Barcelona," Bora boldly quoted from George Orwell's book on his Spanish experience, which he'd avidly read following the civil war. "I joined the militia to reach Teruel. We crossed the Ebro and laid siege around Belchite afterwards, but not under Lister."

The man who did most of the questioning was not the bluebeard, but a man whose facial hair was scant and fiery. Staring critically at Bora, he objected, "The militia, you say. You don't look like a member of Partido Obrero."

"Is there a specific way a member of the Workers' Party should look?"

"*Ya veremos*: do you know who the *Solidarios* are?"

"Buenaventura Durruti's men."

"And who killed Durruti?"

"He was murdered by the communists of PCE while fighting for Madrid. I wasn't in Spain at that time, but I heard that half a million marched at his funeral."

"Half a million *and more.*"

Durruti's death had embittered the struggle between anarchists and PCE communists, causing a bloodbath. Bora caught the ball in mid-air. "*Y ustedes son faistas?*" He meant "members of FAI," the Anarchist Federation of Catalonia.

They didn't say, and continued to sound him out. Having followed his Spanish stint with debriefing in Germany, and refined his study of the conflict at the War Academy, Bora acquitted himself credibly, careful not to be so precise and all-knowing as to seem to have learnt a part. No one asked his name, but that was not unusual. In Spain, Bora had fought as "Douglas", and everyone around him had been under some kind of cover or disguise.

These were fellows he'd shot at and had been fired on by in the misery of sub-zero winter and the blaze of summer, purely on ideological grounds, and as a Catholic. At twenty-three, being a Spanish Foreign Legion lieutenant was about as glorious as he could imagine. At Belchite as in Teruel, he'd been among the besieged, not the attackers; from Belchite he'd sneaked out with a few companions just before the city surrendered. It was easy to talk about common experiences of hardships; he only had to mind the way he described them, through the eyes of his own enemies of those days. It surprised him to find how much more they shared: idealism first of all, and fierce endurance.

Meanwhile, the bluebeard had presented the Browning to his red-haired companion, who appreciatively hefted it. "How come that you, an English monarchist, served the Republic in Spain?"

Bora rushed to mix truth and fiction. "Well, my mother's family is Scots: ask the Scots about English rule." *Yes. Yes. That's believable. Waldo Preger's resentment about social rank comes to mind, and how it affects his angry idea of the Fatherland.* "When your own country doesn't recognize your legitimate aspirations, you have a right to seek them elsewhere." *My Scots ancestors died against and for the King of England. You wonder what obstacles a hybrid like Lieutenant Patrick Krishnamurti Sinclair must have confronted in his own life and career, remaining stiff-backed and loyal to His Majesty.* "Her, too." Bora glanced at the frowning Allen. "Although she's American, she's also been seeking a purpose elsewhere."

"Why are you looking for the English, then?"

"I mean to take her where they are hiding, so she'll be safer."

"And where will you go afterwards?"

"I don't know. It depends on what the English say, or do." Which was true enough.

This seemed to satisfy the Catalans for the moment. The travellers were escorted to the bottom of the gully, where no wind or clouds reached. Here there was food, which the men offered in exchange for the cigarettes which they divided among themselves. Cold meat, honey, wine and Kyriakos' cheese came out. Rice milk, too. Bora shared soluble coffee and lemonade powder. Amused to be smoking what they took for stolen German Army tobacco, they laid out a comfortable place for the surprised Allen to sit.

"We're *faistas*," the fiery head told Bora. "Good thing you put down your gun, *camarada*, we'd have blown you away if you hadn't. What's happening on the island's north coast?"

Bora had no problem saying it was solidly in German hands.

"We keep an eye on the English," they told him, "but won't serve under them. We were among those who signed up back in Syria because we'd have to fight with the fascists if we stayed in the French Foreign Legion. But as far as we here are concerned, our fight is as much against English capitalism as against the fascists."

Without enquiring further, Bora understood. The Catalans were among the troops transferred by the British from the Middle East to the island at the end of 1940. Clearly, this handful had jumped ship the moment they'd had a chance, and now waited for the opportunity to fight for the revolution; never mind a war that didn't help proletarians. Altogether, the best possible comrades, unaware of what had gone on since, and ignorant of British units.

"Why don't you stay with us, *ingles*, and wait for the revolution?"

Bora nodded towards Allen, meaning his obligations to a wife. "*Debo cuidar de ella.*"

When he sat next to her and summarized how things stood, she looked up from her roast kid. "I might not know Spanish," she said irritably under her breath, "but I heard you, back there. Why did you say I'm embarrassed?"

"I didn't say you're embarrassed. *Embarazada* in Spanish means pregnant."

"Preg – what? What did you just *say*?"

"Look, Ma'am, I really don't want to discuss this or other matters, and I don't care whether you approve or not. I said it with good reason. These are men who deserted the French Foreign Legion. They aren't used to seeing women in knee-length trousers. They could get ideas. I don't know about you, but I don't need it."

She filled her mouth with food. "This is really *egregious*! I'm not pregnant and I don't plan on getting pregnant."

"You're ahead of me on planning, Mrs Sidheraki: I only plan to get back alive."

The time spent with the Catalans at Meltemi trickled like sand in an hourglass. Overhead, the breeze that spared the hideout tore to shreds what remained of the passing clouds, until a jagged cut-out of clear, gold-blue marked the sky under which seven men waited for the revolution to reach Crete. Bora resorted to all he'd observed about the British presence in and around Iraklion, staying credibly vague when it came to the Germans. "It cost them to take the island," he admitted. He was much more generous when it came to Spanish recollections: he spoke in detail of the Hill of Santa Barbara in Teruel as if he'd been among those surrounding it, not one of its reduced defenders. Although his side had won in the end, he spoke of his worst moments there in order to sound as glum as his listeners were about it. To them – and to Bora, too – this wasn't Crete any more. In the eyes of the men around him, it was that other land, fought over tooth and nail, lost and regained, and finally lost. To him, it was all that Spain had meant to him as a soldier and a very young man.

The Catalans didn't know where the closest Britons might be holing up. They did advise Bora to avoid Krousonas ("Where there are Greeks who shoot on sight, *quienquiera que sea*"). Although they didn't speak the local language, they understood from villagers that there was a chieftain called Satanas down there, who sided with the *ingleses*. All they knew was that a few injured Englishmen, some of them badly injured, were licking their wounds in a place they showed Bora on their crumpled map.

"*Se llama* Agias Irinis."

Bora was very interested in this. At last. It was not impossible that Powell might be among them; if not, army medics or local practitioners tending to the lot could be prevailed upon to give further directions. He learnt that peasants provided supplies for most of the runaways, an activity that made them into reliable couriers back and forth. Word of mouth travels rapidly, and Agias Irinis was definitely the next stop.

It took the Catalans two hours to trust Bora enough to send him on his way, although they wouldn't return his pistol until it was time for them to separate, and only because he left behind his Esbit cooker in exchange.

A stunning afternoon met the travellers at the mouth of the gully. Up there, the wind blew as fiercely as before; it ground the webbed leaves of the fig trees and bent the spiny bushes; southward, clear vistas stretched to other mountains and down towards the plain of Messarà, beyond which lay the Libyan Sea.

If she appreciated Bora's ploy to guard her from unwanted attentions, Frances Allen did not gratify him with a thank you. She handed him his things back, and listened as they walked to a summary of his conversation with the Catalans. "Agias Irinis is a common place name on the island. Which one are we speaking of?"

Bora showed on his map the general location he'd been pointed to.

"So it's not the nunnery south-west of Krousonas. There's another place by the same name higher up, about – here. Not easy to reach. I know of it because John Pendlebury built and outfitted a shed there, where we stored equipment and sat to draw during our spring campaigns."

"Remote, and with a roof over their heads. If they survived the hike, it stands to reason that wounded men would try to find shelter in such a place. Which way from here?"

"If you want to avoid Krousonas, we have to keep diagonally along this slope to that saddle, and then I have to figure it out." Bora must appear newly confident he could accomplish his task, because she hastened to take him down a peg or two. "And *who* are you going to pretend you are, this time?"

They'd come a short distance from Meltemi, and already the heat was oppressive. Bora watched the American defiantly blow the rebel curl off of her sweaty forehead, and let her wait for an answer. His lack of attraction for her was at risk of becoming rudeness: she only needed to push him half a step more.

"If and when I meet Powell, I'll identify myself as a German."

"Are you out of your mind?"

"As a German *with* an American hostage."

"You're out of your mind. If they don't buy it, we can both end up dead."

Bora, who preceded her, turned and stopped. His stare was unreadable behind the dark lenses, and so were his spare gestures, the slow precision of his words. "The moment you take me to Powell, you can go."

"You're doubly out of your mind." Looking up at him, her eyes were grey-blue, he noticed, incredulous and younger than the rest of her face.

"The fact is, ma'am, I'm in a hurry to wind this up. You slow me down. Killing you wouldn't appreciably improve my chances of getting back, so, unless you make me change my mind, off you go when I find Sergeant Powell."

"I've never been told I'm *not useful*."

"Well, I'm telling you now."

"You wouldn't have made it this far without me."

"I'm a resourceful fellow, I'd have managed somehow." Was it possible she felt so piqued by his evaluation of her that she had overlooked (or disbelieved) his promise to let her go? Bora resumed walking. He decided he would not inform her that her husband was a free man, and on the island. His small vendetta in letting her go was just that – keeping the detail to himself.

The detour needed to bypass Satanas' rebel stronghold more than doubled the travel time to Agias Irinis. Bora disliked the idea, but had no choice. As it was, some fifty minutes after leaving Meltemi, an incident occurred that could easily nullify his efforts so far.

A third of a mile or so away, between here and where, far below, Krousonas flickered with its white houses on its knoll, Bora caught a movement and then a worrisome sight. A single file of men was advancing from the right along the dirt road leading down to Krousonas. Against the patched, pale green of a deeply rolling landscape, they proceeded unhurriedly, at a lower altitude than Bora's, but each in full view of each other. Black *vragha* and the bristle of barrels on their shoulders promised nothing good. Used to looking for their herds across the mountainous grazing land, even without field glasses Cretan peasants could easily spot two travellers moving on higher ground. Bora recognized MAB 38 submachine guns from their perforated barrel jackets. He told Allen to keep down, and crouched so that his own khaki clothing would melt into the dryness around him.

Thirteen men. All he needed was for the American to attempt a getaway at this time, or call out to them. *Here and now, those must be Satanas' bandits. Only her husband's feud with the* kapetanios *would keep her from pulling a fast one. I have four-teen shots in the Browning, at the maximum precision range for a*

handgun: if she cries out and they see us, I'd have to hit all fourteen
targets to clear my path.

For now, she sat motionless, with legs drawn up and an unlit cigarette stuck to her lower lip, squinting in the direction of the men. Minutes passed as the line kept its deliberate pace, nothing but wind and heat separating it from the observers. The squad would eventually have to turn around a hairpin bend and lose sight of the slope before regaining it at a lower level, where the road scissored the rocky slope in the opposite direction. Meanwhile, any one of the men could at any time look up and to the left, and *see* them. Bora felt sweat lace his neck, but wouldn't so much as wipe it off. His aversion to being trapped, a cavalryman's habit of pursuing aggressively made him squirm inside. On the outside, he was stock-still. Sergeant Powell, hiding in the brook bed, must have felt the same helplessness before Waldo's paratroopers, and he hadn't even been armed.

The men did seem to be dawdling, the slow gait of either weariness or reconnaissance duty. Out of the corner of his eye, Bora kept watch on his travel companion. It was singular that not even at times like this did they develop any form of solidarity or closeness; only the pragmatic concurrence of behaviour that could allow both to escape danger. She stared at the line and moistened her lower lip with the tip of her tongue, pushing the unlit cigarette to the side of her mouth.

At one point, the last man in the row broke out, heading at a quicker pace to the front where the leader was likely to be. All stopped. *Worse luck, they've seen us.* Bora unlatched the holster and noticed immediately in his peripheral vision that Frances Allen stiffened in alarm.

A confabulation took place below. No alarm; the tail man seemed to be asking for a break, right where the entire squad could, by paying attention, see that they were not alone. Flasks or other water containers came out, were passed around. Rifles slid off shoulders.

Bora spoke under his breath. "When they huddle to drink, start moving slowly to your right, and for God's sake don't knock any pebbles downhill."

"What's to the right?" she whispered back.

"A slight bulge that'll keep us out of sight. Go."

Her first motion – it was awkward, sliding sideways in a sitting position, propping oneself on both hands – caused a loose stone to wobble under her sandal. Bora lunged to catch it with his foot before it started rolling down.

"*Sorry*. What do you expect?" she said, irritably.

In a laborious stretch, he reached for the stone and steadied it. "We have one minute or less: keep moving."

The new position, useful as it was, had the disadvantage of blocking the view of the road. Bora crawled on his belly to where he could observe the men by raising his head. Only when the squad resumed its journey and started down the next curve did he pull back and latch his holster. His anger at her clumsiness, bottled while a threat was imminent, risked fogging his lucidity.

And because it was too much of a risk to start an argument now, he closed himself into the hard-mouthed, hostile silence he'd resorted to as a boy with adults, namely his stepfather, whenever he felt wronged and still had to go along with it.

Before things grew better, they grew worse. Frances Allen lost her way in the admittedly wild sequence of crags and seamed ravines between Mount Voskerò and the other peaks. They struggled up and down chaotic, repetitious passages that became indistinguishable as the afternoon advanced. Twice they hiked past the same small monument to some massacre by the Ottoman Turks. A dilapidated, ghostly hamlet marked the place, and he wondered why any army would care to come this far to kill peasants. *But* we *do it, don't we,* Bora told himself. *We did it here in Crete, perhaps in Ampelokastro as well.*

It became obvious as daylight began to wane that they would not reach Agias Irinis before dark. "There it is, up there." As a means of consolation, Frances Allen pointed to a cliff still bathed in orange light. "If we hadn't gone all around Krousonas, we'd have reached it already."

Bora had to bite his tongue. "How long will it take, from here?"

"Another hour, hour and a half."

"All right, we'll stop, then."

Below, and in view of, Agias Irinis, 7.09 p.m. I can see why *chaos* in Greek also means "deep valley, abyss". They must have been looking into a place like this when they invented the word. It's only understandable that the tales of southern brigands we read as children keep echoing in my mind now that we're out of reach of the squad. I imagined them dark and hairy in those days, and weren't the Catalans dark and hairy, or Satanas' black-trousered men? It's the close of the second day out, and it feels like ages since I left Iraklion, not to speak of Moscow. Agias Irinis is at hand! With the mind's eye, I can see Powell up there, unaware that his role as a witness is about to be revived. But I can also see the blood-spattered walls of Ampelokastro, worthy of a Greek tragedy yet banal. I see Rifat Bey, rid of his despised neighbour, readying to buy his property for a song. He counts money, pets his ferocious dogs. Kostaridis sits somewhere and wonders whether he'll have to change his socks one of these days. It was he who mentioned Satanas and Krousonas to me, and made sure the cobbler escaped before I could ask him for directions. I see Waldo Preger anticipating a medal that reads "Crete" on it, and Lieutenant Sinclair, whose entire life and career are determined by his crossbreed nature as much as by his loyalty to the Empire. Does he consider it unjust, or is he proud of being who he is? If I pry into the distance, my mind's eye glimpses Major Busch guzzling Afri-Cola in his Lublin exile. At the edge of it all, I can make out NKVD chief Lavrenti Pavlovich Beria, impatient for his Dafni and Mandilaria wine...

"Do you have any cigarettes left?"

Bora looked over from the diary page. "I'm down to two packets. You're getting one, and that's it."

"One cigarette, or one pack?"

"One ten-pack, and that's it."

"Same price as the last one?"

"I don't recall charging for the last one."

She smiled a little. "I *talked* to you, didn't I?"

Bora was on the point of blurting out that he wasn't so desperate for conversation. Instead, he retrieved the pack and tossed it to her as he would to an army colleague, with a certain familiar impoliteness. *She'll wait until I finish my entry and then she'll start chatting. Which I actually don't mind. After all, optimism aside, I have as many chances of – how does she put it? – "ending up dead" in the next few hours as I do of completing my task.*

The place where they camped was a rugged ravine bottom, wider than a river gorge, much narrower than a valley. Evening shadows filled it, lending a lilac tinge to the air. (Maggie Bourke-White's blooms, far away in Moscow!) Soon it would degrade into purple, and finally to a leaden grey. High in the pale remnant of sky overhead, a single cargo plane threaded through space like a bright meteor.

There was water at the low point of the boulder-strewn ravine, a stingy run smothered by grass and reeds which Bora surveyed before allowing Frances Allen to go there and wash. Vegetation granted her some privacy, but no practical chance of sneaking away. When she returned, her dripping hair was a rat's nest of curls, and the blouse – rinsed and worn as it was – clung to her breasts.

"Can I have a smoke?"

Although it was too dark even to reread, Bora kept his eyes on the vanishing lines of his diary as he handed her the lighter.

"There's an outcrop in the Texas Hill Country called Enchanted Rock," she said, "where I used to hike with my father. All granite, bald. It smells dry and clean like this place."

There she goes, paying for the cigarettes. "Oh, yes?" Bora meticulously smoothed the blotting paper over his completed diary entry, but would not look up.

She neared the tip of her cigarette to the flame, and laid the lighter where he could recover it without touching her. "Yes. You may or may not know how it is growing up with a soldier for a father: etiquette, rank, the things you're expected to do and especially those you're not. Keeping up the stupid discipline at home as at the army camp, dress code and all."

"I have an idea." Bora put away the cloth-bound book and sat so as not to face her. "Mine is a military family as well."

"But I bet we had a very different upbringing: I didn't grow up in Berlin."

"I didn't grow up in Berlin either."

"Then let's say you weren't raised in Texas, by Texan pioneers."

"That doesn't mean I don't know the frontier, or what borders look like."

"Well, France and Belgium aren't Old Mexico."

Memories flowed. Her words, meant to kill time, or to distract him, or to allay her own fears, primed the irresistible time machine this island held in its heart. Blandly at first, Bora became interested in what they were saying. "France and Belgium are nowhere near where we live," he objected. "When we summered in East Prussia, we had borders all around: Lithuania past the Russ River, and the Polish frontier surrounding us from the Rominte Plain to Marienwerder, Marienburg and the other strongholds of the Teutonic Knights. Westward, the Polish-held Danzig Corridor separated us from the motherland."

Memories flowed and had to be cauterized, like a cut vein. What Bora did not say was that his stepfather refused to cross the contended strip of land. The family had to hire a boat from Kolberg or Stolpmünde to Pillau. Or else, averse as he was to fliers and aircraft, the general would pack wife and boys on a train and fly over "the damned Poles". Nor did Bora add how, during the Great War, invading Russians overran the estate. The general still kept on the wall a map of the Trakehnen countryside printed by the Czar's Army General Staff, as a reminder that Poland and Russia were the enemy. Bora only spoke of borders in general. "And what about your family?"

"Well," she sighed, "there's one of the Alamo patriots on Father's side. Mother's from New Braunfels in the Texas Hill Country: a Grinke, and friends with the Nimitzes and the Hohmanns."

"They're German names."

"Don't fool yourself. Most of the Hill Country is, but by name only, and maybe by the patois the old folks still talk. Father served at Fort Sam Houston in San Antonio with the First US Volunteer Cavalry that gathered there before invading Cuba in '98 – Teddy's Terrors, you know, the Rough Riders. Saw action under Colonel Leonard Wood; was at Peking in 1901 and fought the Spanish in the Philippines a year later. A regular American hero."

Dusk made it safe to sit in the company of a woman who buttons her blouse over her naked torso. Bora turned to her, stretching his legs. "There's much to be said for having an officer-rank father."

"Do you think so? In 1916, the war hero took me 200 miles by train to watch a lynching. Whose? Oh well, he was a young Negro called Jesse Washington, accused of murdering and raping a white woman. You've never seen pictures of it? The 'Waco Horror' was attended by thousands. He admitted to the crimes, and Mayor Dollins smelt re-election if he just let the mob do as they pleased. So, they dragged the fellow out of jail and beat him with anything they could lay their hands on. Then they castrated him, poured coal oil on him and cut off his fingers so he couldn't climb the chain that held him over a slow fire. Oh, yes. Charred bits of his body were sold as souvenirs afterwards, and ladies bought postcards of the scene. Oh, sure, it was much criticized as well as defended throughout the south and the US. As far as my old man was concerned, white Texans aren't to be messed with, and 'let it be a lesson anyways' for a rebellious teenager like me. Wasted breath. I hung over my bed a photo of Elizabeth Freeman of the NAACP, a white woman who took on the Lone Star State by reporting on a Negro's lynching."

"I wasn't aware there were lynch mobs in Texas as late as 1916."

"What do you mean? The last one was eleven years ago." She extinguished the consumed butt of her cigarette before tossing it into the dry grass. "That's why as soon as I had the chance I applied to and was accepted by Syracuse University, to get as far as possible from home. After good old 'Cuse and New York State came France. After France, Italy, then Greece. Father can keep his retirement ranch in Stonewall with all his Longhorns, the 'Sunday houses', Enchanted Rock, the German patois and the old Comanche trails. I don't forgive a wrong either, and I'm never going back."

Bora played with the wedding band on his right forefinger. He did not voice his reaction to what she said, but felt that in a way he, too, was "never going back", something he wouldn't share with her or anyone else: the secret world, the closely guarded skeleton key.

"What's a Sunday house?"

She took off her sandals. "A small residence ranchers built in town so they could spend the weekend and piously go to church."

"I suppose that's what your parents had in mind for you."

"Precisely. Why couldn't I be a good girl and stay close to home, as my father wanted? Why wouldn't I marry one of his younger colleagues, and keep house as the good officer's wife Mother had always been? Why did I go east and *study*, of all things? Studying never helped a woman get a husband, in Father's mind." She slipped off her socks and began to massage the arch of her right foot, with strong kneading motions. "He didn't know his younger colleagues had taken me to bed ever since I was fifteen, and if I didn't lose my virginity until later, it was only because I didn't go all the way with them, but did everything else. Does that shock you?"

"No, no." The only thing that surprised Bora was the flow of her words. *She is afraid. Afraid of me, of what could happen to her. Talking builds a barrier against fear.*

"I'd left home long before leaving Texas. Not that I didn't feel guilty about it – I did. But when I first came to Crete ten years ago, the scales fell from my eyes. It was like being born a second time, into a world where everything had more colour, more sound, more taste to it. Still, it took me a whole year before I realized that a colonel's daughter could go barefoot, pee behind a bush, dispose forever of petticoat and hat." (And not only those, Bora thought.) "In Crete I could do things the free and large way. Eat large without worrying about my figure, drink large, do without all those dumb things even we 'free girls' in college back home hung on to, like flirting to get a fellow's attention. Everything is natural here. It's corny to say, but in Crete you eat, you make love, you die."

"Forgive me, but that's a rather romantic delusion of what life is, on this island or anywhere else."

"How would you know? I bet your female relatives drink their tea with their little finger sticking out."

Bora was amused. "I wouldn't say so. Great-grandmother Carrick was a middle-aged widow when Graf Zeppelin taught her to fly, and died in Katmandu at nearly ninety years of age. 'A woman must be able to converse with the crown prince and preserve fine pickles.' That was her motto. Women in my family look sweet but do what they want."

"Maybe." She was sinking into the darkness, disappearing; her voice came as if disembodied. "*You* don't look like you know what freedom is. You're all spick and span and ramrod, conversing in your first-rate English as you converse in your first-rate German. Don't you think war will end up ruffling you?"

"I hope it does more than ruffle me, frankly. But in the dispute between Apollo and Dionysus, Mrs Sidheraki, you'll excuse me if I choose order over irrationality."

She started to massage her left foot. "Does your wife agree?"

"My wife is exactly like me."

"Ooh, I bet you have fun."

"Be sure, my wife and I have more fun than you'd imagine."

And Dikta is nearly young enough to be your daughter, was on the tip of Bora's tongue, where it stayed.

There was a pause, and then low, throaty laughter on her part. "Are you offended?"

"You couldn't *possibly* offend me, Ma'am."

"Come, give me a light and say something about yourself. Didn't you have a place like Enchanted Rock in your childhood?"

Bora did not respond at once. She smoked, and the tip of burning tobacco was like a winking red eye in the gathering dark.

"Well," he chose to say in the end, "when I was twelve, one day my brother Peter and I got it into our heads to ride to a place called Serpenten, for no other reason than the name fascinated us."

"Serpenten as in 'snakes'?"

"Right. From the Trakehnen train station you could go north and cross the highway. Leaving the great turf beds of East Prussia to your right, you'd then take any of the lanes intersecting along the banks of the Rominten. We didn't want to waste time, so we followed the route to Dalneitschen and cut across the field past the crossroads, because there was no track leading west on that side. Where the woods began, the track began again, and we reached the few large farms, estates and country homes that made up the village. It goes without saying our parents didn't know where we were. Peter felt safe because he was with me, and I just never felt lost. What a disappointment. In Serpenten, fabulous name notwithstanding, there wasn't much to do. So we decided to take a detour to the river bank. It was then an easy bike ride down the country road to Szirguponen, and along the Rodupp Canal back home."

"Tongue-twister place names aside, is that all?"

"That's all."

"It's not much of a story."

It was all Bora was willing to say. In truth, as he and his brother had lazily sat in the grass at Serpenten, out of the blue – having just studied the geological eras at school – he'd lightly commented, "One day this place will no longer exist." Peter, who was tender-hearted those days, burst out crying at the words. Martin made things worse by adding, with a wickedness he didn't know he had, "One day *we*'ll no longer exist, and neither will our parents and our horses and everything." By which time he felt rather sorry and in need of weeping himself. He'd always tried to avoid hurting his brother. To this day, he couldn't imagine why he'd acted that way in Serpenten.

"That can't be all," Frances Allen insisted. "What kind of a recollection was that? Is that how boring your childhood was?"

Bora drew back his legs, rested his elbows on his knees. "Compared with yours, I think so. The land bordering our place in East Prussia belonged to my stepfather's family. After the properties were combined, there was no end to the rides, walks and rowing trips we could take then. No wild Indians, of course, but as long as the general stayed behind in Leipzig (or Dresden, or Berlin), Peter and I ran wild. We came within inches of drowning, breaking our necks, sinking in bogs. Our mother and especially our grandmother, if she was there, gave us reasonable advice and let us go. With Father on the premises – well, you imagine the routine, being from an army family. Flag-raising in the presence of the entire family and staff at six in the morning, followed by a prayer for Germany. Barracks – punctual meals, one hour minimum of reading and commentary of Clausewitz's *On War*, music practice – Peter threw his violin out of the window twice – plus lessons personally supervised by Father: horse care, dead reckoning, bookkeeping – here *I* threw the ledger out of the window – and endless tours of barley, rye and potato fields. We largely behaved until he left again. The moment the train moved out of the station, off went shoes and shirts and on came the warpaint. It was – what's the right word? – *blissful* fighting with the local boys and playing tricks on their sisters until his next visit."

"That's a little more like it." She jealously sucked on her cigarette stub to the end. "But it's hard to see you as someone who made a ruckus as a child."

"Depends on what a ruckus is."

"A free-for-all, a brawl. A fracas."

Bora smiled to himself. *But, dear Ma'am, I did. With and without a good reason in the world. If I could only call to mind why once Waldo and I flew at each other, in a roundabout way I'm sure I could even begin to understand why Wimpy Villiger had to die.* Out loud, he said only, "Ruckus. I'll remember the word."

Minutes later, Frances Allen, tired as she must be, was already lying down, with her head propped on her canvas bag. When Bora quietly reached over for her sandals, she muttered, "I'm not going anywhere," half-asleep. Around them, the evening was coming to a solitary, exquisite end in the ravine, lead-grey muting into blue.

At night, fireflies came.

PART THREE
Returning

9

SATURDAY 7 JUNE, BELOW AGIAS IRINIS

Dear Martin,

Thank you again for being there at my wedding, brother. Duckie insisted that I drop you a note to tell you that she and I are very much enjoying the gift you and Dikta gave us: Titus and Tilly are on their way to becoming our favourite mounts.

Didn't you say marriage is fun? I'm head over heels!

Here at the squadron all is well. I have fantastic superiors and colleagues, and we're in superlative high spirits. Our machines, I'm crazy about, and every day that passes I'm more convinced that I was born to do this job.

But guess what? Given that I'm the only young male in Duckie's family, her father is dropping hints about my taking over his paper mills after the war. "Having a scientific mind," he says, "you're cut out for the position. An excellent aviator has all he needs to lead a large business." Well, we pilots call it "flying a desk", short of being shot down the worst fate that a man can meet! He fancies me as chief engineer and partner, eventually proprietor, anticipates grandsons to compensate him for his failure to produce male heirs. Quite the responsibility: he wants a stud and a racehorse at the same time. Duckie plays coy but she's flattered, anxious to have kids. I think I'll have to break it to her sooner or later that we had better soft-pedal on a large family until I know what my next assignment will be, same as you and Dikta have done. I'm awfully glad she agreed to go and

285

stay in Leipzig with our parents, because Dikta is there and she'll be a good influence on her. Duckie needs to learn style-consciousness from your beautiful wife. Her parents kept her on a short leash, as you know (I had to do somersaults to put a hand inside her bra once during our engagement – I was going mad). Her sisters, minus the one who's a novice, are still years away from marriage. Is it a wonder if my father-in-law already sees me in spats, with a cigar in my mouth, pacing up and down an immense office in Hanover and putting out as much paper as he did in 1923, "when the government printed 700 times as many banknotes as it'd ever had"?

Anyhow, as you can tell I feel like the luckiest dog around. I'm even catching a concert now and then or a lecture: I don't want you to be the only intellectual brother (ha)! I've seen a grand film I recommend to you. Its title is *Riding for Germany*, and tells the story of Captain named von Brenken, a champion horseman who is reunited with his horse Harro after they both gloriously served on the Russian front in the Great War...

At second reading, after a quick browse during take-off from Moscow, Peter's letter appeared to Bora the merry product of a world he less and less belonged to. Superlatives, expectations of civilian life, things to do after the war... He could sit in the clean-scented ravine under Agias Irinis with the thickly written page in hand and wonder whether the two of them, the *seal brown* and the *sorrel*, had anything in common with the children they once were. Peter had gone from being an overly sensitive boy to sunniness itself. The testily compliant Martin was evolving into a stoic with his own mind, as self-directed as he was outwardly restrained. Frances Allen had asked what disguise he'd be wearing next, and it was true that he'd travelled across Crete like a modern-day Ulysses. None of those he met – saving perhaps Waldo Preger – knew who he was, deep down. Waldo himself remembered another Martin

Bora, and his view was outdated. What mattered now was the impression he'd make on Sergeant Powell, who was elusive in spite of himself. *He has to bring me closer to solving Villiger's death. He has to trust me enough that he'll tell.* Bora did not look beyond the meeting, as sure it would take place that very day as if it were part of his destiny to confront a British non-com in a place called Agias Irinis.

By the time his travel mate awoke, he'd thoroughly washed, shaved, and made coffee on a small fire of twigs, already doused. She took the hot tin he handed her and said, "What happens if we don't find Powell?"

"To you, you mean?"

"Right."

Bora sipped his coffee standing, visibly ready to go. "I'll find Powell."

The route to Agias Irinis, a cliff where according to the American nothing existed but a place name and Pendlebury's tool shed, consisted of a narrow track carved into the rocky flank. There were spots where, in the flood of dawn light, the way ahead resembled a nearly perpendicular ladder.

She adjusted the visored cap on her head. "If you don't lose your grip, you can reach it in half an hour. Are you afraid of heights?"

"No. Are you?"

"No, but I'm wearing sandals."

"That's true. Is there another way to the top?"

"Around the northern slope. That's why I said 'an hour, an hour and a half' last night."

If I were alone I'd already be climbing. Bora understood what was on her mind. "I'm not willing to let you go just yet, Ma'am. We'll do as you say."

As they started out, Frances Allen – already short of cigarettes

– reverted to the talkativeness she had left over from the previous evening.

"You know," she said at one point, "one of the sites in the photos you showed me is in the highland that extends behind this cliff. A mountaintop shrine dating to the Middle Minoan period. In a layer of ashes and black earth we discovered clay figurines of girls in bell skirts and fellows in codpieces."

Bora was moderately interested. "Is that why Pendlebury built the shed here?"

"…Yes."

Her sudden hesitation, no longer than a wink, made him suspect that Agias Irinis could have also served the young vice-consul as a rallying place for would-be partisans, even before Crete was invaded. Britons had long been currying favour with the locals through OSS operatives.

Were the shed still used as a redoubt, guards would have been posted on the cliff, and the alarm would have already been given. It made more sense that, as the Catalans had reported, only wounded runaways would call it home now.

Bora led the way out of the ravine. This far into his task, he effectively blocked unrelated considerations regarding the aftermath, as he'd done in combat. One step, and then another: only the certainty of success mattered, largely unfounded as it was. What he'd tell Powell once he met him remained a nebulous sketch. *I'll find the words; I'll make myself credible. There's no alternative.* Ulysses stepped into the hall where the suitors caroused and slaughtered them to the last: the bloodshed at Ampelokastro was nothing to the sea of gore in which the avenger waded up to his ankles once he had finished killing. *I'm not moved by vengeance, so my future actions stay vague until I carry them out. Far from being weakness, it's readiness for anything.*

Now at his side, Frances Allen cast a long undulating shadow as she walked. It occasionally merged with Bora's own taller shadow, and both gave the impression of pointers, racing to mark time across a sundial made of scattered rocks.

It took them close to forty minutes to negotiate the seamed, cleft terrain skirting the bottom of the cliff. Once out of the ravine, they faced an incline in full sun, hairy with drying grass and like the hump of a great albino bison. It was from this north side that Agias Irinis could be reached, by a natural ramp that sloped gradually into baldness; its foot instead was bushy, filled with cicadas, pristine. A scent of wild thyme rode the breeze from it.

The place was no lonelier than others Bora had crossed ever since arriving in Crete. Its shape, however, arching in a single line against the brilliant sky, set it apart from all others, and assigned it to the realm of sights and objects both unknown and familiar.

Bora had never come this way before, of course; he doubted he ever would again, in future travels. He'd seen no photographic images of the rise. It surprised him, when he reached its threshold, to feel something like a thin surge of energy run through him from his feet upward, rooting him there, as if a substance lodged in the earth were sending delicate, pervasive roots into his body.

On the swell of the incline stood three peasant girls. Outlined against the sheen of the sky, far enough so that their features could not be clearly made out, they lingered waist-high in silvery grass, which the wind caused to rise and fall around them in waves. They were singing, and seemed unaware of the coming strangers.

They sang in unison a tune unknown to Bora, with harmonious drawn-out incomprehensible words. The sound, God knows why, reminded him of places so remote and different from this, only a predisposition of his mind could justify the nostalgia awakened by those mournful young voices.

Seeing him, the girls interrupted their song. Unlike those

who in past days had fled like sparrows at the sight of strangers, they stayed. Looking back at him, as if in recognition, they hailed him from afar. White kerchiefs on their heads, they resembled one another like sisters, floating over the grey-blue shiny billows; the invisible lower half of their bodies, dark skirts no doubt, could be scaly fishtails or feathers for all Bora knew.

"They want you to go over and talk to them," Frances Allen said. "They want you to climb the ridge and join them."

Ah, there's home here, their soft wave of arms said. What you're looking for, what you've been trying to recall, what you wondered about and wished-feared to know ever since Spain, ever since Remedios foretold your suffering and death. Join us, and it will be revealed, though we're only girls singing and standing in the tall grass. Home is here, though you don't see it: childhood and love sought-lost, the sound of fists striking, the green wet plains and the river, the burning cities, the thing like an arrow that is called Destiny. We no longer sing, but you hear us: aren't you weary, four years into the war? Will you go on, and have to stand four years more? Stay, and it all ends here. Why, so often, is not doing things more painful than actually doing them, even though they would hurt you?

They're only girls, Bora reasoned, *only girls,* while the lure of their voices told him otherwise. *Didn't old Professor Lohse teach us of the Sirens, "Three seabirds, three half-goddesses, three half-maidens…"?* Ten times, in the brief space of time since seeing them, he had to restrain himself from heeding the call on the strength of their song. Rationality alone held him back, by a tendril that rooted him fast and would not let go.

"They want you to climb the ridge and join them," Frances Allen said.

"I don't think I will."

The northern rim of Agias Irinis was reached by a last moderate climb. No ancient shrine was recognizable where Allen indicated, only a blooming spread of low bushes like a green herd. On the opposite cliff side, the shed lay instead in full view. Bora halted long enough to snap his shoulder boards on, pass the string of his identification tag around his neck, and put on his German officer's side cap. Doing so before making sure only the wounded occupied Agias Irinis was risky, but he'd gone past considering risk. Frances Allen watched his every move; when she tried to lag behind, he gruffly called her back to his side. "We're not done yet."

The shed, built with stacked fieldstone and strips of corrugated iron, stood at the eastern end of the tongue-shaped hilltop, in a field of rocks and sparse grass. Between it and the scruffy area where the shrine Allen spoke of must have existed once, only a careful eye would notice signs of treading back and forth.

No evidence of activity from the outside meant little; the day was young and it was not a given that runaways would be watching out for intruders in this remote location. They could still be asleep. A lack of openings on the north side meant that one could approach unseen. This was what Bora did, Browning in hand, keeping his travel companion half a step ahead of him and slightly to his right, where he could fire and not miss if he needed to. She walked, surly under her visored cap, hands in her pockets.

A roll of bedding cloth sat against the wall, to the left of the entrance, as well as sticks to start a fire and an empty cooking pot. No sounds whatever from within.

The door gave way under the pressure of Bora's foot. Instantly, the early sun flooded the interior, revealing an empty space maybe twenty feet square. Pallets lined three walls, enough to have accommodated five or six people when fully occupied. A stack of shovels, spades, trowels, pails and a measuring rod lay on the floor under the small back window. Remnants of medical supplies, mostly bandages, sat on a solid little table.

Bora's frustration peaked for a brief angry minute. The shed had been occupied until recently, very recently. So much so that tea in a battered metal cup was cold but not musty, and tea leaves were still wet inside the kettle. Under the table, what at first had seemed to be bundled-up bedding turned out to be a makeshift travel bag. Bora was on the point of undoing it to look inside when Allen's reaction – she said nothing, but gave a start – alerted him to something that must have come into view through the back window.

Past the flimsy glass, looking west toward the ruins of the shrine, the ground cover of broom and other flowering shrubs gave signs of life. From the greenness, a single human figure rose as if it had been crouching so far to heed some physiological need, and slowly started towards the shed. Bora stepped back from the window, signalling to the woman to do the same. *He doesn't look like a Minotaur, down there, but may play the part. At every step I take, more and more things and people take the shape of myth: unwittingly, I myself, the Wanderer, with no place to rest my head, here to avenge the dead...*

A gangling man in khaki trousers and a collarless white shirt came forward without haste, visibly unaware the shed had been occupied. Under a receding grey-blonde hairline, his youthful features set him at an imprecise age between thirty and fifty, probably midway between them. He looked down and wiped his hands on a handkerchief as he walked.

Next to Bora, Frances Allen spoke up. "That's Geoffrey, John's right-hand man at Knossos! What's he doing here?"

Bora hushed her. Quickly, he pulled the door to, as he had found it, and took his place at the ready just to the side, so as not to be blinded by the sun when it was pushed open.

Allen's colleague simply raised his eyes when he set foot inside. He froze, seemingly as surprised to see Frances there as he was to face an armed German officer standing with her.

British understatement allowed him to recover enough to exchange a polite, stiff nod with Bora and at once turn to his colleague.

"How are you, Frances?"

"As well as can be expected, Geoff. I'm not here of my own accord."

In their brief exchange, Bora intuited something he could not quantify for now, and had to ignore at his own risk.

"Are you alone here?" he enquired.

The man nodded, still turned to the American. "Half an hour more, and you wouldn't have found me, either."

"Fine." Bora holstered the Browning. "Captain Martin Bora, German *Wehrmacht*. I come on behalf of the German Army War Crimes Bureau, and of the International Red Cross as well."

"Geoffrey Caxton, MA, assistant to the Director of Knossos Antiquities. Is it fair to ask whether you, too, are alone?"

Bora latched the holster, careful to let the question pass him by. "I seek the whereabouts of a British Army non-com, reported to have escaped German captivity with a fellow soldier in the Iraklion area on 31 May. Has he been here? His name is Sergeant Major Powell."

"Powell? No."

"He is about five feet ten inches in height, with a slight build and sandy hair. Possibly from Yorkshire. May have an arm wound due to gunfire."

Being addressed in impeccable English did not appreciably modify Caxton's rigid displeasure. Was he wondering if his colleague had risked her life, or on the other hand had easily been convinced to lead a German to this mountaintop?

She stood there restlessly. "Tell him *something*, Geoff."

The eagerness of her tone convinced him. "Well, there was someone here answering to that description. But his name was Albert 'Bertie' Cowell."

"Not Powell?"

"No. See for yourself." From his back pocket Caxton produced a British Army identification disc. "If you're the bearer of news for Sergeant Cowell, sir, I'm afraid you're eight hours late. I come from burying him. The other tag, I left with his body."

Bora looked. On the red fibre disc, suspended by a makeshift cord – actually a bootlace – a few upper-case letters and numbers were clearly impressed.

"Is there a chance you mistook Powell for Cowell?"

Not I. But Sinclair possibly mistook the sergeant's name in the confusion of the moment. Bora tightened his fist around the disc before giving it back. Hiding his great disappointment took an effort, and he only partially succeeded. "I had to see the sergeant on an important matter of military justice. What happened to him, exactly?"

"*Exactly,* I can't tell. At first Cowell seemed no more severely injured than the others. But an infection developed: there was nothing that could be done." Caxton made a desolate gesture. "Transporting him was impossible. Toward the end, he begged me not to leave him, not even to ask for help. Besides, I'm not sure where I'd have got help."

"Other than from us, that is." Bora critically ran his eyes around the shed. "I understand this was a sort of infirmary."

"It's a campaign shed originally equipped to sleep six; we kept a number of medical supplies in our first-aid kit. I helped build it – didn't I, Frances? – so it made sense for me to come here when Crete was first invaded. I'm no physician. While excavating in Syria and elsewhere I'd gained some basic competencies as a medic – you know how it is out in the field, you can find yourself weeks from anywhere. In the days following the invasion, supplies ran low and it was mere luck, not my doing, if the handful of men who transited through here survived their injuries. Thank God they're safely elsewhere now. What we had a surplus of were the digging tools used in our work. Unfortunately, the shovel at least served its purpose this morning." Caxton's attention returned from Frances, who nervously drank from her canteen, to the German. "What do you mean by 'military justice'?" And because Bora didn't seem inclined to reply, he added, "I have a reason for asking. Sergeant Cowell was – how to put it? – deeply troubled by an incident he witnessed south of Iraklion before his capture. He rather dwelled on it." Instantly, Bora's hopes were up.

"An *incident?*"

This time Caxton looked him straight in the eye. "An atrocity."

"So." Bora coldly sustained the stare. "What sort of atrocity?"

"Civilians gunned down in their own house. The sicker Cowell fell, the more obsessed with the shock of the event he became. He lucidly ruminated over it until last night, when he slipped into his final delirium."

"'Gunned down' by whom? Did he say?"

"He did say." But nothing followed by way of explanation.

Bora shifted his glance away from Caxton. Frances Allen stood motionless by the open door with her back to the outside, to freedom. *She knows that closeness to salvation is no guarantee.* When he walked up to her, her eyes focused on him, both hopeful and hostile; his sentiments exactly, for different reasons. He fished out of his pocket and offered her the last ten-pack.

"Go, now."

She grabbed the cigarettes, squirrelled them away and then hesitated, either in fear of a last-minute snare or wondering if she ought to say something. On neither side was a handshake even attempted. Bora impatiently nodded towards the door. "You had better go, Mrs Sidheraki. Don't make me change my mind."

She turned around, and the morning sun seemed to set her ablaze. *The Firebird,* Bora thought, *fleeing the hunter.* He watched her walk away, cautiously at first and then gaining confidence, looking around, smelling the wind, truly like an animal set free. *She'll be running soon; Crete will once more open like a flower under her steps. She'll race unscathed past the singing girls, who aren't meant for her.*

With her gone from the doorstep, inside the shed the sun opened bright fans of light.

"Mr Caxton, let's make one thing clear: I haven't hiked to this remote location to take prisoners. I promise you I have no intention of hindering your withdrawal further inland if you so choose. But I demand a full report of what Sergeant Cowell told you, on the authority of those I represent."

Again, no answer. Through the small window, Caxton's gaze after the woman had a forlorn intensity Bora did not misread this time. *Imagine. There's a story there. Did he pursue her, unrequited? Were they bedmates before Sidheraki muscled in? She didn't even say goodbye to him.*

"I'm waiting, Mr Caxton."

The balance between youth and middle age on Caxton's face was imperceptibly, sadly altered by a twist of the lips. "All right. It can hurt no one at this point. Sergeant Cowell said he saw German paratroopers enter the house and shoot everyone in it. Yesterday morning, when he was still in his right mind, he asked that I write the story down."

"Did you?"

"Naturally, I obliged him."

Bora held back a sigh. He was in one of those moods when you don't know if the sensation you feel is pain or pleasure, or a mixture of both. It pinpricked him all over his body. "He actually *saw* the soldiers cross the threshold and open fire? Show me your notes."

From a cardboard folder surfaced a large sheet of graph paper, such as archaeologists use when drawing in scale. Sentences had been pencilled on the back of the sheet, without breaks.

Caxton ran his eyes across it then turned it over to Bora. "Fourth line."

Bora read aloud. "'I huddled in the brook bed outside, but clearly saw the Jerries enter the garden gate.' Which is not the same as entering the house. I need to know if Cowell ever said he saw them step inside."

"I don't know." Caxton shook his head. "I don't recall him saying those exact words."

The account, taken down in a neat, slanted hand, did not differ appreciably from the version Sinclair had given the War Crimes Bureau. Fear, disgust, the decision to conquer both in order to bear witness to the slaughter through photography were all there. Cowell's anguish came through like a bloody print.

But often when note-taking one summarizes or condenses. Details judged irrelevant may be left out. Bora angled for minutiae. "Did Cowell mention running into enemy patrols or civilians when he first approached the villa?"

"No."

"What about being confronted by a large dog?"

"A watchdog, you mean? No, he didn't. Well – he did speak of a dead dog lying on the front steps after the shooting. Frankly, I found the detail irrelevant in view of the human tragedy, and excised it."

While Caxton spoke, Bora had gone ahead in his reading, through a story he knew well by now. Goose pimples multiplied. One element towards the end made him look up from the sheet. "It reads here that Cowell was 'fired upon and wounded' as he hastened away from the villa along the road."

"Why, yes. That's right. That's how he received the injury that killed him eventually."

Bora paused. The detail did not match his information that the man was shot by guards while escaping from the queue of prisoners. "There's no word about the provenance of the shot."

"I doubt he saw anyone, Captain. Obviously, he took it to be a German concealed in the brushwood with the intention of eliminating a witness."

Frowning came naturally to Bora, as if suddenly the account were in a language he struggled to understand. "What is this about his having halted 'to take more photographs' when the shot reached him?"

Caxton craned his neck to read. "You must understand that Cowell waffled and rambled on. I only wrote down what was directly related to the atrocity. I understood he'd stumbled across the bodies of two British soldiers as he wandered through the area. He didn't think much of it, given the violence of the fighting up to that day."

"Why stop to photograph them on the way back, then?"

"I believe he referred to it as a 'scruple'."

"A *scruple*. A scruple implies a doubt, or a moral call. Was there something unusual about the dead soldiers, maybe?"

Wearily, Caxton poured himself the last of the cold tea into the battered cup. "You ask too much of a secondary source, Captain. All he said is that they were shot at close range, which hardly qualifies as 'unusual'. My impression is that Cowell assumed they were killed by those who gunned down the civilians. That would explain his decision to have a photographic record of the two bodies as well."

Bora swallowed, which was his sole visible reaction. A corner of the shed, where sunlight did not reach and the shade seemed by contrast dark as night itself, fascinated him, as if his inner turmoil were projected and now cowered there. He saw himself, heard his boyhood self running from the "house with eyes", frightened and thrilled at the same time. "But he did not snap the photos."

"No. A bullet fired from the brushwood struck his right arm above the elbow. It made it impossible for him to operate the camera, and surely discouraged him from lingering in the neighbourhood. Seeing how it ended, I can't say it was fortunate for him that the injury did not hinder his escape from his German captors, a few hours later. Had he remained a POW, who knows, he could have been cured."

"Were you the one who extracted the bullet?"

"I was, for better or for worse. He thought it could be a proof of sorts, and asked that I keep it."

"May I see it?"

Caxton put down his cup, dug in his back pocket for the lead fragment. "I'm no judge, but I dare say it comes from a handgun."

Bora nodded and gave it back. *A paratrooper who means to bring down somebody does not use a handgun, and does not let the wounded quarry go.* He read the last line. "'I wandered in a daze until the afternoon, at which time I was spotted by Jerries by a gully near Kato Kalesia and was taken prisoner.' The notes end at this point. Did Cowell add anything else?"

In Caxton's hands, the cup showed rusted chips through the enamel. He turned it round and round, staring at it. "There's nothing else of interest. Cowell said that while in a queue with other prisoners, he reported what he'd witnessed to the only man among them who held officer rank, also enquiring if he should surrender his camera to the German authorities or not."

"And…?"

"The officer – a first lieutenant, I believe – assured him he would take over. Cowell was considerably relieved to hear he could entrust another with the account and its documentary proof. Evidently, the officer must have followed through with the German authorities as promised, given that you're here and know the story."

Bora found that he could evenly split himself between his query and a private observation of the man before him. *Did he ever bring her here? He hoped – for a moment, he hoped she was here for him. Even with a gun in my hand, I surprised him less than Frances Allen, now Sidheraki's wife. She was cruel to him, I can tell.*

"There's still the detail of Cowell's escape, Mr Caxton."

"The escape!" Bora's words stirred the archaeologist out of proportion. "Now, *there*'s something you should report to the International Red Cross! I heard it told by the soldier who came here with Sergeant Cowell. No, *he* was only grazed during the getaway; he was able to move on after medication. The two had survived by the skin of their teeth and were indignant about the whole matter. *I* am indignant about it. No sooner did the lieutenant volunteer to take over from Cowell, than he overheard the German guards mutter of a plan not to transfer the prisoners but machine-gun them en route to the prison camp. He translated for the men, so Cowell – wounded as he was – and others in the lot didn't waste time and decided to make a run for it. It's what they did, and the guards did open fire."

"On the runaways or on the entire group of prisoners?"

"On the runaways, to be sure. But maybe the others were executed as well, we don't know."

"Well, the lieutenant in question is very much alive." Bora studiously folded the graph paper, slipped it into his chest pocket and buttoned the flap over it. Either Cowell or Sinclair, or both, were confused about the circumstances of the escape. Unless one of them, or both, had lied.

"Please walk me to the grave."

Once they had started toward the scruffy area, the compact, rocky soil in between made Bora newly suspicious. "It cannot have been simple, digging a grave on this hilltop without help."

"I was spared the effort, Captain. There's a Middle Minoan shrine down there, which we excavated over two campaigns. I made the most of an underground deposit for cult-related objects, a *favissa*, technically speaking. Once poor Bertie Cowell lay inside, it was only a matter of heaping dirt from a pile over the hole. Dragging him inside a blanket across this distance was the strenuous part."

Through the ground cover, they reached a clearing invisible from the shed. Low walls, little more than foundations, criss-crossed it; remnants of steps, pillar bases; here and there gaped the round mouths of buried jars. The heap over the grave, scattered with shards, was marked by a cross of white pebbles. At its foot, the shovel was still stuck in the dirt. Prudently, Bora took it out and tossed it where the Briton would not be tempted to wield it, though Caxton kept his arms folded tightly and did no more than stare into the distance.

She's gone by now; he must know how she clambers when she wants to. A kind of male affinity, less than sympathy but not by much, caused Bora to relent his own harshness. "You've been helpful, Mr Caxton. Soon you'll be free to go."

"Yes?"

"Just answer a few more questions as we walk back."

"I reported everything Cowell told me. You have the written account. I don't see what else —"

"Come along. It may seem unrelated, but bear with me. You must be familiar with Crete's intelligentsia: have you ever heard of a Swiss scholar by the name of Alois Villiger?"

A rising of brows showed how mundane the question must seem to Caxton. "Wimpy Villiger? Who hasn't? I thought he was German. Fancies photographing blonde peasants. He's got a residence outside Iraklion."

"*South. South* of Iraklion, to be precise."

The way Bora said it was so suggestive, Caxton stopped in his tracks. "He's not the one who —"

"He's 'the one who', and so are his housekeeper and field hands."

"Good God. Well, he was a bit queer and a secretive bastard, but – good God, not that he deserved… or anyone, for that matter. Won't John Pendlebury be shocked to hear this, much as he didn't like him?"

Pendlebury? He may be as dead and buried as Bertie Cowell. But we'll leave that alone for now.

Bora was silent until they reached the shed again. Letting Caxton precede him inside, he freed himself of his rucksack. "Since you've been tending the injured," he said, "I presume you're not squeamish. I wish to show you some of the photos taken by Sergeant Cowell." Soon he had the folder on the table. "That's why I came this far, and needed to meet him."

Caxton looked through the images. "Ah, poor fellow. Poor fellow. And his people, too. I hadn't seen Wimpy Villiger in months. How he'd aged! Was he ill?"

"I have no idea, I didn't know him." But Bora made yet another mental note as he flipped the next photograph, and the next.

"Hullo," Caxton's utterance interrupted him. "That's Raj!"

Bora looked. "What, the dog?"

"Yes, the dog. How on earth did it come to die at Villiger's doorstep? It never left its master's side."

Leaning on the table, Bora held his breath. *Rifat Bey, too, claimed one of his dogs ran away. An Englishman's pet can be lost as well.* He slowly let air out of his lungs to control his voice. "It must have strayed that once. Why, who's its master?"

"Anglo-Indian officer, prize fellow. Raj was his pet, and became the unit mascot. Yes, it must have run off, and look what happened."

Bora only appeared even-tempered. In the struggle to keep calm, his thoughts were running away with him. Until now, nothing, *nothing* whatsoever had put Sinclair or his men anywhere remotely near the crime scene. He posed the next question as if he didn't know there could be a logical answer for it. "I thought you withdrew here when we first landed. How would you have met a British officer and his mascot before our landing?"

"*Please*, Captain. It was no secret to your army or to anyone else that British troops already manned the island. Pat was among them, and God willing he's made it out of Crete by now. Educated chap, well-travelled. Drank with us occasionally. That's all. He'll be devastated to know of Raj's end."

Bora felt like someone coming up for air after nearly drowning. Ideas overlapped faster than he could formulate them. Composing himself caused him a strain similar to pain. "Academia must be a strange milieu. I heard that Professor Villiger was *persona non grata* at social gatherings among you scholars – the Knossos basement bar being a favourite location. Yet non-scholars, like British Army officers, were invited."

"As for that, Pat's a Valencian who sailed through Cambridge's Pembroke College on hard-earned scholarships. Fully equipped to sit with us, Captain. I know, I did the Classical Tripos at Pembroke myself." Caxton observed Bora carefully returning the photos to his rucksack. "Gentlemen have a right to select their drinking fellows, and all this has no relevance as far as the atrocity is concerned, has it? Nothing Cowell reported exonerates German paratroopers from it."

"Nothing Cowell reported indicts them beyond doubt, either."

Suddenly, Bora was in a frantic hurry to leave, to go back to Iraklion. *What did Frances Allen say? "When British officers first came from Souda last winter and offered a round of drinks… he crawled out of the room." Why was Villiger afraid of them, and was he*

303

afraid of one of them *in particular? Is that why he meant to leave Crete? It makes no sense, but I won't find out in these mountains.* He nodded towards the bundle under the table. "You're free to backpack out of here or stay, Mr Caxton – your choice. I will ensure the appropriate British authorities are acquainted with the location of Sergeant Cowell's grave through the International Red Cross. Will you trust me with his identification disc and the bullet you extracted from his arm?"

Caxton surrendered both without saying that he trusted Bora. He picked up his bundle and shouldered it. "Right," he said, assenting to nothing in particular. "But I don't think I should thank you for it."

Bora understood, and was not offended. He looked at Frances' colleague directly, with a kind of spiteful empathy.

"And I don't think *she*'s quite worth it, Mr Caxton."

8.45 a.m., British fieldwork shed, Agias Irinis. Caxton's gone, heading south with his tea kettle and broken heart. I'm taking a few minutes here to update my diary and jot down the latest in this intricate story. From here, a place called after a saint whose name means "peace", it is between twenty and thirty miles to the north coast. On the map, all roads seem to lead to Iraklion, if you only reach them safely. I will in a moment sketch a few possible return itineraries, but first I *must* write what really matters (in case they stop me permanently, and the diary becomes the sole Ariadne's clue to solve the case).

Excluding the possibility that Preger's men really did kill Villiger and his household, all other reconstructions of the events at Ampelokastro have pros and cons. I list them without privileging one over the others, with possible motives, and arguments against them as well:

First hypothesis: The housekeeper's in-laws, intent on avenging their brother's honour, somehow secure MAB 38 submachine guns and – unseen and unheard by Sgt Cowell – enter the villa and carry out the murder. No one knows them in the neighbourhood, and as Cretans they can flit in and out without arousing suspicions. Moreover, if they double as "freedom fighters", they have ready access to weapons supplied by the Brits, or stolen from dead Germans. To them, it is Siphronia and Villiger who deserve death, but they can't leave the field hands alive to testify against them. Besides, submachine guns aren't hunting rifles, and once you start firing you may do more damage than planned.

Objections: the brothers had to have already been hiding in the garden when the paratroopers walked through. Alternatively, they entered through the rear gate (invisible to Cowell) right after the troopers walked out, and left the same way afterwards. But why would one of them shoot Cowell (and with whose pistol?) as he tried to photograph two dead Englishmen north of Ampelokastro?

(Variation on the theme: Cretan rebels, armed with war weapons such as Sidheraki concealed at home, are responsible for the murder. Motives? Because a German speaker is a German to a Greek, and/or for whatever other reasons of hatred toward the Swiss scholar, a foreigner with strange habits. Sidheraki himself could have led the commando.

Objections: none to speak of. This would be the worst possible scenario for an investigator in a hurry.)

Second hypothesis: Although it's hard to imagine how he would find someone to do the dirty work for him, I can't leave Professor Savelli out of the list, because he was rummaging through Villiger's house after his death. We know he detested the Swiss because of plagiarism, probably with some good reason. Was he looking for books, as he said, or for the roll of photographs? Or for Signora Cordoval's calling card (and if so, why)? It would be dangerous to appear to have frequented a Jewess, especially once Germans occupied the island. He may have turned her in to Villiger out of rancour or greed, and then regretted it – or regretted the fact that he could at some point be exposed as an informer. The card was in the safety deposit box, but if Savelli gave it to Villiger, he had no way of knowing it had been removed from Ampelokastro, where he's likely to have delivered it. Perhaps he forgot the calling card was in a book he lent Villiger, and wanted it back.

Alternatively, it was Villiger who discovered Signora's presence on the island. If Savelli had in the meantime made up with her, it would justify the need to keep the Swiss from harming her, though I don't exactly see how. In either case, the snapshot of the woman – among the "stolen" photos of archaeological sites – plays a role, whenever it was taken and whoever of the two men took it.

Objections: Savelli seems less equipped than others to have carried out the deed. However, if he is (or was) involved with Italian espionage in Rhodes at any level, he may be a wolf in sheep's clothing. If such is the case, motives and reasons may multiply and remain undiscovered.

Note: Kostaridis, when asked directly, refused to reveal Cordoval's whereabouts, and when he gave me the prints before I left for the interior, he pretended to ignore where the snapshot was taken. He knows more than he lets on. He doesn't seem the type of official who covers up cold-blooded murder, and he declares himself anti-communist: but what if a band of non-communist Cretan "patriots" is behind the deaths? Wouldn't he then keep his mouth shut, or even mislead me?

Third hypothesis: Rifat Bey, Villiger's hostile neighbour, commissioned the murder with thugs. The fact that he was away at his town home means little: he's known to keep firearms at Sphingokephalo, can count on men without scruples who'll do his bidding and keep silent, and can probably buy the local authorities as well. His motives? If I have to believe Kostaridis, the Turk didn't need much of an excuse to bump off shop owners or others on the island who were in his way. But if the woman photographed on the terrace is the Jewess, and the terrace is Zimbouli, Rifat Bey's Place of Hyacinths… It's possible that Villiger, during one of his stays in Iraklion, took a snapshot of the handsome blonde. Wouldn't he, ever the classifier, be curious about her? Wouldn't he ask around? The Sphinx-loving Turk might have had a far stronger argument for killing than hostility, water rights or pilfering of ancient shards from his vineyard.

He may have heard that Villiger – known to work for Germany – was enquiring about his Jewish lover, and had to act quickly. The invasion gave him a chance to get rid of the Swiss and all in his household who might talk. His thugs slipped unseen into the garden while the field hands were inside, busy receiving their pay (a fact they would likely know). They had to drop out of sight when German paratroopers unexpectedly marched through the front gate, but as soon as they were out of earshot, they burst in shooting. The use of military weapons and tactics would make the murder appear an act of war. And while the terrified Cowell bided his time in the brook bed until all became safe, Rifat Bey's thugs withdrew from the rear gate to their master's vineyards.

Fourth hypothesis: Sergeant Bertie Cowell lied to Sinclair regarding his real surname and the murder scene at Ampelokastro; later he also lied to Caxton about the two dead soldiers on the road, and being shot while next to them. In fact, he carried out the murder, alone or in the company of others.

Objections: Why would Cowell tell such an elaborate lie to a British officer, and to his caretaker Caxton, when he was already close to death? Most of all, why would a Briton – any Briton – kill locals and their employer, a citizen of a neutral country? He would (and likely should) have done only if he knew that Villiger was more than an expert in racial theory; indeed, if he knew that Villiger, while working officially for the *Ahnenerbe*, spied for *Reichskommissar* Himmler (and perhaps others as well). This would imply that the Briton himself is an operative, informed about Villiger and with orders to dispose of him. But you don't send a single man to do this kind of work unless you're sure he'll find his victim alone and unprotected. Could there have been three men in the commando, with Cowell ready to clean up after himself, to the extent of shooting his own companions? It would explain why he didn't mention them to Sinclair (their bodies were reported to Kostaridis by the War Crimes Bureau), and lied to Caxton about being shot while photographing them.

Other objection: if guilty, why photograph the scene and then surrender the camera to us Germans? Answer: in order to divert suspicions from himself, as the photos clearly show German paratroopers entering the garden. MAB 38 submachine guns use the same cartridges as English Sten guns!

Note: Lieutenant Sinclair did not recognize Raj in the photo. But he had no reason to lie, and the photo was slightly blurry. Dogs do stray in times of battle, and recognizing it would not be riskier than surrendering the camera to us, since his unit was nowhere near the Ampelokastro area.

Besides, can I trust Geoffrey Caxton's memory regarding the mascot's appearance? Caxton was Pendlebury's "right-hand man", and may be one of those scholars recruited by His Majesty's secret service as spies or SOE agents. His story to me – including the detail regarding the dog – could be as fallacious as Cowell's deathbed confession.

Thus, unless the Turk's behind the massacre, in pursuing Cowell I may have unwittingly been after an executioner, not a witness, and he's dead (unless Caxton lied about that too: I saw a grave, not Cowell's body)!

It is a labyrinth, and I am right back where I started. As for exiting it, now that I no longer have the girl with a skein of yarn leading me…

I must speak again to Sinclair and to Rifat Bey; and to Kostaridis as well. My goal is the valley bottom, safer for me and likely to be patrolled by German troops. Going back the way I came, I'd have wandered between Mount Voskerò and other peaks whose names I ignore, and reached the treeless slope where Allen and I saw the armed Cretans (the spot overlooks Krousonas, which I must at all costs stay clear of). At that point, I should be more or less an hour from the Catalans' hideout at Meltemi, also to be avoided. No need to retrace my steps to the site of the Upper Palace with its painted shards, to *mesa pharangi* or Kyriakos' *mandra*. Not even to the chapel of Agios Minas on the south slope of Mount Pirgos, or to Chorafi and the olive grove where the old man in a dazzling shirt wove baskets on the doorstep.

I have marked on the map three possible routes leading north to Iraklion, one of which has the advantage of taking me through Kamari (where I could pay a visit to Savelli) and Ampelokastro, from which, through Kavrochori and Gazi, I might travel the last ten miles to the coastal route near Agias Marinas, and reach Iraklion from the west, through the Chanià Gate.

Once more, I have removed the national insignia from my person, save the identification disc. At this point – should I be captured or wounded, and not killed outright – wearing it is the sole thing that would keep me from being shot as a spy (Major Busch thinks that's what happened to Pendlebury). That is, if Germans or Brits catch me: if it's Cretans or the Catalans, the disc means a sure bullet through the nape of the neck.

The ink was still wet on Bora's last worried consideration when a sound reached him through the open door of the shed. He tensely listened as it began hollowly, like the knocking about of skittles, grew into a distinctive clatter magnified by echoes, and then roared like a waterfall. In the utter silence of Agias Irinis, above the level frequented by herds, cicadas and most chirping insects, the shock of stones that rolled and struck others might or might not indicate a significant landslide: but something or someone brought it about.

Bora knew when acting was better than thinking. He quickly pressed the blotting paper onto the page, threw diary and pen into his rucksack and left the shed. Outside a wind had risen. It carried the rumbling sound from somewhere below the cliff, where a ghostly sparkle of powdered stone wafted across the air. No one was in sight on the tongue-shaped plateau. Far on the northern horizon, a dark grey thing in the sky like a giant, hammer-headed worm meant remote storm clouds, a squall out at sea.

Bora strapped on his rucksack. The landslide could have been caused by goatherds grazing their animals on the neighbouring heights. Frances Allen herself had stumbled twice on unsteady rocks. He decided to reach the edge of the cliff and crawl to its lip to look down. He saw no humans, no animals; only that shifting, sparkling ghost of particles in the air. The last rocks touched bottom now, not far from the place where he and Allen had camped the night before. He thought how easy it had been gathering twigs to build a fire, as in the dry season branches grew brittle and snapped off. A badly anchored mountain shrub, torn by wind that channelled in the ravine, could have come loose and initiated the landslip. If not – Bora was uneasy. *As if anyone ready to attack wouldn't huddle out of sight as soon as he'd accidentally made himself heard.* In that case, the risk of being shot while climbing down the cliff was high, with both hands busy and no chance to reach for his gun if need be. Not appreciably safer was descending the unprotected grassy hump where he'd seen the mermaid girls; worst of all would be attempting other routes, because he had no idea of what lay west and south, other than impassable mountainsides.

The wind, a nor'easter gaining intensity, dissuaded him from braving the steep way down. Bora withdrew from the cliff and headed for the whale-back slope, whose silvery grass, bright like spun metal at this hour, rippled like a curving sea. He did not run but kept a fast steady pace, aiming for the relative protection of the wooded bottom. The three girls, the sisters, had disappeared. *Where have those singing girls gone to?* he wondered. *They weren't in my imagination; Frances Allen saw them and heard them. Could they have ventured onto the mountain and lost their footing? No, goddesses do not miss their step, and neither do Cretan shepherd girls.*

There was a place at the foot of the slope where shrubbery gave way to a chaos of rocks, the way he'd followed out of the ravine earlier this morning. Arriving there safely convinced Bora that after all, on the unfathomable scale of his personal destiny, his leniency toward Caxton –and Frances Allen before him – weighed on the right side. A lingering veil of dust was all that remained of the landslide. As he entered the ravine, dark shapes half-seen on spurs and between bushes suggested a herd, such as he'd envisioned grazing and displacing rocks. He counted them: one, three. Six. Eight, no, ten. Thirteen. Plus one.

On the scales of Bora's personal destiny, something did more than tip the balance. Meltemi and the wild Catalans were nothing to the dark men with machine guns and rifles pointed at him from three sides; the boulders of the run's bed effectively blocked escape on the fourth side. Yes, they were as he'd spotted them marching single file above Krousonas, and next to one of them – the leader of that sombre rank? – bareheaded, stood Frances Allen. *Christ, she fell into their hands as soon as she left Agia Irinis.* Bora's anxiety extended to her. *I can't help her any more than I can help myself.* Reaching for the holster meant a burst of machine-gun fire from one or more of them.

Behind the slow wraith of dust, sparkling like a fluid partition where the sun reached, she looked down towards him.

She neither wept nor called. Her small figure was remote. Beyond his reach, she seemed as lost as Orpheus' wife sinking back into Hades. Only when she deliberately, defiantly passed her arm around the man's waist did Bora understand he had himself tipped the scales of his own fate.

How wrong could I be? Orpheus has *retrieved his wife from the kingdom of the dead!* So, that was Andonis Sidheraki. Smiling Andonis, whom she'd known for the last twenty-four hours to be alive and free. *She's known ever since Krousonas, when she pretended not to recognize him, and misplaced a rock. I caught it, but it might have been too late. Then she "lost her way", and slowed me down. That's why in the shed she had nothing to say when I let her go. She was confident her husband was in the vicinity, or that they'd find each other soon. The moment they found each other, she led him where he might catch me unawares.* In seconds, Bora saw it all. Her fixed attention when they'd spied the men above Krousonas, and – after recognizing her husband – her control over the storm of emotions she no doubt felt, realizing she'd been lied to about his captivity; her coolness of continuing as if nothing had happened while Sidheraki, alerted to her presence by the last man in the row, also pretended ignorance. Surely, he'd simulated a halt for drinking, and then moved out of sight so as to avoid both Satanas' village and the hostage-carrying German. Following from a safe distance, he must have fallen behind at some point, otherwise he'd have attacked earlier, an easy task, thirteen against one. It was mere chance that Bora had had time to interrogate Caxton.

Sidheraki's men were a rough lot; you'd mistake them for heavily armed rustlers or brigands, but sophisticated advisors like Pendlebury had trained them for months. Only a misstep and a slippage of rocks betrayed their approach. If they still kept him under aim, it could only mean they wanted him alive. Bora did not delude himself that gratitude was in Frances

Allen's bones. Or compassion. Her disregard of Caxton, who clearly still felt for her, was nothing to the revenge she must be savouring now...

How had she put it? "I don't forgive a wrong, either." Well, I'm her German taskmaster. Ten seconds into the trap, one frantic thought after the next, Bora was careful not to move a muscle. *And her story about lynching, was it a late evening confession, or a cautionary tale? "I don't forgive a wrong either." Cretans do mutilate the enemy, and to Sidheraki I'm more than an invader: I'm the man who forced his wife to follow him alone, day and night.* Seeking cover seemed impossible, but his only chance to attempt a defence, or disengage. *Even if she doesn't accuse me of anything beyond pushing her forward, he'll suspect I tried to go for her. And she's bleeding, too.* He ached to do something, but a convulsion of boulders clogging the run was all he could spy to his right, the sole unguarded side. The grotesque quality of his predicament (and all of it for sixty bottles of Greek wine!) made him furious. *I should be in Moscow, listening to embassy titbits and avoiding overdrinking, due for leave that will actually bring me to East Prussia for the invasion. I should be in Athens reporting to Busch, or at the very least in Iraklion telling frog-face Kostaridis that I've just about solved this case. I should be doing any one of a million things in a thousand different places: kissing my wife, smelling Maggie Bourke-White's lilacs, reading* Ulysses, *asking that bloody Waldo Preger what was it,* what was it *that we brawled about that summer day in Trakehnen. But hell, I've got fourteen shots and extra cartridges; I'll force them to open fire against me, if things turn out beyond salvation.*

The wind kept blowing from the north-east. *Meltemi,* Bora thought. *Der Nordost wehet,* said the poem in Heidegger's essay. The nor'easter blows on the lonely, feisty sea traveller, not to be confused with commonplace sailors. It wove through the ravine and caused a constant, palsied tremor to the few trees clinging to the rocks; specks of dust still twirled in the draught, handfuls of arid dirt rode it in powdery waves. Unmoved, Sidheraki's men stood or crouched. From his lookout above the place where Bora and Frances had camped the night before, Sidheraki shouted an order Bora did not understand. At once, his wife stepped back. *Is she getting out of the way before they shoot?* There was no more time. To Bora's right – glimpsed before but discarded, as it would hardly cushion a fall – a squat cedar-like bush emerged from his peripheral vision, spreading its blue-green limbs a good ten feet below him. Bora literally dived into it, while machine-gun fire swept the rock and shot splinters everywhere. He crashed through a tangle of sharp-smelling aromatic branches, barbed twigs, exposed roots, which bent and snapped before he struck rock, but only for the time it took to roll off it to the next hard place below. *No resistance, dead weight, hurts less.* It had been the lesson of his boyhood tumbles, never resisted and therefore seldom dangerous. Angry bursts of gunfire pulverized stone, mowed down the wind-tossed heads of reeds and canes around him.

Bora's plunge into the run bruised him, nothing more. Only a ribbon of water threaded the bottom of the ravine, where – encumbered and yet shielded by the rucksack – he scrambled on all fours, crawled and slid with bullets whizzing around him. He ran bent double, without looking, at the risk of wedging his foot any time in the slippery jumble of water and rocks.

Water flows downhill, and that was all he needed to know for now, even though, he warned himself, *They're after me. I'm only delaying the moment and making them more rabid.* Sleek moss made Bora lose his footing as he stumbled headlong down the tormented course of the run. Shots, throaty calls followed him from the left bank; shrubs and a rock face impossible to climb loomed to his right. *Am I racing to a shelter from where to fire back, or what? They know the mountains far better than I do, and wherever I go they'll keep up and even outflank me, guessing my next move.*

He hadn't travelled this way with Frances Allen; any notion of the interior at this stage of his flight was useless. Bora was aware that the stormy nor'easter was picking up, because light dimmed in the ravine; he glanced skyward as a cloud reached the sun and swallowed it like a great fish eating a coin. Just ahead, the ravine opened into a conch-like basin, a motionless tumult of bare rocks and treeless banks, where Bora could not hope to escape capture or death. *Had the suitors caught Ulysses alone in his palace, he couldn't have prevailed, one against many. And I do not exactly have Athena at my side.*

The run became little more than moisture across broad shingle, the banks yawned and flattened on both sides. *Am I the same fellow, the same boy, the same child...? Did it all lead here, Serpenten and the house with eyes, Waldo's dead brother, the beam Pastor Wüsteritz dangled from?* A bullet missed him by a hair, though the hair was wide as a gulf, being the difference between death and life. *Did I ignore the red-headed girl, the singing maidens for nothing, and still was meant to end here?* The stormy wind carried voices, like strident sounds of seabirds caught in the squall. *Sirens, mermaids are often portrayed as human-headed seabirds, and so are Sphinxes; their calls aren't necessarily melodious voices, either.*

Some of the voices, closer in, coming from the opposite direction to that of the pursuing Greeks, told him that more enemies had joined in, and there was really no salvation. *They overtook me, or else Sidheraki called the English, or maybe Caxton did.* Bora couldn't make out the words, other than that they sounded full of anger and were ordering him to do something. *What are they saying? I don't speak their language; why do they shout at me, and* what?

The voices, powerful, from men studding the shingly banks like sailors who hail a shipwrecked brother from the shoals, were bellowing in Catalan.

"*Fuites, angles, fuites!*"

It was as unhoped-for an encouragement as Bora could dream of. Had they been watching over him, his would-be comrades from the Spanish days? They must have, ever since in Meltemi they'd shared bread and remembrance. For all they knew, the Englishman who fought on their side was under attack, and that was enough for them. Wild firing broke out from all sides, and in the midst of it Bora did not stop for the one or the other. He tripped and nearly fell but kept to his staggering flight until a wooded slope provided him a safety ladder up from the shingle. He scaled a cascading incline of pebbles with two of Sidheraki's men at his heels.

Large drops of rain stung like grapeshot as he scrambled to the top, with just enough advantage to steady himself, fire and not miss, before burrowing into the scrubland above.

10

The headwind was fierce. Because of it, or because his pursuers had fallen behind, shots rang less and less frequently after him, and then thunder overtook all sounds. They were probably fighting one another now (Bora hoped the Catalans would win the day). Under a sky convulsed with lightning, he kept climbing among dwarf trees and bushes, into the squall. No rain followed the first rabid drops, and for nearly an hour he wandered uphill, seeking the sheets of rain as they undulated to meet him. Others would keep out of the rain; he had to hide in the storm. From one moment to the next, he entered it as you enter an open floodgate. Instantly, the landscape vanished around him. In the blinding downpour Bora struggled to stand; he had to feel around for tree trunks, rocks, anything; he slipped and lost his footing and was literally brought to his knees. Water swept over him like waves flooding a deck; there was nothing to do but crouch down and wait it out.

By the clock, the storm did not last long. In minutes it dissolved into a lively shower while the squall rode westward to the massif of Psiloritis, to die there or overflow around it, seeking the Plain of Messarà. The thunderstorm still raged on the higher reaches of the island, lightning struck – huts? Solitary trees? – against a pitch-black sky. Thunder rumbled from one valley to the next. Rain on the parched mountainsides caused a thick sea of vapours, above which Bora now found himself.

Looking around, he discovered that he'd come to a crest woolly with dwarf trees. A single eye of sunlight through the clouds pierced the rain and a glorious rainbow arched into the sky, right where Agias Irinis was already an unrecognizable cliff among cliffs, like a wave among waves. Too much adrenaline flowed for him to feel tired, but he was drenched, and it kept raining. Lucky that he had kept the paper items in his rucksack inside waterproof slips, as he had done with his diary in Moscow. In his plunge to escape the gunfire, his wrist compass had struck a boulder and was useless. It would be the last of his problems now, except that he still had to keep away from Sidheraki's men as well as from the well-meaning Catalans, let alone others a shoot-out might have drawn from their territory, like Satanas' men: if they found him, it would be the end. German patrols might be alerted too, but Bora couldn't count on it as long as the weather was prohibitive.

He needed to consult his map – impossible to do without soaking it. Getting away without knowing the direction did not necessarily mean he'd put a useful distance between himself and his pursuers. It was not his plan to climb indefinitely; he had to seek the lowland instead if he meant to regain a safe road leading to the north coast. *Frances Allen knows the way we came, she probably told her husband the direction I'm likely to take; she'll expect me to retrace the steps followed in the past two days, as I'm not familiar with the island and will think twice about trying new paths.*

That was, of course, what he'd have to do. But Cretan rebels would know all the paths, and any peasant or goatherd seeing him might inform them.

Bora saw no sense in wandering in and out of crags filled with vapours. *The run under Agias Irinis flows N–S, so at first I headed south, then I climbed the bank eastwards; after that, I lost track.* How far he'd come, he tried to calculate by the sombre massif in the distance. Those were the wild reaches of Mount

Psiloritis, to the west. But which side of the massif was he facing? The land beneath frothed with mist like a cauldron; until visibility improved below him it would be close to impossible to orient himself. The rainfall had a tropical quality about it. As it thinned, steam rose from the overheated rocks and earth; if the sun didn't turn it into a blinding wall when it came out, he'd have a sense at least of where he had to go.

His watch read – and he was surprised to see it – a few minutes to eleven.

The tail of the storm swung lazily over him as Bora came to a place that resembled what Frances called the Upper Palace – some other such site, mapped no doubt by the ubiquitous British archaeologists but otherwise abandoned until better times would allow new digs. He walked through it in search of any structure that might provide temporary shelter. No wall stood more than four courses from the ground. A square stairwell, with steps leading down to a landing or underground floor, seemed vaguely more promising. The steps sat askew, cleft in the middle as if struck by a powerful giant fist trying to halve them. Why not: earthquakes still rattled the island occasionally; cataclysms had torn it down and reshaped it over thousands of years. The partly excavated stairwell led down to a jumble of collapsed lintels, beyond which gaped a void. It could serve to get out from under the rain, but made as good a trap if discovered as he could think of. Tomb or cellar or treasure chamber, it was all the same to Bora at the moment. It wasn't the first and wouldn't be the last burrow he scuttled into uninvited. *I need a dry place to check my map, and that's all there is to it.*

Peering in, he saw a dark space that looked like a chute. It reminded him of the mildewy air shaft behind the canteen in Iraklion, the one that came down and spewed the customers out into the street. How new to Crete he was then, to Villiger, to all that had happened between then and now!

Inside you could crouch, sit, nearly stand up; but not see someone coming until he stood at the mouth of the stairwell, by which time it would be too late to save yourself.

Bora glanced at the quickly receding rain clouds, and decided not to go in. Up the steps, he regained the ledge, where a sound of voices through the windy drizzle stopped him dead. Men out of sight just below the paved shelf were heatedly speaking Greek. He quickly sank back, threw in his rucksack first, climbed inside the hole, and hoped no one would join him to get out of the rain.

He counted on lying low for the time it would take the Greeks, whoever they were, to move on. As soon as his sight grew used to the dark, a flicker of light – from a fissure among the uneven flagstones above – caught his attention. If he half-stood, hunching uncomfortably, it would provide a spyhole at eye level. With his forefinger, Bora removed enough dirt from the cleft to glimpse a handful of men climb onto the ledge. Their animated exchange made him suppose they were arguing whether to stop here or not, but it was a southern habit to speak loudly, so who knew.

They did stop. Huddled in the last of the rain, miserable and patient, at one point they must have lit cigarettes under their tarpaulin capes, because Bora made out the spark of matches. No. They had lighters, not matches, and wore pieces of British equipment, dark *vragha*. In his cramped position, Bora fretted. They could be Satanas' lot or some of Sidheraki's men, spread out after him like a pack of dogs. Unless he'd wandered alongside his pursuers without knowing, and without knowing they had all caught up here. The possibility that he'd trapped himself made him furious.

On the ledge, the mutable light suggested that wide stretches of clear sky had opened overhead. The rain died down, but the men only shook their waterproofs and sat. After sunlight escaped the clouds, and puddles on the ancient pavement seemed to catch fire, they laid out their shirts on the drying flagstones and stretched out to rest. One, armed with a sub-machine gun, stood vigilantly by.

Bora gave up watching what they were up to. Only if he betrayed himself would the Greeks instantly assume – or resume – the role of hunters. He crouched in the dark, staring at the red-green dot stamped on his retina by looking through the hole. Still soaked through and hungry, he felt inside his rucksack for the cellophane bag where he'd stored a little zwieback, opened it and munched on a biscuit.

He'd learnt in Spain that fatalism and boredom, at least as far as he was concerned, were twin brothers. *I wanted to read my map? I have time now.* He took out his torch, stuck it in the criss-cross of fallen blocks that framed his shelter and turned it on; the light of day would make it impossible for those outside to notice the small glare, unless they got it into their heads to look down the steps. Hunching over the map, Bora pencilled the approximate trail followed after leaving Agias Irinis, down the stony bed of the run. Where he'd wandered next was impossible to trace, but he was high up from the valley. *I'm as stuck in this hole as Ulysses in the Cyclops' lair, except that there's no woolly ram I might crawl under to escape.*

Bora put away the torchlight and sat, thinking a prisoner's thoughts. In a place like this – one of the few times when he could say that, unseen by all, he was as if non-existent – the world seemed to him an indistinct immensity marked by a handful of meaningful spots.

Ampelokastro, Sphingokephalo, Iraklion. Moscow. Anything in between, including Trakehnen, where Dikta summered with his parents, belonged to that indistinct immensity. *I carry out tasks and figure things out, precisely because I do see the world as a set of discrete points which can be individually mastered. That's why today the bloody room where Villiger and his household lay is known to me in its essence – not as it is, sacked and tramped through, but for what it means.*

Bora closed his eyes. Two nights spent awake had begun to weigh on him, and he couldn't afford weariness at this point. He forced himself to think, to keep his mind vigilant, to make something of this forced interval. *I keep going back to it. If I think of the reason why we fought as boys, Waldo and I, I'll be one step closer to understanding – not just him, or myself, because we became men regardless of that row.* One step closer to understanding in general, as if that episode were a vital part in a larger image, like the plaster fragment with the fierce eye of a bull.

Places *were* pointers. He'd grown up among the privileged signs and pointers of his family homes. He'd island-hopped among them, keeping each wholly separate from the others, recognizable, memorized, as if the space intervening were no more differentiated than the ocean's surface. Thus, his parents' place in Leipzig-Lindenau was a port in the archipelago, and the Borna family seat another. *And so our place in East Prussia, each as minutely known as a boy could know any place, with nothing in between.* In a way he still was island-hopping, with hints left in every harbour for him to sail to the next. *Just as the chalk masks ("Shepherd girl, Gonies?") led unwittingly to* mesa pharangi *and to the ivory-skinned girl looking out of the window, and this to the one-eyed goatherd, and this to the Catalans, and to Agias Irini and to here. This place too has to lead to something, although it may not be what I expect, not yet. But this forced time in the hole has a meaning, is a place marked on the indistinct immensity of the earth, and it may be that it makes me remember what it was that Waldo and I argued about, surely something more meaningful than I thought, or perhaps both of us realize. No place is without meaning, no time is without meaning. You only have to find it.*

Tedium (or weariness) overtook fatalism in him. What if the men above were not just drying their clothes or having a smoke? They could be waiting for others to join them, and it could take hours. Feeling less cramped, less uncomfortable only meant the coming of drowsiness. Bora fought it at first, but it was a losing battle. He eventually drew up his knees and rested his back against the wall of his unlikely shelter.

My world as a boy was that archipelago of known places, in which I moved protected and safe. I was aware, however, that there were others who existed in dense peripheral worlds. Waldo lived in one of them, Herr Hitler in another; Pastor Wüsteritz had lived and died in another yet. If I consider our boyhood fight as a focus I might discover what brought it about, because it is clearly a marker that directed us both here, where Preger's men are accused of having killed in cold blood and I've been ordered to prove they did not. Or did.

If he could – by thinking – connect like dots on a map, or tiles in a mosaic, the broken recollections about that summer long ago and his row with Waldo Preger… The tiles scattered, dots danced round like sparks or fireflies. Falling asleep was easier than thinking.

…I am twelve. I am twelve, pure in mind and body. I am twelve and for some reason have a row with Waldo Preger behind the abandoned factory. That's where it was, the factory with the doves, where Pastor Wüsteritz hanged himself. And there we are, Waldo and I. We go from arguing to shoving each other, less and less in control of our boyish tempers.

Why am I so angry?

I can't recall the words we shout; what this means to both of us we won't know for years to come, though he'll know before I do.

The need to draw blood is not part of my childhood. Or hasn't been until now. I hardly recognize myself; anger turns the familiar place around me into a fog. We fight but hardly see each other; each one of us becomes his own anger, larger than himself.

Why am I so angry? Is it because—?

I am twelve, and I save money to buy the first volume of Herr Hitler's Mein Kampf, *hot off the press. Shortly thereafter, the story of the forbidden book comes up in confession.*

Monsignor Hohmann makes me hand it over to my stepfather. The Leica camera is taken from me as a punishment regarding Herr Hitler's book: I will not be allowed to use it again until the following year.

I am twelve and I hate my stepfather (and Monsignor Hohmann). I am confirmed at St Mary's church, Plagwitz-Lindenau, but I lied about feeling sorry about Herr Hitler's book, so if I die, I'll go to hell. Peter offers me the use of his camera on the sly, but I refuse: I will suffer the indignity to the last.

I am twelve and have a row with Waldo Preger behind the abandoned factory...

It was a woman's voice that startled him into awakening. Dream images collapsed, deflated, had to be preciously stored for later. Bora recognized Frances Allen though she spoke Greek, and was instantly lucid and aware. By his watch he'd slept only minutes, enough for her to join those who had until now occupied the ledge. He looked through the spyhole. *So, it's Sidheraki's band. Damn her, I was so close to understanding why Preger and I fought. She's going to get me killed yet.*

Andonis was there, too. Frances spoke and as far as Bora could see the men stirred themselves, but gave no sign of readiness to march on. The couple came briefly into view through the spyhole. The way her husband held her close, one hand spread on her buttock – Bora recognized the possessive touch. The group, he thought, hadn't simply separated in the storm: the two had taken time away from the others. What was it? They'd found a shelter somewhere to make love? Why not. In a hurry, furiously, whether she was bleeding or not. "In Crete you eat, you make love, you die."

And you lead the pack after me, Mrs Sidheraki, or so you think. The men can hardly appreciate your making them wait in the rain, and now your presumption to guide them. Bora tried to disregard the possibility that she or her husband – the archaeologist and the freedom fighter – might be curious to look down the steps into his hole. He held his breath and hoped against hope for a disagreement among the Greeks. This morning he'd counted thirteen in Sidheraki's band; with her, all told, they came to six or seven now. Two he'd fired on; the rest must have fallen to the Catalans in the shoot-out – he'd seen in Spain how deadly a republican marksman could be. Along with the taking of his wife, losing half of his men would enrage Sidheraki into seeking German blood. Seeking blood, *buscar sangre* – Bora hadn't thought of the expression since Spain. And she, too, the Texan adolescent outraged – *not* squeamish – before a lynching. *Does she want me dead? She'll do nothing to stop him from killing me, at any rate.* Bora furtively buckled his rucksack. *But the men might not welcome more risk over a single German.*

His reduced field of vision limited his understanding. Was there more than southern vehemence to the exchange? *Óchi*, which meant no, was thrown back and forth. The men still sat. He could only hear Frances now, not see her. At one point she switched to English, no doubt to exclude the others from what she told her husband. And though only some words came clearly to Bora's ears, he grasped that she was angry and disappointed and insisted that they continue the hunt. The men, it stood to reason, saw no point in doing so. Sidheraki – also invisible and speaking broken English – sounded ambivalent, and unhappy about it. His contrariness showed in his altered voice. Bora heard Frances say out loud, "You've got to choose," and him shout back, "I don't have to choose, I *decide*."

There was hope after all. *He can't be seen giving in to his wife before his men, but he doesn't want to frustrate her.* In Spain, in a similar situation, volunteers would have irritably gone off, because a single enemy or a woman aren't worth fighting over. *Sidheraki's dilemma is nothing to mine, but Frances Allen has to do with both.*

The discussion continued in Cretan dialect. Eventually the men picked up their weapons and stood facing the slope with the waterproofs draped over their shoulders. A tight-lipped Frances flitted in and out of sight; still, Bora could understand that she'd won the argument at a price, or her husband was annoyed with her, or both.

Curiously, for the first time since they'd met he felt close to her, in an adversarial way. Something tied them, an imaginary rubber band or rope or length of yarn that forced them to look out for each other now, as they had when she was to all intents and purposes his prisoner. Bora found that he almost liked her for her obstinacy, and even if he had no intention of letting her have the upper hand, still he recognized the tie.

Soon, with Sidheraki in the lead, she and the others abandoned the ledge. Silence trailed them. When Bora emerged into the brightness of a clear, lonely day, far to his left the unaware Greeks trudged away from the ledge across the mountainside. *She knows I'll be seeking the valley, and* he'll *tell them to string along so they'll catch me as I head downhill. For now, they think I'm still too far inland to risk it, and will keep after me at this level. How close to the coast will they push before turning back?* It was the welcome sight of a foil-like trembling sheen, a long shimmering line on the northern horizon, that made his heart leap.

There it is, the sea: how lovely, even if you're not a Greek. That's where I'm going. In the sun, Bora's wet clothes began to steam. Out came his sunglasses, and the world became tenderly green. *Now that I know where the north is, I need to know where Krousonas is, nothing else. Frances and her man expect everything but that* I *will be following* them.

Krousonas perched below, to the north in a convulsed bubbling up of hills. Looking tame but demonized because they said the devil holed up there, or because it really meant great danger, it was one in a handful of unidentified little burgs. From where Bora stood, every hill, bare or sparsely treed, appeared to be crowned by a solitary farmhouse or a reduced village, what his Scots grandmother termed "a blinking sort o' place" (quoting Thomas Hardy: she said it of Trakehnen, too). In between, dark oaks grew close to the ground like a pelt, pale opuntia bushes sent up their flukes, trails ran thinner than pencil marks. The half-seen white thread far below, which Bora called for want of better words *the valley road*, did not run on flat land at all: it only wormed among lower ranges and single knolls. And he'd heard Kostaridis call it *basilikos dromos*, the high road or royal way! Sarchos must be the whitewashed hamlet beyond Krousonas, and Agios Mironas beyond that, or Kato Asites. Diminutive churches, bleached like mosques – former mosques, maybe – sat under oppressive tile roofs. Above everything, the midday heat was stifling after the rain; cicadas crowded it with endless noise. Distances trembled as moisture went up from shrinking puddles and all the storm had soaked to the bone.

Anxious to reach a place where he could risk leaving the mountain, Bora kept trailing the Greeks, careful to keep out of sight but never losing the last man. He now had the impression they were slowing down in search of a spot for mess time. It meant he'd have to halt as well, whether he liked it or not.

Ahead, a single dead tree marked the wind-beaten incline, next to the remnants of a dry wall. Bora saw it from afar and it was ominous, with those few naked branches, one of which stretched out like a gibbet. Eaten by landslides all around, the slope was unsafe, the passage near the tree clearly una-voidable: the Greeks filed through and continued in a single line. Bora let a minute go by, studying the ruinous state of the trail. Yes, one could continue northward only by toeing a margin narrow as a gymnast's beam, further reduced to a ribbon of stony soil between the tree and the dry wall. *If I make it past,* Bora told himself, *if I make it past unharmed, I will reach a different place from the one travelled thus far. Perhaps safer, perhaps not: but different.*

Well, nothing happened to him in the passage. Once he was beyond the tree, whose outstretched branch forced him to bow his head, he found himself on a ragged slope identical to the previous one. Yet the sense of having crossed a threshold stayed with him.

The place Sidheraki's men made for was a dilapidated, flat-roofed stone house, guarded by a leafy fig tree and over-looking the valley. Bora watched them stealthily go in with weapons at the ready and come out again, reassured. Still they chose to camp in the open, 200 feet below on a shelf of pastureland. While his men ate, Sidheraki stood surveying the valley. Frances Allen stood next to him, earnestly, if Bora was able to judge from where he was, even anxiously entreating him. She implacably pointed the way to follow, playing Ariadne as she never had with her German captor. *As soon as they are past Krousonas, now that the countryside is less wild she'll clamber left and right to ask this and that farmer or shepherd, and adjust her course accordingly. If I keep to the heights, sooner or later she'll meet someone who'll tell her he's sighted the likes of me, even though I may never even have noticed him. I'm the Minotaur in her labyrinth, but unlike the Minotaur I can move and fight freely outside of the maze.*

Daringly, Bora gained on the group until he was level with it, only higher. Picking his steps, keeping low, he crawled to the house the Greeks had discarded, and slipped in through a breach in the wall. The passing of time, not the hand of man, had wrecked it beyond use. What the hand of man did was steal door and window frames, yanking out the bricks laid out as floor tiles. Tender shoots of the fig tree fingered upward from the ground and sought the bright clefts in the ceiling. All furniture had been removed except for a broken-down table. In a corner, a rope with a long frayed end coiled like a snake. A clay jug, once fitted with two handles, lay forlorn in a rich growth of nettles. Through a storm of crickets and small flies Bora ventured across the ground floor in search of steps or a ladder to the roof.

What he found was a masonry ramp bereft of stepping stones. Once upstairs, the tumbledown planking of the flat roof was a disappointment: the potential observation point would never hold a man's weight.

Within reach, however, the richly leaved fig tree offered an alternative. Only a little unbalanced by the rucksack, Bora jumped from the edge of the roof, easily swung to the fork in the trunk, and straddled it. The trunk squeaked and moaned under him. He knew from boyhood how easy fig trees were to get up, but you couldn't trust their grey limbs, rough like elephant skin, because they could snap under you. Not that he'd hurt himself falling from this gnarled specimen, nine feet at most from the ground. What mattered was its sheltered vantage point.

Beyond the tangle of leaves that oozed a milky liquid as their stems broke, few landmarks were recognizable to him aside from Iraklion and its harbour. Týlissos, Ampelokastro and Sphingokephalo lay to the north-west behind the brow of the mountain, impossible to consider as destinations from here. If he did cut downhill, straight down across crumbling slopes and wooded ledges, it would be half an hour to Krousonas, and an hour more through unknown terrain to the *valley road*, such as it was.

I haven't much choice. I must outguess a woman who knows every inch of this island if I want to reach it. With Krousonas in the way, it's foolish for me to break out here, but I must be back in Iraklion today. Whatever the risk. Frances thinks the same way: she wants to bag me today, whatever the risk. But her husband – he's more logical, or more responsible. His war is bigger than Martin Bora. There's one thing he knows I will not do unless I'm out of my mind – no, there are two: *approaching Krousonas, and going back inland.*

It suddenly seemed so clear: the dangers involved were irrelevant. Bora climbed down, mindful not to shake the branches and call attention to the tree from below. He stole back inside the house to grab the coil of rope from the corner and the single-handled jug; he stuffed them in his rucksack, and left. Crawling at first and then placing one foot after the other on the narrow margin, he moved to his right, keeping low but without hesitation. He backtracked, headed south, away from his goal for the moment. *There are three harbours in my interior map at this time: Iraklion, Moscow and East Prussia. I must get away from the three of them if I want to reach them – which is what Ulysses did time and again: came within sight of Ithaca only to be tossed back.*

Half a mile from the house, Bora faced the passage between the dead tree and dry wall. He took the rope out of his rucksack, uncoiled it, threw it twice over the gibbet branch to form a loop. The hanging ends, he tied around the jug so that today or tomorrow, when Sidheraki's men filed through, they would find it dangling in front of their eyes. He then creased and neatly divided in two his diary's blotting paper. On the cleaner half he scribbled the Greek verses from the Iliad, remembered when he flew over in the ambulance plane.

A dawn will come, an evening, a midday / when someone will bereave me of life in battle / by the stroke of a spear or a bow's arrow. Below, he added in English, *But not now, Mrs Sidheraki,* and his signature.

He wrapped the paper around the shard with the magic eye, and slipped both inside the jug.

From here to the valley, there were lengths of steep rocky soil, winding trails, huts reduced to stone heaps. Mastic trees stood incredibly green and fresh-looking; poppies and evergreens filled the hollows like red and green fires. Unnamed villages, lonely chapels, endless rubble walls reminiscent of Aragon dressed the tormented foot of the mountain. Bora could not see it beyond the shrubbery, but Krousonas squatted just north of here, he was sure.

There was nothing obvious in what he was preparing to do; it was foolhardy to think that running headlong towards the valley would result in anything but a ruinous fall or a haphazard rifle shot. But it lingered in him, that idea of places like islands, each reachable in turn if you dare to take the risk, and if it is your destiny. He eyed the drop of the land as if an imaginary sinking and swelling line connected the spot where he stood to a single desired spot far below.

Mountains, yes, but not high mountains. *Perfect for fell running, as Peter and I learnt – more or less – in the Grampians from our Cargill cousins.* Bora carefully put away his sunglasses, latched the pistol holder, fastened the straps of his rucksack. He took a few quick breaths like a sportsman before a race. *This is no Ben Nevis, but going down is all I have to do.*

The moment he took off, it was as if he had wings on his heels. He jumped, straddled, cut across. Fences and stony brinks fled under him; he let himself slide and free fall, whenever sliding and free-falling were quicker than climbing down. Wherever the descent led, he went there, he sped up saddles and cliffs only to gain the next plunge. A red throb of sun and shadow went past him, zigzags of dusty roads, forlorn houses or empty barnyards. Under his mountain boots, rock, grass, pebbles, drying mud made no difference. He heard rifle shots as the running hare hears them, like a background noise left behind. Thorns, nettles, burs, spiky heads of thistles stuck to him or took their toll as he trod on them. Not that it mattered: not even as a boy had he run with such abandon, save perhaps when he had fled in terror from the house with eyes. *Only there's no family garden waiting to let me in at the end of the race. Or maybe there is, as a distant harbour beyond Iraklion. Beyond Villiger's bloody room, Gorky Boulevard, East Prussia, the war – all of those I must go past to return home. If I ever return.*

VALLEY ROAD, 2.35 P.M.

How he reached the bottom safely, he couldn't have said. Suddenly, there was no more downward slope. Bora stopped at the verge of a blinding white dirt road, barely in touch with his body. The roar of blood in his ears took a few endless moments to subside; it felt until then like keeping his head under water. The sky pulsed red; the mountain he'd come from, red and remote, safe, fluttered before his eyes with his heartbeat. He knelt down to regain his breath; feeling his body coalesce around him slowly, one sense at a time, without pain. *Hell, if along with the supplies at the depot I'd got the cap of invisibility, I couldn't have done better. The shard with the Minotaur eye brought me luck, or the ivory-white girl at* mesa pharangi*: I did well to avoid the singing girls in the high grass…*

That's Kato Asites up there, not Krousonas. The place was south of Krousonas, he was sure, far inland, and the road ahead forked like a wishbone. Beyond the fork, a handful of one-storeyed ramshackle houses baked in the sun. Still lightheaded, Bora walked in that direction. No soldiers, no army equipment around, only signs in German script pointing in different directions. The left branch of the fork diverged toward the foot of the mountain, to Skala and Kavrochori (and Ampelokastro between them), no distances given. As for the main road, it led south to Agias Varvaras, 8km. To the north, lay Agios Mironas, 7km. Iraklion, too, 30km away.

Bad news. Even in an area nominally under German control, those eighteen or so miles posed a major problem without transportation to be had. *I'm still deep in the labyrinth, with twenty-four hours at most to find the exit by solving this case. Agios Mironas rings a bell, but I'll be damned if I know why.* Bora eyed a miserly fountain by the roadside, where he went to wash off sweat and dirt as best he could and rinse the dust out of the scrapes and cuts on his limbs. Piece by piece, he regained his identity: shoulder boards, identification disc, side cap. Curiously, he felt no pain in his muscles, as if his body were putting off discomfort and exhaustion until he could afford them. The raging haste that until now had made him function was on hold too.

Villiger, Kostaridis, Preger and Sinclair seemed so unreachable from here, only a blessed numbness kept him from despair. The moment you see Ithaca like a cork bobbing over the ocean, she's taken from you.

The nameless handful of houses along the road received him with the usual complement of elders seated on low walls and girls sliding away, hiding their faces behind black or white kerchiefs. Announcing that he had money – *Echo parades* – would not conjure a vehicle or a horse out of thin air. Bora could only hope that a German patrol would pass through, but waiting here wouldn't improve his chances of meeting one. Trailed by careless glances, he started north, and had covered nearly a mile before the grinding of a truck engine behind him caused him to look back.

The truck was a Petropoulos Diamond T, black and red like a carnival Lucifer, and Bora found himself face-to-face with Rifat Bey Agrali.

11

That's what it was – Agios Mironas is where the Turk keeps his trucks... Wasn't I told he has trucks crossing the island from Iraklion to Ierapetra?

The Turk was riding with a driver of his, not the same one Bora had conscripted, but one destined to be commandeered all the same. At a tilt of his employer's head, the man turned off the engine, got down and started walking. Another tilt of the head invited Bora to take his place in the cab.

"Come."

Bora slipped the rucksack off his shoulders and climbed in. No sooner had the engine started again than he felt the muzzle of the Subay against his ribs, and started to laugh.

"Are you stupid, you stupid *frangos*?"

"If you wanted to shoot me, you wouldn't be giving me a lift."

"You think? I'll kill you and throw you out of this truck."

The threat went beyond unsociability. Rifat Bey acted as though he'd learnt things in the meantime (from Kostaridis?) and was determined to square accounts now that there was a chance. For Bora it was like fingering the clue out of the labyrinth after dropping it in the dark, provided the clue was not a noose. He found himself thinking clearly, and yet suspended in that physical state between ache and stupor where excitement vies with fatigue, and prudence crumbles.

He reached into his chest pocket for a photograph, which he held where the Turk could see it well. "This is – what do you call it, Zimbouli? – your place just outside Iraklion."

"I *will* kill you and throw you out of this truck."

"But you don't know whether I made copies of it."

"You didn't. You just have this one."

Yes, Kostaridis tattled about the film roll Savelli stole at Ampelokastro. Bora kept smiling. More and more, he felt a certain demented irrepressible merriment with the gun against his side. Danger gratified him nearly as much as the first taste of pain across his muscles. Slowly, with thumb and forefinger he lifted Signora Cordoval's calling card out of the same pocket. "This, too." He showed it. "I thought you were hiding guns, or objects you'd swiped from your dead neighbour, but you were – you are – hiding *her.*"

Rifat Bey kept one eye on him, the other on the road. The Subay dragged up Bora's side. When it met the hollow under his ear, Bora simply slipped photo and card back into his pocket and buttoned it. "What I don't understand is when you picked her up from Savelli, and whether he knows, or suspects you did. Maybe not. I think he stole the film roll because Villiger had the bad habit of claiming other scholars' digs and finds."

"I could have killed Savelli ten times over."

"Why didn't you? One way or another, Signora's card fell into Villiger's hands. I'd kill Savelli, if I thought he might be a problem."

On the lonely road, Rifat Bey drove, glowering at his passenger while the truck swerved at will across the tarmac. "You're a funny one."

"Is that a promotion from 'bastard son of an infidel German whore'?"

The pressure of the Subay changed at every lurch but never left Bora's neck. "Stop smiling! It's not a time for smiling."

Whether it was tension that was making him smile, or relief that he was beginning to feel *some* pain, Bora did not react when the Subay abruptly dropped down and dug once more into his ribs. At the side of the road, now that they were approaching Agios Mironas, there was a German presence. Armed paratroopers gathered under a shady tree stared at the advancing truck; they seemed on the point of stepping out to halt it, but changed their minds when Bora nodded a greeting from the passenger seat.

"You *are* touched in the head," the Turk grumbled. "Why didn't you call out to them? Now you'll have have to lie dead by the road."

He knows I'm armed, knows what sort of handgun I carry. Does he judge from my muddled appearance that I may not be quick to react? He's right. Bora sighed. "Look, Agrali. I need to know who killed your neighbour. You had good reason for it, if Kostaridis went as far as telling you not only that Signora had been spotted in Iraklion, but also that the Swiss was asking about her. Small town, big gossip."

"Kostaridis is just a *sbirro.*"

"But we know how things go between honourable men. If Kostaridis could prove anything against you – regarding the murder or anything else – he'd clap you in jail. He doesn't, so I assume he has no proof. He owes you nothing, you're not Greek." During the headlong tumble, Bora's hands had picked up thorns and splinters from the brushwood; he was only now starting to notice the sharp tingle drilling up his nerves from his fingertips. "Did Villiger demand money so he wouldn't turn your girl in?" With his thumbnail, he began scraping a sliver of wood from under his skin. "In your boots, I'd have shot him dead before I gave him a penny."

"I'm not going to tell you anything about anything." Agrali's green eyes, narrow and bloodshot, showed a state of mind close to murder. "You're wrong if you're hoping I'll put away my gun."

"I don't care about that; you can leave it there if you can keep to the road with one hand."

"I'll tell you nothing, *frangos*."

An abandoned house was coming up, with a blooming roadside garden that overflowed the fence. Bora recognized a pink haze of lilacs. He closed his eyes as they rode by. Through the open window, scent bathed him for a moment so fleeting and superb that he was surprisingly tempted by a thought. *It could be more merciful and much quicker than other deadly moments. All I need to do is make a rash move, and he'll kill me.*

Ever since childhood, and especially on the verge of adolescence, in the fullness of energy or happiness he'd had those momentary death wishes, aware in a small way that things would never be so perfect again. As if he didn't have his destiny as a soldier before him! Bora was deeply ashamed for indulging in such thoughts.

"Listen, Agrali. I think you met Signora Cordoval in Rhodes years ago, when you trafficked with the Italian Tobacco Manufacture there. I think it was on your account, not the family brooch's, that Savelli raged at her to the extent that the police intervened, both in Rhodes and in Crete four years ago. I think you brought her here somehow, before or after your Greek wife died, and – until we landed – felt pretty safe about it. Kostaridis knew the arrangement and kept his mouth shut. Of late, she probably visited you in the country off and on; the story of being reclusive because you were in mourning isn't credible in the least." When the prod of steel against his ribs increased, Bora was provoked but would not show it. "Your 'missing' dog was taken to Zimbouli to guard her, wasn't it? It was never lost. Is it still there, and do you go and feed it yourself, from time to time? You probably sneaked Signora to your hilltop home just in time, before German troops had a chance to look for billets in Iraklion and find Jewish women instead. I do believe you'd have shot Kostaridis and me, too, had we tried to enter that day."

"You talk too much."

Every curve brought the truck closer to Iraklion. Bora began to recognize ridges, the shape and lie of hills, the profiles of Mount Voskerò, Mount Pirgos... Were they still looking for him, up there, or had they given him up? Had Frances read his message, raking the rebel curl off her forehead? It was as if part of him was still running for his life in the mountains and always would, as if that existence had a separate path of its own and this was another self, with a different fate. *In that life they catch me, I die. In this one...* Bora studiously dug out a thorn from the palm of his hand.

"Villiger could have taken that photo on an impulse, during one of his monthly forays into town, merely because she's a blonde and he judged her – imagine – an Aryan beauty. It was enquiring about her that did not go unnoticed. Did Savelli supply the calling card? It's irrelevant now. The Italian was trying to retrieve *something* when Kostaridis and I walked in on him at Ampelokastro. The details on the card were written in Italian. But the language is still widely spoken in Crete; I have no time to investigate who wrote them, or why. They could be street directions as much as a tip that there'd be money to be extorted from the Cordoval family. For your information, the card was in Villiger's safe-deposit box, so – whether or not he had time to match the blonde in the photo with her racial profile – he clearly put some value on it."

"You talk too much. I think now I have to kill you."

The cab was roomy, but not enough for two tall men. Of the entire experience, Bora found that he resented the threat less than the discomfort of sitting here, cramped by the rucksack at his feet. "I heard you the first time." The fragment in the palm of his left hand lay under a resilient veil of skin, and he used his teeth to dislodge it. "But I'm right, am I not? Not because he likes you, but because he doesn't like *us*, Kostaridis dropped the hint that your neighbour in German employ was curious about Signora Cordoval, so you tried to frighten Villiger into leaving the island. He didn't leave, or didn't do it quickly enough for you. Whatever Kostaridis believes, *I* want to know whether you had Villiger murdered, and all those with him."

"So you can turn me in to your army? I should be as stupid as you are, *frangos*."

Bora spat the thorn out of the window. *This morning I was at Agias Irinis, and the rain was yet to come. Now we're past the storm. Everything is dry at the sides of the road, so it's possible the downpour only lashed the heights. Past Krousonas, past the gibbet tree. Has Frances Allen found the message?* Unhurriedly, he undid the button of his chest pocket. "Actually, there's someone else it would be more useful for me to blame for the deaths." He amiably handed the snapshot and card to the Turk. "Take 'em both, I don't need them. She doesn't interest me in the least. Keep her away from Iraklion, though, and away from terraces where she can be photographed."

The Subay nosed up and wavered as Rifat Bey snatched the papers without letting go of the grip. "I don't understand any of it."

"No? I don't understand *some* of it. Were you really in town during the shooting at Ampelokastro?"

"No."

"At least we made that clear."

They were entering Agios Mironas. There, a requisitioned British truck had broken down and partially blocked the way, forcing Rifat Bey into a series of manoeuvres, changing gears and steering hard. The Subay came to rest on the seat, within easy reach of either man. Bora glanced at it, and away from it. *After this village,* he remembered from studying the map, *there's a place called Voutes, and the turn-off for Kato Kalesia, where Cowell and Sinclair queued as prisoners of war. Beyond there's Týlissos. I don't see it from here, but the Sphinx monument is somewhere up there also, like a frozen beacon.*

At last, they negotiated the hurdle. Past the garage marked *Eipikeirese Rifat Agrali,* the Turk drove with his eyes on the road, gloomily biting the blond whiskers on his upper lip.

"Well, I'm going to kill you, so it makes no difference what I tell you. I did *not* have that German-speaking swine shot. I did *not* frighten him into leaving Crete. If I wanted him dead, I'd strangle him with my own hands without scaring him first, and without asking my boys to do the job for me. Had I heard he was after Signora, or had he come to me asking for money, I'd have cut his throat and fed him to my dogs. The peasants working for him – I spit on them. I was never bothered by witnesses; why should I dirty my hands with field hands and a house servant? If you were less stupid than you are, you'd know that in Crete witnesses keep their mouths shut regardless."

"So, I'm wrong nearly all along the line. Good. Since you were at Sphingokephalo, then, suppose you tell me what you heard, or saw, that day."

Saturday 7 June, 4.04 p.m. Written in pencil to avoid ink blotches on this bumpy road, en route to Iraklion in Rifat Bey's truck. With the excuse that no place is quite right, the Turk keeps delaying the moment of my execution. It's a game he plays, and besides he can't be sure I'd go down gently – I have fourteen shots in my gun. He calls me stupid, and at the moment I can't in good faith disagree with him. I'm not saying I could have wrapped this up on my second day in Crete; still, the clue to get in and out of the labyrinth was dangling in front of me, and I didn't go for it. I can only console myself with thinking that only now do I have all the elements. Well, all except for a motive that would stick in a courtroom. At any rate, Preger's men are off the hook, which is what this investigation – for all its high-minded name – was expected to prove.

Although he still hates our German guts, this ogre of a Turk tells a credible tale, summarized below.

Saturday 31 May, late morning: Rifat Bey Agrali is at home at Sphin-gokephalo. His dogs are nervous because of sporadic cannon- and gunfire. On and off they bark, but when they start to howl, which they do when strangers approach the neighbourhood, he makes the most of his hilltop perch to look through his field glasses in all directions.

To the west, he sees in the distance what he'll later identify as German paratroopers, apparently heading on foot toward the Iraklion–Skala–Kato Asites road (that is, the N–S road both Sphin-gokephalo and Ampelokastro overlook). What provokes his mastiffs, however, is somewhat closer in: a dog, which three men in British uniforms, wandering from the north along the same road, have with them.

To my question, "Were the Britons heavily armed, and did any of them hold a rank?" he premises that vegetation and curves in the road limited his observation, but two of them carried Sten guns. Not sure about their respective ranks. Anticipating there will be an ambush or a shoot-out between paratroopers and Britons, Rifat Bey decides to lock himself indoors with weapons at the ready. As he is making fast the glass door of his terrace, two pistol shots heard in quick succession from the direction of the Brits accelerate his decision.

He hears nothing else for a while, "maybe twenty minutes", then "one or two machine guns" open fire below. Shortly, curiosity gets the better of him, and he sneaks out to the terrace with his field glasses. The first thing that strikes him is that the paratroopers are already quite far southbound on the road to Skala. Who did the shooting, then? The Turk lets "less than fifteen more minutes" elapse before he arms himself and leaves the house. Once he reaches the bottom of the hill and crosses the brook between the two properties, he sees no dead Germans or Brits on the road. All he notices is a lone Briton staggering away from Ampelokastro, towards Iraklion.

To my questions, "Was he wounded? Did he have a photographic camera with him?" he answers he doesn't know if he had a camera, the man had his back to him. Pressed for details, he adds he doesn't believe the man was wounded, but "walking in a daze" (Cowell's own words, according to Geoffrey Caxton).

Suspecting that an ambush of sorts has taken place in his neighbour's property, Rifat Bey stealthily approaches the garden. Once past the front gate, he spots the dead dog. "Inside, you know what there was. I took a look from the door and backed out."

By this time, he is confused as to what he has just witnessed. As he leaves Villiger's garden, fully intending to pretend ignorance about the whole affair, he's startled by a last pistol shot.

Because it comes from the north, the direction taken by the dazzled Briton, his immediate thought is that the man has killed himself.

Looking up from the page, Bora interrupted his furious pencilling. "Where are we?"

"Voutes."

"Ah. You had better kill me, then. That's not far from Iraklion."

Rifat Bey pointed with his chin to Bora's diary. "You should add that I barred doors and windows and when some of yours came knocking the following day I made them think there was nobody home. I only drove to Iraklion later that day, with a case of Malvasia for my friends in town so they'd all swear I'd been at Zimbouli on the thirty-first."

"'Some of mine' were military judges looking into the shooting. You would have done well to have let them in and told them what you told me."

"What for? It's not like I care who killed that son of a bitch of a neighbour."

On both sides of the road more and more German vehicles and buildings requisitioned by Germans now appeared. Paratroopers and mountain Jäger sat in the shade sipping beer and clear liquor.

"Did you get your wine?"

Bora put away his diary. It annoyed him to admit it had been stolen and drunk by other Germans, but his silence spoke of some difficulty in that regard. Rifat Bey grinned under his moustache. "You should have listened to me and gone to buy from the Spinthakis widow near Agia Ekaterini. It's too late now. Some local patriot decided to cut her throat because she did business with you all, and smash everything she had in her shop."

"I'll buy what I find."

"You'll have to."

Before entering the Chanià Gate, Rifat Bey nodded for Bora to leave. "Get down. I don't want to be seen in town with a German."

Bora opened the door, jumped off and shouldered his rucksack. By the side of the road, a giant opuntia shrub stretched its blooming paddles, yellow buds against the blue bar of the sea. The afternoon air was thick with the odour of brine.

As he started walking to town, for a while the truck kept up with him. With his elbow out of the driver's side Rifat Bey watched him from above. *He could yet fire a shot into my head,*

343

Bora thought, *just as I am about to enter the last frantic hours in Crete.* He looked up at the cab, so that he wouldn't be killed unawares if Rifat Bey had a mind to.

Nothing of the kind.

From his Lucifer-coloured truck, the Turk said before giving it some gas, "You think you're so smart. Why don't you ask yourself if my wives died a natural death?"

7 JUNE, 4.40 P.M., IRAKLION

Kostaridis looked like a frog that had sighted a dragonfly too large to swallow. He stood up from behind his desk, and – too clever to manifest his surprise – greeted Bora as if they'd left each other ten minutes earlier. Only a strangled flush stayed on his face. He wore an off-white shirt, assuming it wasn't just dirty, and a tie like a rat's tail.

"*Capitano.*"

On his walk to the police station, Bora had mentally gone from the strange lull of the truck ride to a near-desperate state of alacrity. For two days he'd been as if spellbound, and now there seemed to be not enough time in the world for him to get things done before leaving Crete.

Which was why he couldn't enjoy the moment of Kostaridis' wonder. "*Epitropos.*"

"Anything I can help you with?"

"I'll let you know after I see the British prisoner again. Take me there."

"Take you where? He'll have been transferred back to the Galatas camp!"

"Not if I didn't leave word I was done with him. He had better be still under guard at the airfield. Take me there; I don't have time to call ahead."

A lesser man would have observed something obvious but inopportune, like "Where's the American woman?" or "Have you taken a look at yourself?" Kostaridis grabbed his jacket from the back of his chair, and the car keys from his desk. "Let's go." He cracked open an inner door, said something in Greek to a subordinate, and followed Bora outside.

On the doorstep, he seemed to recall something. "Two days ago the International Red Cross was here asking for you."

Bora turned. "Asking for *me*? How would they know I was the one looking into Villiger's death?"

"They didn't. Their information was that Major Voos was handling matters, so they went to the Megaron, and the German Air Force commander routed them here. I believe that's where your name was first mentioned. Major Voos' replacement hasn't arrived yet, so I had to escort them to Ampelokastro, although there's even less left in the house than when you and I went." Kostaridis let Bora into the car, and sat behind the wheel. "No, they found nothing useful."

"And what did you tell them about me?"

"Forgive me, but that's police business."

"*What did you tell them about me?*"

"Not knowing where you were, I said you were out of town. They had a flight out the same evening, so they had to content themselves with that. I explained I don't speak German, which kept them from further enquiries. Anything else?"

"No."

It was all they said during the trip to the airfield. Bora moodily picked burs and bits of straw from his socks, as if that would make a difference to the sorry state of his outfit. Something like a dark mountain, so high he couldn't see its top, stood between him and the morning. He was so afraid of raising his eyes and really seeing it that he didn't even look at the road, instead busy removing prickly bits from the wool. Meeting Sinclair. Radioing Bruno Lattmann in Athens… *Then I must confer with Kostaridis. And then acquaint Preger with the unofficial version of the story. Find out when the next flight out will be. Write my report. And the wine? Hell, I mustn't forget the wine. I must get the wine too.*

The German airmen at the gate wouldn't let Kostaridis through, so – on the promise that the inspector would wait there for him – Bora left the car, and crossed the perimeter under the curious stares of the guards.

It relieved him to hear that Sinclair was still being held at the airfield, although he'd been transferred to more liveable quarters. "The Red Cross gave us grief about it," the same *Feldwebel* who'd escorted Bora the previous time informed him. "First thing in the morning the prisoner is due for transport to the mainland, where the IRC will oversee his treatment. A few more hours, sir, and you'd have missed him."

"Is he alone?"

"He's alone."

"Leave me with him."

"Don't you need an interpreter?"

Sinclair was confined to an inner service room, with a cot, table and chair. When Bora entered, the prisoner was standing in the middle of the floor, where a naked light bulb cast enough glare on the newspaper he was reading.

"I'm here to thank you, Lieutenant." The opening of the door had not induced Sinclair to look up from the printed page; the greeting did.

"Your English is much improved."

Bora had no time to exchange quips. He gave a crisp salute and took one step forward, careful, however, to remain just outside the lit centre of the room. The worn appearance of his uniform had nothing to do with it: his experience as an interrogator, ever since the Polish days, made him automatically seek the shade.

"Following your directions, I obtained the eyewitness' written statement about the deaths at Ampelokastro."

"That's quite impossible."

"That's quite possible. I am about to forward it to the War Crimes Bureau and the International Red Cross."

The newspaper was a month-old issue with headlines in English on the German invasion of Yugoslavia and Greece. Sinclair doubled it over, looking at Bora with the same spare, polite aloofness of their first meeting. His watch had not been returned to him, but in the three days since then, the bruises on his elbow and wrist had been attended to. "Won't you take a seat, Captain?"

"No."

One had to admire his aplomb. Bora said, "I also bring regards from your old fellow student Geoffrey Caxton, to whom I'm indebted for the right spelling of the NCO's surname. It's Cowell. Albert 'Bertie' Cowell. Not Powell, as you told me."

"Forgive me." The newspaper was carefully folded once more. "I don't know who Mr Caxton is, and the man I spoke to, the man with the camera, was a Sergeant Major Powell."

In the back of his mind, Bora knew he was inches away from giving in to exhaustion. It might show, if Sinclair offered him a chair. A verbal skirmish was the last thing he needed. Without raising his voice, he chose to change tactics. "Speaking of surnames, at this time I will need those of the brave men in your unit who stayed behind with you. I have reason to believe they came to grief not far from Ampelokastro, but as they were missing identification discs, their bodies were regrettably interred in nameless graves."

Sinclair seemed genuinely surprised. "It was wrongly reported to you: the two men were not in my unit, I merely enrolled them on the spot to carry out the delaying action. And they were nowhere near the place you call Ampelokastro when they died."

"They were, and so was Raj. Or at least, that's what Caxton calls your dog."

"I'm not acquainted with Mr Caxton, and never owned a dog named Raj. It would be banal for an Anglo-Indian to choose such a name for a pet." Under the light, Sinclair's impeccable dark hair flashed with a blue sheen when he turned to toss the tightly folded newspaper onto the cot. "The men and I held the rearguard near Gazi, west of Iraklion. Whatever else these individuals, Caxton and Cowell, told you is a fabrication or a mistake."

If he closed his eyes, Bora could see the steep mountainside roll before him, and felt unbalanced. A reaction of the nerves, but in a manner of speaking he was still going downhill without a certain destination. "Well, Sergeant Cowell apparently told the truth when he said you speak German."

"I *do not* speak it."

"Then how would you understand what the soldiers manning the queue were discussing? With a few others, Cowell attempted a getaway after they heard you say the guards planned to shoot the prisoners en route. And all despite already having a pistol shot in his arm."

"Pure nonsense. Why are you saying these things? Powell was fired on by the guards."

I could show him Caxton's notes, but I want him to think Cowell is still alive, and in a position to confront him in person. "It'll be your word against his – and Caxton's."

Sinclair straightened up and set his shoulders a little, like a patient schoolmaster who begins to feel annoyance at a pupil's chatter. "If any of this were true, Captain, you would have brought your witnesses here. This ingenious tale, patently concocted to clear your fellow Germans of a war crime, will not stand up in any court, military or civilian. Without me, the massacre would have never come to the attention of the authorities. Without me, you would have nothing to go by."

"Yes, yes. *Domenikos qui et Minos.* The cobbler tried to kill me. But you warned me he was unsavoury."

"I also took it upon myself to alert the Red Cross representatives, when they visited on Thursday, that you might be under orders to supply an alternative reconstruction of those odious deaths. The IRC will no doubt be curious to hear you out, seeing that British soldiers had no motive to murder local civilians and a Swiss national in cold blood."

A motive? There was no motive. Bora played it by ear, trying not to lose his assuredness. He was like one who opens a door and finds there's a drop yawning in front of him. *He's clever, to the extent of committing small inaccuracies that make him appear sincere. Unless he is.*

The need to grasp something solid and keep from falling became anxiously physical. *If I could only trust Geoffrey Caxton more than I'm tempted to trust a brother officer… Caxton had a written statement, but could have lied about the rest. Cambridge is a place where intelligence fishes for agents. With us, sincerity and what is expedient to say are the same thing. It's all in freeing oneself from a concept of truth as "concordance with the facts".*

"I agree," he forced himself to say. "That's not exactly what happened at Ampelokastro. If anything, the British Army has been wronged in this matter as much as our own paratroopers. That's the detail I am striving to clarify." The sense of being off balance made him seek proof that he was still in his body, and in touch with reality. Driving his hands deeply into his pockets, Bora rubbed the splinters in his fingertips against the cloth, awakening small throbs of pain up his arms. Despite the lack of windows, from the runway the rumble of a cargo plane taking off reached the room, and he shamelessly wished he were on it.

In the pool of artificial light, Sinclair relaxed his shoulders. "I see you're frustrated." He came as close to expressing collegial sympathy as a British officer was likely to do, with a tinge of condescension. "Believe me, Captain, I appreciate your dilemma. In my present state, frustration daily threatens to get the better of me. But as soldiers we can't give in to emotional responses, even when confronted with failure."

"How do you know the nationality of the dead man? I never told you."

"How? The Red Cross representatives informed me."

"I will verify that."

"Please do. But they're not well-disposed towards you."

He's an operative. Bora looked from the imaginary threshold at the void below him, trying to judge if it was unfathomable. He decided it wasn't. *Whose he is, and why he's here, I don't know, but I'd bet my life on it. He's not military counter-espionage.* The gulf could be crossed, but he had to wait before jumping.

Sinclair had been granted cigarettes, the same German issue that Bora and Frances Allen had used as exchange goods in the mountains. He pulled out a pack and lifted it questioningly to Bora, who shook his head. He then placed a cigarette in his mouth, lit it with a match (another concession), and when he tilted back his head to blow out smoke, the ruddiness of his western countenance formed such a contrast with his dusky hair, he seemed to consist of two mismatched people in one. He observed Bora as one would a slightly younger acquaintance, judging whether it is worth measuring oneself against him.

"I'm looking at months, perhaps years of detention in a prison camp. Ahead of you, Captain, there's the privilege of whatever the war will bring." He glanced away from his interlocutor as the cargo plane roared overhead. "I think you and I know what privilege is. Who has it, who does not, and what it means. How detestable it is having privileges denied, or taken away. Count your blessings. I am Prometheus, bound to the rock for the duration. You are Ulysses, ready to unfurl your sails —"

"Maybe not," Bora interrupted him. "I work at the German Embassy in Moscow."

As from a newly safe perch, he watched the seemingly neutral statement kill the metaphor on the prisoner's lips. The word "Moscow" was a calling card, a sign of mutual recognition that apparently said nothing but implied everything. It did not demolish but made irrelevant the boundary between truth and lie. It did not abolish categories: it went beyond them.

Moscow was where games were played, and only players were invited. Sinclair's hesitation (like Busch's when he'd heard Bora had never been to Crete, or Bora's when Kostaridis had surprised him by offering his services) told him he'd done the equivalent of scoring the surface of one diamond with another. That line, barely scratched, thinner than a hair, was wide enough for Bora's confidence to drive a steel wedge through it.

"And whomever *you* work for, Lieutenant, *you* are behind the deaths at Ampelokastro. The woman and the field hands were incidental victims; as a soldier, I understand that. What disgusts me is that you lured away two men unawares from your unit to carry out your plans. Did they become suspicious along the way that you might be trying to desert, or give yourself up? Or did they really believe you needed them – and the faithful mascot – to 'hold the rear'? Their submachine guns were what you needed, and to get them you didn't hesitate to dispose of the men after they'd accompanied you nearly to your destination. As luck would have it, Sten and MAB 38 models both use 9×19 Parabellum cartridges, so – like every-body else – I assumed MAB 38s had been used: after all, we had photos of German paratroopers marching into the garden with those weapons. By the way, at what point did you take the collar off Raj's neck? Before or after stripping your soldiers of all identification? The dog still trusted you, followed you, and you killed it on the doorstep before barging into the house." Bora took out and showed Cowell's ID disc and the deformed bullet. "I promise you, for your men's deaths if not for the others, I will make sure the War Crimes Bureau *and* the Red Cross *and* the British Army are fully informed, demanding if need be that Cowell and your men be exhumed, along with the unit mascot."

"And what would my *motive* be for this mayhem?" Sinclair sounded no more than surprised. The sight of the two objects left him unconcerned. Others would have stepped back or aside, fled the circle of artificial light: he stood at the centre of it as before. The only discordant element in his scrupulous self-control was that he spoke with the cigarette in his mouth, like Frances Allen. "Without a motive it's all preposterous rubbish. I am shocked and advise you against making empty threats when you can't prove any of it."

"Don't underestimate me." Bora feared losing his temper to the same extent as Sinclair had regained his composure. He knocked on the door to be let out of the room.

Sinclair's tranquil voice followed him past the threshold. "Don't underestimate *me*, Captain. Tomorrow I'll be beyond reach of your malicious impostures, and you had better find your culprit somewhere else."

Bora walked out of the building, angry with himself. He resented having wasted time not understanding earlier, being unable to snap the last link of the chain, and now having the

Red Cross against him to boot. The still-bright afternoon sun engulfed him, with the wearying impression this day would never come to an end. He went next door to the next hurdle, securing from his Air Force colleagues an outgoing flight and access to a telegraph. Busch's clearance obtained both.

The coded exchange with Bruno Lattmann in Athens had the quality of urgent familiarity between them. Lattmann had "some material" for Bora, and Bora asked him to be on the Dekeleia runway at 1.30 in the morning. In comparison, asking about "Soviet operatives in 1928–30 Shanghai, better if English-speaking" seemed a tame request.

Lattmann was famous for his unmilitary retorts, coded or clear. "Don't get greedy."

It was nearly six o'clock before Bora looked for Kostaridis' car outside the gate. Kostaridis, however, had been ordered by the guards to park at a distance, at the end of an oven-hot strip of tarmac that melted under the studded soles of the mountain boots.

The inspector drove back without asking questions. At one point, he said, "I'll have your things and papers returned to Ithaca Street this evening," and, "There's some bottled water in the back. You had better drink."

Bora automatically reached for the bottle, uncapped it, and swigged it dry. "There's another."

Bora drained that, too. "Thank you."

Suddenly fatigue threatened to overwhelm him. Only a word, knocking about in his head, made him restless enough not to fall asleep during the ride. *Privilege. Privilege. Sinclair is right; it's about privilege. With me, and him, and Waldo Preger, each in our way. It was privilege fifteen years ago at Trakehnen, that summer day.*

Privilege is the key to remembering.

Yes. Yes, of course. It comes to me now, that row behind the abandoned factory, where Pastor Wüsteritz hanged himself.

I am twelve, and have a row with Waldo Preger behind the abandoned factory because of the book. The book. How could I forget? It's because – although I don't believe a word of what I'm saying – on principle and out of family obedience I defend my stepfather's prohibition to read Mein Kampf, *Herr Hitler's book. The one I saved money to buy, and read before it was taken from me, for which I was punished. Doggedly, blindly I stand for the prohibition, so much so that finally Waldo punches me in the face.*

The blow brings me to my senses. I strike back with both fists, in my heart wishing Herr Hitler could see me now because, even though I outwardly justify my stepfather's action, I believe I'm the sort of young German the Fatherland is looking for. My own divided loyalties enrage me, while my playmate has no doubts and newly sees me as the enemy.

Why did I imagine him as a monarchist? I may be the master's son, but he belongs to the master race.

Peter steps in just as we roll furiously on the ground and blood has started to flow.

I am twelve, and am dragged in a sorry state by my stepfather to apologize to the Pregers: old privilege demands it. Thankfully, Waldo isn't there (he's licking his wounds), but he'll hear about it and gloat. That's new privilege.

I am twelve and I know absolutely nothing about the world.

12

"Is there a place to eat in Iraklion where there are no Germans?"

They were close to the turn-off for Ithaca Street when Bora asked. Kostaridis looked over as if he were confronted with a rhetorical question. "None where a German would eat."

"*Epitropos*, I'm tired. Is there such a place, or not?"

"It's not even six-thirty; Greeks dine much later." Bora's insistence must appear odd to him, but aggressive enough to require a solution. "We could go to my house," Kostaridis suggested. And immediately, to prevent objections to his offer, he hastened to add, "You know how it is with us bachelors. I never married. The absence of a woman in the house..."

Bora was well past being finicky. He'd eat anything set in front of him at this point. "I accept. Can we go immediately? I need to talk to you."

Between there and Kostaridis' house they stopped by the depot long enough for Bora to pick up a few additional supplies for dinner, and also for the air journey.

The house front was unassuming, squeezed between centuries-old massive buildings of the Venetian type. Once inside, it was like turning off the heat of day. The twilit interior was several degrees cooler than the street, and once the shutters yawned open, the spotless picture of order.

Regardless of whether or not Bora seemed surprised, Kostaridis explained, "This is actually my brother's house. He's a civil servant presently in the mainland. I room upstairs."

His scruffiness, the way the hair sat on his head pasted down by sweat and brilliantine, looked out of place on the dignified ground floor. And if he indirectly apologized for them, Bora was torn between regretting his dirty boots and thinking, *I can't imagine what* his *rooms look like upstairs.*

Pointing to a flight of steps, Kostaridis said, "I'm going to my studio to phone the office and let them know I'll be back later. Feel free to freshen up and make yourself comfortable, *capitano.*"

Bora took the invitation literally. His old habit of checking the premises led him to glance discreetly into middle-class spaces where family photos shared the walls with watercolours, and inherited furniture had glassed-in shelves with embroidered doilies under stacks of plates. In an oval frame there was a photo portrait of a couple, certainly the Kostaridis elders. A grumpy, faded pair sitting next to each other, a moustached old man (the Smyrna hotel employee) and a woman with a sad and forceful look about her. And everything impeccably clean, cool, due to those thick walls and louvred shutters. When he glanced into the bedroom, the door of the wardrobe, partly open, offered a view of neatly hung suits, ties, summer and winter shoes.

A fastidious brother assigned to a government post justified the spotlessness; the only concession to Vairon was the encased Olympics pistol on a table, and his bronze medal under glass. In the immaculate bathroom, where Bora went to wash and quickly pass the razor blade over his face, the mirror above the basin returned a pitiless, sunburnt image of dust and strain. Dining took a matter of minutes. Kostaridis wanted to set the table, but Bora was anxious to summarize his findings, so they ate as single men ever did, standing in the kitchen.

"*Epitropos*, do you recall when we discussed the weapons used at Ampelokastro, and we resolved that two men were involved?

You said something to the effect that one of the two shooters might have hesitated to open fire on defenceless civilians."

"Judging from the evidence on the back wall, yes. It looked as though one of the two submachine guns struck mostly the wall."

"I say there was only one shooter, who used two submachine guns so that a commando action would be hypothesized. The ammunition used, 9×19 mm, matches the Italian-made MAB 38s, which our paratroopers carry along with the Schmeisser, as the witness photos clearly show. Well, I thought, what are the alternatives? We have to exclude Italian troops, nowhere around Iraklion. After the first week of battle, those effective Breda guns might have been easy to come by: dead Germans were stripped of more than just their weapons. Even a hothead like Sidheraki managed to swipe a few."

"Yes, but —"

Bora interrupted him. "Bear with me, *Epitropos*. The only flight out I could find between now and the day after tomorrow leaves at midnight, and there's still much I must do before I leave. I'll make it short. The photos of the paratroopers kept me thinking 'MAB 38', while I knew very well that other machine guns take the same calibre, including our enemies' favourite Sten. But why would British troops kill harmless locals?"

Kostaridis listened silently, with a glass of wine and water in his hand that would remain half full throughout, and a pained look of attention on his face. "Well, one of them was not local, *capitano*. And since, shall we say, he worked for Germany – I don't know, the money, the deposit box under another name – perhaps not even harmless."

"True. Which is why a Briton might open fire on him."

The inspector leaned against the wall circling the glass in his pale hands, staring at Bora with his bulging eyes. No mention of espionage was made, although it stood to reason that it might be involved. He heard the summary of the past three days without interrupting. All he then said was, "But short of a clear motive you have to be able to prove that the relationship between killer and intended victim *was* the motive."

"Right." It was the hurdle, undeniably.

"The lieutenant could have mistaken the sergeant's name in good faith, and one dead dog may resemble another. The photos tell a credible story. Where would the killer come from, and how could he not have run into the paratroopers or his compatriot, already hiding near the villa?"

Behind Kostaridis, above the tiled half of the wall hung a colourful calendar, showing a photograph of the Parthenon. Bora looked at it as he spoke. "I recalled your telling me, as we approached Ampelokastro from the high ground, that by another trail you could rejoin the road to Skala and enter Villiger's garden through the rear gate. That's what the killer did, as a precaution, and incidentally why he and Sergeant Cowell, who stumbled on his own to the property from the north, missed each other. Both had to lie low when German paratroopers unexpectedly approached from across the brook. The soldiers were due elsewhere and uninterested in wasting time with civilians. Seeing the bad state of the road along the brook, they took the shortcut through the garden, proceeding in silence as we generally do on patrol. The household probably never even noticed their passage. I learnt in Poland that, at war, often civilians leave gates and doors open: soldiers won't hesitate to break them down, and you might as well not bother with locks."

"The island was swarming with troops those first few days."

"Precisely. From his vantage point above the villa, Sinclair watched the Germans come and go. As soon as they were out of earshot, he entered the garden. In true army fashion, he did in minutes all he had to do. On the front steps his dog might have grown nervous, so he shot it point-blank, kicked the door in, and opened fire." The wall calendar hung slightly crooked; one could imagine the Parthenon sliding from its podium like a cake from a platter. "I've seen it done, *Epitropos*. It's really very easy with petrified civilians. He surprised his victims from the doorstep and missed none of them. Still, he crossed the floor and fired from the opposite side of the room, so we'd imagine the presence of an accomplice. He exhausted both cartridge belts, which is why later he had to use his handgun against the photographer."

"And where did the Sten guns end up?"

"Open-ended question. He surely rid himself of them: but if you can – your words – drop 10,000 men on this island and lose track of them, you can lose track of two rifles. The Turk could have found them, or they may lie smashed into pieces somewhere." Bora looked at his watch, as if looking at it could slow down the passing of time. "First, however, whether or not Sinclair was looking for someone else – or something – in the house, I believe he went upstairs, and was still there ten or fifteen minutes later, when the unwary Sergeant Cowell stumbled in and photographed the scene. Remember, you and I never heard Savelli above us until he dropped a book on the floor. Naturally, Sinclair meant to head back north and give himself a credible alibi by 'falling into enemy hands'. His intention was from the start to make the killing seem like a military action, possibly our doing – we Germans certainly haven't been above suspicion, even in Crete. But if he spied unseen his compatriot taking pictures, he realized that under certain circumstances photographic proof could be useful. Cowell unwittingly obliged him by photographing Breda-toting German troops entering the garden!"

Kostaridis put away the glass without drinking. A frown made his forehead into a criss-cross of folds, his mouth stayed half-open and a bit slack in contemplation before he said,

"Clear enough. The ammunition calibre was consistent with German weapons. So you say the killer crept after the photographer out of the house, and both headed north. But why shoot him a few minutes later – and not kill him?"

Bora looked away from the calendar. "Actually, he did kill him in the end: the man died of his wound. Sinclair had to intervene when Cowell stopped to photograph the two dead Britons on the side of the road. Should the roll of film end up in British hands, the dead soldiers could be identified and traced to his delaying action, and he didn't want the two to be in any way connected to what happened at the villa. I doubt, *Epitropos*, that he knew the dead mascot had been photographed, because – even without a collar – it might be recognized, and in fact was. Had Sinclair known, he'd have made sure Cowell did not survive. All the more, it was remarkable how he didn't bat an eyelid when I showed him Raj's image, by which time he could only pretend he wasn't familiar with the dog. He also had to take a risk and assume *he* hadn't been photographed. If he didn't kill Cowell, it's because he thought he'd be useful. Remember, the photos 'proved' a German war crime and had to reach a recipient."

Kostaridis seemed restless. But he was only looking for cigarettes, which he found next to the gas stove. "It was a big risk."

"But worth it. The only thing Sinclair did not plan on was finding himself elbow to elbow with the wounded sergeant in the same queue at Kato Kalesia. But he readily went along when Cowell confided to him he'd photographed German paratroopers entering the garden before the shooting. An excellent addition to his scenario. And no mention whatever of British officers or dead dogs! Still, with Cowell alive matters could become sticky eventually, so – once he had secured the camera – Sinclair encouraged him and a few others to make a run for it. Some were killed right off. As for Cowell, who escaped the bullets this time, stumbling away with an untreated arm wound could and did result in death."

Kostaridis took out an Italian coffee maker and heaped it with enough fine grounds for six people. "Part of this you reconstructed from what Rifat Bey told you. Will he confirm it before the authorities? He's not to be trusted."

"I gather as much." It was all Bora said about the Turk's parting quip about his dead wives. "My task was to clear German soldiers of the accusation, which I think I did. I placed Sinclair at Ampelokastro at the time of Villiger's death. The War Crimes Bureau or the IRC would be able to prove that the men in his detail and the unit's mascot were killed by his pistol, if a full investigation were launched."

Kostaridis used his cigarette to light the gas under the coffee maker. "And you think it will?" Above the gas stove, he noticed the crooked calendar and raised his arm to right it. "As a policeman I see total lack of a motive, shall we say, and only circumstantial evidence. Once your paratroopers are cleared, with all that's going on…"

"That's what frustrates me most. I can't prove Sinclair's guilt before he's removed to the mainland. I leave from the airfield in the middle of the night; he sails on a hospital ship at seven-thirty from Iraklion's harbour. There's nothing I can do about it; the Red Cross has taken an interest in him and might even see that he is handed to the soft-hearted Italians." Bora shook his head in disgust. He ached all over, and refused to sit down only because it would be painful to have to get up again. When Kostaridis nodded with his head toward the coffee maker, Bora took a Thermos flask out of his rucksack and handed it to him. "By the way, Andonis Sidheraki is alive and well in the interior; you won't shake him – or his wife – off any time soon. And if Signora Cordoval isn't the only one of her kind in Crete, *Epitropos*, do me the favour of telling me nothing. I don't want to know. It's clear you're an old hand at keeping quiet about things." The inspector's look of dumb innocence unexpectedly amused him. "When you dropped in uninvited at the cobbler's, I meant it when I accused you of conniving to stop me. But you have to forgive me; I have a German's prejudice against southern Europeans. The truth is that you didn't need to lead me by the nose; I did it very well by myself." Bora glanced around the well-kept kitchen. "Your self-effacing act, so down at heel... I should have known when you wouldn't even drop a spent match on the floor of Villiger's library. A man who sets straight a crooked calendar while murder is being discussed. There's no civil servant brother, is there? And I wager that in peacetime, when there are no Germans around, your elegance is a small legend in Iraklion."

Kostaridis looked down, very pleased, but he didn't say yes or no.

"It confirms what I thought, *Epitropos* – that you and Rifat Bey were in touch regarding Signora: otherwise when we climbed to his terrace he'd have remarked on your unprecedented shabbiness." Bora swallowed a yawn. "I really should go; it's just over four hours to my flight. Thanks for the coffee, I'll put it to good use. Won't you have any?"

"I never drink coffee at night. It's off to Ithaca Street, then. Your things are back there, and the door to the apartment was repaired."

"Yes. I do need to change before I see my colleague in the Airborne. I'll walk to the Megaron from the lodgings. I need to stay awake."

When they left the house, a pastel tinge in the sky softened all colours, and would turn to shadow before long. A nearly full moon had risen. The transient quality of the hour, between day and night, made the indifferent street view memorable somehow, as the mind at times ascribes value to plain images and stores them away for later. Bora's discontent must have been palpable, because Kostaridis paused after taking the car keys out of his pocket.

"Other than fetching you later tonight, is there any last thing I can do for you in Crete?"

Bora would think about this moment in the weeks and months to come, wondering. What there was in the look they exchanged had no special name: Bora looked straight at Kostaridis, and the policeman returned the stare. Then Bora averted his eyes, and spoke as if not expecting a reply: more, as if no reply were needed, or the subject was peripheral instead of being the reason for his being here. "Not unless you can favour me with thirty bottles of good Mandilaria, and the same with Dafni."

"Ah! *Capitano*, the widow Spinthakis —"

"She's dead, I know."

"The rest sell average wine, nothing you want to give as a gift."

"I was hoping to buy in Athens, but not at half past one in the morning."

"Good Dafni and Mandilaria in Athens?" For all his acting scandalized, Kostaridis still had the expression of their mutual stare. "You might as well buy from Panagiotis, although it is true what the Turk says, that he deals in dishwater. Sorry, I can't help you."

They got in the car.

"Well, hell then. I'll stop by Panagiotis' before I go to the Megaron."

Bora tried to sound casual about it. In fact, now that the investigation was drawing to an end and time was running frightfully short, the matter of satisfying Lavrenti Pavlovich, Deputy Chairman of the Council of People's Commissars and NKVD Chief, resumed crushing dimensions. Not even in Moscow had he felt so put upon. It was as if he had awakened from one nightmare straight into another. *I can't go back to Moscow without highest quality goods. What am I going to do?*

He brooded over it during the short ride, down streets patrolled by Germans and streets where life sank back into normality. Swallows and noisy swifts dipped and soared across the paling sky. Elders sat and smoked; women kept out of sight or leaned crossing their arms on windowsills. The middle class, the professionals, were away or collaborating or keeping aloof. Fear faded into resignation, turned inescapably into indifference.

And yet out there stood a disquieting wilderness. Mount Pirgos, Mount Voskerò, one-eyed shepherds, red-haired girls, mermaids dressed as young peasants, the solitary birthplace of Zeus – a grand theatre of dead temples and ghostly sites around this small harbour of the many names.

It was as if Kostaridis read Bora's mind, because he said, "Remember, after you leave: Mount Ida is an ancient name that means 'The Wooded One'. Now it's called 'Psiloritis', Bare Mountain. That's the summary of Crete's history, *capitano*, so long and so troubled – all was taken from us."

"I'll remember."

They were already turning into the narrow street where Bora roomed. Kostaridis braked, and said, "Let me see you in."

"It's not necessary."

"I lost two men on this street, whether or not it was on your account."

"Maybe Minos tried to get done by day what he failed to do at night."

"One more reason to let me see you in."

"As you wish."

Bora found the precaution annoying, but when he touched the lock with the key, and the street door gave way, both he and Kostaridis took out their pistols. A gradual push of the wooden door showed it was dark and quiet inside.

"*Capitano*, let me go in first."

"No."

"Then let me flash the electric torch in."

Bora shouldered Kostaridis aside to enter, and the cone of light shining behind him did not keep him from stumbling and skinning his shin on something hard and immovable just inside the entrance.

Once the stairway light was flipped on, they faced a stack of wooden crates, filled with bottles of wine, straw-packed and ready to go. "Export quality," Kostaridis said in admiration. "Mandilaria from the Spinthakis winery, and Dafni with the Minotaur label! The pride of Crete. It doesn't get any better than this, *capitano*." And because Bora didn't answer, busy counting to make sure the bottles came to sixty, he reasoned, "That whoreson of a Turk must have dipped into his personal cellar. And he forced the lock to get in."

"I don't care if he passed through walls, *Epitropos*. It saves my neck!"

"Not unless you find a truck to get them to the airfield."

Bora had until now scrupulously kept tab of every drachma he'd spent from the cache in Villiger's deposit box. "Here." He dug out the remaining bills, without counting them, and shoved them in Kostaridis' hand. "Buy one if you have to, will you?"

Washing thoroughly and changing into his Moscow uniform were the next steps. Bora went through them mechanically, pushing forward the time when he'd allow himself to crash as if it were the notch on a slide rule. Riding breeches and boots on, tunic on. Immediately the evening seemed much warmer.

At the Megaron, where he arrived shortly after eight, he spoke to a non-com in Preger's company, a fellow with a splinted middle finger on his left hand, who said he'd enquire if the captain was in. Bora waited in the lobby, ignoring the glances at his impeccable riding boots. Already the hotel was taking the appearance of stable occupation, with thumbnail-studded noticeboards on walls and typewriters ticking behind closed doors. It seemed ages since Major Busch had sipped Afri-Cola in the back room and broken window glass was heaped on this polished floor.

Who knows where the portraits of the Greek royals had ended up? Certainly, coffee cups were being regularly washed now, and beds made upstairs for the officers.

The non-com returned in minutes. "Sorry, *Rittmeister*, the commander isn't in. Do you have a message for him?"

"No, never mind."

"I'll take a message if the *Rittmeister* has one."

The solicitous insistence meant Preger was in the building and curious to know what his colleague had to say, but would not meet him. Through the thickness of Bora's exhaustion anger mounted slowly. He further delayed it by avoiding the man's face, with his eyes on the ridiculous splinted finger.

"There's no message."

He'd done well walking there; he needed to breathe in the tart sea air and bracing saltiness as he returned to Ithaca Street. In less than three hours, Kostaridis would send a truck and driver. He had time to start drafting a report in longhand, and with a four-hour stopover in Bucharest, would have time to type it as well. In Lublin, Bora only had half an hour. God willing, that's where he would hand it in, to be forwarded as needed.

At eleven o'clock, a Fiat delivery van was idling below. Kostaridis met Bora on the doorstep, and with the help of the driver they loaded the cases. Bora had bundled up the clothing he'd worn in Crete, and left it upstairs with the mountain boots and whatever he no longer needed. The rucksack, with maps and food for the long journey, he took along with his briefcase. The driver climbed in the back and Kostaridis himself drove to the airfield.

Along the way, as often happens when departure is near, the two had nothing to say to each other. Bora's mind was already in Athens, where Lattmann would await him on the runway, and in Bucharest and beyond. Soon Max and Moritz would be following him to his Moscow hotel. He'd soon walk by Maggie Bourke-White's door, and smell lilacs. Already, notwithstanding the incompleteness of his task, he was leaving Crete behind. He kept his eyes closed to avoid seeing the few flickering lights, the phosphorescent trim of the backwash. Kostaridis would think he was asleep, and that was fine. But at one point, out of that darkness, Bora thought of the wax candles he'd seen among the ruins at Týlissos, whose presence Frances Allen wouldn't explain. That point, at least, he could make clear to himself by asking.

"I thought you were sleeping," Kostaridis commented. "In places like Týlissos, at Easter time folks make pilgrimages to the cemetery. They burn candles, bring food for the dead as in ancient times. What you saw at the archaeological site were probably tapers left by those who camped overnight among the ruins." He deftly changed gears. "It's a strange relationship we have with the departed. As I told you, poor Siphronia, who died a violent death as a married woman living in the house of a *frangos*, had to be buried before she started haunting. At times not even a hastily dug grave is considered sufficient. In the twentieth century, *capitano*, we had best leave alone what practices are occasionally carried out to make sure the dead don't 'walk'."

But for those who investigate, the dead walk, and how! At the airfield, the van was let in because of its cargo and Bora's satisfactory paperwork. A Ju 52 sat on the runway. There were no pilots around, but an airman confirmed it was the outgoing flight to Athens.

"Call me when you're ready to go."

The wind from the sea was nearly cold. It came with the deep breathing noise of the undertow; white ghastly fringes marked waves and emerging wrecks. Once he had made sure the bottles were safely loaded, Bora tried hard not to think that Patrick Sinclair was within this same perimeter and that he could do nothing to keep him here. He'd leave Crete first, and it was unlikely he'd ever return.

He gave back the keys to the small apartment to Kostaridis, and Kostaridis returned the bundle of drachmas. "None were necessary. Forgive me, *capitano*, but to a departing German my compatriots will offer free transportation."

Bora nodded, tolerantly. "*For a departing foe, we'll build a golden bridge*: the Italians say and do the same thing." He watched Kostaridis pocket the keys. "How curious, if one thinks about it, rooming on the island of Crete at a place named after the island of Ithaca."

Kostaridis smiled his frog smile. "Not so curious. Every place is Ithaca to the native who longs to return there. And then every road is the road to Ithaca. Isn't it? Just as every wanderer is Ulysses if he is conscious of his roving."

But you never quite return to Ithaca. Or, if you do, it is not forever. Bora didn't voice his thought. What he said, was, "Hm. *Das Gewissen-haben-wollen wird Bereitschaft zur Angst:* the desire for a conscience prepares one for anguish – that's how Professor Heidegger, one of my teachers, nicely put it."

"I'm not a learned man, *capitano*. But we Greeks call Ulysses 'long-suffering', so he must have had a conscience."

"Not when he first started out. Boyhood is where most of us stop being virtuous, and the need to develop a conscience comes in. You had better go, *Epitropos*. I have kept you up far too long, and I apologize." Bora saluted, they shook hands. "So long. How do you say it in Greek?"

"*Adio*. But it's best to say *kalì andàmossi* – until next time."

"Until next time, then."

But they still stood irresolute in front of each other. "Are you sure the Englishman is guilty, *capitano*?"

"More than sure."

"And that, shall we say, you'll be able to prove it?"

"Not so sure."

Kostaridis made a vague gesture and turned away. "*Kalì andàmossi*, then."

"*Kalì andàmossi*."

Half an hour to departure. Bora walked into the terminal with the intention of jotting down an update in his diary. The last person he expected to see entering after him was Preger – so soon he must have been waiting in the dark until now to catch him alone.

The crude neon light of the room made his suntanned face look ashen. And so, Bora thought, must his own face seem.

He said, "I came to the Megaron to let you know I am convinced that your men had nothing to do with the deaths at Ampelokastro, and, God willing, will be able to prove it soon."

Under the ugly glare, Preger heard him out with an unreadable blankness on his hard face. Just a few sentences, no details, and when Bora finished, both men remained standing unemotionally, stiff-shouldered. Not close enough to touch each other, as if it were wise to keep out of striking distance. Bora was running on empty, but was perfectly capable of hiding his weariness and disappointment. Preger – hard to say what Preger was concealing. Surprise, unplanned gratitude? He picked his words as one gathers small change after buying something.

"I'm not going to thank you because there's nothing my men did that needed to be disproved, by you or by anyone else."

"Fine with me. I didn't come here to do what I ended up doing, so we're even."

"That we can never be."

Neither surprise nor gratitude – it was hostility that lay under Preger's lack of expression. Bora kept himself even from blinking.

"'Even' is a word that doesn't work between us, *Rittmeister*. Not because of the spat we had as kids, the blows and all that. I'm not so small-minded. The reason, Martin-Heinz Douglas *Freiherr* von Bora, is that you are all that we're striving to leave behind, the kind of Germany of lords and ladies and generals' sons and estates. You weren't in the streets of Königsberg in '32, as I was. You didn't build any of the Germany we have now. I'm not even sure you're fighting for the same Germany I'm fighting for."

Through the open door, the wingtips of the aeroplane, green and red, flickered as it taxied slowly towards the runway.

It was as if Preger had secured a tool and now was digging inside him to scoop up anger from where it rested. Bora swallowed the provocation, but barely. "Germany is one. It pre-dates both of us. Unless we really make a mess of things, it'll continue after us. Are you really certain we'd be having this conversation if we hadn't punched each other that day?"

"Fuck you, *Rittmeister*, you kept vacationing with the family at Trakehnen. I was packed off to Königsberg."

There it was, the sore, unforgiven spot. Not so abstract after all. Not small-minded but not high-minded, either. Bora blinked. In all these years he had never connected the row to Waldo's school transfer. "Did my parents send you?"

"Worse. *My* parents sent me."

"Come on. We fought just that once!"

"Ha. *Hegemeister* Preger, whose father and grandfather had been managing Herr Baron's estate, couldn't bear the shame of seeing his dead master's son apologizing to him. That was Germany then. I'm sure your parents didn't even notice I had gone."

Saying that no doubt his parents had taken notice would ruin the picture of Waldo's resentment, so Bora did not suggest the possibility. *If I know my mother, not only would she have enquired about Waldo; having learnt what happened, it would have been just like Nina to urge the Pregers to let him come back: but it would have been just like old Preger to insist that a man's a guardian of his good name, and he's entitled to rule his family as he sees fit.* He wished he could say that, if it was any consolation, he'd been mortified by his punishment as well, but it wasn't the case. *And I admit that after asking about Waldo the following summer, I accepted the fact that he lived elsewhere now. Soon Peter was old enough to become my privileged playmate, and on our bikes we were gone from the estate most of the day.*

Should he feel sorry? At the moment Bora was totally unwilling to see himself and his old playmate as anything but expendable: they were two among millions of soldiers; they'd live or die fighting in spite of their different childhoods.

"*Hauptmann* Preger, please know that I'm not going to justify myself for my family, or my upbringing, or anything else that doesn't relate directly to what you and I are today within the German armed forces. Much less will I apologize for being who I am."

"As if you ever could."

Bora was not above spite, and could be ungenerous. To himself, he admitted what he never would out loud, that in a way Preger was right. The Germany they lived in had been built on street brawls and fisticuffs he hadn't taken a part in, just as he hadn't participated in intimidations, set books or synagogues on fire, jailed political adversaries or silenced his conscience. Preger was right about that. He recalled the hostility of police inspector Weidlich in Leipzig, little more than two years earlier. There, too, under the ideological varnish, there was class-related resentment waiting to explode. The scores might be settled in that regard as well, sooner or later. He chose to retaliate by keeping from Preger that he had remembered the reason for the row.

The airman looked in out of the darkness. "When you're ready, *Rittmeister*."

Bora nodded and turned back to Preger. "Well, comrade, if you're done, I have a flight to catch."

"So you can go back to your cushy embassy job?" Preger sneered. "I'm done, I'm done. The blood we spilt on this island has nothing to do with your kind."

The three dead von Blüchers were "my kind". This, Bora did no more than think. Walking out onto the dark runway, he felt as resentful as on the day he'd apologized in the Pregers' living room, with his stepfather looming behind him. He'd imagined then that the general stood for all the ties and rules and traditions he was hankering to be rid of. And yet Sickingen also embodied the connections, the beliefs, the solid network of those who would not, it's true, let go of power and influence so easily, but at the same time wouldn't bow to gangsters' methods and would fight back. Since then, how many times had he disagreed with the old man, disobeyed him, and for all of his achievements and first career successes, let him down? It couldn't be helped, it was generational, and for many years deep down he'd told himself contemptuously that Sickingen wasn't his father after all, and couldn't tell him what to do.

Aside from the cases of wine, the plane carried to the mainland CreForce paperwork found here and there on the island.

Bora would be the sole passenger. "Climb in, *Rittmeister*," the co-pilot said, inviting him in. "Ten minutes, and we set off."

Bora answered the co-pilot's summons, climbed the ladder and found a place to sit. The truth of the matter was that generations of German and Scots ancestors had parented him. They weighed on him more than they bolstered him. Preger needed to feel superior at this time.

And, who knows, maybe he *was* ahead of Bora in today's Germany.

And so, farewell to Crete and its time machine, to the metaphor of the Wanderer, to the question of truth and untruth, and the many masks we wear, whether we're heroes or not, to go through life.

In the air, despite some turbulence, he anchored his torch so that he could write in his diary, as he'd done at night as a boy, under his bed.

Sunday 8 June, 12.14 a.m., above the Aegean Sea. I don't think I ever was so foolish as I was in Spain. Can Waldo Preger have been so much more conscious than I? We were there for the bloody feast, because it wasn't our country after all, it wasn't our civil war. We could go at it with all we had and feel enthused about it. I was fighting for decency, religion and the Holy Mother Church, to stop Bolshevism from taking over the western world, and so on. I'm sure Waldo took to Spain the same twin-fisted aggressiveness he'd practised on German streets and refined as a policeman.

Was it true? Was it what we were there for? I wonder what the hell it was that we learnt in Spain. Surely we didn't learn humility, something a man if not a soldier should become familiar with. If anything, we came away from it believing ourselves invincible. We'll see. It's something I still want to believe, although travelling in and out of Russia I'm all too aware of the size of the mouthful we're about to take. Will our jaws stand up to our appetite?

England has ruled wide portions of the world, including India. Can't Germany rule the vastness of Russian Eurasia? In Spain we'd just got our nose bloodied, skinned our knees and elbows. We were a frustrated, mutilated country coming back from the dead after Versailles. Preger, with his fallen brother and social expectations, was a substantial part of it. I was a part of the Reich that lost the Great War and was unbearably oppressed by the Allies. Together, he and I formed a whole. Now we're coming apart, we don't see eye to eye, we discern darkly, in a dark mirror, a different Germany from each other's. If we win the war, it won't matter which one of us was right. If – I don't even know why I go on thinking of it – if by any remote chance we should not prevail, Captain Preger's Reich stands to be punished much more severely than my stepfather's Germany ever was.

Enough. He and I might not be there to see the outcome in any case, so it's all in the lap of the gods at this point. The question is: am I foolish now?

13

Viel täuschet Anfang
Und Ende.

Full of deceit is the beginning
And the end.

F. HÖLDERLIN,
"ONCE I ASKED OF THE MUSE"

1.49 A.M., DEKELEIA AIRPORT, ATHENS

In the stifling, small airport office where they met, Lattmann wasted no time. He pulled out his notebook and flipped through it. His unreadable miniature longhand was reminiscent of Carolingian script, with round lower-case letters and exaggeratedly tall ascenders.

"I made no promises, mind you. Major Busch, who's still overseeing matters from Lublin, hounded me more than you did, because he wants you to hand him the full report there. This is what I've got."

"Well, Bruno, I'm off in forty-five minutes, so it's good if it's short, and hopefully useful."

"Judge for yourself. Under his own name, notwithstanding his love story with Heini Himmler, your Switzer comes out as clean as unused underwear. Don't know why they lifted his file from our central office."

"Except that he was more than just Alois Villiger."

Lattmann yawned, which was the only reminder to Bora that he'd got him up from a comfortable bed. "And in fact

Duvoin is more interesting. First of all, the Lucerne address on his passport belongs to a shop, not a residence. He travelled via what was then Austria to Italy in the spring of 1938, officially on an antiquarian bookselling trip, but seems to have done little and moved little from the Hotel Miramare in Ostia, just outside Rome. We were checking on foreigners on Italian soil due to the Führer's visit, so details are pretty certain."

"The Miramare? That's where I lunched, and where Bondarenko's Comintern colleague 'Paolo' was reported to work out of!"

"Right. Did you ever get to meet him, or see him at least?"

"That wasn't my charge. I was supposed to find out whether Bondarenko or other personnel from the Soviet embassy ever visited the hotel – which they didn't."

"So it isn't enough to say that Villiger-Duvoin could have been 'Paolo' to the Italian secret service, and 'Emma' to ours. All we know is that he was lodging there at the time…"

Bora took notes himself, hunching because the neon light was bothering him and he had to shield his weary eyes from it. "…and travelled under a false name. What can you tell me about Federico Steiger?"

"You hit the nail on the head: one of our Moscow informants, although *not* a resident of Hotel Lux. No existing photos of him at the time. Seems to have worked for us exclusively. His stint in China as a merchant in raw silk goes back thirteen years. He appears to have been dormant at the time. The unusual thing for a *kaltgestellt*, and the only detail I could find, is that he did not mix much. He didn't frequent bars or restaurants patronized by other foreigners. That's all I have."

"If he wasn't as dormant as we thought, he might have had his favourite meeting places elsewhere." Bora felt like he was scooping the dregs at the bottom of a container, and the dregs were his mental energy. "Let me sum this up: Villiger worked above water as Professor Alois Villiger of the *Ahnenerbe*, M. A. Duvoin might or might not have served the Soviets in Italy; Federico Steiger spied for us in Moscow and possibly Shanghai. The *Reichskommissar* won't be glad to hear it. No wonder Villiger was 'jittery', as they reported to me. If indeed he was or had been a double agent and planned a trip away from Crete to escape trouble, he'd have to go as far as the moon. Depending on Emma's identity, Germany could have had as good a reason to eliminate him as the Soviet Union. Twice a double-crosser: no wonder the *Abwehr* wanted to look into his death. I don't mean to sound ungrateful, Bruno, but what I really hoped you'd tell me —"

"I'm getting there. In 1928 Shanghai, a leading contact for the Reds was rumoured to be a British subject, supposedly a military man in the so-called Volunteer Corps. We never discovered his real name, and – you can bet your boots – neither did the Brits. There were others in Soviet employ we never figured out, like the one they used to call 'Tin Man'. In this case, the codename was 'Valencia'. You'd think he'd be Spanish."

What did Caxton say about Cambridge's Pembroke College students? That they're nicknamed Valencians. And Sinclair was one of them.

"Wait. No other details about the Englishman in Moscow's employment?"

"No." Lattmann had to decipher his own handwriting, mouthing the words. "Unless you consider useful that he'd previously served with the Shanghai Defence Force whose British-led troops guarded the International Settlement during the local troubles. When the Force was withdrawn at the close of 1927, he must have stayed on with the Volunteer Corps. Both he and Steiger incidentally resided on Nanking Road, but we know it was a foreign enclave. Not nearly enough to

377

make a connection between them, and besides 'Valencia' was transferred shortly thereafter."

"Where, do we know?"

"We *don't* know. He probably left the service."

That confirms why Sinclair, an Anglo-Indian with a good education but no military school training, a draftee to all effects, was still a first lieutenant in his mid-thirties.

"You've got to find me something more about him, Bruno."

"Why?"

"Because if Patrick Sinclair was in Shanghai for the Reds and used the codename 'Valencia', I'd have a ready-made motive for his silencing a double-crosser and all the witnesses."

Lattmann fanned himself with the notebook, frowning. "It's not something I can do at the drop of a hat."

"It'll take me until nearly six to reach Bucharest. There, I have a four-hour stopover. What if I get in touch with you from there?"

"It depends on what it is that you want. Give me specific questions, and I'll radio you at Baneasa airport if and when I have something. After eight o'clock in any case. And keep in mind I promise even less than before."

Bora took the notebook from his colleague and wrote: *Was the 14th Infantry Brigade among the units of the Shanghai Defence Force? Was there an India connection with other reported Soviet spies in town?*

"I don't understand your last point," Lattmann observed.

"We know that Chatto, the Indian communist executed by Stalin in the Great Purge, was in Shanghai at the time. See if you can find a link between Indian revolutionaries and 'Valencia'. Also, anything else. Anything. Including the language he used in his coded messages."

Lattmann snorted. "Why do I end up giving in to you?"

"I'll make it up to you, Bruno."

"My foot. I'm going back to bed."

6.00 A.M. BANEASA AIRPORT, BUCHAREST

The moment they came in view of the Danube, it started to pour. Bora's first hour of stopover in Bucharest was spent enquiring about his next flight, unlikely because of the weather to take off before 10.30 or later. He then went to sit in the Romanian Air Force mess hall, where he'd awaited his flight to Greece a few days earlier.

A handful of pilots in uniforms very similar to German ones, with belt compasses, drank coffee at a long table by a rainy window. Bora overheard their chatter as he wrote in longhand the draft of his final report. He requested and obtained a typewriter, although he was still missing the details he hoped to receive from Lattmann when he radioed from Athens in two hours' time.

He kept writing. Just before seven, the Romanian pilots rose from their chairs, exchanged a salute with him, and left. At 8.30 a.m. Bora wasn't yet worried about the delay of Lattmann's call, although by 9 a.m. he was uncomfortable, and downright preoccupied by 9.30. Outside, it thundered enough to make the glass panes rattle. A Luftwaffe Junkers 52 landed in a crown of splashes and crossed the space of the window out of sight only to reappear from the opposite direction, no closer to the building.

Still no radio contact from Athens. Due to leave Romania in little more than an hour, Bora decided he'd attempt to contact his colleague himself, and started gathering his unfinished papers. What interrupted him was seeing someone who looked like a very wet Lattmann walk into the room: recognizing him as Lattmann himself plunged him for an impractical second into a reel of assumptions, the most egotistical of them being that war with Russia had begun without him.

Lattmann tossed his rain-limp side cap onto the table. "Hello, Martin. Don't ask. Major Busch sent me after you, and I never had a worse flight in my life. Get me some coffee, will you?" Coffee came. Although they were perfectly alone in the room, Lattmann spoke in a low tone with his lips on the rim of his steaming cup. "Guess what. The 14th Infantry Brigade *was* in the Shanghai Defence Force, and – curiously – the only coded message in our hands that surely originated in Shanghai from 'Valencia' is in Latin. Does that help? I thought so. As far as the 'India connection', as you call it, for our man it has a first and last name, and is not a man: Agnes Smedley, an American socialist with leanings towards Indian independence." (*Yes,* Bora thought, *a meddlesome freethinker of the Frances Allen type.*) "She was Chatto's lover at the time, but also frequented other men in the communist milieu, including 'Valencia'. She reportedly was involved in a row over the fact that 'Valencia' was refused membership of the exclusive, whites-only Shanghai Club, a point I don't quite understand, because he was supposed to be a Briton."

Bora had been taking notes, and now his writing accelerated. "Not enough in the class- and colour-conscious British diaspora, maybe. Excellent! If he's one and the same as 'Valencia', Sinclair might not have qualified as wholly white: he's Anglo-Indian."

"Well, shit. Why didn't you tell me beforehand?"

"You wouldn't have dug up as much as you did, as quickly as you did."

So, privilege had something – or everything – to do with it, Sinclair was right. And so was Waldo Preger. But it wasn't only a matter of being refused access to an exclusive club, or being a hired man's son. Injustice, real or perceived, weighs just the same. A half-breed like Sinclair was likely to have developed just as much anger against the system because of what he was, rather than simply for political reasons. British universities did produce fine operatives. Why shouldn't the Comintern sound even more attractive to a discontented, bright young man than His Majesty's class- and race-bound service?

Bora watched Lattmann finish his coffee. Whatever had happened after Shanghai, things had changed. Sinclair might have gone into civilian life and lain dormant until the war began, or even until he landed in Crete, where Federico Steiger was undoubtedly known to be living under his real name, Alois Villiger. Villiger was now back to serving the Reich exclusively, and there was no telling how much damage he'd already cost the Soviets: blowing his colleagues' covers, bringing about the arrest of comrades in the Greek mainland…Who better than Sinclair, a faultless British subject coincidentally quartered in Crete, to dispose of him? The German invasion had only given the perfect excuse for the massacre.

"That's the final link, Bruno. Sinclair fits the profile perfectly, down to his use of Latin. It's up to our central office now, to do with it as they see fit in regard to the *Reichskommissar*, the War Crimes Bureau and International Red Cross."

"Except that it might have been our central office that made the Villiger file disappear in the first place. I'd hold on to my britches when it comes to the zeal they'll put in it."

"Well, regardless. Let's finish drafting this. I'll type it quickly and hand it in to Major Busch in Lublin."

"He'll be there waiting." Lattmann reached with his spoon into the sugar bowl and fished out a heap of sweet stuff he put in his mouth. "I need the energy," he mumbled. "But wait before you reach your conclusions, I'm not finished. Do you know somebody called Kostaridis in Crete?"

"Yes. Why?"

"I was boarding the plane to come here when a communication reached our Athens office through Cretan Police, from a Police Inspector Kostaridis in Iraklion. He reported that an unknown marksman had just opened fire on British prisoners boarding a German hospital ship at seven this morning. One of them was killed. No, no name given, but he was the only officer in the lot, and I'm willing to bet it was your Anglo-Indian. The rifle was fired from at least 800 yards away, Kostaridis said. Said that from that distance only an Olympic shooter could have hit his target." Lattmann poured himself more coffee. "If I hadn't met you on the Athens runway and well away from Iraklion by seven a.m., Martin…"

Is there any last thing I can do for you in Crete?

Bora said nothing. That moment at sundown the day before, the transient quality of the hour between day and night… the meaningful glance he and Kostaridis had exchanged. He was so relieved, weariness suddenly came down heavily upon him. Like a blow, he had to steady himself under it.

Wet as he was, Lattmann was newly in a good mood. He resembled a rabbit when he smiled. "I *love* this intrigue, don't you?"

"Mostly, I wonder what we're going to tell the *Reichskommissar.*"

"Ah, that's up to Busch. If Heini Himmler has charged us and not his own secret service with this case, it's because he doesn't want to hear what he doesn't want to hear. Busch will cut and paste the findings so that Villiger comes out clean, the mere victim of England's viciousness. As for the War Crimes Bureau, they'll put the murder enquiry back in the drawer, now that our paratroopers are excused. The IRC will have to take note. And to His Majesty's Army, what's there to say? It isn't as if we killed Sinclair."

In Lublin, where Bora landed at 1.45 p.m., Major Busch waited on the runway inside a staff car, so as not to be seen by the pilots of the shiny Russian Lisinov ready to pick up Bora for the last leg of the journey.

Bora was told through the car window to step inside, and in less than ten minutes, the typed final draft passed into the major's hands. Typical of his profession, he only asked, "Is everything in the report?" and when Bora said it was, he slipped it inside a leather portfolio. No other comments, much less compliments. "Good. Go, now."

TUSCHINO AIRPORT, MOSCOW, 7.30 P.M., MOSCOW TIME

Around the capital, the sandy-floored, beautiful birch woods of the Podmoskovye slid under the plane. Lining up with the runway for landing, the Lisinov threaded through the calm evening air. Compared with Crete, the greenness of Russia and Moscow gardens were to Bora like long-awaited draughts of water. He only had to put it to the back of his mind (exhaustion made this possible) that Lavrenti Pavlovich had buried his victims by the thousand in those merry birch woods.

There was an embassy colleague waiting for him – a fellow from the Seelow Hills, with an accent as though every sentence were a question. He sounded as if he was asking him, but he actually told Bora he had to hurry with the wine.

"Come, Bora, you have to change and personally oversee delivery at the Spiridonovka Palace!"

Bora had just come down the ladder and was trying to steady himself after some twenty long hours of travel. "Why? The reception isn't until next Sunday."

"*Was.* It's being held tonight. Big affair. Get moving, I'll give you a ride."

"I've got the wine with me, remember?"

"There's a van waiting. It'll follow us to the National, where you have to change in no time, and then to the Spiridonovka. Is this all the luggage you have?" The colleague nodded towards Bora's small bag and grabbed the rucksack from him. "Good. Let's go."

That haste was at play was proven by the fact that there was no checking of the bags, and they walked out of the terminal undisturbed. The van, an embassy car and a car with NKVD plain-clothes men in it were indeed parked outside.

"Did you hear about Manoschek?"

The question came as if it were possible that – despite days of absence – Bora had an answer. He was too tired to play games. "He's in Berlin as far as I know," he said. "Why?"

"He was killed in a car accident this morning. No, it was a milk truck down the street from his Berlin office. Killed instantly. Ah, here comes the wine: they'll load it in no time. Nice tan, by the way."

The street, and the palace named after it, lay in the Moscow district where houses of rich merchants had been designed in the old days by foreign architects. Bora's natural father had lived on Spiridonovka, as a neighbour to the Morozovs and other patrons of the arts.

It was a place of official receptions where Czarist era crystals and silver hadn't changed since those days, and tonight's affair lived up to tradition. Representatives of friendly or neutral nations and anybody who was anybody in town attended. The latest (occupied) Paris gowns found their way there, splashes of Chanel perfume, the favourite with wives of Soviet officials, music by award-winning Artists of the Soviet Union. You'd expect Erskine Caldwell and Maggie Bourke-White to be invited, but apparently they'd left for the south of Russia on one of their triumphal tours of the workers' paradise.

The entire German diplomatic mission in Moscow was present, including General Köstring, too ailing to do his job as attaché but well enough to be there and outrank his stand-in Colonel Krebs, not to speak of Krebs' aide Martin Bora (quickly briefed and handed a list of ladies he was expected to dance with). Foreign Minister Molotov, Stalin's secretary Poskrebyshev (he of the jailed wife), and a swarm of lesser officials trickled in. Deputy Chairman Lavrenti Beria was expected no earlier than eleven o'clock, which would be still more than four hours before the entertainment was likely to end. Getting to bed at four in the morning was not unusual after these bashes. In such cases, depending on the day of the week, usually Bora showered and gulped the sugarless contents of a coffee pot before preparing to go directly to work.

Tonight, after all the week in Crete had demanded of him, he only gave the impression of being in control. In fact, his head swam; drinking the smallest amount of alcohol would knock him under one of the Czar's tables. He hung on to a half-filled glass of Dafni for dear life. "What is it, *Kapitan*, you don't like the wine? You're not drinking."

The idea that Deputy Chairman Beria should care enough to ask about him was as credible as the claim that Manoschek had died in an accident.

"Mr Deputy Chairman, the wine is excellent."

"Then drink it." Standing on a carpeted dais that allowed him to see eye-to-eye with the tall German, Lavrenti Pavlovich had a mean smile. "You travelled nearly four thousand miles to secure it, did you not? Do justice to this fine vintage."

Bora drank. In an unprecedented reaction, he could feel the small amount of alcohol erode his lucidity as it slid down his throat. Already the Deputy Chairman was flipping his fingers for the waiter to approach with a full glass. "It's worth it: it has all of Crete inside."

After the second glass, a third followed, and a fourth. The only hope was to be rescued by someone from the German

Embassy, as it wasn't thinkable to admit weariness to the Deputy Chairman, much less disinclination to drink. Even Foreign Minister Molotov, who declared himself a teetotaller, was "doing justice" to the Dafni – or Mandilaria, or both.

Bora kept his countenance because there was no alternative. Had he not been so exhausted and sleep-deprived he could have put away wine and hard liquor without blinking. As it was, the white gown of a western official's wife dazzled him; it hurt his eyes as the Greek sun had done when he landed in Athens. Lavrenti Pavlovich looked at him maliciously through his round lenses and made him drink.

It was minutes but seemed hours. Finally, Colonel Krebs, of his own accord or on Köstring's suggestion, tactfully started out to reclaim his aide; but not before the Deputy Chairman cornered Bora. His round, swarthy face gave the impression of being twisted, as if his friendly, deadly smile were produced by someone turning his nose like a knob.

"*Kapitan, Kapitan…* You shouldn't be spying on your own boss."

Bora wasn't sure he'd heard right. Lavrenti Pavlovich mouthed the words more than saying them; conversation was loud all around, the award-winning Artists of the Soviet Union had struck up the first of many dance tunes by Alexander Tsfasman ("On the Sea Shore", crooned by Pavel Mikhailov). He followed Krebs as in a dream, all the while giving the impression of utter self-control. He fulfilled the duties of dance partner with all the ladies listed for him, moved around, addressed those he had to address and kept from addressing those he was supposed to ignore. But it was as if another Martin Bora, sober and proper, were doing all that. The real one watched the first and needed to throw up.

Thankfully, several of the Russian guests had to attend a ceremony the following morning, so the party wound down early, at 1 a.m. Bora had time to stumble back to his hotel room, where he vomited with exhaustion and fell asleep with his dress uniform on.

MONDAY 9 JUNE, GERMAN EMBASSY, MOSCOW

The reception was a major success. It was all Bora heard about coming to work the following morning. The Cretan wine had won out over Georgian and Crimean reds and vodka from the Kuban.

A civilian pointed out to him a beribboned bottle of Starka on Bora's desk. "From the office of the Deputy Chairman."

It was a high compliment, even though the idea of a blend of vodka, port wine, brandy and fruit flavours made him feel nauseous just as his stomach was settling.

Bora's Monday morning was as busy as always, until nine o'clock, at which time Colonel Krebs called him in.

He expected a routine debriefing by the acting military attaché after the party. What else? Even if they leaked as far as Moscow, in no way could Major Busch's preposterous opinions regarding Ambassador von der Schulenburg be considered official, and he, Bora, had received no specific warning from his own *Abwehr* referents in Moscow. Rumours abounded. If asked expressly about any given remarks by the Deputy Chairman, he'd reply truthfully that he took Lavrenti Pavlovich's comment ("You shouldn't be spying on your own boss") as mere provocation, or angling for God knows what hesitation on his part.

Krebs, however, did not bring up the reception. He soberly surveyed Bora from behind the desk, and then walked around it to the balcony door, open despite the nip of the early hour. He wordlessly signalled to follow him outside, where their words were less likely to be intercepted. Leontyevsky Lane was in the shade, and breath condensed in small clouds before the men's faces.

"You're being expelled from the Soviet Union." The words, tersely spoken, travelled the brief space of the balcony between them as if from an unfathomable distance. "Not that it would make much difference to you at this point, all things considered, but Ambassador Count von der Schulenburg believes it would be best if we reassigned you before the demand is made official."

Bora knew he was holding his breath because no cloud materialized in front of him. He had to force himself to breathe.

"Herr Oberst, was there a reason given for my expulsion?"

"No." Unlike Busch, Krebs really did wear a monocle, which lent a distinguished air to his otherwise commonplace frown. "We can guess at it," he said, "that's all. Don't take it personally. Count von der Schulenburg and General Köstring – and I too, for that matter – think highly of you, and care about your career. The Deputy Chairman agreed to consider himself satisfied if you leave Moscow at once, better if today. There are no planes flying out of the city in the next few hours, so a seat was secured for you on the next train bound for Brest-Litovsk. You have thirty-five minutes to pack and reach the Baltic and Byelorussia Station. Don't worry about saying your farewells, I will make sure everyone here is informed that you wish them your best."

Bora had no real reason to feel as hurt as he did. Such instant transfers were frequent in the diplomatic world, and junior officers could be shuffled without notice from one end of the world to the other. He was simply being sent to Poland, within easier reach of his regiment.

The programme change might even give him an extra night with Dikta. And in less than two weeks he'd be crossing the Soviet border again as an invader.

So, why was it that he now stood perfectly still in front of his superior, letting out no emotion either way, while he felt that one more word from Krebs would bring him close to tears? For a moment, he was a touchy, introverted twelve-year-old who was being told no.

Half an hour later, he was riding to Smolensk Station (its Russian name), whose westward rails forked outside the city, the northern going to the Baltic, the other to Russian-occupied Poland. In the mile and a half from the hotel to the station his chauffeured automobile followed Gorky Boulevard past the double ring of garden-rich avenues. Tribuk stared at the road ahead and not once did his ferret eyes seek him through the rear-view mirror.

That's what it's like becoming a persona non grata. *It's like losing one's body, turning into a ghost.* How muted, how anomalous his state in Moscow had become in the space of an hour was proven by the fact that his NKVD shadows, Max and Moritz, did not follow him. He wished they, at least, would see him off.

But they didn't.

At the station, a long train idled by the platform. Except for a single passenger coach behind the locomotive, it was an uninterrupted sequence of freight cars, bringing supplies from the Soviet Union to the country about to attack it. Once on it, there would be no getting off before leaving Russian territory, of course, which would not happen until daybreak, considering the break-of-gauge at the border with Soviet-held Poland.

Bora climbed aboard, stored away his bag, took his seat. The coach was empty, and it seemed highly improbable anyone would join him between here and the border. It consoled him to discover that the window at least did open.

He knew the routine. Last station on Russian territory, Niegoreloje, change trains at Stolpce; a guard would climb in, pull the curtains closed and sit with him until they reached the Bug River border with German-occupied Poland. From Brest-Litovsk on to Warsaw (Krebs' orders), and then take a different train to the Legionowo–Rakowice–Jamielnik line, the border with East Prussia. First station there, Deutsch Eylau, then east to Insterburg, divisional HQ, a short train ride away from Trakehnen.

Perfectly on time, the train moved out of the station. Bora thought how, at the crossroads between Gorky Street and Garden Boulevard, he'd glimpsed a glory of blooming lilacs frothing through an ornate iron fence. While still in the automobile he had tried to take Maggie's dry sprig out of his wallet and let it fall out of the window, but the back windows were blocked.

Dropping anything on a Moscow street was unthinkable. Any motion in that sense would be highly suspicious. So, the sprig that could not be returned to its owner remained in his wallet, behind his wife's photograph.

Presently, the long sheds of the "Year of the Revolution 1905" Repair Works went by, in this district of engine and machinery factories and aeroplane assembly works. *We'll bomb them in two weeks*, he thought. The idea excited him, troubled him. It troubled him more than it excited him. He liked Moscow. It had been his father's city for years. As Krebs put it, he regretted leaving it without saying his farewells. But was it really worse than having time to savour his departure?

Link after link, the train gained speed. If he glanced back from the open window, Bora could see the long chain of freight cars carrying grain, timber and ore complete a grand curve as they followed him to the Fatherland. As he grasped the reality of the moment, he couldn't help wondering whether, beneath or beyond patriotism, he felt up to what was coming.

Mentally, he did what he'd done many times as a boy. He tossed down a pebble to see how far it rolled down, how many rocks it would displace before becoming anchored by exposed roots or reaching a ledge. While the train took him away from Moscow, the imaginary pebble slid in dust, hit a stone, bounced, fell much further down where he could not lean out to see without risking his neck. *I'm the pebble,* he thought. *Didn't even need a hand to drop me over the rim: I volunteered for it. There'll be roots and ledges on the way down, or not even that; I might take many with me or perform a solitary slide into oblivion. Less than two weeks and the plunge begins. I can't wait; but have I got what it takes?*

The thought of the vast expanse to be travelled day and night (factories, fields, coal seams, farms, ore, densely populated cities), the reports circulating at the embassy (two million Soviet troops massed at the western border, though it was surely more than that), took his breath away.

Am I sure of my own resolve? Will I accept what comes?

Will I? In his luggage he still had Joyce's *Ulysses* with him, and he now took it out. He'd have time to read it during the long journey. Ahead, right and left, the old racing track and Presnenskoe districts ran separated by the railroad. Ahead, the tracks crossed the Moskva and then sped alongside green spaces, where trees and hedges were in full bloom.

If Martin Bora had known that in a thousand days he'd lose all he had (and was), his actions that day wouldn't have appreciably changed. Today things were as they were.

So it was where trees and hedges were in full bloom that he decided to let go of the lilac sprig. He took it out of his wallet and stood up to drop it outside. In the metallic window frame there was a small imperfection or notch, and speed, as the train accelerated, pushed Bora's arm back so that his left hand rapped against it. Just as he let go of the flower, the sharp metal cut the back of his hand.

Nothing but a small wound. But after Crete, after churning through the island's pitiless time machine, it was hard not to take the incident, minor as it seemed, as a portent of sorts. *I start my journey away from Russia with blood on my hand, even though it's just a tear in the skin.* Bora pressed his lips on the cut to stop the bleeding, and sat back for the journey.

Will I accept what comes with this war? Will I?

Ulysses, on the seat where he'd tossed it, had randomly flipped open on the last page. Bora was – and was not – one to read the end of a novel first. His eyes fell on the final words, that was all. He didn't even know to which character the inner monologue belonged, or if it mattered. The words were few, disconnected apparently from his present state, but Bora instantly made them his own.

They read,

And yes I said yes I will yes.

Afterword

One thousand days would make a difference to all of them. Some would lose their lives, among them Bora's enthusiastic brother in 1943 Ukraine, and Andonis Sidheraki, killed by the Greek Army in the bloody civil war that racked Greece at the close of the conflict. The same fate awaited the Catalan anarchists, fighting for their unachievable revolution.

Ambassador von der Schulenburg and his son would be executed by the Nazis for their part in the anti-Hitler resistance, along with most members of the espionage ring known as "Red Orchestra". Hans Krebs, promoted to the rank of general, would sign Germany's unconditional surrender to the Soviets in 1945 Berlin, and then commit suicide. Waldo Preger would survive the war, only to die in 1954 fighting with the French Foreign Legion at Dien Bien Phu, when Vietnam was still called Indochina. One year earlier, a politically disgraced Lavrenti Beria had followed the fate of thousands of his victims.

Others were more fortunate.

Once widowed, Frances Allen returned to the United States and became a professor at her alma mater. Always active in the civil rights movement, she was arrested by the FBI several times in her own country. She continued never to forget or forgive a wrong.

In 1946, Vairon Kostaridis escaped the Greek communists' blacklist by joining his relatives in New York, where he eventually opened an investigation agency specializing in marital infidelity: The Minotaur Private Investigation Agency.

The return of the victorious British found Rifat Bey still in Crete. He never married Signora, which was probably the reason why he did not kill her, and spent the rest of his life with her. Pericles Savelli went back to Italy after the war. There, he used his close friendship with a politician's wife to be chosen as head curator at a museum of Renaissance art, about which he knew close to nothing. When his mistakes caught up with him, he blamed them on his assistant, and kept his honourable post until retirement.

Major Emil Busch profitably worked for years as a Mercedes automobiles executive in South Africa, and never lost his predilection for soft drinks.

In the 1980s, after a fine career as a journalist, the elderly Bruno Lattmann headed his own radio station in West Berlin: when the Wall came down in 1989, he broadcast worldwide an unforgettable live report of the event.

Martin Bora, as the mermaid-maidens foretold, had four more years of fighting ahead of him. In the process, he was to lose the war, love and physical integrity, but never his moral integrity. That distant day in Serpenten, during his bike ride with Peter, he'd somehow seen into the future. In 1945, the family estate in East Prussia would be lost to the Soviets, along with the entire region, Leipzig and all of Saxony. Today Serpenten no longer exists on the map. And Trakehnen is called Yasna Polyana, in the Russian province of Kaliningrad.

Glossary

Abwehr (Amt/Ausland Abwehr): German Army counter-espionage service in World War II.

Ahnenerbe: "Society of the Research of Ancestral Heritage". Created in 1935 by Heinrich Himmler as a part of the SS, its task was to "research the places, spirit, acts and heritage of the Indo-German race".

Au courant: diplomatic French for "informed of the situation".

Bouzouki: traditional Turkish–Greek string instrument.

Comintern: international organization of communist parties, led by Moscow and active from 1919 to 1943.

CreForce: military forces of the British Commonwealth in 1941 Crete.

Epitropos: police inspector, in Greek.

Ex libris: a label with one's name applied to a book, to show ownership.

Feldwebel: a sergeant in the German Army.

Frangos: a Greek expression for "foreigner".

Freiherr: German nobility title, the equivalent of a British baron.

Gestapo (*Geheime Staatspolizei*): secret police in the Third Reich.

GPU (*Gosudarstvennoe politicheskoe upravlenie*): secret police in the Soviet Union.

Hauptmann: in German, army captain.

Hegemeister: in German, an estate superintendent.

Jäger: German mountain trooper.

Kafeneio: in Greek, a coffee shop or a bar.

Kapetanios: in Greek, Commander.

Luftwaffe: German Air Force.

Marshrutka: a shared taxi in the old Soviet Union.

NAACP (National Association for the Advancement of Colored People): civil rights association founded in 1909.

Narkomindel: Ministry of Foreign Affairs in the Soviet Union.

NKVD: military and civilian security service in the Soviet Union.

Oberführer: SS Brigadier General.

Ouzo: in Greek, strong aniseed-flavoured alcoholic drink.

Perinde ac cadaver. Jesuit Latin motto: (As compliantly) "as a corpse".

Poprusk: in Russian, a safe conduct.

Raki: Turkish brandy.

Reichskommissar: high administrative rank in the Third Reich.

Rittmeister: Captain in the German Cavalry during World War II.

Sepoys: native troops in British-ruled India.

SOE (Special Operations Executive): World War II British secret service office, with the special task of carrying out sabotage behind enemy lines.

Sphakiotes: originally, fighters for Greek independence from Ottoman rule; later, the term was often used merely to indicate rough characters.

SS (*Schutzstaffeln*): paramilitary corps of the National Socialist Party.

Starka*:* vodka produced in Poland and Lithuania.

Valencian: nickname for a student attending Pembroke College of Cambridge University.

vragha: loose trousers traditionally worn by Greek peasants.

Wehrmacht: World War II German armed forces.